Critical acclaim for *The Storyteller* and Jodi Picoult:

'The first person accounts about what happened in the Holocaust are absolutely harrowing . . . there are descriptive passages that make you catch your breath' *Sunday Express*

'Jodi Picoult's new book will leave you thinking about its story for a long time . . . it is an emotional and compelling tale' *Sun*

'Another great read' *Cosmopolitan*

'If you think you know Jodi Picoult, her latest novel will make you think again . . . a powerful and unexpected climax' *Good Housekeeping*

'Simply stunning' *Image Magazine*

'A beautifully woven story . . . the humour and characters wrap themselves around you, daring you to stop reading' *My Weekly*

'It's the twistiest of page turners. You'll be gripped from start to finish.' *Easy Living*

'Picoult's pitch and pace are masterly and hardly conducive to a good night's sleep' *Financial Times*

'This is Picoult's greatest strength; her ability to inhabit other people's feelings, relishing the bits that are complex and contradictory . . . She is a master of her craft . . . and humanity is what Picoult does best' *Daily Telegraph*

'Impossible to put down and stayed in my mind long after I had finish

'Picoult is

Also by Jodi Picoult

JODI PICOULT

The Storyteller

HODDER

First published in America in 2013 by Atria Books
An imprint of Simon & Schuster, Inc.

First published in Great Britain in 2013 by Hodder & Stoughton
An Hachette UK company

First published in paperback in 2013

13

Copyright © Jodi Picoult 2013

A CIP catalogue record for this title is available from the British Library

B-format paperback ISBN 978 1 444 76666 0
A-format paperback ISBN 978 1 444 76667 7
Ebook ISBN 978 1 444 76665 3

Typeset in Miller Text by Palimpsest Book Production Limited,
Falkirk, Stirlingshire

Printed and bound in Great Britain by Clays Ltd, St Ives plc

Hodder & Stoughton policy is to use papers
that are natural, renewable and recyclable products and
made from wood grown in sustainable forests. The logging
and manufacturing processes are expected to conform
to the environmental regulations of the country of origin.

Hodder & Stoughton Ltd
338 Euston Road
London NW1 3BH

www.hodder.co.uk

For my mother, Jane Picoult,
because you taught me there is nothing more
important than family.
And because after twenty years, it's your turn again.

Acknowledgments

This book began with another: *The Sunflower*, by Simon Wiesenthal. While a prisoner in a Nazi concentration camp, Wiesenthal was brought to the deathbed of an SS soldier, who wanted to confess to and be forgiven by a Jew. The moral conundrum in which Wiesenthal found himself has been the starting point for many philosophical and moral analyses about the dynamics between victims of genocide and the perpetrators – and it got me thinking about what would happen if the same request was made, decades later, to a Jewish prisoner's granddaughter.

To undertake a novel grounded in one of the most horrible crimes against humanity in history is a daunting task, because even when one is writing fiction, getting the details right becomes an exercise in honoring those who survived, and those who did not. I am indebted to the following people for their assistance in bringing to life both Sage's world in the present day and Minka's world in the past.

For teaching me to bake bread, and the most delicious research session of my career, thanks to Martin Philip. Thanks to Elizabeth Martin and One More Page Books in Arlington, Virginia, for teaching me how to bake with nefarious intent.

For anecdotes about Catholic school, thanks to Katie Desmond. For helping me spell Darija's dance terminology, thanks to Allyson Sawyer. For teaching me the dynamics of a grief group, thanks to Susan Carpenter. For preliminary legal, law enforcement, and war tribunal questions, thanks to Alex Whiting, Frank Moran, and Lise Gescheidt.

While writing this book, I auctioned off a character name to help raise money for the Gay and Lesbian Advocates and Defenders. Thanks to Mary DeAngelis for her generosity, and for providing her name to Sage's best friend.

Eli Rosenbaum, Director of Strategy and Policy for the Human Rights and Special Prosecutions Section of the Department of Justice, is a real-live Nazi hunter who found the time to teach me what he does, let me create a character based on his experiences, and still managed to slay dragons. I am incredibly grateful to know someone like him is out there tirelessly doing what he does. (And I appreciate the fact that he let me take artistic license on the speed it takes for historians to get information from NARA. In real life it would be days, not minutes.)

I am grateful to Paul Wieser, who gave me my first lesson on Third Reich history, and to Steffi Gladebeck, who provided the German perspective. But I am most indebted to Dr. Peter Black, Senior Historian at the United States Holocaust Memorial Museum, who suffered my endless questions, corrected me with great patience, helped me cobble together a viable Nazi upbringing, and read sections to help ensure historical accuracy. I mean it wholeheartedly when I say I could not have written this book without his input.

I am grateful to Team Jodi at Emily Bestler Books/Simon & Schuster: Carolyn Reidy, Judith Curr, Kate Cetrulo, Caroline Porter, Chris Lloreda, Jeanne Lee, Gary Urda, Lisa Keim, Rachel Zugschwert, Michael Selleck, and the many others who have helped my career grow. Thanks to the crackerjack PR team of David Brown, Valerie Vennix, Camille McDuffie, and Kathleen Carter Zrelak, who are so good at getting everyone else as excited about a new book as I always am. To Emily Bestler, I value your guidance, your friendship, your commitment to my writing, and your ability to find the best shopping websites ever.

Laura Gross, happy anniversary. Thanks for the information on Oneg Shabbat, for letting Sage get under your skin, and most of all for being my wingman.

Thanks to my father, who did indeed conduct a Seder in a Donald Duck voice when we were small. As for my mother – I knew she was formidable, but when I asked if maybe she could find me some Holocaust survivors, I had names and numbers within a day. She paved the way for this book, and I am grateful.

It is to those men and women, however, that I owe the greatest debt. The extensive research I conducted for this novel included speaking to a group of amazing people – Holocaust survivors, whose experiences during the war in the ghettos, in villages, in cities, and in concentration camps fed my imagination and allowed me to create the character of Minka. Although Minka suffers similar horrors as those described to me by survivors and Nazi hunters, she is not based on any one person I met or heard about; she is truly a work of fiction. So, to the survivors who opened their homes and their hearts, I am honored that you chose to share *your* stories with me. Thank you, Sandy Zuckerman – who provided me with the transcript of her mother, Sylvia Green's experiences during the Holocaust. Thank you, Gerda Weissman Klein, for your courage and your creativity as a writer. Thank you, Bernie Scheer, for your honesty and your generosity of spirit while telling me your experiences. And thank you, Mania

Salinger, for your bravery, for letting me rifle through the bits and pieces of your life, and for becoming a treasured friend.

And last, thanks to my family: Tim, Kyle (who had the great foresight to take German while I was writing this book), Jake, and Samantha (who penned a few vampiric paragraphs for me to use). The four of you are the story of *my* life.

*M*y father trusted me with the details of his death. 'Ania,' he would say, 'no whiskey at my funeral. I want the finest blackberry wine. No weeping, mind you. Just dancing. And when they lower me into the ground, I want a fanfare of trumpets, and white butterflies.' A character, that was my father. He was the village baker, and every day, in addition to the loaves he would make for the town, he would create a single roll for me that was as unique as it was delicious: a twist like a princess's crown, dough mixed with sweet cinnamon and the richest chocolate. The secret ingredient, he said, was his love for me, and this made it taste better than anything else I had ever eaten.

We lived on the outskirts of a village so small that everyone knew everyone else by name. Our home was made of river stone, with a thatched roof; the hearth where my father baked heated the entire cottage. I would sit at the kitchen table, shelling peas that I grew in the small garden out back, as my father opened the door of the brick oven and slid the peel inside to take out crusty, round loaves of bread. The red embers glowed, outlining the strong muscles of his back as he sweated through his tunic. 'I don't want a summer funeral, Ania,' he would say. 'Make sure instead I die on a cool day, when there's a nice breeze. Before the birds fly south, so that they can sing for me.'

I would pretend to take note of his requests. I didn't mind the macabre conversation; my father was far too strong for me to believe any of these requests of his would ever come to pass. Some of the others in the village found it strange, the relationship I had with my father, the fact that we could joke about this, but my mother had died when I was an infant and all we had was each other.

The trouble started on my eighteenth birthday. At first, it was just the farmers who complained; who would come out to feed their chickens and find only an explosion of bloody feathers in the coop, or a calf nearly turned inside out, flies buzzing around its carcass. 'A fox,' said Baruch Beiler, the tax collector, who lived in a mansion that sat at the bottom of the village square like a jewel at the throat of a royal. 'Maybe a wildcat. Pay what you owe, and in return, you will be protected.'

He came to our cottage one day when we were unprepared for him, and by this I mean we did not manage to barricade the doors and douse the fire and make it seem as if we were not at home. My father was shaping loaves into hearts, as he always did on my birthday, so that the whole town knew it was a special day. Baruch Beiler swept into the kitchen, lifted his gold-tipped cane, and smacked the worktable. Flour rose in a cloud, and when it settled I looked down at the dough between my father's hands, at that broken heart.

'Please,' said my father, who never begged. 'I know what I promised. But business has been slow. If you give me just a little more time—'

'You're in default, Emil,' Beiler said. 'I hold the lien on this rathole.' He leaned closer. For the first time in my life, I did not think my father invincible. 'Because I am a generous

man, a magnanimous man, I will give you till the end of the week. But if you don't come up with the money, well, I can't say what might happen.' He lifted his cane, sliding it between his hands like a weapon. 'There have been so many . . . misfortunes lately.'

'It's why there are so few customers,' I said, my voice small. 'People won't come to market because they fear the animal that's out there.'

Baruch Beiler turned, as if noticing for the first time that I was even present. His eyes raked over me, from my dark hair in its single braid to the leather boots on my feet, whose holes had been repaired with thick patches of flannel. His gaze made me shiver, not in the same way that I felt when Damian, the captain of the guard, watched me walk away in the village square – as if I were cream and he was the cat. No, this was more mercenary. It felt like Baruch Beiler was trying to figure out what I might be worth.

He reached over my shoulder to the wire rack where the most recent batch of loaves was cooling, plucked one heart-shaped boule from its shelf, and tucked it beneath his arm. 'Collateral,' he pronounced, and he walked out of the cottage, leaving the door wide open simply because he could.

My father watched him go, and then shrugged. He grabbed another handful of dough and began to mold it. 'Ignore him. He is a little man who casts a big shadow. One day, I will dance a jig on his grave.' Then he turned to me, a smile softening his face. 'Which reminds me, Ania. At my funeral, I want a procession. First the children, throwing rose petals. Then the finest ladies, with parasols painted to look like hothouse flowers. Then of course my hearse, drawn by four – no – five snowy horses. And finally, I'd like Baruch Beiler to be at the end of the parade, cleaning up the dung.' He threw back his *head and laughed. 'Unless, of course, he dies first. Preferably sooner rather than later.'*

My father trusted me with the details of his death . . . but in the end, I was too late.

Part One

It is impossible to believe anything in a world that has ceased to regard man as man, that repeatedly proves that one is no longer a man.

– Simon Wiesenthal, *The Sunflower*

Sage

On the second Thursday of the month, Mrs. Dombrowski brings her dead husband to our therapy group.

It's just past 3:00 p.m., and most of us are still filling our paper cups with bad coffee. I've brought a plate of baked goods – last week, Stuart told me that the reason he keeps coming to Helping Hands isn't the grief counseling but my butter-scotch pecan muffins – and just as I am setting them down, Mrs. Dombrowski shyly nods toward the urn she is holding. 'This,' she tells me, 'is Herb. Herbie, meet Sage. She's the one I told you about, the baker.'

I stand frozen, ducking my head so that my hair covers the left side of my face, like I usually do. I'm sure there's a protocol for meeting a spouse who's been cremated, but I'm pretty much at a loss. Am I supposed to say hello? Shake his handle?

'Wow,' I finally say, because although there are few rules to this group, the ones we have are steadfast: be a good listener, don't judge, and don't put boundaries on someone else's grief. I know this better than anyone. After all, I've been coming for nearly three years now.

'What did you bring?' Mrs. Dombrowksi asks, and I realize why she's toting her husband's urn. At our last meeting, our facilitator – Marge – had suggested that we share a memory of whatever it was we had lost. I see that Shayla is clutching a pair of knit pink booties so tightly her knuckles are white. Ethel is holding a television remote control. Stuart has – again – brought in the bronze death mask of his first wife's face. It has made an appearance a few times at our group, and it was the creepiest thing I'd ever seen – until now, when Mrs. Dombrowski has brought along Herb.

Before I have to stammer my answer, Marge calls our little group to order. We each pull a folding chair into the circle, close enough to pat someone on the shoulder or reach out a hand in support. In the center sits the box of tissues Marge brings to every session, just in case.

Often Marge starts out with a global question – *Where were you when 9/11 happened?* It gets people talking about a communal tragedy, and that sometimes makes it easier to talk about a personal one. Even so, there are always people who don't speak. Sometimes months go by before I even know what a new participant's voice sounds like.

Today, though, Marge asks right away about the mementos we've brought. Ethel raises her hand. 'This was Bernard's,' she says, rubbing the television remote with her thumb. 'I didn't want it to be – God knows I tried to take it away from him a thousand times. I don't even have the TV this works with, anymore. But I can't seem to throw it out.'

Ethel's husband is still alive, but he has Alzheimer's and has no idea who she is anymore. There are all sorts of losses people suffer – from the small to the large. You can lose your keys, your glasses, your virginity. You can lose your head, you can lose your heart, you can lose your mind. You can relinquish your home to move into assisted living, or have a child move overseas, or see a spouse vanish into dementia. Loss is more than just death, and grief is the gray shape-shifter of emotion.

'My husband hogs the remote,' Shayla says. 'He says it's because women control everything else.'

'Actually, it's instinct,' Stuart says. 'The part of the brain that's territorial is bigger in men than it is in women. I heard it on John Tesh.'

'So that makes it an inviolable truth?' Jocelyn rolls her eyes. Like me, she is in her twenties. Unlike me, she has no patience for anyone over the age of forty.

'Thanks for sharing your memento,' Marge says, quickly interceding. 'Sage, what did you bring today?'

I feel my cheeks burn as all eyes turn to me. Even though I know everyone in the group, even though we have formed a circle of trust, it is still painful for me to open myself up to their scrutiny. The skin of my scar, a starfish puckered across my left eyelid and cheek, grows even tighter than usual.

I shake my long bangs over my eye and from beneath my tank top, pull out the chain I wear with my mother's wedding ring.

Of course, I know why – three years after my mom's death – it still feels like a sword has been run through my ribs every time I think of her. It's the same reason I am the only person from my original grief group still here. While most people come for therapy, I came for punishment.

Jocelyn raises her hand. 'I have a real problem with that.'

I blush even deeper, assuming she's talking about me, but then I realize that she's staring at the urn in Mrs. Dombrowski's lap.

'It's disgusting!' Jocelyn says. 'We weren't supposed to bring something dead. We were supposed to bring a memory.'

'He's not a *something*, he's a *someone*,' Mrs. Dombrowski says.

'I don't want to be cremated,' Stuart muses. 'I have night-mares about dying in a fire.'

'News flash: you're already *dead* when you're put into the fire,' Jocelyn says, and Mrs. Dombrowski bursts into tears.

I reach for the box of tissues, and pass it toward her. While Marge reminds Jocelyn about the rules of this group, kindly but firmly, I head for the bathroom down the hall.

I grew up thinking of loss as a positive outcome. My mother used to say it was the reason she met the love of her life. She'd left her purse at a restaurant and a sous-chef found it and tracked her down. When he called her, she wasn't home and her roommate took the message. A woman answered when my mom called back, and put my father on the phone. When they met so that he could give my mother back her purse, she realized he was everything she'd ever wanted . . . but she also knew, from her initial phone call, that he lived with a woman.

Who just happened to be his sister.

My dad died of a heart attack when I was nineteen, and the only way I can even make sense of losing my mother three years later is by telling myself now she's with him again.

In the bathroom, I pull my hair back from my face.

The scar is silver now, ruched, rippling my cheek and my brow like the neck of a silk purse. Except for the fact that my eyelid droops, skin pulled too tight, you might not realize at first glance that there's something wrong with me – at least that's what my friend Mary says. But people notice. They're just too polite to say something, unless they are under the age of four and still brutally honest, pointing and asking their moms what's wrong with that lady's face.

Even though the injury has faded, I still see it the way it was right after the accident: raw and red, a jagged lightning bolt splitting the symmetry of my face. In this, I suppose I'm like a girl with an eating disorder, who weighs ninety-eight pounds but sees a fat person staring back at her from the mirror. It isn't even a scar to me, really. It's a map of where my life went wrong.

As I leave the bathroom, I nearly mow down an old man. I am tall enough to see the pink of his scalp through the hurricane whorl of his white hair. 'I am late again,' he says, his English accented. 'I was lost.'

We all are, I suppose. It's why we come here: to stay tethered to what's missing.

This man is a new member of the grief group; he's only been coming for two weeks. He has yet to say a single word during a session. Yet the first time I saw him, I recognized him; I just couldn't remember why.

Now, I do. The bakery. He comes in often with his dog, a little dachshund, and he orders a fresh roll with butter and a black coffee. He spends hours writing in a little black notebook, while his dog sleeps at his feet.

As we enter the room, Jocelyn is sharing her memento: something that looks like a mangled, twisted femur. 'This was Lola's,' she says, gently turning the rawhide bone over in her hands. 'I found it under the couch after we put her down.'

'Why are you even here?' Stuart says. 'It was just a damn dog!'

Jocelyn narrows her eyes. 'At least I didn't *bronze* her.'

They start arguing as the old man and I get settled in the circle. Marge uses this as a distraction. 'Mr. Weber,' she says, 'welcome. Jocelyn was just telling us how much her pet meant to her. Have you ever had a pet you loved?'

I think of the little dog he brings to the bakery. He shares the roll with her, fifty-fifty.

But the man is silent. He bows his head, as if he is being pressed down in his seat. I recognize that stance, that wish to disappear.

'You can love a pet more than you love some people,' I say suddenly, surprising even myself. Everyone turns, because unlike the others, I hardly ever draw attention to myself by volunteering information. 'It doesn't matter what it is that leaves a hole inside you. It just matters that it's there.'

The old man slowly glances up. I can feel the heat of his gaze through the curtain of my hair.

'Mr. Weber,' Marge says, noticing. 'Maybe you brought a memento to share with us today . . .?'

He shakes his head, his blue eyes flat and without expression.

Marge lets his silence stand; an offering on a pedestal. I know this is because some people come here to talk, while others come to just listen. But the lack of sound pounds like a heartbeat. It's deafening.

That's the paradox of loss: How can something that's gone weigh us down so much?

At the end of the hour, Marge thanks us for participating and we fold up the chairs and recycle our paper plates and napkins. I pack up the remaining muffins and give them to Stuart. Bringing them back to the bakery would be like carting a bucket of water to Niagara Falls. Then I walk outside to head back to work.

If you've lived in New Hampshire your whole life, like I have, you can smell the change in the weather. It's oppressively hot, but there's a thunderstorm written across the sky in invisible ink.

'Excuse me.'

I turn at the sound of Mr. Weber's voice. He stands with his back to the Episcopal church where we hold our meetings. Although it's at least eighty-five degrees out, he is wearing a long-sleeved shirt that is buttoned to the throat, with a narrow tie.

'That was a nice thing you did, sticking up for that girl.'

The way he pronounces the word *thing*, it sounds like *think*.

I look away. 'Thanks.'

'You are Sage?'

Well, isn't that the sixty-four-thousand-dollar question? Yes, it's my name, but the double entendre – that I'm full of wisdom – has never really applied. There have been too many moments in my life when I've nearly gone off the rails, more overwhelmed by emotion than tempered by reason.

'Yes,' I say.

The awkward silence grows between us like yeasted dough. 'This group. You have been coming a long time.'

I don't know whether I should be defensive. 'Yes.'

'So you find it helpful?'

If it were helpful, I wouldn't still be coming. 'They're all nice people, really. They each just sometimes think their grief is bigger than anyone else's.'

'You don't say much,' Mr. Weber muses. 'But when you *do* . . . you are a poet.'

I shake my head. 'I'm a baker.'

'Can a person not be two things at once?' he asks, and slowly, he walks away.

I run into the bakery, breathless and flushed, to find my boss hanging from the ceiling. 'Sorry I'm late,' I say. 'The shrine is packed and some moron in an Escalade took my spot.'

Mary's rigged up a Michelangelo-style dolly so that she can lie on her back and paint the ceiling of the bakery. 'That moron would be the bishop,' she replies. 'He stopped in on his way up the hill. Said your olive loaf is heavenly, which is pretty high praise, coming from him.'

In her previous life, Mary DeAngelis was Sister Mary Robert. She had a green thumb and was well known for maintaining the gardens in her Maryland cloister. One Easter, when she heard the priest say *He is risen,* she found herself standing up from the pew and walking out the cathedral door. She left the order, dyed her hair pink, and hiked the Appalachian Trail. It was somewhere on the Presidential Range that Jesus appeared to her in a vision, and told her there were many souls to feed.

Six months later, Mary opened Our Daily Bread at the foothills of the Our Lady of Mercy Shrine in Westerbrook, New Hampshire. The shrine covers sixteen acres with a meditation grotto, a peace angel, Stations of the Cross, and holy stairs. There is also a store filled with crosses, crucifixes, books on Catholicism and theology, Christian music CDs, saints' medals, and Fontanini crèche sets. But visitors usually come to see the 750-foot rosary made of New Hampshire granite boulders, linked together with chains.

It was a fair-weather shrine; business dropped off dramatically during New England winters. Which was Mary's selling point: What could be more secular than freshly baked bread? Why not boost the revenue of the shrine by adding a bakery that would attract believers and nonbelievers alike?

The only catch was that she had no idea how to bake.

That's where I come in.

I started baking when I was nineteen years old and my father died unexpectedly. I was at college, and went home for the funeral, only to return and find nothing the same. I stared at the words in textbooks as if they had been written in a language I could not read. I couldn't get myself out of bed to go to classes.

I missed one exam, then another. I stopped turning in papers. Then one night I woke up in my dorm room and smelled flour – so much flour I felt as if I'd been rolling in it. I took a shower but couldn't get rid of the smell. It reminded me of Sunday mornings as a kid, when I would awaken to the scent of fresh bagels and bialys, crafted by my father.

He'd always tried to teach my sisters and me, but mostly we were too busy with school and field hockey and boys to listen. Or so I thought, until I started to sneak into the residential college dining hall kitchen and bake bread every night.

I left the loaves like abandoned babies on the thresholds of the offices of professors I admired, of the dorm rooms of boys with smiles so beautiful that they stunned me into awkward silence. I left a finial row of sourdough rolls on a lectern podium and slipped a boule into the oversize purse of the cafeteria lady who pressed plates of pancakes and bacon at me, telling me I was too skinny. On the day my academic adviser told me that I was failing three of my four classes, I had nothing to say in my defense, but I gave her a honey baguette seeded with anise, the bitter and the sweet.

My mother arrived unexpectedly one day. She took up residence in my dorm room and micromanaged my life, from making sure I was fed to walking me to class and quizzing me on my homework readings. 'If I don't get to give up,' she told me, 'then neither do you.'

I wound up being on the five-year plan, but I did graduate. My mother stood up and whistled through her teeth when I crossed the stage to get my diploma. And then everything went to hell.

I've thought a lot about it: how you can ricochet from a moment where you are on top of the world to one where you are crawling at rock bottom. I've thought about all the things

I could have done differently, and if it would have led to another outcome. But thinking doesn't change anything, does it? And so afterward, with my eye still bloodshot and the Frankenstein monster stitches curving around my temple and cheek like the seam of a baseball, I gave my mother the same advice she had given me. *If I don't get to give up, then neither do you.*

She didn't, at first. It took almost six months, one bodily system shutting down after another. I sat by her side in the hospital every day, and at night went home to rest. Except, I didn't. Instead, I started once again to bake – my go-to therapy. I brought artisan loaves to her doctors. I made pretzels for the nurses. For my mother, I baked her favorite – cinnamon rolls, thick with icing. I made them daily, but she never managed a bite.

It was Marge, the facilitator of the grief group, who suggested I get a job to help me forge some kind of routine. Fake it until you make it, she said. But I couldn't stand the thought of working in broad daylight, where everyone would be staring at my face. I had been shy before; now I was reclusive.

Mary says it's divine intervention that she ran into me. (She calls herself a recovering nun, but in reality, she gave up her habit, not her faith.) Me, I don't believe in God; I think it was pure luck that the first classifieds section I read after Marge made her suggestion included an ad for a master baker – one who would work nights, alone, and leave when customers began to trickle into the store. At the interview Mary didn't comment on the fact that I had no experience, no significant summer jobs, no references. But most important, she took one look at my scar and said, 'I'm guessing when you want to tell me about that, you will.' And that was that. Later, as I got to know her, I'd realize that when she gardens, she never sees the seed. She is already picturing the plant it will become. I imagine she thought the same, meeting me.

The only saving grace about working at Our Daily Bread (no pun intended) was that my mother was not alive to see it. She and my father had both been Jewish. My sisters, Pepper and Saffron, were both bat mitzvahed. Although we sold bagels and challah as well as hot cross buns; although the coffee bar attached to the bakery was called HeBrews – I knew my mother would have said: *All the bakeries in the world, what made you decide to work for a* shiksa?

But my mother also would have been the first to tell me that good people are good people; religion has nothing to do with it. I think my mom knows, wherever she is now, how many times Mary found me in the kitchen in tears, and delayed the opening of the bakery until she helped me pull myself together. I think she knows that on the anniversary of my mother's death, Mary donates all the money raised at the bakery to Hadassah. And that Mary is the only person I don't actively try to hide my scar from. She isn't just my employer but also my best friend, and I like to believe that would matter more to my mother than where Mary chose to worship.

A splat of purple paint drops on the floor beside my foot, making me look up. Mary's painting another one of her visions. She has them with staggering regularity – at least three a year – and they usually lead to some change in the composition of our shop or our menu. The coffee bar was one of Mary's visions. So was the greenhouse window, with the rows of delicate orchids, their flowers draped like a string of pearls over the rich green foliage. One winter she introduced a knitting circle at Our Daily Bread; another year, it was a yoga class. Hunger, she often tells me, has nothing to do with the belly and everything to do with the mind. What Mary really runs isn't a bakery, but a community.

Some of Mary's aphorisms are painted on the walls: *Seek and ye shall find. All who wander are not lost. It's not the years in your life that count, but the life in your years.* I sometimes wonder if Mary really dreams up these platitudes or if she just memorizes the catchy phrases on *Life Is Good* T-shirts. I guess it doesn't much matter, though, since our customers seem to enjoy reading them.

Today, Mary is painting her latest mantra. *All you knead is love,* I read.

'What do you think?' she asks.

'That Yoko Ono is going to sue you for copyright infringement,' I reply.

Rocco, our barista, is wiping down the counter. 'Lennon was brilliant,' he says. 'If he were alive today / Can you *Imagine?*'

Rocco is twenty-nine years old, has prematurely gray dreadlocks, and speaks only in Haiku. It's his *thing,* he told Mary, when he applied for his job. She was willing to overlook that little verbal tic because of his prodigious talent creating foam art – the patterned swirls on top of lattes and mochaccinos. He can make ferns, hearts, unicorns, Lady Gaga, spiderwebs, and once, on Mary's birthday, Pope Benedict XVI. Me, I like him because of one of Rocco's other *things*: he doesn't look people in the eye. He says that's how someone can steal your soul.

Amen to that.

'Ran out of baguettes,' Rocco tells me. 'Gave angry folks free coffee.' He pauses, counting syllables mentally. 'Tonight make extra.'

Mary begins to lower herself from her rigging. 'How was your meeting?'

'The usual. Has it been this quiet all day?'

She hits the ground with a soft thud. 'No, we had the preschool drop-off rush and a good lunch.' Getting to her feet, she wipes her hands on her jeans and follows me into the kitchen. 'By the way, Satan called,' she says.

'Let me guess. He wants a special-order birthday cake for Joseph Kony?'

'By Satan,' Mary says, as if I haven't spoken, 'I mean Adam.'

Adam is my boyfriend. Except not, because he's already someone else's husband. 'Adam's not *that* bad.'

'He's hot, Sage, and he's emotionally destructive. If the shoe fits . . .' Mary shrugs. 'I'm leaving Rocco to man the cannons while I head up to the shrine to do a little weeding.' Although she's not employed there, no one seems to mind if the former nun with the green thumb keeps the flowers and plants in good form. Gardening – sweaty, machete-hacking, root-digging, bush-dragging gardening – is Mary's relaxation. Sometimes I think she doesn't sleep at all, she just photosynthesizes like her beloved plants. She seems to function with more energy and speed than the rest of us ordinary mortals; she makes Tinker Bell look like a sloth. 'The hostas have been staging a coup.'

'Have fun,' I say, tying the strings of my apron, and focusing on the night's work.

At the bakery, I have a gigantic spiral mixer, because I make multiple loaves at a time. I have pre-ferments in various temperatures stored in carefully marked canisters. I use an Excel spreadsheet to figure out the baker's percentage, a crazy math that always adds up to more than 100 percent. But my favorite kind of baking is just a bowl, a wooden spoon, and four elements: flour, water, yeast, salt. Then, all you need is time.

The Storyteller

Making bread is an athletic event. Not only does it require dashing around to several stations of the bakery as you check rising loaves or mix ingredients or haul the mixing bowl out of its cradle – but it also takes muscle power to activate the gluten in the dough. Even people who wouldn't be able to tell a poolish from a biga know that to make bread, you have to knead it. Push and roll, push and fold, a rhythmic workout on your floured countertop. Do it right, and you'll release a protein called gluten – strands that let uneven pockets of carbon dioxide form in the loaves. After seven or eight minutes – long enough for your mind to have made a to-do list of chores around the house, or for you to replay the last conversation you had with your significant other and what he really meant – the consistency of the dough will transform. Smooth, supple, cohesive.

That's the point where you have to leave the dough alone. It's silly to anthropomorphize bread, but I love the fact that it needs to sit quietly, to retreat from touch and noise and drama, in order to evolve.

I have to admit, I often feel that way myself.

Bakers' hours can do strange things to a brain. When your workday begins at 5:00 p.m. and lasts through dawn, you hear each click of the minute hand on the clock over the stove, you see movements in the shadows. You do not recognize the echo of your own voice; you begin to think you are the only person left alive on earth. I'm convinced there's a reason most murders happen at night. The world just feels different for those of us who come alive after dark. It's more fragile and unreal, a replica of the one everyone else inhabits.

I've been living in reverse for so long now that it's not a hardship to go to bed when the sun is rising, and to wake when it's low in the sky. Most days this means I get about six hours of sleep before I return to Our Daily Bread to start all over again, but being a baker means accepting a fringe existence, one I welcome wholeheartedly. The people I see are convenience store clerks, Dunkin' Donuts drive-through cashiers, nurses switching shifts. And Mary and Rocco, of course, who close up the bakery shortly after I arrive. They lock me in, like the queen in Rumpelstiltskin, not to count grain but to transform it before morning into the quick breads and yeasted loaves that fill the shelves and glass counters.

I was never a people person, but now I actively prefer to be alone. This setup suits me best: I get to work by myself; Mary is the front man responsible for chatting up the customers and making them want to return for another visit. I hide.

Baking, for me, is a form of meditation. I get pleasure out of slicing up the voluminous mass of dough, eyeballing it to just the right amount of kilos on a scale for a perfect artisan loaf. I love how the snake of a baguette quivers beneath my palm as I roll it out. I love the sigh that a risen loaf makes when I first punch it down. I like curling my toes inside my clogs and stretching my neck from side to side to work out the kinks. I like knowing there will be no phone calls, no interruptions.

I am already well into making the one hundred pounds of product I make every night by the time I hear Mary return from her gardening stint up the hill and start to close up shop. Rinsing my hands in the industrial sink, I pull off the cap I wear to cover my hair while I'm working and walk to the front of the shop. Rocco is zipping up his motorcycle jacket. Through the plate-glass windows, I see heat lightning arc across the bruise of the sky.

'See you tomorrow,' Rocco says. 'Unless we die in our sleep. / What a way to go.'

I hear a bark, and realize that the bakery isn't empty. The one lone customer is Mr. Weber, from my grief group, and his tiny dog. Mary sits with him, a cup of tea in her hands.

He struggles to get to his feet when he sees me and does an awkward little bow. 'Hello again.'

'You know Josef?' Mary asks.

Grief group is like AA – you don't 'out' someone unless you have his permission. 'We've met,' I reply, shaking my hair forward to screen my face.

His dachshund comes closer on her leash to lick at a spot of flour on my pants. 'Eva,' he scolds. 'Manners!'

'It's okay,' I tell him, crouching down with relief to pat the dog. Animals never stare.

Mr. Weber slips the loop of the leash over his wrist and stands. 'I am keeping you from going home,' he says apologetically to Mary.

'Not at all. I enjoy the company.' She glances down at the old man's mug, which is still three-quarters full.

I don't know what makes me say what I say. After all, I have plenty to do. But it has started to pour now, a torrential sheet of rain. The only vehicles in the lot are Mary's Harley and Rocco's Prius, which means Mr. Weber is either walking home or waiting for the bus. 'You can stay until Advanced Transit shows up,' I tell him.

'Oh, no,' Mr. Weber says. 'This will be an imposition.'

'I insist,' Mary seconds.

He nods in gratitude and sits down again. As he cups his hands around the coffee mug, Eva stretches out over his left foot and closes her eyes.

'Have a nice night,' Mary says to me. 'Bake your little heart out.'

But instead of staying with Mr. Weber, I follow Mary into the back room, where she keeps her biker rain gear. 'I'm not cleaning up after him.'

'Okay,' Mary says, pausing in the middle of pulling on her chaps.

'I don't *do* customers.' In fact when I stumble out of the bakery at 7:00 a.m. and see the shop filled with businessmen buying bagels and housewives slipping wheat loaves into their recycled grocery bags, I am always a little surprised to remember there is a world outside my industrial kitchen. I imagine it's the way a patient who's flatlined must feel when he is shocked back into a heartbeat and thrown into the fuss and bustle of life – too much information and sensory overload.

'*You* invited him to stay,' Mary reminds me.

'I don't know anything about him. What if he tries to rob us? Or worse?'

'Sage, he's over ninety. Do you think he's going to cut your throat with his dentures?' Mary shakes her head. 'Josef Weber is as close as you can get to being canonized while you're still alive. Everyone in Westerbrook knows him – he used to coach kids' baseball; he organized the cleanup of Riverhead Park; he taught German at the high school for a zillion years. He's everyone's adoptive, cuddly grandfather. I don't think he's going to sneak into the kitchen and stab you with a bread knife while your back is turned.'

'I've never heard of him,' I murmur.

'That's because you live under a rock,' Mary says.

'Or in a kitchen.' When you sleep all day and work all night, you don't have time for things like newspapers or television. It was three days before I heard that Osama bin Laden had been killed.

'Good night.' She gives me a quick hug. 'Josef's harmless. Really. The worst he could do is talk you to death.'

I watch her open the rear door of the bakery. She ducks at the onslaught of driving rain and waves without looking back. I close the door behind her and lock it.

By the time I return to the bakery's dining room, Mr. Weber's mug is empty and the dog is on his lap. 'Sorry,' I say. 'Work stuff.'

'You don't have to entertain me. I know you have much to do.'

I have a hundred loaves to shape, bagels to boil, bialys to fill. Yes, you could say I'm busy. But to my surprise I hear myself say, 'It can wait a few minutes.'

Mr. Weber gestures to the chair Mary had occupied. 'Then please. Sit.'

I do, but I check my watch. My timer will go off in three minutes, then I will have to go back into the kitchen. 'So,' I say. 'I guess we're in for some weather.'

'We are always in for some weather,' Mr. Weber replies. His words sound as if he is biting them off a string: precise, clipped. 'Tonight however we are in for some *bad* weather.' He glances up at me. 'What brought you to the grief group?'

My gaze locks on his. There is a rule that, at group, we are not pressed to share if we're not ready. Certainly Mr. Weber hasn't been ready; it seems rude that he'd ask someone else to do what he himself isn't willing to do. But then again, we aren't at group.

'My mother,' I say, and tell him what I've told everyone else there. 'Cancer.'

He nods in sympathy. 'I am sorry for your loss,' he says stiffly.

'And you?' I ask.

He shakes his head. 'Too many to count.'

I don't even know how to respond to that. My grandma is always talking about how at her age, her friends are dropping like flies. I imagine for Mr. Weber, the same is true.

'You have been a baker long?'

'A few years,' I answer.

'It is an odd profession for a young woman. Not very social.'

Has he *seen* what I look like? 'It suits me.'

'You are very good at what you do.'

'Anyone can bake bread,' I say.

'But not everyone can do it well.'

From the kitchen comes the sound of the timer buzzing; it wakes up Eva, who begins to bark. Almost simultaneously there is a sweep of approaching lights through the glass windows of the bakery as the Advanced Transit bus slows at its corner stop. 'Thank you for letting me stay a bit,' he says.

'No problem, Mr. Weber.'

His face softens. 'Please. Call me Josef.'

I watch him tuck Eva into his coat and open his umbrella. 'Come back soon,' I say, because I know Mary would want me to.

'Tomorrow,' he announces, as if we have set a date. As he walks out of the bakery he squints into the bright beams of the bus.

In spite of what I have told Mary, I go to collect his dirty mug and plate, only to notice that Mr. Weber – Josef – has left behind the little black book he is always writing in when he sits here. It is banded with elastic.

I grab it and run into the storm. I step right into a gigantic puddle, which soaks my clog. 'Josef,' I call out, my hair plastered to my head. He turns, Eva's beady little eyes poking out from between the folds of his raincoat. 'You left this.'

I hold up the black book and walk toward him. 'Thank you,'

he says, safely slipping it into his pocket. 'I don't know what I would have done without it.' He tips his umbrella, so that it shelters me as well.

'Your Great American Novel?' I guess. Ever since Mary installed free WiFi at Our Daily Bread, the place has been crawling with people who intend to be published.

He looks startled. 'Oh, no. This is just a place to keep all my thoughts. They get away from me, otherwise. If I don't write down that I like your kaiser rolls, for example, I won't remember to order them the next time I come.'

'I think most people could use a book like that.'

The driver of the Advanced Transit bus honks twice. We both turn in the direction of the noise. I wince as the beams of the headlights flash across my face.

Josef pats his pocket. 'It's important to remember,' he says.

One of the first things Adam told me was that I was pretty, which should have been my first clue that he was a liar.

I met him on the worst day of my life, the day my mother died. He was the funeral director my sister Pepper contacted. I have a vague recollection of him explaining the process to us, and showing us the different kinds of caskets. But the first time I really noticed him was when I made a scene at my mother's service.

My sisters and I all knew my mother's favorite song had been 'Somewhere over the Rainbow.' Pepper and Saffron had wanted to hire a professional to sing it, but I had other plans. It wasn't just the *song* my mother had loved, it was one particular rendition of it. And I'd promised my mother that Judy Garland would sing at her funeral.

'News flash, Sage,' said Pepper. 'Judy Garland isn't taking bookings these days, unless you're a medium.'

In the end, my sisters went along with what I wanted – mostly because I framed this as one of Mom's dying wishes. It was my job to give the CD to the funeral director – to Adam. I downloaded the song from the *Wizard of Oz* soundtrack on iTunes. As the service began, he played it over the speaker system.

Unfortunately it wasn't 'Somewhere over the Rainbow.' It was the Munchkins, performing 'Ding Dong! The Witch Is Dead.'

Pepper burst into tears. Saffron had to leave the service, she was so upset.

Me, I started to giggle.

I don't know why. It just spurted out of me, like a shower of sparks. And suddenly every single person in that room was staring at me, with the angry red lines bisecting my face and the inappropriate laughter fizzing out of my mouth.

'Oh my God, Sage,' Pepper hissed. 'How *could* you?'

Feeling panicked, cornered, I stood up from the front pew, took two steps, and passed out.

I came to in Adam's office. He was kneeling next to the couch and he had a damp washcloth in his hand, which he was pressing right against my scar. Immediately, I curled away from him, covering the left side of my face with my hand. 'You know,' he said, as if we were in the middle of a conversation, 'in my line of work, there aren't any secrets. I know who's had plastic surgery, and who's survived a mastectomy. I know who had their appendix out and who had surgery for a double hernia. The person may have a scar, but it also means they have a story. And besides,' he said, 'that wasn't what I noticed when I first saw you.'

'Yeah, right.'

He put his hand on my shoulder. 'I noticed,' he said, 'that you were pretty.'

He had sandy hair and honey-brown eyes. His palm was warm against my skin. I had never been beautiful, not before everything happened, and certainly not after. I shook my head, clearing it. 'I didn't eat anything this morning . . .' I said. 'I have to get back out there—'

'Relax. I suggested that we take a fifteen-minute break before we start up again.' Adam hesitated. 'Maybe you'd like to borrow a playlist from my iPod instead.'

'I could have sworn I downloaded the right song. My sisters hate me.'

'I've seen worse,' Adam replied.

'I doubt it.'

'I once watched a drunk mistress climb into a coffin with the deceased, until the wife dragged her away and knocked her out cold.'

My eyes widened. 'For real?'

'Yeah. So this . . .?' He shrugged. 'Small potatoes.'

'But I *laughed*.'

'Lots of people laugh at funerals,' Adam said. 'It's because we're uncomfortable with death, and that's a reflex. Besides, I bet your mother would much rather know you were celebrating her life with a laugh than know she had you in tears.'

'My mother would have thought it was funny,' I whispered.

'There you go.' Adam handed me the CD in its sleeve.

I shook my head. 'You can keep it. In case Naomi Campbell becomes a client.'

Adam grinned. 'I bet your mom would have thought that was funny, too,' he said.

A week after the funeral, he called me to see how I was doing. I thought this was strange on two counts – because I'd never heard of that kind of customer service from a funeral home, and because Pepper had been the one to hire him, not me. I was so touched by his concern that I baked him a quick babka and took it to the funeral home one day on my way home from work. I'd hoped to drop it off without running into him, but as it turned out, he was there.

He asked me if I had time for coffee.

You should know that even that day, he was wearing his wedding ring. In other words, I knew what I was getting into. My only defense is that I never expected to be adored by a man, not after what had happened to me, and yet here was Adam – attractive and successful – doing just that. Every fiber of morality in me that said Adam belonged to someone else was being countermanded by the quiet whisper in my head: *Beggars can't be choosers; take what you can get; who else would ever love someone like you?*

I knew it was wrong to get involved with a married man, but that didn't stop me from falling in love with him, or wishing he would fall in love with me. I had resigned myself to living alone, working alone, being alone for the rest of my life. Even if I had found someone who professed not to care about the weird puckering on the left side of my face, how would I ever know if he loved me, or pitied me? They looked so similar, and I had never been very good at reading people. The relationship between Adam and me was secretive, kept behind closed doors. In other words, it was squarely in my comfort zone.

Before you go and say it's creepy to let someone who's been embalming people touch you, let me tell you how wrong you are. Anyone who's died – my mother included – would be lucky to have that last touch be as gentle as Adam's. I sometimes think that because he spends so much time with the dead, he is the only person who really appreciates the marvel of a living body. When we make love, he lingers over the pulse of my carotid, at my wrist, behind my knees – the spots where my blood beats.

On the days when Adam comes to my place, I sacrifice an hour or two of sleep in order to be with him. He can pretty much sneak away anytime, thanks to the nature of his business, which requires him to be on call 24/7. It's also why his wife hasn't found it suspicious when he disappears.

'I think Shannon knows,' Adam says today, when I am lying in his arms.

'Really?' I try to ignore how this makes me feel, as if I am at the top of the roller coaster hill, and I can no longer see the oncoming track.

'There was a new bumper sticker on my car this morning. It says I ♥ MY WIFE.'

'How do you know she put it there?'

'Because *I* didn't,' Adam says.

I consider this for a moment. 'The bumper sticker might not be sarcastic. It could just be blissfully ignorant.'

Adam married his high school girlfriend, whom he'd dated through college. The funeral home where he works is his wife's family business and has been for fifty years. At least twice a week he tells me he is going to leave Shannon, but I know this isn't true. First, he'd be walking away from his career. Second, it is not just Shannon he'd be leaving, but also Grace and Bryan, his twins. When he talks about them, his voice sounds different. It sounds the way I hope it sounds when he talks about me.

He probably *doesn't* talk about me, though. I mean, who would he tell that he's having an affair? The only person *I've* told is Mary, and in spite of the fact that we are both at fault for getting involved, she acts as if he was the one to seduce me.

'Let's go away this weekend,' I suggest.

On Sundays, I don't work; the bakery is closed on Mondays. We could disappear for twenty-four glorious hours, instead of hiding in my bedroom with the shades drawn against the sunlight and his car – with its new bumper sticker – parked around the corner at a Chinese restaurant.

Once Shannon came into the bakery. I saw her through the open window between the kitchen and the shop. I knew it was her, because I've seen pictures on Adam's Facebook page. I was certain she had come to ream me out, but she just bought some pumpernickel rolls and left. Afterward, Mary found me sitting on the floor of the kitchen, weak with relief. When I told her about Adam, she asked me one question: *Do you love him?*

Yes, I told her.

No you don't, Mary said. *You love that he needs to hide as much as you do.*

Adam's fingers graze my scar. Even after all this time, although it's not medically possible, the skin tingles. 'You want to go away,' he repeats. 'You want to walk down the street in broad daylight with me, so everyone can see us together.'

When he puts it like that, I realize it's not what I want at all. I want to squirrel away with him behind the closed doors of a luxury hotel in the White Mountains, or in a cottage in Montana. But I don't want him to be right, so I say, 'Maybe I do.'

'Okay,' Adam says, twisting my curls around his fingers. 'The Maldives.'

I come up on an elbow. 'I'm being serious.'

Adam looks at me. 'Sage,' he says, 'you won't even look in a mirror.'

'I Googled Southwest flights. For forty-nine dollars we could get to Kansas City.'

Adam strokes his finger down the xylophone of my rib cage. 'Why would we want to go to Kansas City?'

I push his hand away. 'Stop distracting me,' I say. 'Because it's not *here*.'

He rolls on top of me. 'Book the flights.'

'Really?'

'Really.'

'What if you're paged?' I ask.

'They're not going to get any deader if they have to wait,' Adam points out.

My heart starts to beat erratically. It's tantalizing, this thought of going public. If I walk around holding the hand of a handsome man who obviously wants to be with me, does that make me normal, by association? 'What are you going to tell Shannon?'

'That I'm crazy about you.'

I sometimes wonder what would have happened if I'd met Adam when I was younger. We went to the same high school, but ten years apart. We both wound up back in our hometown. We work alone, at odd hours, doing jobs most ordinary people would never consider for a career.

'That I can't stop thinking about you,' Adam adds, his teeth raking my earlobe. 'That I'm hopelessly in love.'

I have to say, the thing I adore most about Adam is exactly what's keeping him from being with me all the time: that when he loves you, he loves you unerringly, completely, overwhelmingly. It's how he feels about his twins, which is why he is home every night to hear how the biology test went for Grace or to see Bryan score the first home run of the baseball season.

'Do you know Josef Weber?' I ask, suddenly remembering what Mary said.

Adam rolls onto his back. *'I'm hopelessly in love,'* he repeats. *'Do you know Josef Weber?* Yeah, that's a normal response . . .'

'I think he worked at the high school? He taught German.'

'The twins take French . . .' Suddenly he snaps his fingers. 'He was a Little League umpire. I think Bryan was six or seven at the time. I remember thinking that the guy must have been pushing ninety even back then, and that the rec department was off its rocker, but it turned out he was pretty damn spry.'

'What do you know about him?' I ask, turning on my side.

Adam folds his arms around me. 'Weber? He was a nice guy. He knew the game backward and forward and he never made a bad call. That's all I remember. Why?'

A smile plays over my face. 'I'm leaving you for him.'

He kisses me, slow and lovely. 'Is there anything I can do to change your mind?'

'I'm sure you'll think of something,' I say, and I wrap my arms around his neck.

In a town the size of Westerbrook, which was derived of Yankee *Mayflower* stock, being Jewish made my sisters and me anomalies, as different from our classmates as if our skin happened to be bright blue. 'Rounding out the bell curve,' my father used to say, when I asked him why we had to stop eating bread for a week roughly the same time everyone else in my school was bringing hard-boiled Easter eggs in their lunch boxes. I wasn't picked on – to the contrary, when our elementary school teachers taught holiday alternatives to Christmas, I became a virtual celebrity, along with Julius, the only African-American kid in my school, whose grandmother celebrated Kwanzaa. I went to Hebrew school because my sisters did, but when the time came to be bat mitzvahed, I begged to drop out. When I wasn't allowed, I went on a hunger strike. It was enough that my family didn't match other families; I had no desire to call attention to myself any more than I had to.

My parents were Jews, but they didn't keep kosher or go to services (except for the years prior to Pepper's and Saffron's bat mitzvahs, when it was mandatory. I used to sit at Friday night services listening to the cantor sing in Hebrew and wonder why Jewish music was full of minor chords. For Chosen People, the songwriters sure didn't seem very happy). My parents did, however, fast on Yom Kippur and refused to have a Christmas tree.

To me, it seemed they were following an abridged version of Judaism, so who were they to tell me how and what to believe? I said this to my parents when I was lobbying to not have a bat mitzvah. My father got very quiet. *The reason it's important to believe in something,* he said, *is because you* can. Then he sent me to my room without supper, which was truly shocking because in our household, we were encouraged to state our opinions, no matter how controversial. It was my mother who sneaked upstairs with a peanut butter and jelly sandwich for me. 'Your father may not be a rabbi,' she said, 'but he believes in tradition. That's what parents pass down to their children.'

'Okay,' I argued. 'I promise to do my back-to-school shopping in July; and I'll always make sweet-potato-marshmallow casserole for Thanksgiving. I don't have a problem with tradition, Mom. I have a problem going to Hebrew school. Religion isn't in your DNA. You don't believe just because your parents believe.'

'Grandma Minka wears sweaters,' my mother said. 'All the time.'

This was a seemingly random observation. My father's mother lived in an assisted living community. She had been born in Poland and still had an accent that made it sound like she was always singing. And yes, Grandma Minka wore sweaters, even when it was ninety degrees out, but she also wore too much blush and leopard prints.

'A lot of survivors had their tattoos surgically removed, but she said seeing it every morning reminds her that she won.'

It took me a moment to realize what my mother was telling me. My father's mother had been in a concentration camp? How had I made it to age twelve without knowing this? Why would my parents have hidden this information from me?

'She doesn't like to talk about it,' my mother said simply. 'And she doesn't like her arm to show in public.'

We had studied the Holocaust in social studies class. It was hard to imagine the textbook pictures of living skeletons matching the plump woman who always smelled like lilacs, who never missed her weekly hair appointment, who kept brightly colored canes in every room of her condo so that she always had easy access to one. She was not part of history. She was just my grandma.

'She doesn't go to temple,' my mother said. 'I guess after all that, you'd have a pretty complicated relationship with God. But your father, he started going. I think it was his way of processing what happened to her.'

Here I was, trying desperately to shed my religion so I could blend in, and it turned out being Jewish was truly in my blood, that I was the descendant of a Holocaust survivor. Frustrated, angry, and selfish, I threw myself backward against my pillows. 'That's Dad's issue. It has nothing to do with me.'

My mother hesitated. 'If she hadn't lived, Sage, neither would you.'

That was the one and only time we ever discussed Grandma

Minka's past, although when we brought her to our house for Chanukah that year, I found myself scrutinizing her to see some shadow of the truth on her face. But she was the same as always, picking the skin off the roasted chicken to eat when my mother wasn't looking, emptying her purse of perfume and makeup samples she'd collected for my sisters, discussing the characters on *All My Children* as if they were friends she visited for coffee. If she had been in a concentration camp during World War II, she must have been a completely different person at the time.

The night my mother told me about my grandmother's history, I dreamed of a moment I hadn't remembered, from when I was very tiny. I was sitting on Grandma Minka's lap while she turned the pages of a book and read me the story. I realize now that it wasn't the right story at all. The picture book was of Cinderella, but she must have been thinking of something else, because her tale was about a dark forest and monsters, a trail of oats and grain.

I also recall that I wasn't paying much attention, because I was mesmerized by the gold bangle bracelet on my grandmother's wrist. I kept reaching for it, pulling at her sweater. At one point, the wool rode up just far enough for me to be distracted by the faded blue numbers on her inner forearm. *What's that?*

My telephone number.

I had memorized my telephone number the previous year in preschool, so that if I got lost, the police could call home. *What if you move?* I asked.

Oh, Sage, she laughed. *I'm here to stay.*

The next day, Mary comes into the kitchen while I'm baking. 'I had a dream last night,' she says. 'You were making baguettes with Adam. You told him to put the loaves in the oven, but instead, he stuck your arm inside. I screamed and tried to pull you out of the fire but I wasn't fast enough. When you stepped away, you didn't have a right hand. Just an arm made out of bread dough. *It's fine,* Adam said, and he took a knife and hacked your wrist. He sliced off your thumb and your pinkie and each finger, and each one was soaked with blood.'

'Well,' I say. 'Good afternoon to you, too.' Then I open the refrigerator and take out a tray of buns.

'That's it? You don't even want to speculate on what it meant?'

'That you had coffee before you went to bed,' I suggest. 'Remember when you dreamed that Rocco refused to take off his shoes because he had chicken feet?' I face her. 'Have you even ever *met* Adam? Do you know what he looks like?'

'Even the most beautiful things can be toxic. Monkshood, lily of the valley – they're both in the Monet garden you like so much at the top of the Holy Stairs, but I wouldn't go near them if I weren't wearing gloves.'

'Isn't that a liability for the shrine?'

She shakes her head. 'Most of the visitors refrain from eating the scenery. But that's not the point, Sage. The point is that this dream was a sign.'

'Here we go,' I mutter.

'Thou shalt not commit adultery,' Mary preaches. 'You can't get any more clear than that directive. And if you do, bad things happen. You get stoned by your neighbors. You become an outcast.'

'Your hands become edible,' I say. 'Look, Mary, don't go full-frontal nun on me. What I do with my free time is my own business. And you know I don't believe in God.'

She moves, blocking my path. 'That doesn't mean He doesn't believe in you,' she says.

My scar tingles. My left eye starts to tear, the way it did for months after the surgery. Back then it was as if I were sobbing for everything I would be losing in the future, even though I didn't know it at the time. Maybe it is archaic and – ironically – biblical to believe that ugly is as ugly does, that a scar or a birthmark is the outward sign of an inner deficiency, but in my case, it also happens to be true. I did something awful; every time I catch a glance of my reflection I am reminded of it. Is it wrong for most women to sleep with a married man? Of course, but I am not most women. Maybe that's why, even though the old me would never have fallen for Adam, the new me did just that. It's not that I feel entitled, or that I deserve to be with someone else's husband. It's that I don't believe I deserve anything better.

I'm not a sociopath. I'm not proud of my relationship. But most of the time, I can make excuses for it. The fact that Mary has gotten under my skin today means that I am tired, or more vulnerable than I thought, or both.

'What about that poor woman, Sage?'

That poor woman is Adam's wife. That poor woman has a man I love, and two wonderful kids, and a face that is smooth and scar-free. That poor woman has had everything she wants handed to her on a silver platter.

I reach for a sharp knife and begin slicing the tops of the hot cross buns. 'If you want to feel sorry for yourself,' Mary continues, 'then do it in a way that isn't going to destroy other people's lives.'

I point the tip of the knife at my scar. 'Do you think I *wanted* this?' I ask. 'Do you think I don't wish every day of my life that I could have the same things everyone else does – a job that's nine-to-five, and a stroll down the street without kids staring, and a man who thinks I'm beautiful?'

'You could have all those things,' Mary says, folding me into her arms. 'You're the only one saying you can't. You're not a bad person, Sage.'

I want to believe her. I want to believe her, so much. 'Then I guess sometimes good people do bad things,' I say, and I pull away from her.

In the bakery shop, I hear Josef Weber's clipped accent, asking for me. I wipe my eyes on the hem of my apron and grab a loaf I've set aside and a small package; I leave Mary standing in the kitchen without me.

'Hello!' I say brightly. Too brightly. Josef looks startled by my false good cheer. I thrust the small bag of homemade dog biscuits for Eva into his hands, as well as the loaf of bread. Rocco, who is not used to me fraternizing with the customers, pauses in the act of restacking clean mugs. 'Wonders never cease / From the deepest, darkest bowels / The recluse arrives,' he says.

'*Bowels* is two syllables,' I snap, and I motion Josef toward an empty table. Any lingering hesitation I had about being the one to instigate a conversation with Josef has become a lesser of two evils: I'd much rather be here than be interrogated by Mary. 'I saved you the best loaf of the night.'

'A *bâtard*,' Josef says.

I am impressed; most people don't know the French term for that shape. 'Do you know why it's called that?' I say, as I cut a few slices, trying hard not to think of Mary and her dream. 'Because it's not a *boule*, and it's not a *baguette*. Literally, it's a bastard.'

'Who knew that even in the world of baking, there is a class structure?' Josef muses.

I know it's a good loaf. You can smell it, when an artisanal bread comes out of the oven: the earthy, dark scent, as if you are in the thick of the woods. I glance with pride at the variegated crumb. Josef closes his eyes in delight. 'I am lucky to know the baker personally.'

'Speaking of that . . . you umpired the Little League game of a friend's son. Bryan Lancaster?'

He frowns, shaking his head. 'It was years ago. I did not know all their names.'

We chat – about the weather, about Eva, about my favorite recipes. We chat, as Mary closes up the bakery around us, after hugging me fiercely and telling me that not only does God love me but she does, too. We chat, even as I dart back and forth into the kitchen to answer the calls of various timers. This is extraordinary for me, because I don't chat. There are even moments during our conversation when I forget to disguise the pitted side of my face by ducking my head or letting my hair fall in front of it. But Josef, he is either too polite or too embarrassed to mention it. Or maybe, just maybe, there are other things about me he finds more interesting. This is what must have made him everyone's favorite teacher, umpire, adoptive grandfather – he acts as if there is nowhere else on earth he'd rather be than here, right now. And no one else on earth he'd rather be talking to. It is such a heady rush to be the object of someone's attention in a *good* way, not as a freak, that I keep forgetting to hide.

'How long have you lived here?' I ask, when we have been talking for over an hour.

'Twenty-two years,' Josef says. 'I used to live in Canada.'

'Well, if you were looking for a community where nothing ever happens, you hit the jackpot.'

Josef smiles. 'I think so.'

'Do you have family around here?'

His hand shakes as he reaches for his mug of coffee. 'I have no one,' Josef answers, and he starts to get to his feet. 'I must go.'

Immediately, my stomach turns over, because I've made him uncomfortable – and nobody knows better than I do what that feels like. 'I'm sorry,' I blurt out. 'I didn't mean to be rude. I don't talk to many people.' I offer him an unhemmed smile, and make amends the only way I know how: by revealing a piece of myself that I usually keep under lock and key, so that I am equally exposed. 'I also have no one,' I confess. 'I'm twenty-five, and both of my parents are dead. They won't see me get married. I won't get to cook them Thanksgiving dinner or visit them with grandkids. My sisters are totally different from me – they have minivans and soccer practices and careers with bonuses – and they hate me even though they say they don't.' The words are a flood rushing out of me; just speaking them, I am drowning. 'But mostly I have no one because of this.'

With a shaking hand, I pull my hair back from my face.

I know every detail he's seeing. The pocked drawstring of skin flapping the corner of my left eye. The silver hatch marks cutting through my eyebrow. The puzzle-piece patchwork of grafted skin that doesn't quite match and doesn't quite fit. The way my mouth tugs upward, because of how my cheekbone healed. The bald notch at my scalp that no longer grows hair, that my bangs are brushed to carefully cover. The face of a monster.

I cannot justify why I've picked Josef, a virtual stranger, to reveal myself to. Maybe because loneliness is a mirror, and recognizes itself. My hand falls away, letting the curtain of my hair cover my scars again. I just wish it were that easy to camouflage the ones inside me.

To his credit, Josef does not gasp or recoil. Steadily, he meets my gaze. 'Maybe now,' he replies, 'we will have each other.'

The next morning on my way home from work, I drive by Adam's house. I park on the street, roll down my window, and stare at the soccer nets stretched across the front yard, at the welcome mat, at the lime-green bike tipped over and sunning itself in the driveway.

I imagine what it would be like to sit at the dining room table, to have Adam toss the salad as I serve the pasta. I wonder if the walls in the kitchen are yellow or white; if there is still a loaf of bread – probably store-bought, I think with mild judgment – sitting on the counter after someone has made French toast for breakfast.

When the door opens, I swear out loud and slink lower in my seat, even though there is no reason to believe that Shannon sees me. She comes out of the house still zipping her purse, hitting the remote control so that her car doors unlock. 'Come on,' she calls. 'We're going to be late for the appointment.'

A moment later Grace stumbles out, coughing violently.

'Cover your mouth,' her mother says.

I realize I am holding my breath. Grace looks like Shannon, in miniature – same golden hair, same delicate features, even the same bounce to their walk. 'Do I have to miss camp?' Grace asks miserably.

'You do if you have bronchitis,' Shannon says, and then they both get into the car and peel out of the driveway.

Adam hadn't told me his daughter was sick.

Then again, why would he? I don't hold claim to that part of his life.

As I pull away, I realize that I'm not going to book those airline tickets to Kansas City. I never will.

Instead of driving home, though, I find myself looking up Josef's address on my iPhone. He lives at the end of a small cul-de-sac, and I am parked at the curb trying to concoct a reason that I might be dropping by when he knocks on the window of my car. 'So it *is* you,' Josef says.

He is holding the end of Eva's leash. She dances around his feet in circles. 'What brings you to my neighborhood?' he asks.

I consider telling him that it is a coincidence, that I took a wrong turn. Or that I have a friend who lives nearby. But instead, I wind up speaking the truth. 'You,' I say.

A smile breaks across his face. 'Then you must stay for tea,' he insists.

His home is not decorated the way I would have expected. There are chintz couches with lace doilies on the backs, photographs on top of a dusty mantel, a collection of Hummel figurines on a shelf. The invisible fingerprints of a woman are everywhere. 'You're married,' I murmur.

'I was,' Josef says. 'To Marta. For fifty-one very good years and one not-so-good.'

This must have been the reason he started coming to grief group, I realize. 'I'm sorry.'

'I am, too,' he says heavily. He takes the tea bag from his mug and carefully wraps a noose around it on the bowl of the spoon. 'Every Wednesday night she would remind me to take the garbage can to the curb. In fifty years, I never once forgot, but she never gave me the benefit of the doubt. Drove me crazy. Now, I would give anything to hear her remind me again.'

'I almost flunked out of college,' I reply. 'My mother actually moved *into* my dorm room and dragged me out of bed and made me study with her. I felt like the biggest loser on earth. And now I realize how lucky I was.' I reach down and stroke Eva's silky head. 'Josef?' I ask. 'Do you ever feel like you're losing her?

Like you can't hear the exact pitch of her voice in your head anymore, or you can't remember what her perfume smelled like?'

He shakes his head. 'I have the opposite problem,' he says. 'I can't forget him.'

'Him?'

'Her,' Josef corrects. 'All this time, and I still mix up the German words with the English.'

My gaze lands on a chess set on a sideboard behind Josef. The pieces are all carefully carved: pawns shaped like tiny unicorns, rooks fashioned into centaurs, a pair of Pegasus knights. The queen's mermaid tail curls around its base; the head of the vampire king is tossed back, fangs bared. 'This is incredible,' I breathe, walking closer for a better look. 'I've never seen anything like it.'

Josef chuckles. 'That is because there is only one. It is a family heirloom.'

I stare with even more admiration at the chessboard, with its seamless inlay of cherry and maple squares; at the tiny jeweled eyes of the mermaid. 'It's beautiful.'

'Yes. My brother was very artistic,' Josef says softly.

'He *made* this?'

I pick up the vampire and run my finger over the smooth, slick skull of the creature. 'Do you play?' I ask.

'Not for years. Marta had no patience for the game.' He looks up. 'And you?'

'I'm not very good. You have to think five steps ahead.'

'It's all about strategy,' Josef says. 'And protecting your king.'

'What's with the mythical creatures?' I ask.

'My brother believed in all sorts of mythical creatures: pixies, dragons, werewolves, honest men.'

I find myself thinking of Adam; of his daughter, coughing

as a pediatrician listens to her lungs. 'Maybe,' I say, 'you could teach me what you know.'

Josef becomes a regular at Our Daily Bread, showing up shortly before closing, so that we can spend a half hour chatting before he leaves for the night and I start my workday. When Josef shows up, Rocco yells to me in the kitchen, referring to him as 'my boyfriend.' Mary brings him a cutting from the shrine – a daylily – and tells him how to plant it in his backyard. She starts assuming that even after she locks up, I will make sure Josef gets home. The dog biscuits I bake for Eva become a new staple of our menu.

We talk about teachers that I had at the high school when Josef was still working there – Mr. Muchnick, whose toupee once went missing when he fell asleep proctoring an SAT test; Ms. Fiero, who would bring her toddler to school when her nanny got sick and would stick him in the computer lab to play Sesame Street games. We talk about a strudel recipe that his grandmother used to make. He tells me about Eva's predecessor, a schnauzer named Willie, who used to mummify himself in toilet paper if you left the bathroom door open by accident. Josef admits that it is hard to fill all the hours he has, now that he isn't working or volunteering regularly.

And me: I find myself talking about things that I have long packed up, like a spinster's hope chest. I tell Josef about the time my mother and I went shopping together, and she got stuck in a sundress too small for her, and we had to buy it just so that we could rip it off. I tell him how, for years after that, even uttering the word *sundress* made us both collapse with laughter. I tell him how my father would read the Seder every year in a Donald Duck voice, not out of irreverence, but because it made his little girls laugh. I tell him how, on our birthdays, my mother let us eat our favorite dessert for breakfast and how she could touch your forehead if you were feverish and guess your temperature, within two-tenths of a degree. I tell him how, when I was little and convinced a monster lived in my closet, my father slept for a month sitting upright against the slatted pocket doors so that the beast couldn't break out in the middle of the night. I tell him how my mother taught me to make hospital corners on a bed; how my father taught me to spit a watermelon seed through my teeth. Each memory is like a paper flower stowed up a magician's sleeve: invisible one moment and then so substantial and florid the next I cannot imagine how it stayed hidden all this time. And like those paper flowers, once they've been let loose in the world, the memories are impossible to tuck away again.

I find myself canceling dates with Adam so that I can instead spend an hour at Josef's house, playing chess, before my eyelids droop and I have to drive back home and get some rest. He teaches me to control the center of the board. To not give up any pieces unless absolutely necessary, and how to assign arbitrary point values to each knight and bishop and rook and pawn so that I can make those decisions.

As we play, Josef asks me questions. Was my mother a redhead, like me? Did my father ever miss the restaurant industry, once he went into industrial sales? Did either of them ever get a chance to taste some of my recipes? Even the answers that are hardest to give – like the fact that I never baked for either of them – don't burn my tongue as badly as they would have a year or two ago. It turns out that sharing the past with someone is different from reliving it when you're alone. It feels less like a wound, more like a poultice.

Two weeks later, Josef and I carpool to our next grief

group meeting. We sit beside each other, and it is as if we have a subtle telepathy between us as the other group members speak. Sometimes he catches my gaze and hides a smile, sometimes I roll my eyes at him. We are suddenly partners in crime.

Today we are talking about what happens to us after we die. 'Do we stick around?' Marge asks. 'Watch over our loved ones?'

'I think so. I can still feel Sheila sometimes,' Stuart says. 'It's like the air gets more humid.'

'Well, I think it's pretty self-serving to think that souls hang around with the rest of us,' Shayla says immediately. 'They go to Heaven.'

'Everyone?'

'Everyone who's a believer,' she qualifies.

Shayla is born-again; this isn't a surprise. But it still makes me uncomfortable, as if she is specifically talking about my ineligibility.

'When my mother was in the hospital,' I say, 'her rabbi told her a story. In Heaven and Hell, people sit at banquet tables filled with amazing food, but no one can bend their elbows. In Hell, everyone starves because they can't feed themselves. In Heaven, everyone's stuffed, because they don't have to bend their arms to feed each other.'

I can feel Josef staring at me.

'Mr. Weber?' Marge prompts.

I assume Josef will ignore her question, or shake his head, like usual. But to my surprise, he speaks. 'When you die you die. And everything is over.'

His blunt words settle like a shroud over the rest of us. 'Excuse me,' he says, and he walks out of the meeting room.

I find him waiting in the hallway of the church. 'That story you told, about the banquet,' Josef says. 'Do you believe it?'

'I guess I'd like to,' I say. 'For my mother's sake.'

'But your rabbi—'

'Not my rabbi. My mother's.' I start walking toward the door.

'But you believe in an afterlife?' Josef says, curious.

'And you don't.'

'I believe in Hell . . . but it's here on earth.' He shakes his head. 'Good people and bad people. As if it were this easy. Everyone is both of these at once.'

'Don't you think one outweighs the other?'

Josef stops walking. 'You tell me,' he says.

As if his words have heat behind them, my scar burns. 'How come you've never asked me,' I blurt out. 'How it happened?'

'How what happened?'

I make a circular gesture in front of my face.

'Ach. Well. A long time ago, someone once told me that a story will tell itself, when it's ready. I assumed that it wasn't ready.'

It is a strange idea, that what happened to me isn't my tale to tell, but something completely separate from me. I wonder if this has been my problem all along: not being able to dissect the two. 'I was in a car accident,' I say.

Josef nods, waiting.

'I wasn't the only one hurt,' I manage, although the words choke me.

'But you survived.' Gently, he touches my shoulder. 'Maybe that's all that matters.'

I shake my head. 'I wish I could believe that.'

Josef looks at me. 'Don't we all,' he says.

The next day, Josef doesn't come to the bakery. He doesn't come the following day, either. I have reached the only viable conclusion: Josef is lying comatose in his bed. Or worse.

In all the years I've worked at Our Daily Bread, I've never left the bakery unattended overnight. My evenings are ordered to military precision, with me working a mile a minute to divide dough and shape it into hundreds of loaves; to have them proofed and ready for baking when the oven is free. The bakery itself becomes a living, breathing thing; each station a new partner to dance with. Mess up on the timing, and you will find yourself standing alone while chaos whirls around you. I find myself compensating in a frenzy, trying to produce the same amount of product in less time. But I realize that I'm not going to be of any use until I go to Josef's house, and make sure he's still breathing.

I drive there, and see a light on in the kitchen. Immediately, Eva starts barking. Josef opens the front door. 'Sage,' he says, surprised. He sneezes violently and wipes his nose with a white cloth handkerchief. 'Is everything all right?'

'You have a cold,' I say, the obvious.

'Did you come all this way to tell me what I already know?'

'No. I thought – I mean, I wanted to check on you, since I hadn't seen you in a few days.'

'Ach. Well, as you can see, I am still standing.' He gestures. 'You will come in?'

'I can't,' I say. 'I have to get back to work.' But I make no move to leave. 'I was worried when you didn't show up at the bakery.'

He hesitates, his hand on the doorknob. 'So you came to make sure I was alive?'

'I came to check on a friend.'

'Friends,' Josef repeats, beaming. 'We are friends, now?'

A twenty-five-year-old disfigured girl and a nonagenarian? I suppose there have been stranger duos.

'I would like that very much,' Josef says formally. 'I will see you tomorrow, Sage. Now you must go back to work so that I can have a roll with my coffee.'

Twenty minutes later, I am back in the kitchen, turning off a half dozen angry timers and assessing the damage caused by my hour AWOL. There are loaves that have proofed too much; the dough has lost its shape and sags to one side or the other. My output for the whole night will be affected; Mary will be devastated. Tomorrow's customers will leave empty-handed.

I burst into tears.

I'm not sure if I'm crying because of the disaster in the kitchen or because I didn't realize how upsetting it was to think that Josef might be taken away from me, when I've only just found him. I just don't know how much more I can stand to lose.

I wish I could bake for my mother: boules and pain au chocolat and brioche, piled high on her table in Heaven. I wish I could be the one to feed her. But I can't. It's like Josef said – no matter what we survivors like to tell ourselves about the afterlife, when someone dies, everything is over.

But *this*. I look around the bakery kitchen. This, I can reclaim, by working the dough very briefly and letting it rise again.

So I knead. I knead, I knead.

The next day, a miracle occurs.

Mary, who at first is tight-lipped and angry at my reduced nightly output, slices open a ciabatta. 'What am I supposed to do, Sage?' she sighs. 'Tell customers to just go down the street to Rudy's?'

Rudy's is our competition. 'You could give them a rain check.'

'Peanut butter and jelly tastes like crap on a rain check.'

When she asks what happened, I lie. I tell her that I got a migraine and fell asleep for two hours. 'It won't happen again.'

Mary purses her lips, which tells me that she hasn't forgiven me yet. Then she picks up a slice of the bread, ready to spread it with strawberry jam.

Except she doesn't.

'Jesus, Mary, and Joseph,' she gasps, dropping the slice as if it's burned her fingers. She points to the crumb.

That's a fancy term for the holes inside bread. Artisanal bread is judged on its variegated crumb, other breads – like Wonder (which is barely even a bread, nutritionally) have uniform, tiny crumb.

'Do you see Him?'

If I squint, I can make out what looks like the shape of a face.

Then it becomes more clear: A beard. A thorny crown.

Apparently I've baked the face of God into my loaf.

The first visitors to our little miracle are the women who work in the shrine gift shop, who take a picture with the piece of bread between them. Then Father Dupree – the priest at the shrine – arrives. 'Fascinating,' he says, peering over the edge of his bifocals.

By now, the bread has grown stale. The half of the loaf that Mary hasn't cut yet, of course, has a matching picture of Jesus. It strikes me that the thinner you cut the slices, the more incarnations of Jesus you would have.

'The real question isn't that God appeared,' Father Dupree tells Mary. 'He's always here. It's why He chose to appear *now*.'

Rocco and I are watching this from a distance, leaning on the counter with our arms folded. 'Good Lord,' I murmur.

He snorts. 'Exactly. Looks like / You baked the Father, the Son / And the Holy Toast.'

The door flies open and a reporter with frizzy brown

hair enters, trailed by a bear of a cameraman. 'Is this where the Jesus Loaf is?'

Mary steps forward. 'Yes, I'm Mary DeAngelis. I own the bakery.'

'Great,' the reporter says. 'I'm Harriet Yarrow from WMUR. We'd like to talk to you and your employees. Last year we did a human-interest piece on a logger who saw the Virgin Mary in a tree stump and chained himself to it to keep his company from stripping the rest of that forest. It was the most watched piece of 2012. Are we rolling? Yes? Great.'

While she interviews Mary and Father Dupree, I hide behind Rocco, who rings up three baguettes, a hot chocolate, and a semolina loaf. Then Harriet sticks her microphone in my face. 'Is this the baker?' she asks Mary.

The camera has a red light above its cyclopean eye, which blinks awake while filming. I stare at it, stricken by the thought of the whole state seeing me on the midday news. I drop my chin to my chest, obliterating my face, even as my cheeks burn with embarrassment. How much has he already filmed? Just a glimpse of my scar before I ducked my head? Or enough to make children drop their spoons in their soup bowls; for their mothers to turn off the television for fear of giving birth to nightmares? 'I have to go,' I mutter, and I bolt into the bakery office, and out the back door.

I take the Holy Stairs two at a time. Everyone comes to the shrine to see the giant rosary, but I like the little grotto at the top of the hill that Mary's planted to look like a Monet painting. It's an area nobody ever visits – which, of course, is exactly how I like it.

This is why I'm surprised when I hear footsteps. When Josef appears, leaning heavily on the railing, I rush over to help him. 'What is going on down there? Is someone famous having coffee?'

'Sort of. Mary thinks she saw the face of Jesus in one of my loaves.'

I expect him to scoff, but instead Josef tilts his head, considering this. 'I suppose God tends to show up in places we would not expect.'

'You believe in God?' I say, truly surprised. After our conversation about Heaven and Hell, I had assumed that he was an atheist, too.

'Yes,' Josef replies. 'He judges us at the end. The Old Testament God. You must know about this, as a Jew.'

I feel that pang of isolation, of *difference*. 'I never said I was Jewish.'

Now Josef looks surprised. 'But your mother—'

'Is not me.'

Emotions chase over his features in quick succession, as if he is wrestling with a dilemma. 'The child of a Jewish mother is a Jew.'

'I suppose it depends on who you're asking. And I'm asking you why it matters.'

'I did not mean to offend,' he says stiffly. 'I came to ask a favor, and I just needed to be certain you were who I thought you were.' Josef takes a deep breath, and when he exhales, the words he speaks hang between us. 'I would like you to help me die.'

'What?' I say, truly shocked. *'Why?'*

He is having a senile moment, I think. But Josef's eyes are bright and focused. 'I know this is a surprising request . . .'

'Surprising? How about *insane*—'

'I have my reasons,' Josef says, stubborn. 'I ask you to trust me.'

I take a step backward. 'Maybe you should just go.'

'Please,' Josef begs. 'It is like you said about chess. I am thinking five steps ahead.'

His words make me pause. 'Are you sick?'

'My doctor says I have the constitution of a much younger man. This is God's joke on me. He makes me so strong that I cannot die even when I want to. I have had cancer, twice. I survived a car crash and a broken hip. I have even, God forgive me, swallowed a bottle of pills. But I was found by a Jehovah's Witness who happened to be passing out leaflets and saw me through the window, lying on the floor.'

'Why would you try to kill yourself?'

'Because I *should* be dead, Sage. It's what I deserve. And you can help me.' He hesitates. 'You showed me *your* scars. I only ask you to let me show you *mine*.'

It strikes me that I know nothing about this man, except for what he has chosen to share with me. And now, apparently, he's picked me to help him carry out his assisted suicide. 'Look, Josef,' I say gently. 'You do need help, but not for the reason you think. I don't go around committing murder.'

'Perhaps not.' He reaches into his coat pocket and pulls out a small photograph, its edges scalloped. He presses it into my palm.

In the picture, I see a man, much younger than Josef – with the same widow's peak, the same hooked nose, a ghosting of his features. He is dressed in the uniform of an SS guard, and he is smiling.

'But I did,' he says.

*D*amian held his hand high, as his soldiers laughed behind him. I tried to leap to reach the coins, but I couldn't, and stumbled. Although it was only October, there was a hint of winter in the air, and my hands were numb with the cold. Damian's arm snaked around me, a vise, pressing me along the length of his body. I could feel the silver buttons of his uniform cutting into my skin. 'Let me go,' I said through my teeth.

'Now, now,' he said, grinning. 'Is that any way to speak to a paying customer?' It was the last baguette. Once I got his money, I could go back home to my father.

I looked around at the other merchants. Old Sal was stirring the dregs of herring left in her barrel; Farouk was folding his silks, studiously avoiding the confrontation. They knew better than to make an enemy of the captain of the guard.

'Where are your manners, Ania?' Damian chided.

'Please!'

He tossed a glance at his soldiers. 'It sounds good when she begs for me, doesn't it?'

Other girls rhapsodized about his striking silver eyes, about whether his hair was as black as night or as black as the wing of a raven, about a smile so full of sorcery it could rob you of your thoughts and speech, but I did not see the attraction.

Damian might have been one of the most eligible men in the village, but he reminded me of the pumpkins left too long on the porch after All Hallows' Eve – lovely to look at, until you touched one and realized it was rotten to the core.

Unfortunately, Damian liked a challenge. And since I was the only woman between ten years and a hundred who wasn't swayed by his charm, he had targeted me.

He brought down his hand, the one holding the coins, and curled it around my throat. I could feel the silver pressing into the pulse at my neck. He pinned me against the scrubwood of the vegetable seller's cart, as if he wanted to remind me how easy it would be to kill me, how much stronger he was. But then he leaned forward. Marry me, *he whispered,* and you'll never have to worry about taxes again. *Still gripping me by the throat, he kissed me.*

I bit his lip so hard that he bled. As soon as he let go of me, I grabbed the empty basket I used to carry bread back and forth to the market, and I started to run.

I would not tell my father, I decided. He had enough to worry about.

The further I got into the woods, the more I could smell the peat burning in the fireplace of our cottage. In moments, I would be back home, and my father would hand me the special roll that he had baked for me. I would sit at the counter and tell him about the characters in the village: the mother who became frantic when her twins hid beneath Farouk's bolts of silk; Fat Teddy, who insisted on sampling the cheese at each market stall, filled his belly in the process, and never bought a single item. I would tell him about the man I had never seen before, who had come to the market with a teenage boy who looked to be his brother. But the boy was feebleminded; he wore a leather helmet that covered his nose and mouth, leaving only holes for breathing, and a leather cuff around his wrist, so that his older brother could keep him close by holding tight to a leash. The man strode past my bread stand and the vegetable seller and the other sundries, intent on reaching the meat stall, where he asked for a rack of ribs. When he did not have enough coins to pay, he shrugged out of his woolen coat. Take this, *he said.* It's all I have. *As he shivered back across the square, his brother grabbed for the wrapped parcel of meat.* You can have it soon, *he promised, and then I lost sight of him.*

My father would make up a story for them: They jumped off a circus train and wound up here. They were assassins, scoping out Baruch Beiler's mansion. *I would laugh and eat my roll, warming myself in front of the fire while my father mixed the next batch of dough.*

There was a stream that separated the cottage from the house, and my father had placed a wide plank across it so that we could get from one side to the other. But today, when I reached it, I bent to drink, to wash away the bitter taste of Damian that was still on my lips.

The water ran red.

I set down the basket I was carrying and followed the bank upstream, my boots sinking into the spongy marsh. And then I saw it.

The man was lying on his back, the bottom half of his body submerged in the water. His throat and his chest had been torn open. His veins were tributaries, his arteries mapped a place I never wanted to go. I started to scream.

There was blood, so much blood that it painted his face and stained his hair.

There was blood, so much blood that several moments passed before I recognized my father.

Sage

In the picture, the soldier is laughing, as if someone has just told him a joke. His left leg is braced on a crate, and he is holding a pistol in his right hand. Behind him is a barracks. It reminds me of photos I have seen of soldiers on the eve of being shipped out, wearing too much bravado like a cloying aftershave. This is not the face of someone ambivalent about his role. This is someone who enjoyed what he was doing.

There are no other people in the picture, but outside the white borders, they hover like ghosts: all the prisoners who knew better than to make themselves visible when a Nazi soldier was near.

This man in the photo has pale hair and strong shoulders and an air of confidence. It is hard for me to reconcile this man with the one who told me once that he had lost too many people to count.

Then again, why would he lie about something like this? You lie to convince people you are *not* a monster . . . not that you *are* one.

For that matter, if Josef is telling the truth, why would he have made himself such a visible member of the community: teaching, coaching, walking around in broad daylight?

'So you see,' Josef says, taking the picture from me again. 'I was SS-Totenkopfverbände.'

'I don't believe you,' I say.

Josef looks at me, surprised. 'Why would I confess to you that I did horrible things if it were not true?'

'I don't know,' I reply. 'You tell me.'

'Because you are a Jew.'

I close my eyes, trying to wade through the whirlpool of wild thoughts in my head. I'm *not* a Jew; I haven't considered myself one in years, even if Josef believes that to be a technicality. But if I'm not a Jew, why do I feel so viscerally and personally offended by this photograph of him in an SS uniform?

And why does it make me sick to hear him label me; to think that, after all this time, Josef would still feel that one Jew is interchangeable for another?

In that moment, a tide of disgust rises inside me. In that moment, I think I *could* kill him.

'There is a reason God has kept me alive for this long. He wants me to feel what *they* felt. They prayed for their lives but had no control over them; I pray for my death but have no control over it. This is why I want you to help me.'

Did you ask any Jews what they wanted?

An eye for an eye; one life for many.

'I'm not going to kill you, Josef,' I say, pushing away from him, but his voice stops me.

'Please. It's a dying man's wish,' he begs. 'Or perhaps the wish of a man who wants to die. They are not so different.'

He's delusional. He thinks he's some kind of vampire, like the king in his chess set, who is trapped here by his sins. He thinks that if I kill him biblical justice will be served and a karmic debt will be erased, a Jew taking the life of the man who took the life of other Jews. Logically, I know that's not true. Emotionally, I don't even want to give him the satisfaction of thinking I would consider it.

But I can't just walk away and pretend this conversation never happened. If a man came up to me on the street and confessed to a murder, I wouldn't ignore it. I'd find someone who knew what to do.

Just because that murder occurred nearly seventy years ago doesn't make it any different.

It is still a complete disconnect for me – looking at this photo of an SS officer and trying to figure out how he became the man standing in front of me. The one who has hidden, in plain sight, for more than half a century.

I had laughed with Josef; I had confided in Josef; I had played chess with Josef. Behind him is Mary's Monet garden, the one with dahlias and sweet peas and stem roses, hydrangea and delphinium and monkshood. I think about what she told me weeks ago, how sometimes the most beautiful things can be poisonous.

Two years ago, the John Demjanjuk case was in the news. Although I hadn't followed it, I remember the image of a very old man being removed from his home in a wheelchair. Clearly someone, somewhere, is still out there prosecuting former Nazis.

But who?

If Josef is lying, I need to know why. But if Josef is telling the truth, then I have unwittingly just become a part of history.

I need time to think. And I need him to believe I'm on his side.

I turn back and hand him the photograph. I think about young Josef in his uniform, lifting his gun and shooting at someone. I think about a picture in my high school history book, an emaciated Jewish man carrying the body of another.

'Before I decide whether or not to help you . . . I have to know what you did,' I say slowly.

Josef lets out a breath he has been holding. 'So it is not a no,' he says cautiously. 'This is good.'

'This is *not* good,' I correct, and I run down the Holy Stairs, leaving him to fend for himself.

I walk. For hours. I know that Josef will come down from the shrine and try to find me in the bakery, and when he does, I don't want to be there. By the time I get back to the shop, all heaven has broken loose. A trickle of the frail, the elderly, the wheelchair-bound snakes out the front door. A small knot of nuns kneeling in prayer have gathered by the oleander bush in the restroom hallway. Somehow, in the short time I've been gone, the word about the Jesus Loaf has gotten out.

Mary stands beside Rocco, who has pulled his dreadlocks into a neat ponytail and who is holding the bread on a platter covered with a burgundy tea towel. In front of them is a mother pushing her twenty-something son in a complicated motorized wheelchair. 'Look, Keith,' she says, lifting the loaf and holding it against his curled fist. 'Can you touch Him?'

Seeing me, Mary signals Rocco to take over. Then she slips her arm through mine and leads me into the kitchen. Her cheeks are glowing; her dark hair has been brushed to a high sheen – and holy cow, is she wearing *makeup*? 'Where have you *been*?' she chides. 'You've missed all the excitement!'

That's what she *thinks.* 'Oh?'

'Ten minutes after the midday news aired, they started coming. The old, the sick, anyone who wants to just touch the bread.'

I think about the petri dish that the loaf must be now, if that many hands have been all over it.

'Maybe this is a stupid question,' I say, 'but why?'

'To be healed,' Mary replies.

'Right. Because all this time the CDC should have been looking for the cure for cancer in a slice of bread.'

'Tell that to the scientists who discovered penicillin,' Mary says.

'Mary, what if it has nothing to do with a miracle? What if it's just the way the gluten happened to string together?'

'I don't believe that. But anyway, it would *still* be a miracle,' Mary says, 'because it gives desperate people some hope.'

My mind unravels back to Josef, to the Jews in the camp. When you are singled out for torture because of your faith, can religion still be a beacon? Did the woman whose son had profound disabilities believe in the God of this stupid loaf who could help him, or the God who had let him be born that way in the first place?

'You should be thrilled. Everyone who's come through here to see the loaf has taken away something else you've baked,' Mary says.

'You're right,' I mutter. 'I'm just really tired.'

'Then go home.' Mary looks at her watch. 'Since I think tomorrow we'll have twice as many customers.'

But as I leave the bakery, passing someone who's filming an encounter with the loaf on a Flip Video camera, I already know I'm going to find a sub to take over my shift.

Adam and I have an unwritten agreement to not show up at each other's place of business. You never know who's going to be passing by, who's going to recognize your car. Plus, his boss happens to be Shannon's father.

As I park my car a block away from the funeral home, for this very reason, I think again about Josef. Had a new acquaintance ever waggled a finger at him, genially saying, 'I know you from somewhere . . .' and made him break out in a sweat? Did he look in every window not to see his own reflection but to make sure no one was watching him?

And, of course, it makes me wonder whether our connection was pure chance, or if he'd been hunting for someone like me. Not just a girl descended from a Jewish family in a town with precious few Jews, but one with the added bonus of a damaged face, too self-conscious to draw attention to herself by going public with his story. I had never told Josef about Adam, but had he still recognized in me a guilty conscience, like his own?

Luckily, there isn't a funeral going on. Adam's business is a steady one – he'll always have clients – but if he were in the middle of a service I wouldn't be rude enough to disturb him. I text Adam when I am hovering outside the back of the building, near the recycling bins and the Dumpster. *I'm out back. Need to talk.*

A moment later he appears, dressed like a surgeon. 'What are you *doing* here, Sage?' he whispers, although we are alone. 'Robert's *upstairs.*'

Robert, the father-in-law.

'I'm having a really bad day,' I say, close to tears.

'And I'm having a really long one. Can't this wait?'

'Please,' I beg. 'Five minutes?'

Before he can reply, a tall man with silver hair appears in the doorway beside him. 'Maybe you'd like to tell me, Adam, why the embalming room door is wide open with a client on the table? I thought you kicked the cigarette habit—' Spying me, he registers the Picasso half of my face and forces a smile. 'I'm sorry, may I help you?'

'Dad,' Adam says, 'this is Sage—'

'McPhee,' I jump in, turning slightly so that my scar is better hidden. 'I'm a reporter for the *Maine Express.*'

I realize too late that sounds like a train, not a newspaper.

'I'm doing a story about a day in the life of a mortician,' I say.

Adam and I both watch Robert scrutinize me. I'm still wearing my baking outfit: loose T-shirt, baggy shorts, Crocs. I'm sure no self-respecting reporter would be caught dead at an interview looking like this.

'She called me last week to arrange a time to shadow me,' Adam lies.

Robert nods. 'Of course. Ms. McPhee, I'm happy to answer any questions that Adam can't.'

Adam visibly relaxes. 'Why don't you follow me?' He puts his hand on my arm, steering me into the facility. There is a shock as his hand touches my bare skin.

When he leads me down the hall, I shiver. It's cold in the basement of the funeral home. Adam enters a room on the right and closes the door behind us.

On the table is an elderly woman, naked beneath a sheet.

'Adam,' I say, swallowing. 'Is she . . .?'

'Well, she's not taking a nap,' he says, laughing. 'Come on, Sage. You know what I do for a living.'

'I didn't plan on watching you *do* it.'

'*You're* the one who came up with the reporter angle. You could have told him you were a cop and that you needed to take me down to the station.'

It smells like death in here, and frost, and antiseptic. I want to fold myself into Adam's arms, but there is a window in the door and at any moment, Robert or someone else could walk by.

He hesitates. 'Maybe you could just look the other way? Because I sort of have to get to work, especially in this heat.'

I nod, and stare at the wall. I hear Adam sorting through metallic instruments, and then something buzzes to life.

I am holding Josef's story like an acorn, tucked away. I don't want to share it yet. But I don't want it to take root, either.

At first I think Adam must be using a saw, but then I peek from the corner of my eye and realize he is shaving the dead woman. 'Why are you doing *that*?'

The electric blade growls as he rounds her chin. 'Everyone gets shaved. Even kids. Peach fuzz makes the makeup more noticeable, and you want that "memory picture" – the last image you have of a loved one – to be natural.'

I am fascinated by his economy of movement, by his efficiency. This is a part of his life I know so little about, and I'm hungry for any tidbit of him I can take away. 'When does the embalming happen?'

He looks up, surprised by my interest. 'After we shape the face. Once the fluid enters the veins, the body firms up.' Adam slips a piece of cotton between the left eye and the eyelid, and then sets a small plastic cap on top, like a giant contact lens. 'Why are you here, Sage? It's not because you have a burning desire to be a mortician. What happened to you today?'

'Do people ever tell you things you wish they wouldn't?' I blurt out.

'Most of the people I meet can't talk anymore.' I watch Adam thread a suture string onto a curved needle. 'But their relatives give me an earful. Usually they say what they should have said to their loved one before she died.' He slips the needle through the jaw below the gums and threads it through the upper jaw into a nostril. 'I guess I'm the last stop, you know? The repository of regret.' Adam smiles. 'Sounds like a Goth band, doesn't it?'

The needle passes through the septum into the other

nostril, and back into the mouth. 'What brought this on?' he asks.

'I had a conversation with someone today that really rattled me. I'm not sure what I should do about it.'

'Maybe he doesn't want you to *do* anything. Maybe he just needed you to listen.'

But it isn't that simple. The confessions Adam hears from the relatives of the deceased are *should-have*s and *wish-I'd*s, not *I did*s. Once you are given a grenade with the pin pulled out, you have to act. You have to pass it off to someone who knows how to disable it, or press it back into the hands of the person who's relinquished it. Because if you don't, you're bound to explode.

Adam gently ties the sutures so that the mouth cannot drop open but looks naturally set. I imagine Josef dying, his mouth being sewn shut, all his secrets trapped inside.

On the way to the police station, I call Robena Fenetto. She's a seventy-six-year-old Italian woman who retired in Westerbrook. Although she doesn't have the stamina to be a baker full-time anymore, I've called her once or twice to fill in for me when I was down for the count with the flu. I tell her which pre-ferments to use, where my spreadsheets are with the baker's percentage that will yield enough output to keep Mary from firing me.

I tell her to tell Mary I'll be a little late.

I haven't been to the police station since my bike was stolen when I was a senior in high school. My mother took me in to file a report. I remember that at the same time, the father of one of the most popular girls in the school was being brought in, disheveled and reeking of alcohol at 4:00 p.m. He was the head of a local insurance company, and they were one of the few families in town who could afford an inground pool. It was the first time I remember learning that people are never who they seem to be.

The dispatcher at the little glass window has a nose ring and a buzz cut, which is maybe why she doesn't blink twice when I approach. 'Can I help you?'

How do you just come out and say *I think my friend is a Nazi* without sounding insane?

'I was hoping to talk to a detective,' I say.

'About?'

'It's complicated.'

She blinks. 'Try me.'

'I have information about a crime that was committed.'

She hesitates, as if she is weighing whether or not I'm telling the truth. Then she writes down my name. 'Take a seat.'

There's a row of chairs, but instead of sitting, I stand and read the names of the deadbeat dads who fill the Wanted posters on a giant bulletin board. A flyer advertises a class for fire safety.

'Ms. Singer?'

I turn around to see a tall man with cropped gray hair and skin the color of one of Rocco's mocha lattes. He's wearing a gun holstered on his belt, and a badge around his neck. 'I'm Detective Vicks,' he says, staring just a beat too long at my face. 'Would you mind coming inside?'

He punches in a key code and opens a door, leading me down a narrow hallway to a conference room. 'Take a seat. Can I get you a cup of coffee?'

'I'm all set,' I tell him. Even though I know I'm not being interrogated, when he closes the door behind me, I feel trapped.

Heat rushes up my neck, and I break out in a sweat. What if

the detective thinks I'm lying? What if he starts asking me too many questions? Maybe I shouldn't get involved. I don't really know anything about Josef's past, and even if he's telling the truth, what could possibly be done after almost seventy years?

. And yet.

When my grandma was being taken by the Nazis, how many other Germans had turned a blind eye, making the same kinds of excuses?

'So,' Detective Vicks says. 'What's this about?'

I take a deep breath. 'A man I know may be a Nazi.'

The detective purses his lips. 'A neo-Nazi?'

'No, the kind from World War Two.'

'How old is this guy?' Vicks asks.

'I don't know, exactly. In his nineties. The right age, anyway, for the math to make sense.'

'And what is it that led you to believe he's a Nazi?'

'He showed me a photograph of himself in uniform.'

'Do you know that it was authentic?'

'You think I'm making this up,' I say, so surprised that I meet the detective's gaze head-on. 'Why would I do that?'

'Why would a thousand crazy people call in to a tip line that runs on the news about a missing kid?' Vicks says, shrugging. 'Far be it from me to figure out the human psyche.'

Stung, I feel my scar burn. 'I'm telling you the truth.' I am just leaving out, conveniently, the fact that this same man asked me to kill him. And that I chose to let him believe I was entertaining the possibility.

Vicks tilts his head, and I can see that he's already making a judgment – not about Josef but about *me*. Clearly I'm trying my damnedest to hide my face; he must be wondering if there's more I'm concealing. 'Is there anything in this man's behavior that would indicate he was actually involved in Nazi activities?'

'He doesn't wear a swastika on his forehead, if that's what you're asking,' I say. 'But he has a German accent. In fact he used to teach the language at the high school.'

'Hang on – are you talking about Josef *Weber*?' Vicks says. 'He goes to my church. Sings in the choir. He led the Fourth of July parade last year, as the Citizen of the Year. I've never even seen the guy swat a mosquito.'

'Maybe he likes bugs more than he liked Jews,' I say flatly.

Vicks leans back in his chair. 'Ms. Singer, did Mr. Weber say something that upset you personally?'

'Yes,' I say. 'He told me he was a Nazi!'

'I mean an argument. A misunderstanding. Maybe even an offhand comment about your . . . appearance. Something that might have warranted . . . such an accusation.'

'We're friends. That's why he confided in me in the first place.'

'That may be, Ms. Singer. But we're not in the habit of arresting someone for alleged crimes without having a valid reason to believe he might be a person of interest. Yes, the guy speaks with a German accent, and he's old. But I've never even experienced a whiff of racial or religious prejudice from him.'

'Isn't that the point? I thought serial killers were supposed to be totally charming in public; that's why nobody guesses they're serial killers. You're just going to assume I'm crazy? You're not even going to investigate what he did?'

'What did he do?'

I look down at the table. 'I don't know, exactly. That's why I'm here. I thought you could help me find out.'

Vicks looks at me for a long moment. 'Why don't you write

down your contact information, Ms. Singer,' he suggests, passing me a piece of paper and a pen. 'I'll look into things, and we'll be in touch.'

Without a word I scribble down my information. Why would anyone believe me, Sage Singer, a damaged ghost who only comes out at night? Especially when Josef has spent the past twenty-two years gilding his reputation as a beloved Westerbrook community member and humanitarian?

I hand the paper back to Detective Vicks. 'I know you're not going to contact me,' I say coolly. 'I know you're going to toss that piece of paper into the trash as soon as I walk out the door. But it's not like I walked in here saying I found a UFO in my backyard. The Holocaust *happened*. Nazis *existed*. And they didn't all just evaporate into thin air when the war ended.'

'Which was nearly seventy years ago,' Detective Vicks points out.

'I thought there was no statute of limitations on murder,' I say, and I walk out of the conference room.

My nana only serves tea in a glass. For as long as I can remember, she has said this is the only way to drink it properly, the way her parents used to serve it when she was a young girl. It strikes me, as I sit at her kitchen table, watching her bustle around the kitchen with her cane to set the kettle and arrange rugelach on a plate, that although she talks openly and easily about being a child and about her life with my grandfather, there is a caesura in the time line of her life, a break of years, a derailment. 'This is some surprise,' Nana says. 'A nice one, but still a surprise.'

'I was in the area,' I lie. 'How couldn't I stop by?'

My grandmother sets the plate on the table. She is tiny – five feet, maybe – although I used to think of her as tall. She always wore the most beautiful set of pearls, which my grandfather had given her as a wedding gift, and in the old photo of the ceremony that sat on her mantel, she looked like a movie star with her dark hair in victory rolls and slim figure hugged by a confection of lace and satin.

She and my grandfather used to run an antiquarian bookstore, a tiny hole-in-the-wall that had narrow aisles jammed with hundreds of old tomes. My mother, who would always buy her books new, hated the vintage hardcovers with their cracked spines and threadbare cloth covers. True, you couldn't go in there and find the latest bestseller, but when you held one of those volumes in your hands, you were leafing through another person's life. Someone else had once loved that story, too. Someone else had carried that book in a backpack, devoured it over breakfast, mopped up that coffee stain at a Paris café, cried herself to sleep after that last chapter. The scent of their store was distinctive: a slight damp mildew, a pinch of dust. To me, it was the smell of history.

My grandfather had been an editor at a small academic press before buying the bookstore; my grandmother had allegedly wanted to be a writer, although in my childhood I never saw her write anything longer than a letter. But she loved stories, that much was true. She would sit me on the glass counter beside the cash register and take the A. A. Milne and the J. M. Barrie books from their locked case and show me the illustrations. When I was older, she would let me wrap customers' purchases in the brown butcher paper she kept on a giant roll, and she taught me to tie it with string, just like she did.

Eventually my grandparents sold the bookstore to a developer who was bulldozing a host of mom-and-pop stores to make way for a Target. Whatever money they made was enough for my nana to live on, even all these years after Poppa was gone.

'You were not *really* in the area,' she says now. 'You look just like your father used to look when he lied to me.'

I laugh. 'How's that?'

'Like you've swallowed a lemon. Once, when your father was maybe five, he stole my nail polish remover. When I asked him about it, he lied. Eventually I found it in his sock drawer and told him so. He became hysterical. Turned out he read the label and thought it would make me – someone Polish – disappear. He hid it before it could do its job.' Nana smiles. 'I loved that boy,' she sighs. 'No mother should outlive a child.'

'It's no party to outlive your parents, either,' I reply.

For a moment, there is a shadow veiling her features. Then she leans down and hugs me. 'See, now you are not lying. I know you are here because you're lonely, Sage. That's nothing to be ashamed of. Maybe now, we will have each other.'

They are the same words, I realize, that Josef said to me.

'You should cut your hair,' my nana announces. 'No one can see you properly.'

A small snort escapes me. I think I'd rather run naked through the street than cut my hair, and leave my face exposed. 'That's the point,' I say.

She tilts her head. 'I wonder what magic could make you see yourself the way the rest of us do,' she muses. 'Maybe then you'd stop living like a monster who comes out only after dark.'

'I'm a baker. I *have* to work at night.'

'Do you? Or did you pick the profession *because* of the hours?' Nana asks.

'I didn't come here to be grilled about my career choice . . .'

'Of course not.' She reaches over and pats my face, the bad side. She lets her thumb linger on the ridged flesh, to let me know that it doesn't bother her – and that it shouldn't bother me. 'And your sisters?'

'I haven't talked to them lately,' I mutter.

That is an understatement. I actively avoid their calls.

'You know they love you, Sage,' my grandmother says, and I shrug. There is nothing she could possibly say that can convince me Pepper and Saffron don't hold me responsible for the fact that our mother isn't alive.

A timer goes off on the oven, and my grandmother pulls out a braid of challah. She may have given up formal religion, but she still adheres to the culture of Judaism. There is no ailment her matzo ball soup cannot fix; there is no Friday she doesn't have fresh bread. Daisy, the home health aide Nana refers to as her 'girl,' is the one who mixes the dough in the KitchenAid and sets it to rise before Nana braids it. It took two years for Nana to trust Daisy enough to give her the family recipe, the same one I use at Our Daily Bread.

'Smells good,' I say, desperate to change the course of the conversation.

My grandmother drops the first challah down on the counter and goes back, in turn, for each of the other three. 'You know what I think?' she says. 'I think that even when I do not remember my own name anymore I will still know how to make this challah. My father, he made sure of it. He used to quiz me – when I walked into our apartment after school, when I was studying with a friend, when we were strolling together into the city center. *Minka*, he'd say, *how much sugar? How many eggs?* He'd ask what temperature the water should be at, but that was a trick question.'

'Warm to dissolve the yeast, boiling to mix the wet ingredients, cold to balance it out.'

My grandma looks over her shoulder and nods. 'My father, he would have been very happy to know his challah is in good hands.'

This, I realize, is my opportunity. I wait until Nana has brought one of the braids to the table on a cutting board. As she slices it with a bread knife, steam rises like a passing soul. 'Why didn't you and Poppa start a bakery, instead of a bookstore?'

She laughs. 'Your poppa couldn't boil water, much less a bagel. To bake bread, you have to have a gift. Like my father did. Like you do.'

'You hardly ever talk about your parents,' I say.

Her hand trembles the slightest bit where she holds the knife, so slightly that had I not been watching so carefully, I might never have noticed. 'What's there to say?' She shrugs. 'My mother, she kept house, and my father was a baker in Łódź. You know this.'

'What happened to them, Nana?'

'They died a long time ago,' she says dismissively. She hands me a piece of bread, no butter, because if you've made a truly great challah you don't need any. 'Ah, look at this. It could have risen more. My father used to say that a good loaf, you can eat tomorrow. But a bad loaf, you should eat now.'

I grasp her hand. The skin is like tissue, the bones pronounced. 'What happened to them?' I repeat.

She forces a laugh. 'What is with these questions, Sage! All of a sudden you're writing a book?'

In response, I turn her arm over and gently push up the sleeve of her blouse so that the blurry edge of her blue tattoo is exposed. 'I'm not the only one in the family with a scar, Nana,' I murmur.

She pulls away from me and yanks down the cotton. 'I do not wish to talk about it.'

'Nana,' I say. 'I'm not a little girl anymore—'

'No,' she says abruptly.

I want to tell her about Josef. I want to ask her about the SS soldiers she knew. But I also know that I won't.

Not because my grandma doesn't want to discuss it, but because I am ashamed that this man I've befriended – cooked for, sat with, laughed with – might have once been someone who terrified her.

'When I got here, to America, this is when my life began,' my grandmother says. 'Everything before . . . well, that happened to a different person.'

If my grandmother could reinvent herself, why not Josef Weber?

'How do you do it?' I ask softly, and I'm no longer asking just about her and Josef but about myself as well. 'How do you get up every morning and not remember?'

'I never said I do not remember,' my grandmother corrects. 'I said I prefer to forget.' Suddenly, she smiles, cutting the ribbon between this conversation and whatever comes next. 'Now. My beautiful granddaughter did not come all this way to talk about ancient history, did she? Tell me about the bakery.'

I let the *beautiful* comment slide. 'I baked a loaf of bread that had Jesus's face in it,' I announce; it's the first thing to come to mind.

'Really.' My grandmother laughs. 'Says who?'

'People who believe that God might show up in an artisan boule, I guess.'

She purses her lips. 'There was a time when I could see God in a single crumb.'

I realize she is extending an olive branch, a sliver of her past. I sit very still, waiting to see if she'll go on.

'You know, that was what we missed most. Not our beds, not our homes, not even our mothers. We would talk about food. Roast potatoes and briskets, pierogi, babka. What I would have given my life for back then was some of my father's challah, fresh from the oven.'

So this is why my grandmother bakes four loaves every week, when she cannot finish even one herself. Not because she plans to eat it but because she wants to have the luxury of giving the rest away to those who are still hungry.

When my cell phone begins to ring, I grimace – it's probably Mary, giving me hell because Robena's arrived to start the night's baking instead of me. But as I pull it out of my pocket, I realize that the number's unfamiliar.

'This is Detective Vicks, calling for Sage Singer.'

'Wow,' I say, recognizing the voice. 'I wasn't expecting you to call me back.'

'I did a little digging,' he replies. 'We still can't help you. But if you want to take your complaint somewhere, I'd suggest the FBI.'

The FBI. It seems like a massive step up from the local police department. The FBI is the organization that captured John Dillinger and the Rosenbergs. They found the fingerprint that incriminated the murderer of Martin Luther King, Jr. Their cases are high-profile matters of immediate national security, not ones that have languished for decades. They will probably laugh me off the phone before I finish my explanation.

I look up and see my grandmother at the kitchen counter now, wrapping one of the challah loaves in tinfoil.

'What's the number?' I ask.

It's a miracle that I make it back to Westerbrook without driving off the road; that's how tired I am. I let myself into the bakery with my set of keys and find Robena asleep, sitting on a giant sack of flour with her cheek pressed to the wooden countertop. On the bright side, though, there are loaves on the cooling racks, and the smell of something baking in the oven.

'Robena,' I say, gently shaking her awake. 'I'm back.'

She sits up. 'Sage! I just dozed off for a minute . . .'

'It's okay. Thanks for helping me out.' I slip into an apron and tie it around my waist. 'How was Mary, on a scale of one to ten?'

'About a twelve. She got pretty worked up because she's expecting a lot of traffic tomorrow, thanks to the Jesus Loaf.'

'Hallelujah,' I say flatly.

I'd tried the number of the local FBI office while driving home, only to be told that the division I *really* needed to talk to was part of the Department of Justice in Washington, D.C. They gave me a different number, but apparently the Human Rights and Special Prosecutions Section keeps bankers' hours. I got a voice recording telling me to call another number, if this was an emergency.

It is hard to justify this as an emergency, given the length of time that Josef had kept his secret to himself.

So instead, I have decided to finish up the baking, load the loaves into the glass cases, and be gone before Mary arrives to open the shop. I'll call back from the privacy of my own home.

Robena walks me through the timers that she's set around the kitchen, some measuring bake times, some measuring dough that's proofing, some measuring shaped loaves left to rest. When I feel like I'm up to speed, I walk her to the front door, thank her, and lock up behind her.

Immediately my gaze falls on the Jesus Loaf.

In retrospect I won't be able to tell Mary why I did it.

The bread is stale, hard as stone, with the variegations of seed and pigment that created the face already fading away. I take the peel I use to slide bread in and out of the wood-fired oven and toss the Jesus Loaf into the yawning maw of the kiln, onto the red-hot flames in its belly.

Robena has made baguettes and rolls; there are a variety of other breads to be finished before dawn. But instead of mixing according to my usual schedule, I alter the day's menu. Doing the calculations in my head, I measure out the sugar, the water, the yeast, the oil. The salt and the flour.

I close my eyes and breathe in the sweet wheat. I imagine a shop with a bell over the window that rings when a customer enters; the sound of coins dropping like a scale of musical notes into the cash register, which might make a girl look up from the book in which her nose is buried. For the rest of the night, I bake only one recipe, so that by the time the sun simmers on the horizon, the shelves of Our Daily Bread are packed tightly with the knots and coils of my great-grandfather's challah, so much that you could never imagine how hunger might feel.

I kept dozing off in the market. I had not slept since I buried my father, not with any of the bells and whistles and fanfare he had joked of but in a small plot behind the cottage. My insomnia was not born of grief, however. It was out of necessity.

I had no money for taxes. We had no savings, and our only income came from the market where we sold our daily loaves. In the past, my father baked while I trekked into the village square. But now, there was only me.

I found myself living around the clock. At night, I would roll up my sleeves and shape mounds of dough into boules; I would mix more while those rose; I would take the last loaves out of the brick oven as the sun spilled, like an accident, over the horizon in the morning. Then I would fill my basket and hike to the market, where I found myself struggling to stay awake while I hawked my wares.

I did not know how long I could continue this. But I wasn't going to let Baruch Beiler take away the only thing I had left – my father's home and his business.

However, fewer customers were coming into town. It was too dangerous. My father's body had been one of three found this week around the outskirts of the village, including a toddler who had wandered into the woods and had never returned. All had been disfigured and devoured the same way, as if by a ravenous animal. Frightened, the townspeople were opting to live off their own gardens and canned goods. Yesterday I had seen only a dozen customers; today there had been only six. Even some of the merchants had chosen to stay safe behind their locked doors. The market was a gray, ghostly space, the wind whistling over the cobblestones like a warning.

I opened my eyes to find Damian shaking me awake. 'Dreaming of me, darling?' he asked. He reached past me, brushing my face, and ripped the neck from a baguette. He popped the bread into his mouth. 'Mmm. You are nearly the baker your father was.' For just a moment, compassion transformed his features. 'I'm sorry about your loss, Ania.'

Other customers had told me the same. 'Thank you,' I murmured.

'I, on the other hand, am not,' Baruch Beiler announced, coming to stand behind the captain. 'Since it greatly diminishes my chances of ever receiving his tax revenue.'

'It is not the end of the week yet,' I said, panicking.

Where would I go if he turned me out into the streets? I had seen women who sold themselves, who haunted the alleys of the village like shadows and who were dead in the eyes. I could accept Damian's offer of marriage, but that was just a different kind of deal with the Devil. Then again, if I were homeless, how long would it be before the beast that was preying upon the people of our village found me?

From the corner of my eye I saw someone approaching. It was the new man in town, leading his brother on the leather leash. He walked past me without even glancing at the bread, and stood in front of the empty wooden plank where the butcher usually set up his wares. When he turned to me, I felt as if a fire had been kindled beneath my ribs. 'Where is the butcher?' he asked.

'He isn't selling today,' I murmured.

I realized he was younger than I'd first thought, perhaps just a few years older than me. His eyes were the most impossible color I had ever seen – gold, but gleaming, as if they were lit from within. His skin was flushed, with bright spots of color on his cheeks. His brown hair fell unevenly over his brow.

He was wearing only that white shirt, the one that had been beneath the coat he traded the last time he'd been in the village square. I wondered what he had been willing to barter with today.

He didn't say anything, just narrowed his eyes as he stared at me.

'The merchants are running scared,' Baruch Beiler said. 'Just like everyone else in this godforsaken town.'

'Not all of us have iron gates to keep the animals out,' answered Damian.

'Or in,' I murmured beneath my breath, but Beiler heard me. 'Ten zloty,' he hissed. 'By Friday.'

Damian reached into his military jacket and pulled out a leather pouch. He counted the silver coins into his palm and flung them at Beiler. 'Consider the debt paid,' he said.

Beiler knelt, collecting the money. Then he stood and shrugged. 'Until next month.' He stalked toward his mansion, locking the gates behind himself before vanishing into the massive stone house.

From their position in front of the empty meat stall, I could see the man and his brother watching us.

'Well?' Damian looked at me. 'Didn't your father teach you any manners?'

'Thank you.'

'Perhaps you'd like to show *your appreciation,' he said. 'Your debt to Beiler's paid. But now you owe one to me.'*

Swallowing, I came up on my tiptoes, and kissed his cheek.

He grabbed my hand and pressed it against his crotch. When I tried to push away from him, he ground his mouth against mine. 'You know I could take what I want anytime,' he said softly, his hands bracketing my head and squeezing my temples so hard that I could not think, could barely listen. 'I am only offering you a choice out of the goodness of my heart.'

One minute he was there, and the next, he wasn't. I fell, the cobblestones cold against my legs, as the man with the golden eyes yanked Damian away from me and wrestled him to the ground. 'She already chose,' he gritted out, punctuating his words with blows to the captain's face.

As I scrambled away from their fight, the boy in the leather mask stared at me.

I think we both realized at the same time that his leash was dangling, free.

The boy threw back his head and started to run, his footsteps echoing like gunshots as he raced across the deserted village square.

His brother paused, distracted. It was enough of a hesitation for Damian to land a solid punch. The man's head snapped back, but he staggered to his feet and chased after the boy.

'You can run,' Damian said, wiping the blood from his mouth. 'But you can't hide.'

Leo

The woman on the phone is breathless. 'I've been trying to find you for *years*,' she says.

This is my first red flag. We're not that hard to find. You ring up the Justice Department, and mention why you're calling, you'll be routed to the office of Human Rights and Special Prosecutions. But we take every call, and we take them seriously. So I ask the woman her name.

'Miranda Coontz,' she says. 'Except that's my married name. My maiden name was Schultz.'

'So, Ms. Coontz,' I say, 'I can hardly hear you.'

'I have to whisper,' she says. 'He's listening. He always manages to come into the room when I start trying to tell people who he really is . . .'

As she goes on and on, I wait to hear the word *Nazi* or even *World War II*. We're the division that prosecutes cases against people who have committed human rights violations – genocides, torture, war crimes. We're the real Nazi hunters, nowhere near as glamorous as we're made out to be in film and television. I'm not Daniel Craig or Vin Diesel or Eric Bana, just plain old Leo Stein. I don't pack a pistol; my weapon of choice is a historian named Genevra, who speaks seven languages and never fails to point out when I need a haircut or when my tie doesn't match my shirt. I work in a job that gets harder and harder to do every day, as the generation that perpetrated the crimes of the Holocaust dies out.

For fifteen minutes I listen to Miranda Coontz explain how someone in her own household is stalking her, and how at first she thought the FBI had sent him as a drone to kill her. This is red flag number two. First of all, the FBI doesn't go around killing people. Second, if they *did* want to kill her, she'd already be dead. 'You know, Ms. Coontz,' I say, when she breaks to take a breath, 'I'm not sure that you've got the right department . . .'

'If you bear with me,' she promises, 'it will all make sense.'

Not for the first time, I wonder how a guy like me – thirty-seven, top of his class at Harvard Law – turned down a sure partnership and a dizzying salary at a Boston law firm for a government pay grade and a career as the deputy chief of HRSP. In a parallel universe I would be trying white-collar criminals, instead of building a case around a former SS guard who died just before we were able to extradite him. Or, for that matter, talking to Ms. Coontz.

Then again, it didn't take me long in the world of corporate law to realize that truth is an afterthought in court. In fact, truth is an afterthought in most trials. But there were six million people who were lied to, during World War II, and somebody owes them the truth.

'. . . and you've heard of Josef Mengele?'

At that, my ears perk up. Of course I've heard of Mengele, the infamous Angel of Death at Auschwitz-Birkenau, the chief medical officer who experimented on humans and who met incoming prisoners and directed them either to the right, to work, or to the left, the gas chambers. Although historically we know that Mengele could not have met every transport, almost every Auschwitz survivor with whom I've spoken insists it was Mengele who met his or her transport – no matter what hour of the day the arrival took place. It's an example of how much has been written about Auschwitz, how survivors sometimes conflate those accounts with their own personal experiences. I have no doubt in my mind they truly believe it was Mengele they saw when they first arrived at Auschwitz, but no matter how much of a monster the guy was, he had to sleep sometime. Which means that *other* monsters met some of them instead.

'People believe Mengele escaped to South America,' Ms. Coontz says.

I stifle a sigh. Actually, I *know* that he lived, and died, in Brazil.

'He's alive,' she whispers. 'He's been reincarnated, in the form of my cat. And I can't turn my back on him, or go to sleep, because I think he's going to kill me.'

'Good God,' I mutter.

'I know,' Ms. Coontz agrees. 'I thought I was getting a sweet little tabby from the shelter, and one morning I wake up to find scratch marks bleeding on my chest—'

'With all due respect, Ms. Coontz, it's a little bit of a stretch to think that Josef Mengele is now a cat.'

'Those scratch marks,' she says gravely, 'were in the shape of a *swastika.*'

I close my eyes. 'Maybe you just need a different pet,' I suggest.

'I had a goldfish. I had to flush it down the toilet.'

I am almost afraid to ask. 'Why?'

She hesitates. 'Let's just say I have proof that Hitler was reincarnated, too.'

I manage to get her off the phone by telling her that I'll have a historian look into her case – and it's true, I will pass this off to Genevra the next time she does something to piss me off and I want to get back at her. But no sooner do I have Miranda Coontz off my line than my secretary buzzes me again. 'Is your moon out of alignment or something?' she asks. 'Because I've got another one for you on line two. Her local FBI office referred her here.'

I look at the piles of documents on my desk – reports that Genevra has turned in. Getting a suspect to trial is a slow and laborious expedition and in my case, often a fruitless one. The last case we were able to bring to prosecution was in 2008, and the defendant died at the end of the trial. We do the opposite of what police do; instead of looking at a crime and seeing 'whodunit,' we start with a name, and pore through databases to see if there's a match – a person who's alive with that name – and then to figure out what he did during the war.

We have no shortage of names.

I pick up the receiver again. 'This is Leo Stein,' I say.

'Um,' a woman replies. 'I'm not sure I have the right place . . .'

'I'll let you know, if you tell me what you're calling about.'

'Someone I know may have been an SS officer.'

In our office, we have a category for these calls: My Neighbor's a Nazi. Typically, it's the neighbor from hell who kicks your dog when he crosses the property line, and calls the town when the leaves of your oak tree fall in his yard. He's got a European accent and wears a long leather coat and has a German shepherd.

'And your name is?'

'Sage Singer,' the woman says. 'I live in New Hampshire, and so does he.'

This makes me sit up a little straighter. New Hampshire's a great place to hide, if you're a Nazi. No one ever thinks to look in New Hampshire.

'What's this individual's name?' I ask.

'Josef Weber.'

'And you think he was an SS officer because . . .?'

'He told me so,' the woman says.

I lean back in my chair. 'He *told* you that he was a Nazi?' In the decade I've been doing this, that's a new one for me. My job has involved peeling away the disguises from criminals, who think that after nearly seventy years, they should literally get away with murder. I've never had a defendant confess until I've managed to back him so far into a corner with evidence that he has no choice but to tell the truth.

'We're . . . acquaintances,' Sage Singer replies. 'He wants me to help him die.'

'Like Jack Kevorkian? Is he terminally ill?'

'No. He's the opposite – very healthy, for a man his age. He thinks that there's some sort of justice in asking me to be a part of it – because my family was Jewish.'

'Are *you*?'

'Does it matter?'

No, it doesn't. I'm Jewish, but half the staff in our department isn't.

'Did he mention which camp he was in?'

'He used a German word . . . *Toten* . . . Otensomething?'

'*Totenkopfverbände?*' I suggest.

'Yes!'

Translated, it means the Death's Head Unit. It's not an individual location but rather the division of the SS that ran the concentration camps for the Third Reich.

In 1981 my office won a seminal case, *Fedorenko v. United States*. The Supreme Court decided – wisely, in my humble opinion – that anyone who was a guard at a Nazi concentration camp necessarily took part in perpetration of Nazi crimes of persecution there. The camps operated as chains of functions, and for it to work, everyone in the chain had to perform his function. If one person didn't, the apparatus of extermination would grind to a halt. So really, no matter what this particular guy did or didn't do – whether he actually pulled a trigger or loaded the Zyklon B gas into one of the chambers – even confirming his role as a member of the SS-TV in a concentration camp would be enough to build a case against him.

Of course, that's still an enormous longshot.

'What's his name?' I ask again.

'Josef Weber.'

I ask her to spell it and then I write it down on a pad, underline it twice. 'Did he say anything else?'

'He showed me a picture of himself. He was wearing a uniform.'

'What did it look like?'

'An SS uniform,' she says.

'And you know this because . . .?'

'Well,' she admits. 'It looks like the ones you always see in movies.'

There are two caveats here. I do not know Sage Singer; she could be a recent escapee from a mental hospital who is making this entire story up. I also do not know Josef Weber, who himself might be a mental hospital escapee seeking attention. Plus, there's the fact that I've never, in a decade, received a cold call like this from an ordinary citizen about a Nazi in the backyard that actually panned out. Most of the tips we go on to investigate come from lawyers representing women in divorce suits, hoping to allege that their husbands – who are a certain age and from Europe – are also Nazi war criminals. Imagine the payout, if you can get a judge to believe how cruel the guy was to your client. And always, even these allegations turn out to be total crap.

'Do you have that photo?' I ask.

'No,' she admits. 'He does.'

Of course.

I rub my forehead. 'I've gotta ask . . . does he have a German shepherd?'

'A dachshund,' she says.

'That would have been my second choice,' I murmur. 'Look, how long have you known Josef Weber?'

'About a month. He started coming to a grief therapy group I've been going to since my mother died.'

'I'm sorry to hear that,' I say automatically, but I can tell it is a kindness she isn't expecting. 'So, it's not as if you really have a thorough understanding of his character, or why he might say he did something he didn't actually do . . .'

'God, what is *with* you people?' she explodes. 'First the cops, then the FBI – shouldn't you at *least* be giving me the benefit of the doubt? How do *you* know he's not telling the truth?'

'Because it doesn't make sense, Ms. Singer. Why would anyone who's managed to hide for over half a century just suddenly drop the pretense?'

'I don't know,' she says frankly. 'Guilt? A fear of Judgment Day? Or maybe he's just tired. Of living a lie, you know?'

When she says that, she hooks me. Because it's so damn human. The biggest mistake people make when they think about Nazi war criminals is to assume they were always monsters; before, during, and after the war. They weren't. They were once ordinary men, with fully operational consciences, who made bad choices and had to fabricate excuses to themselves for the rest of their lives when they returned to a mundane existence. 'Do you happen to have his birth date?' I ask.

'I know he's in his nineties . . .'

'Well,' I tell her, 'we can try to check his name and see if we get a hit. The records we have aren't complete, but we've got one of the best databases in the world, with over thirty years of archival research in it.'

'And then what?'

'Assuming we get confirmation or for some other reason think there might be a legitimate claim, I'd ask you to talk to my chief historian, Genevra Astanopoulos. She would be able to ask you a host of questions that would help us investigate further. But I have to warn you, Ms. Singer, even though my office has received thousands of calls from members of the public, none have panned out. In fact there was one call, prior to this office's creation in 1979, that led the U.S. Attorney's Office in Chicago to prosecute the alleged criminal – who turned out to not only be innocent but a *victim* of the Nazis. Out of all the tips we've received since then from citizens, not a single one has actually become a prosecutable case.'

Sage Singer is quiet for a moment. 'Then I'd say you're due for one,' she says.

All things considered, Michel Thomas was one of the lucky ones. A Jewish concentration camp inmate, he escaped the Nazis and joined the French resistance and then a commando group before assisting the U.S. Army Counterintelligence Corps. During the last week of World War II, he received a tip about a truck convoy near Munich, believed to be carrying some sort of important cargo. Arriving at a paper mill warehouse in Freimann, Germany, he discovered heaps of documents that the Nazis had planned to have pulped: the worldwide membership file cards of over ten million members of the Nazi Party.

These documents were used at the Nuremberg Trials, and afterward, to identify, locate, and prosecute war criminals. They're the first stop for the historians who work with me at HRSP. That's not to say that if we do not turn up a hit on a name that individual was not a Nazi – but it does make building a case a hell of a lot easier.

I find Genevra at her desk. 'I need you to run a name,' I say.

After Germany was unified in the nineties, the United States returned the Berlin Document Center, the central repository of SS/Nazi Party records that had been seized by the U.S. Army after World War II . . . but not before microfilming the whole damn thing. Between the Berlin Document Center and the information that came to light after the breakup of the USSR, I know Genevra's bound to unearth something.

That is, if there's something to be unearthed.

She looks up at me. 'You spilled coffee on your tie,' she says, pulling a pencil out of the bird's nest of frizzy yellow hair piled on top of her head. 'Better change it before your date.'

'How do *you* know I have a date?' I ask.

'Because your mother called me this morning and told me I should push you out the door with brute force if you were still here at six thirty p.m.'

This doesn't surprise me. No cable, Ethernet, or FiOS system is as blisteringly fast at spreading news as a Jewish family.

'Remind me to kill her,' I tell Genevra.

'Can't,' she muses. 'Don't want to be roped in as an accomplice.' She grins at me over her glasses. 'Besides, Leo, your mom's a breath of fresh air. All day long I read about people who craved world domination and racial superiority. By comparison, wanting grandchildren is sort of sweet.'

'She *has* grandchildren. Three, courtesy of my sister.'

'She doesn't like the fact that you're married to your job.'

'She didn't much like it when I was married to Diana, either,' I say. It's been five years since my divorce was final, and I have to admit, the worst thing about that whole experience was having to admit to my mother that she was right: the woman I believed to be the girl of my dreams was not, in fact, right for me.

Recently, I ran into Diana in the Metro. She's remarried, and she's got one kid and another on the way. We were exchanging pleasantries when my cell phone rang – my sister, asking me if I was going to be able to make it to my nephew's birthday party that weekend. She heard me say good-bye to Diana, and within the hour, my mother had called to set me up on a blind date.

Like I said, Jewish family network.

'I need you to run a name,' I repeat.

Genevra takes the paper from my hand. 'It's six thirty-six,' she says. 'Don't make me call your mother.'

I stop back at my desk to grab my briefcase and laptop, because leaving without them would be as foreign to me as leaving without my arm or leg. I instinctively reach for the holster on my belt to make sure my BlackBerry's there. I sit down for a second, and Google Sage Singer's name.

I use search engines all the time, of course. Mostly it's to see if someone (Miranda Coontz, for example?) is a complete whack job. But the reason I want to find information on Sage Singer is her voice.

It's smoky. It sounds like the first night in autumn when you build a fire in the fireplace and drink a glass of port and fall asleep with a dog on your lap. Not that I have a dog *or* port, but you get what I mean.

This, if nothing else, is proof that I ought to be running out the door to go to that blind date. Sage Singer's voice may have sounded young, but she is probably in her dotage – she did say, after all, that this Josef Weber guy was a friend of hers. Her mother had recently died, after all, probably of old age. And that husky rasp could be the mark of a lifelong cigarette addict.

The only Sage Singer in New Hampshire who pops up, though, is a baker at a small boutique café. Her berry tart recipe is in a local magazine as part of a summer cornucopia piece. Her name appears in the business listing of the newspaper heralding the opening of Mary DeAngelis's new bakery.

I click on the News link and find a video from a local television station – one uploaded just yesterday. 'Sage Singer,' the reporter says in a voice-over, 'is the baker who crafted the Jesus Loaf.'

The what?

The clip is an amateur video of a woman with a messy ponytail, her face turned away from the camera. I can see a mark of flour on her cheek the moment before she completely ducks out of the spotlight.

She isn't what I expected. When ordinary citizens call HRSP, it usually tells you more about them than about the people they are accusing – they want a conflict resolved, they hold a grudge, they want attention. But my gut tells me that's not the case here.

Perhaps Genevra will turn up a hit after all. If Sage Singer can surprise me once, maybe she can do it again.

My car has, I am sure, the world's last eight-track cartridge player. As I sit in traffic on the Beltway, I listen to Bread and Chicago. I like to pretend that everyone in all the cars around me is listening to eight-tracks, too, that the years have been rolled back to a simpler time. I realize how strange this is, given how much smaller the world has become as a result of technology and how my office has benefited from it. Even better, having an eight-track player isn't just strange anymore; it's *retro*.

I'm thinking of this, and whether I should tell my blind date that I'm so tragically hip I buy my music on eBay instead of iTunes. The last time I went out (a colleague who set me up with his wife's cousin) I spent the whole dinner talking about the Aleksandras Lileikis case, and the woman begged a headache before dessert and took the Metro home. The truth is, I'm lousy with small talk. I can discuss the fine points of the Darfur genocide, but the majority of Americans probably can't even tell you the country where that's taking place. (It's Sudan, FYI.) On the other hand, I can't talk football, or tell you the plot of the last novel I read. I don't know who's dating whom in Hollywood. And I don't really care. There are so many things in the world considerably more important.

I check the name of the restaurant against the note in my BlackBerry calendar and walk inside. I can tell it's one of those places where they serve 'precious' food – appetizers the size of a mushroom cap, unpronounceable ingredients listed for each menu item that make you wonder if someone sits around making these up: cod semen and wild-fennel pollen; beef cheeks, meringue grits, ash vinaigrette.

When I give the maître d' my name, he leads me to a table in the rear of the dining room, a place so dark I wonder if I'll even be able to tell if my date is attractive. She is already seated, and as my eyes adjust to the lack of light I notice that yes, she's cute, except for her hair. It's styled with a big pouf on the top, as if she's trying to fashionably mask encephalitis. 'You must be Leo,' she says, smiling. 'I'm Irene.'

She is wearing a lot of silver jewelry, much of it caught in her cleavage. 'Brooklyn?' I guess.

'No,' she repeats, more slowly. 'I-rene.'

'No – I mean, your accent . . . are you from Brooklyn?'

'Jersey,' Irene says. 'Newark.'

'The car theft capital of the world. Did you know more cars are stolen there than in L.A. and NYC put together?'

She laughs. It sounds like a wheeze. 'And my mother's worried about me living in Prince George County.'

A waiter comes over to rattle off specials, and to take our drink order. I order wine, about which I know nothing. I choose one based on the fact that it's not the most expensive one on the list, and it's not the least expensive, either, because that would just look cheap.

'So this is weird, huh?' she says. Either she is winking at me or she has something in her eye. 'Our parents knowing each other?'

The way it has been explained to me, my mother's podiatrist is the brother of Irene's father. It's not like they grew up next door. 'Weird,' I agree.

'I moved here for a job, so I don't really know anyone yet.'

'It's a great city,' I say automatically, although I do not entirely believe this. The traffic is insane, and there's a protest every other day about some cause, which quickly stops being idealistic and starts being a pain in the neck when you need to get somewhere in a timely fashion and all the roads are blocked off. 'I'm sure my mom told me, but I've forgotten – what do you do?'

'I'm a certified bra fitter,' Irene says. 'I'm working at Nordstrom.'

'Certified,' I repeat. I wonder where the legitimizing agency for bra fitters is. If you get grades: A, B, C, D, and DD. 'It sounds like a very . . . unique job.'

'It's a handful,' Irene says, and then she laughs. 'Get it?'

'Um. Yeah.'

'I'm doing bra fitting now so I can put myself through school and do what I *really* want.'

'Mammography?' I guess.

'No, be a court reporter. They're always so stylish in the movies.' She smiles at me. 'I know what you do. My mother told me. It's very Humphrey Bogart.'

'Not so much. Our department isn't Casablanca, just the poor bastard stepchild of the DOJ. We don't actually have Paris. We barely even have a coffeemaker.'

She blinks.

'Never mind.'

'So how many Nazis have you caught?'

'Well, it's a little complicated,' I say. 'We've won court cases against a hundred and seven Nazi criminals. Sixty-seven have been removed from the U.S., to date. But it's not sixty-seven out of a hundred and seven, because not all of them were U.S. citizens – you have to be careful about the math. Unfortunately, few of the people we've deported or have had extradited were ever prosecuted, to which I say, shame on Europe. Three defendants have been tried in Germany, one in Yugoslavia, and one in the USSR. Of those, three were convicted, one was acquitted, and one had his trial suspended for medical reasons and died before it could continue. Before our department was created, one other Nazi criminal was sent from the U.S. to Europe and prosecuted there – she was convicted and imprisoned. We've got five cases currently in litigation and many more people under active investigation and . . . Your eyes are glazing over.'

'No,' Irene says. 'I just wear contacts. Really.' She hesitates. 'But aren't the guys you're chasing, like, really *old* now?'

'Yes.'

'So they can't be moving all that fast.'

'It's not a literal chase,' I explain. 'And they did horrible things to other human beings. That shouldn't go unpunished.'

'Yeah, but it was so *long* ago.'

'It's still important,' I tell her.

'You mean because you're Jewish?'

'The Nazis didn't just target Jews. They also killed Gypsies and Poles and homosexuals and the mentally and physically disabled. Everyone should be invested in what my department does. Because if we're not, what message is America sending to people who commit genocide? That they can get away with it, if enough time passes? They can hide inside our borders without even a slap on the wrist? We routinely deport hundreds of thousands of illegal aliens every year whose sole offense is that they overstayed a visa or came without the right paperwork – but people who were involved in crimes against humanity get to stay? And die peacefully here? And be buried on American soil?'

I don't realize how loud and impassioned I've become until a man who is sitting at the next table starts to clap, slowly but forcefully. A few other folks at tables around me join in. Mortified, I slink lower in my chair, trying to become invisible.

Irene reaches for my hand and threads her fingers through mine. 'It's okay, Leo. Actually, I think it's really sexy.'

'What is?'

'The way you can wave your voice around, like it's a flag.'

I shake my head. 'I'm not some big patriot. I'm a guy who's doing his job. I'm just tired of defending what I do. It isn't obsolete.'

'Well, it *is*, kind of. I mean, it's not like those Nazis are hiding in plain sight.'

It takes a moment for me to realize she is confusing the words *obsolete* and *obscure*. At the same time, I think about

Josef Weber, who – according to Sage Singer – has done just that, for decades.

The waiter arrives with the bottle of wine and pours a taste for me. I swish it around in my mouth, nod my approval. At this point, frankly, I'd have given the thumbs-up to moonshine, as long as there was a valid alcohol content.

'I hope we're not going to talk about history all night,' Irene says breezily. 'Because I'm really bad at it. I mean, who really cares if Columbus discovered America instead of Westhampton—'

'The West Indies,' I murmur.

'Whatever. The natives were probably less bitchy.'

I refill my wineglass, and wonder whether I will survive until dessert.

Either my mother has a sixth sense or else she implanted a microchip in me at birth that allows her to know my comings and goings at all times. It's the only way I can explain the fact that she times her phone calls for the very moment I walk in my front door, without fail.

'Hi, Mom,' I say, pushing the speakerphone button without even bothering to look at the caller ID.

'Leo. Would it have killed you to be nice to that poor girl?'

'That poor girl is completely capable of landing on her feet. And she doesn't need or want someone like me, anyway.'

'You don't know if you're compatible after one lousy dinner,' my mother says.

'Mom. She thought the Bay of Pigs was a barbecue joint.'

'Not everyone had the educational opportunities you did, Leo.'

'You study that stuff in eleventh grade!' I say. 'Besides, I *was* nice to her.'

There is a pause on the other end of the line. 'Really. So you were being nice when you took a phone call and told her it was the office and you had to go because John Dillinger had been captured.'

'In my defense, dinner had lasted two hours already and our entrée plates hadn't even been cleared.'

'Just because you're a lawyer doesn't mean you can twist the story around. I'm your mother, Leo. I could read your thoughts in utero.'

'Okay, (a) That's creepy. And (b) Maybe you and Lucy should just let me find my own dates from now on.'

'Your sister and I want you to be happy, is that such a crime?' she says. 'Plus, if we waited for you to find your own dates you'd be sending your wedding invitation to me at the Sons of Abraham.'

It's the cemetery where my father is already buried. 'Great,' I say. 'Just make sure you leave your forwarding address.' I hold the keypad away from my ear and punch the pound button. 'Got another call coming in,' I lie.

'At this hour?'

'It's an escort service,' I joke. 'I don't like to keep Peaches waiting . . .'

'You're going to be the death of me, Leo,' my mother says with a sigh.

'Sons of Abraham Cemetery. Got it,' I say. 'I love you, Ma.'

'I loved you first,' she replies. 'So what am I supposed to tell my podiatrist about Irene?'

'If she keeps wearing heels she'll wind up with bunions,' I say, and I hang up.

My house is very *GQ*. The countertops are black granite, the couches covered in some kind of gray flannel. The furniture is spare and modern. There's blue lighting under the cabinets in the kitchen that makes the place look like Mission Control at NASA. It looks like the kind of place where an NFL bachelor or a corporate attorney would be comfortable. My sister, Lucy, who does interior design, is responsible for the look. She did it to snap me out of my post-divorce funk, so I can't really tell her that it seems sterile to me. Like I'm an organism in a petri dish, not a guy who feels guilty putting his feet up on the lacquered black coffee table.

I strip off my tie and unbutton my shirt, then carefully hang my suit up in the closet. Realization number one about single life: no one else is going to take your suits to the cleaners on your behalf. Which means if you leave them crumpled in a ball at the foot of the bed, and you work till ten every night, you're screwed.

Wearing my boxers and an undershirt, I put on the stereo – it's a Duke Ellington kind of night – and then find my laptop.

Granted, it might have been more exciting if I had stayed in Boston working in corporate law (and who knows, maybe this décor would be just my cup of tea). I would be out schmoozing with clients instead of reading Genevra's report on one of our suspects right now. God knows I'd be socking away more money for retirement. Maybe I'd even have a girl named Peaches curled up at the end of the sofa. But in spite of what my mother thinks, I *am* happy. I cannot imagine doing anything except what I do and liking it more.

I'd first gotten an internship with HRSP when it was still called OSI, the Office of Special Investigations. My grand-father, a World War II vet, had regaled me with stories of combat my whole life; as a boy my most prized possession was an M35 Heer steel helmet that he gifted to me, with a dark spot on the inside he swore was brain matter. (My mother, disgusted, removed it from my room one night while I was asleep and to this day hasn't told me what she did with it.) In college, hoping to pad my résumé before I went to law school, I took the job at OSI. I expected legal experience I could put on my applications. What I got instead was passion. Everyone in that office was there because they wanted to be, because they truly believed that what they did was important, no matter what the Pat Buchanans of the world said about the U.S. government wasting money to hunt down people who were too old to be a threat to the general population.

I went to Harvard Law and had my choice of offers from Boston firms when I graduated. The one I picked paid me enough to buy fancy suits and a sweet Mustang convertible, which I never had time to joyride in, because I was working furiously on a track toward becoming a junior partner. I had cash, I had a fiancée, and 95 percent of my litigation had resulted in a verdict for the defendant I was representing. But I missed caring.

I wrote to the director of OSI and moved to Washington one month later.

Yeah, I know that my head is more often mired in the 1940s than the 2010s. And true, if you spend too much time living in the past, you never move forward. But then again, you can't tell me what I do isn't necessary. If history has a habit of repeating itself, doesn't someone have to stay behind to shout out a warning? If not me, then who?

The Duke Ellington track ends. To fill the silence, I turn on the television. I watch Stephen Colbert for about ten minutes, but he's too entertaining to be background noise for me. I keep finding myself pulled away from Genevra's report to listen to his patter.

When my laptop chimes with an incoming email, I look down at the screen. Genevra.

Hope I'm not interrupting a lovely sexcapade with the next Mrs. Stein. But just in case you're sitting home alone watching old episodes of Rin Tin Tin like me (don't judge) thought you'd want to know that Josef Weber's name returned no hits. Onward and upward, boss.

I stare at the email for a long moment.

I had told Sage Singer that the odds were against her. For whatever reason, Josef Weber is lying to her about his past. But that's Sage Singer's problem now, not mine.

I've questioned dozens of suspects over the years I've worked at HRSP. Even when I am presenting some of them with the incontrovertible evidence that they were guards at an extermination camp, they always say they had no idea that people were being killed. They insist that they only saw the prisoners on work detail, and they remember them being in good condition. They recall seeing smoke and hearing rumors of bodies being burned, but they never witnessed it themselves and didn't believe it at the time. Selective memory, that's what I call it. And – go figure – it's completely different from the stories of survivors I've interviewed, who can describe the stench from the chimneys of the crematoria: nauseating and acrid and sulfurous, fatty and thick, almost more of a taste than a smell. They say you couldn't help but breathe it in, everywhere you went. That even now, they sometimes wake up with the scent of burning flesh in their nostrils.

Zebras don't change their stripes, and war criminals don't repent.

It doesn't surprise me that Josef Weber, who confessed to being a Nazi, isn't one. After all, it's what I expected. What surprises me is how much I really wanted Sage Singer to prove me wrong.

*W*hen you can prolong the inevitable, it's always better. That's why, for a predator, the wilding begins with a chase. It's not toying with food, as some people think. It's getting the adrenaline level to match your own.

There comes a point, though, where waiting is no longer possible. You hear the prey's heart beating inside your own head, and it is the last conscious thought you will be able to hold. Once you give in to the primeval, you are an observer, watching another part of you feast, shredding the flesh to find the ambrosia. You drink in the victim's fear, but it tastes like excitement. You have no past, no future, no sympathy, no soul. But you knew that before you even started, didn't you?

Sage

When I show up for work the next night, someone else is baking in my kitchen. He is a behemoth of a man, six-foot-something, with Maori-style tattoos on his upper arms. When I walk in, he's cutting slabs of dough and tossing them with incredible precision onto a scale. 'Hey,' he says, in a squirrelly voice that doesn't match his body. 'Howyadoin.'

My mind is a colander, and all the words I need to have this conversation are funneling fast through the sieve. I am so surprised I forget to hide my scar. 'Who are you?'

'Clark.'

'What are you doing?'

He looks at the table, the wall, anywhere but at me. 'The dinner rolls.'

'I don't think so,' I say. 'I work alone.'

Before Clark can respond, Mary enters the kitchen. She was no doubt alerted to my arrival by Rocco, who had greeted me in the front of the bakery with this cryptic observation: 'Dreamed of traveling? / Maybe taking up knitting? / Now may be the time.'

'I see you've met Clark.' She smiles at the giant who is now shaping loaves at a blistering speed. I wonder if he's poked through my pre-ferments and pored over my spreadsheets. It makes me feel as if someone has been rifling through my underwear drawer. 'Clark used to work at King Arthur Flour in Norwich, Vermont.'

'Good. Then he can go back to them.'

'Sage! Clark's just here to help you out. To relieve some of the stress.'

I take Mary by the arm and turn her away, so that Clark can't hear what I say. 'Mary,' I whisper, 'I don't want any help.'

'Maybe so,' she says. 'But you need it. Why don't you and I take a little walk?'

I'm fighting tears, and the uncontrollable urge to throw a tantrum; I'm equal parts angry and hurt. Yes, I took the night off without telling my boss, but I found my own replacement. And maybe I changed the menu without running it by her, either, but that challah I baked was moist and sweet and perfect. But mostly I'm upset because I thought Mary was my friend, not just my boss, which makes her zero-tolerance policy even more devastating.

She leads me past the last few customers in the shop, who are being rung out by Rocco. As we pass the register, I turn away from him. Did Mary tell Rocco she was getting rid of me? Is he her new confidant about this business, the way I used to be?

I follow her through the parking lot and the shrine gates, up the Holy Stairs, until we are standing in the same grotto where Josef told me he was a Nazi.

'Are you firing me?' I burst out.

'Why would you think that?'

'Oh, I don't know. Maybe because Mr. Clean's in my kitchen baking *my* dinner rolls. I can't believe you'd replace me with some drone from a factory . . .'

'King Arthur Flour's hardly a factory, and Clark's not a replacement. He's just here to give you a little flexibility.'

Mary sits down on a granite bench. Her eyes are a piercing blue, with all that monkshood behind her. 'I'm only trying to help, Sage. I don't know if it's stress or guilt or something else, but you're not yourself lately. You've become erratic.'

'I'm still doing my job. I've *been* doing my job,' I protest.

'You baked two hundred and twenty loaves of challah last night.'

'Did you try any? Trust me, no customer could find a better one anywhere else.'

'But they *would* have to go somewhere else if they wanted rye bread. Or sourdough. Or an ordinary wheat loaf. Or any of the other staples you chose not to make.' Her voice grows soft as moss. 'I know you were the one who got rid of the Jesus Loaf, Sage.'

'Oh, for God's sake—'

'I prayed about it. That loaf was a call to save someone, and now, I realize that person is *you.*'

'Is this because I played hooky?' I ask. 'I had to see my grandmother. She wasn't feeling well.' It is amazing, I realize, how quickly lies compound. They cover like a coat of paint, one on top of the other, until you cannot remember what color you started with.

Maybe Josef had actually begun to believe he was the person everyone thought him to be. And maybe *that* was what finally made him tell the truth.

'Look at you, Sage, a million miles away. Are you even listening to me? You're a hot mess. Your hair looks like there are birds nesting in it; you probably haven't showered today; you have circles under your eyes that are so dark it makes me think of kidney failure. You're burning a candle at both ends, working here all night and then committing adultery during the day with that trollop.' Mary frowns. 'What's a male version of *trollop*?'

'*Shimbo*,' I say. 'Look, I know you and I don't see eye to eye about Adam, but you didn't get all up in Rocco's grille when he asked you the best fertilizer for a cannabis crop—'

'If he'd been stoned on the job, I would have,' Mary insists. 'You may not believe this, but I don't think you're immoral for sleeping with Adam. In fact, I think it bothers you deep down, just as much as it bothers me. And maybe that's why it's taking over your life in a way that's affecting your work.'

I start to laugh. Yeah, I'm obsessed with a man. He just happens to be a nonagenarian.

Suddenly an idea lights in my mind, delicate as a beating butterfly. *What if I told her?* What if this burden I've been carrying around – this confession from Josef – wasn't only mine to bear? 'Okay, maybe I *have* been a little upset. But it's not Adam. It's Josef Weber.' I look her in the eye. 'I learned something about him. Something terrible. He's a Nazi, Mary.'

'Josef Weber. The same Josef Weber I know? The one who always leaves a twenty-five-percent tip and who gives half his roll to his dog? The Josef Weber who was given the Good Samaritan award last year by the chamber of commerce?' Mary shakes her head. 'This is exactly what I'm talking about, Sage. You're overtired. Your brain is firing on the wrong cylinders. Josef Weber's a sweet old man I've known for a decade. If he's a Nazi, honey, then I'm Lady Gaga.'

'But, Mary—'

'Have you told anyone else about this?'

Immediately, I think of Leo Stein.

'No,' I lie.

'Well, good, because I don't think there's a novena for slander.'

I feel as if the whole world is looking through the wrong

end of the telescope, and I am the only one who can see clearly. 'I'm not accusing Josef,' I say desperately. 'He *told* me.'

Mary purses her lips. 'A few years ago some scholars translated an ancient text they believed was the Gospel of Judas. They said the information, told from Judas's point of view, would turn Christianity on its ear. Instead of Judas being the world's biggest traitor, he was apparently the only one Jesus trusted to get the job done – which is why Jesus, knowing he would have to die, picked Judas to confide in.'

'So you believe me!'

'No,' Mary says flatly. 'I don't. And I didn't believe those scholars, either. Because I've got two thousand years of history telling me Jesus – who incidentally was one of the good guys, Sage, just like Josef Weber – was betrayed by Judas.'

'History's not always right.'

'But you've got to start there anyway. If you don't know where you've come from, how in Heaven's name will you ever figure out where you're going?' Mary folds me into an embrace. 'I am doing this because I love you. Go home. Sleep for a week. Get a massage. Hike up a mountain. Clear your head. And *then* come back. Your kitchen will be waiting for you.'

I feel dangerously close to sobbing. 'Please,' I beg. 'Don't take this away from me. It's the only thing in my life I haven't screwed up.'

'I'm not taking anything away from you. It's still your bread. I made Clark promise that he'll use your recipes.'

What I'm thinking about, though, is the scoring.

Back in the days of communal ovens, people would bring their own dough from home to bake en masse with the rest of the village. So how could you tell the loaves apart, when they came out of the oven? The way they were cut, by the individual bakers. When you score the outside of the dough, it does two things: it tells the loaf where to open, and helps the interior structure by giving it a place to expand. But it also allows the baker to leave his or her brand. I always score a baguette five times, for example, with the longest cut at one end.

Clark won't.

It's a silly thing, one that our customers probably don't even notice, but it's my signature. It's my stamp, on each loaf.

As Mary walks down the Holy Stairs, I wonder if this is yet another reason Josef Weber picked me as his confessor. If you hide long enough, a ghost among men, you might disappear forever without anyone noticing. It's human nature to ensure that someone has seen the mark you left behind.

'I don't know what got into you today,' Adam says as I roll off him and stare up at the bedroom ceiling. 'But I'm sure as hell grateful.'

I wouldn't call what we just did lovemaking; it was more like trying to crawl beneath Adam's skin, dissolve by osmosis. I wanted to lose myself in him, until there was nothing left.

I trail my fingers along his rib cage. 'Do I seem different to you lately?'

He grins. 'Yes, especially in the last half hour. But I'm fully in favor of the new you.' He glances at his watch. 'I need to get going.'

Today Adam is presiding over a Japanese Buddhist funeral, and he's been doing research to make sure that he gets all the customs just right. Ninety-nine point nine percent of the Japanese are cremated, including the deceased he will be taking care of today. Yesterday was the wake.

'Can't you stay a little longer?' I ask him.

'No – I've got a ton to do,' Adam says. 'I'm terrified I'm going to mess it up.'

'You've cremated hundreds of people,' I point out.

'Yeah, but there's a whole *process* for the Japanese. Instead of grinding down the bone residue like we usually do, there's a ritual. Family members pick up the bone fragments together with a special pair of chopsticks and put them into the urn.' He shrugs. 'Besides, you need your beauty sleep. You've only got a few hours before it's time to make the donuts again.'

I draw the covers up to my chin. 'Actually, I'm taking a few days off work,' I say, as if it were my idea all along. 'Testing new recipes. Reevaluating stuff.'

'How's Mary going to keep her bakery open, if you're here?'

'I have a guy filling in for me,' I reply, again amazed at how smooth a lie feels in my throat, and how much of an aftertaste is left behind. 'Clark. I think he'll do all right. But it also means I get to live like a normal person, with normal hours. So, you know, maybe you'll be able to stay the night. It would be really nice to fall asleep with you.'

'You fall asleep with me all the time,' Adam points out.

But it's different. He waits until I'm out like a light, and then takes a shower and tiptoes out of the house. What I want is what other people take for granted: the chance to feel the night tighten around us like a noose. To ask, *Did you set the alarm?* To say: *Remind me that we are running out of toothpaste.* To have our time together not be so romantically charged but instead, just plain boring.

I wind my arms around Adam and bury my face in the curve of his neck. 'Wouldn't it be fun to pretend we're an old married couple?'

He disengages himself from my embrace. 'I don't have to pretend,' he says, and he gets up from the bed and walks into the bathroom.

As if I needed any reminder of that. I wait until I hear the shower running, and then I throw back the covers and wander into the kitchen. I pour myself a glass of orange juice and sit down at my laptop. On the screen is a spread-sheet I'd used to make a poolish when I first came home from the bakery. Just because I'm not working at Our Daily Bread doesn't mean I can't refine my recipes in my own home test kitchen.

The poolish is fermenting on the counter – it's got a few more hours to go before it's usable, but the yeast has frothed at the top, like the head on a beer. I close out the spreadsheet and open YouTube in my browser.

I am like many twenty-five-year-olds in this country, I imagine. My knowledge of World War II was shaped by high school history classes, my understanding of the Holocaust a combination of assigned readings: Anne Frank's *Diary of a Young Girl* and Elie Wiesel's *Night*. Even knowing that there was a personal connection to my grandmother – or maybe *because* of that – I tended to view the Holocaust in the abstract, the way I viewed slavery: a series of horrors that had happened a long time ago in a world markedly different from the one I lived in. Yes, those were bad times, but really, what did they have to do with me?

I type 'Nazi Concentration Camp' into the search bar, and my screen floods with thumbnail images: of Hitler's pinched face, of a tangle of bodies in a pit, of a room crammed to the rafters with shoes. I pick a video that is a newsreel from 1945, after the liberation. As it loads, I read the comments underneath.

THE HOLOCAUST WAS A HOAX. FUCK KIKES.

FAKE SHIT HOLOCAUST WAS A JEWISH LIE.

My uncle's farm was there and the Red Cross praised the camp conditions. Read the report.

FU you Nazi pig. Stop whining and start admitting.

I guess the witnesses were liars too?

This is still happening all over the world while we look the other way like the Germans did 70 years ago. We have learned nothing.

I click somewhere into the middle of the fifty-seven-minute film. I have no idea what camp I am watching, but I see bodies stacked outside the crematoria, so horrific that it's virtually impossible to believe this wasn't just a Hollywood rendering, that these are real people I am seeing, with their bones protruding so clearly you could map the skeleton beneath the skin; that the face with the eye blown out of it belonged to someone who had a wife, a family, another life. Here are the body disposal facilities, the voice-over tells me. Ovens capable of burning more than a hundred bodies per day. Here are the litters, used to slide a body inside, the way I use a peel to slip an artisanal loaf into my wood-fired oven. I see a fleeting image of a skeleton inside the cavern of one of the ovens; another of a pile of bone fragments. I see the plaque of the proud furnace manufacturers: Topf & Söhne.

I think of Adam's clients, picking the bones of their beloved from the ash.

Then I think of my grandmother and I feel like I'm going to be sick.

I want to close my computer, but I cannot make myself do it. Instead I watch parades of Germans in their Sunday finest being led into the camps, smiling as if they are on holiday. Their faces change, darkening, some even crying, as they are led on the tour of the facility. I watch Weimar businessmen in suits being pressed into service to relocate and rebury the dead.

These were the people who might have known what was going on but didn't admit it to themselves. Or who turned a blind eye, so that they wouldn't have to get involved. The kind of person I'd be if I ignored what Josef has told me.

'So,' Adam says, walking into the kitchen with his hair still damp from the shower and his tie already knotted. He starts to rub my shoulders. 'Same time Wednesday?'

I slam my laptop shut.

'Maybe,' I hear myself reply, 'we should take a break.'

He looks at me. 'A break?'

'Yeah. I need some time alone, I think.'

'Didn't you ask me five minutes ago to act like we were married?'

'And didn't you tell me five minutes ago you already *are*?'

I consider what Mary said, about how being with Adam might bother me more than I want to admit. I think about being the kind of person who stands up for what she believes in, instead of denying what's right before her eyes.

Adam looks stunned, but he quickly smooths away the surprise. 'Take as much time as you need, baby.' He kisses me so gently that it feels like a promise, like a prayer. 'Just remember,' he whispers. 'No one else will ever love you like I do.'

It strikes me, as Adam leaves, that his words could be taken as a vow, or as a threat.

I suddenly remember a girl in my World Religion class in college, a foreign student from Osaka. When we were covering Buddhism, she talked about corruption: how much money her family had to pay a priest for her dead grandfather's *kaimyo,* a special name given to the deceased that he would take with him to Heaven. The more you paid, the more characters were in your posthumous name, and the more prestige your family accrued. *Do you think that matters in the Buddhist afterlife?* the professor had asked.

Probably not, the girl had said. *But it keeps you from coming back to* this *world every time your name is called.*

In retrospect, I realize I should have shared this anecdote with Adam.

Anonymity, I guess, always comes at a price.

When the phone rings, I am having a nightmare. Mary is standing behind me in the kitchen, telling me I am not working fast enough. But even though I am shaping loaves and slipping them into the oven so quickly that I have blisters on my fingers and blood baked into the dough, every time I take out a finished loaf there are only bones, bleached white as the sails of a ship. *It's about time,* Mary scolds, and before I can stop her she picks one up with chopsticks, and bites down hard, breaking all of her teeth into tiny pearls that fall to the floor and roll beneath my shoes.

I am in such a deep sleep, in fact, that even though I reach for the receiver and say hello, I drop it and it rolls underneath my bed.

'Sorry,' I say, after I retrieve it. 'Hello?'

'Sage Singer?'

'Yes, that's me.'

'This is Leo Stein.'

I sit up in bed, suddenly awake. 'I'm sorry.'

'You said that already . . . Did I . . . You sound like I woke you up.'

'Well. Yeah.'

'Then I'm the one who should be apologizing. I figured since it was eleven o'clock—'

'I'm a baker,' I interrupt. 'I work at night and sleep during the day.'

'You can call me back at a more convenient time—'

'Just tell me,' I say. 'What did you find out?'

'Nothing,' Leo Stein replies. 'There are absolutely no records in the SS membership registry for Josef Weber.'

'Then there's been a mistake. Did you try spelling it differently?'

'My historian is very thorough, Ms. Singer. I'm sorry, but I think you might have misunderstood what he was telling you.'

'I didn't.' I push my hair out of my face. 'You're the one who said the records aren't complete. Isn't it possible that you just haven't found the right one yet?'

'It's possible, but without that, we really can't do anything else.'

'Will you keep looking?'

I can hear the hesitation in his voice, the understanding that I am asking him to find an invisible needle in a haystack. 'I don't know how to stop,' Leo says. 'We'll run checks in two Berlin records centers and our own databases. But the bottom line is if there's no valid information to run with—'

'Give me till lunchtime,' I beg.

*　*　*

In the end, it is the way I met Josef – at a grief group – that makes me wonder if Leo Stein is right, if Josef is lying. After all, he lived with Marta for fifty-two years. That's a damn long time to keep a secret.

It is pouring when I reach his house, and I don't have an umbrella. I'm drenched after running to the covered porch, where Eva barks for nearly half a minute before Josef comes to the door. I am seeing double – not a blurriness of vision but a superimposition of this old man with a younger, stronger one dressed in the uniform of the soldiers I have seen on YouTube. 'Your wife,' I say. 'Did *she* know you're a Nazi?'

Josef opens the door wider. 'Come in. This is not a conversation for the street.'

I follow him into his living room, where the chess game we were playing days earlier remains, unicorns and dragons frozen at my last move. 'I never told her,' Josef admits.

'That's impossible. She would have wanted to know where you were during the war.'

'I said I was sent by my parents to study at university in England. Marta never questioned it. You would be surprised at the lengths you will go to to believe the best about someone if you truly love him,' Josef says.

That, of course, makes me think of Adam. 'It must be hard, Josef,' I say coolly. 'To not get tangled up in your lies.'

My words land like blows; Josef shrinks back in his chair. 'This is the reason I told you the truth.'

'But . . . you didn't, did you?'

'What do you mean?'

I can't very well tell him that the reason I know he's been lying is that a Nazi hunter from the Department of Justice checked out his false story. 'It just doesn't add up. A wife who never stumbled over the truth, not in fifty-two years. A history of being a monster, without any proof. Of course the biggest inconsistency of all is why, after over sixty-five years of keeping a secret, you'd blow your own cover.'

'I told you. I want to die.'

'Why now?'

'Because I have no one to live for,' Josef says. 'Marta was an angel. She saw good in me when I couldn't even look in a mirror. I so badly wanted to be the man she thought she had married, that I became him. If she knew what I had done—'

'She would have killed you?'

'No,' Josef says. 'She would have killed herself. I did not care about what happened to me, but I couldn't stand thinking of what it would be like for her, to know she had been touched by hands that would never truly be clean.' He looks at me. 'I know she is in Heaven now. I promised myself that I would be who she wanted me to be until she was gone. And now that this is the case, I have come to you.' Josef folds his hands between his knees. 'Dare I hope this means you are considering my request?'

He speaks formally, as if he has asked me to dance with him at a mixer. As if this is a business proposition.

But I string him along. 'You understand how selfish you're being, right? You want me to risk getting arrested. Basically, I give up the rest of my life, just so you can leave yours.'

'This is not the case. No one is going to think twice if an old man turns up dead.'

'Murder isn't legal, in case you've forgotten in the past sixty-eight years.'

'Ah, but you see, this is why I have been waiting for someone like you. If you do it, it's not murder, it is mercy.' He meets my gaze. 'You see, before you help me die, Sage, I need one more favor from you. I ask you to forgive me first.'

'Forgive you?'

'For the things I did back then.'

'I am *not* the one you should be asking forgiveness from.'

'No,' he agrees. 'But they are all dead.'

Slowly, the cogs turn, until the picture lines up clearly for me. Now I see why he turned to me for his grand confession. Josef does not know about my grandmother; however, I am the closest thing to a Jew he can find in this town. It is, I realize, like the victim's family in a death row case. Do they have the right to seek justice? My great-grandparents had died at the hands of Nazis. Did that make me, by proxy, the next best thing?

I hear Leo's voice, an echo in my mind. *I don't know how to stop.* Is his work vengeance? Or justice? There is the finest line between the two, and when I try to focus on it, it becomes less and less clear.

Repentance might bring peace to the killer, but what about the ones who've been killed? I may not consider myself a Jew, but do I still have responsibility to the relatives of mine who *were* religious, and who were murdered for it?

Josef confided in me because he considers me a friend. Because he trusts me. But if Josef's claims are legitimate, the man I befriended – and trusted – is a shadow puppet, a figment of the imagination. A man who has deceived thousands of people.

It makes me feel dirty, as if I should have been a stronger judge of character.

In that moment I make myself a promise: I will find out if Josef Weber was an SS soldier. Yet if he *does* turn out to be a Nazi, I will not kill him the way he wants. Instead, I will betray him the way he betrayed others. I will pump him for information and feed it back to Leo Stein so Josef will die somewhere in a prison cell.

But *he* doesn't have to know that.

'I can't forgive you,' I say evenly, 'if I don't know what you did. Before I agree to anything, you're going to have to give me some actual proof of your past.'

The relief that floods Josef's features is palpable, almost painful. His eyes fill with tears. 'The photograph—'

'Means nothing. For all I know it's not even you. Or it came from eBay.'

'I understand.' Josef looks up at me. 'So the first thing you will need to know,' he says, 'is my real name.'

If Josef thinks it is strange when I jump up moments later and ask to use his bathroom, he doesn't say so. Instead he directs me down the hall to a small powder room that has wallpaper blooming with cabbage roses and a little dish of decorative soaps still in their plastic wrap.

I run the water in the sink, and then take my cell phone out of my pocket.

Leo Stein answers on the first ring.

'His name isn't Josef Weber,' I say breathlessly.

'Hello?'

'It's me, Sage Singer.'

'Why are you whispering?'

'Because I'm hiding in Josef's bathroom,' I say.

'I thought his name wasn't Josef . . .'

'It's not. It's Reiner Hartmann. With two *n*'s at the end. And I have a birth date for him, too. April twentieth, 1918.'

Same as the Führer, he had said.

'That would make him ninety-five,' Leo says, doing the math.

'I thought you said it's never too late to go after them.'

'It's not. Ninety-five is better than dead. But how do you know he's telling you the truth?'

'I don't,' I say. 'But you will. Stick it in a database and see what happens.'

'It's not quite that easy—'

'It can't be that hard. Where's your historian? Ask her to do it.'

'Ms. Singer—'

'Look, I'm hiding in an old man's bathroom. You told me that with a name and a birth date records are easier to find.'

He sighs. 'Let me see what I can do.'

While I am waiting I flush the toilet. Twice. I am sure that Josef or Reiner or whatever he wants to be called now is wondering if I've fallen in; or maybe he thinks I'm taking a sponge bath in the sink.

After about ten minutes, I hear Leo's voice. 'Reiner Hartmann was a member of the Nazi Party,' he says.

I feel oddly euphoric, knowing that there's been a hit, and also leaden, because it means that the man on the other side of that door was involved in mass murders. I let out the breath I've been holding. 'So I was right.'

'Just because his name turned up in the Berlin Document Center doesn't mean he's a legal slam dunk,' Leo says. 'This is just the beginning.'

'What happens next?'

'That depends,' Leo replies. 'What more can you find out?'

*I*t felt like a blade along the side of my neck.

I heard the rip of my own skin; felt the blood, sticky and hot, dripping down my chest. Again he dove toward me, snapping my vocal cords. All I could do was wait for the razor of his teeth, know that it was coming again.

I had heard the stories of upiory who rose from the dead and ate through their linen shrouds in search of the blood that would sustain them, because they no longer had any of their own. They were insatiable. I had heard the stories, and now I knew they were true.

This was no piercing of fangs, no draining. He gorged on me and brought me to the edge of death, the brink he skated on for eternity. So this was what Hell was like: a slow, silent scream. No strength to move, no voice to speak. Just my other senses heightened: touch and smell and sound, as he shredded my flesh. He banged my head against the ground: once, twice. My eyes rolled back; darkness dropped like a guillotine . . .

Suddenly, I bolted upright. I was bathed in sweat, my cheek dusty with flour where I had fallen asleep waiting for the dough to rise. But that banging was still in my head. I grabbed for my throat, relieved to feel it smooth and whole, and heard it again: someone was knocking on the door of the cottage.

The man with the golden eyes was standing at the door,

silhouetted by the moon. 'I could bake for you,' he said. His voice was deep, soft. Accented. I wondered where he had come from.

I was still partly in a dream state; I did not understand.

'My name is Aleksander Lubov,' he told me. 'I've seen you in the village. I know about your father.' He looked over my shoulder at the baguettes couched in linen, lined up like waiting soldiers. 'During the day, I have to watch my brother. He isn't right in the head, and he'll harm himself if he's left alone. But I have to find work, too. Work I can do at night, when he is asleep.'

'When will you *sleep?' I asked, the first question to pierce like an arrow through the fog of my mind.*

He smiled, and just like that, I could not breathe. 'Who says that I do?'

'I cannot pay you—'

'I'll take what you can give,' he replied.

I thought of how tired I was. I thought of what my father would say if I let a stranger into his bakery. I thought of Damian and Baruch Beiler, and what they each wanted from me.

It is said that you're safer with the devil you know than with the devil you don't. And I knew nothing about Aleksander Lubov. So why would I agree to his proposal?

'Because,' he said, as if he could read my mind. 'You need me.'

Josef

I will not answer to the other name. That person, he is someone I like to think I have never been.

But this isn't true. Inside each of us is a monster; inside each of us is a saint. The real question is which one we nurture the most, which one will smite the other.

To understand what I became you must know where I came from. My family, we lived in Wewelsburg, which was part of the city of Büren in the district of Paderborn. My father was a machinist by trade and my mother kept house. My earliest memory is of my father and mother fighting over money. After the first Great War, inflation spiraled out of control. Their savings, which they had diligently put away for years, were suddenly worth nothing. My father had just cashed in a ten-year insurance policy, and the proceeds did not even cover the cost of a newspaper. A cup of coffee was five thousand marks. A loaf of bread, two hundred billion marks. As a boy, I remember running with my mother to meet my father on payday, and then began the mad rush to the shops to purchase goods. Often, the shops had run out. Then my brother, Franz, and I would be sent at twilight into the fields of farmers who lived outside of Wewelsburg, to steal apples from the trees and potatoes from the ground.

Not everyone suffered, of course. Some had invested in gold

early on. Some speculated in fabric or meat or soap or produce. But most middle-class Germans, like my family, were ruined. The Weimar Republic, shiny and new after the war, was a disaster. My parents had done everything right – worked hard, saved well – and to what end? Election after election, no one seemed to have the answer.

The reason I tell you this is that everyone always asks: How could Nazis come to power? How could Hitler have had such free rein? Well, I tell you: desperate people often do things that they normally would not do. If you went to the doctor and he said you had a terminal disease, you'd probably walk out of that office feeling pretty low. Yet if you shared this news with friends, and one told you, 'You know, I had a friend who was diagnosed with that, too, and Doctor X cured him right away.' Well, maybe he is the biggest quack, maybe he charges two million dollars for a consultation – but I bet you'd still be on the phone to him immediately. No matter how educated you are, no matter how irrational it seems, you will follow a glimmer of hope.

The National Socialist German Workers' Party, it was that ray of light. Nothing else was working to fix Germany. So why not try this? They promised to get people back to work. To get rid of the Treaty of Versailles. To regain the territory we'd lost in the war. To put Germany back in its rightful place.

When I was five years old, Hitler tried to take over the government at a beer hall – the Munich Putsch – and failed miserably by most accounts. But he learned that the way to lead a revolution was not violently but legally. And at his trial in 1924, every word Hitler spoke was reported in the German newspapers, the National Socialist Party's first propaganda onslaught.

You will notice I say nothing about the Jews. That is because most of us didn't know a single Jew. Out of sixty million Germans, only 500,000 were Jews, and even those would have called themselves Germans, not Jews. But anti-Semitism was alive and well in Germany long before Hitler became powerful. It was part of what we were taught in church, how two thousand years ago, the Jews had killed our Lord. It was evident in the way we viewed Jews – good investors, who seemed to have money in a bad economy when no one else had any. Selling the idea that the Jews were to blame for all of Germany's problems was just not that difficult.

Any military man will tell you that the way to pull a divided group together is to give them a common enemy. This is what Hitler did, when he came to power in 1933 as chancellor. He threaded this philosophy through the Nazi Party, directing his diatribes against those who leaned left politically. Yet the Nazis pointed out the linkage between Jews and the left; Jews and crime; Jews and unpatriotic behavior. If people hated Jews already for religious reasons or economic reasons, giving them another reason to hate them was not really going to be difficult. So when Hitler said that the biggest threat to the German state was an attack on the purity of the German people, and so her uniqueness must be guarded at all costs – well, it gave us something to be proud of again. The threat of Jews was in the mathematics. They would mingle with ethnic Germans in order to raise their own status and in doing so, would bring down Germany's dominance. We Germans needed *Lebensraum* – living space – to be a great nation. Without room to expand, there was little choice: you went to war to conquer territory and you got rid of the people who were a threat to Germany, or who weren't ethnic Germans like you.

By 1935, when I was already a young man, Germany had left the League of Nations. Hitler announced that Germany would be rebuilding its army, which had been forbidden after the first Great War. Of course, had any other country – France, England – stepped in and stopped him, what happened might not have happened. But who wanted to go back to war that quickly? It was easier just to rationalize what was happening, to say he was only taking back what had once belonged to Germany. And in the meantime, in my country, there were jobs again – factories for munitions and guns and planes. People were not making as much money as they used to, and they were working longer hours, but they were able to support their families. By 1939, the German *Lebensraum* extended through the Saar, the Rhineland, Austria, the Sudetenland, and the Czech lands. And finally, when the Germans moved into Danzig, Poland, the English and French declared war.

I will tell you a little bit about myself as a boy. My parents desperately wanted their children to have a better life than they had – and the answer, they believed, was in education. Surely people who had learned how to invest better would not have found themselves in such dire financial straits. Although I wasn't particularly bright, my parents wanted me to test into *Gymnasium*, the most academic education possible in Germany, the one whose graduates were university-bound. Of course, once there, I was always picking fights or clowning around, anything to hide the fact that I was in way over my head. My parents would be called into school weekly to see the headmaster, because I had failed another test, or because I'd come to blows with another student in the hall over a petty dispute.

Luckily, my parents had another star to hitch their wagon to – my brother, Franz. Two years younger than me, Franz was studious, his head always buried in a book. He would scribble away in notebooks that he hid underneath his mattress and that I would routinely steal to embarrass him. They were full of images I did not understand: a girl floating in an autumn pond, drowned because of a lost love; a deer hollowed by hunger picking through the snow for a single acorn; a fire that started in a soul and consumed the body, the bedding, the house surrounding it. He dreamed of studying poetry at Heidelberg, and my parents dreamed with him.

And then, one day, things began to change. At *Gymnasium*, there was a contest to see which class could first get 100 percent participation in the Hitler-Jugend. In 1934, joining the Hitler Youth was not mandatory yet, mind you. It was a social club, like your Boy Scouts, except we also swore allegiance to Hitler as his future soldiers. Under the guidance of adult leaders, we would meet after school, and go camping on weekends. We wore uniforms that looked like those the SS wore, with the Sig Rune on the lapel. I, who at age fifteen chafed at sitting at a desk, loved being outside. I excelled at the sports competitions. I had a reputation for being a bully, but that was not necessarily fair – half of the time I was beating someone to a pulp because he had called Franz a sissy.

I desperately wanted my class to win. Not because I had any great allegiance to the Führer but because the local leader of the HJ *Kameradschaft* was Herr Sollemach, whose daughter, Inge, was the prettiest girl I had ever seen. She looked like an ice queen, with her silver-blond hair and her pale blue eyes; and she and her friends did not know I existed. This, I realized, was an opportunity to change that.

For the competition, the teacher put everyone's names on the board, erasing those of the boys who joined the HJ, one by one. There were some who joined out of peer pressure; some who joined because their fathers said they had to.

There were more than a dozen, however, who joined because I threatened to pound them in the school yard if they did not.

My brother refused to join the Hitler-Jugend. In his classroom, he and one other boy were the only ones who didn't. We all knew why Artur Goldman did not join – he *could* not. When I asked Franz why he would align himself with a Jew, he said he didn't want his friend Artur to feel like he was being left out.

A few weeks later, Artur stopped going to school and never came back. My father encouraged Franz to join the Hitler-Jugend, too, to make new friends. My mother made me promise to watch over him at our meetings. 'Franz,' she would say, 'isn't strong like you.' She worried about him camping out in the woods, getting sick too easily, not connecting with the other boys.

But for the first time in her life, she didn't have to worry about me. Because as it turned out, I was the poster child for the Hitler-Jugend.

We would hike and sing and do calisthenics. We learned how to line up in military formations. My favorite activity was *Wehrsport* – military marching, bayonet drills, grenade throwing, trench digging, crawling through barbed wire. It made me feel like a soldier already. I had such enthusiasm for the Hitler-Jugend that Herr Sollemach told my father I would make a fine SS man one day. Was there any greater compliment?

To find the strongest among us, there were also *Mutproben*, tests of courage. Even individuals who were afraid would be compelled to do what we were told to do, because otherwise the stigma of being a coward would cling to you like a stench. Our first test was climbing the rock wall at the castle, without any safety harness. Some of the older boys scrambled to be in the front of the line, but Franz held back and I stayed with him, as per my mother's orders. When one of the boys fell and broke his leg, the training was aborted.

A week later, as part of our tests of courage, Herr Sollemach blindfolded the group of us. Franz, sitting next to me, held tightly on to my hand. 'Reiner,' he whispered, 'I'm scared.'

'Just do what they say,' I told him, 'and it will be over soon.'

I had come to see a beautiful liberation in this new way of thinking – which was, ironically, not having to think for myself. At *Gymnasium* I wasn't clever enough to come up with the right answer. In Hitler-Jugend, I was told the right answer, and as long as I parroted it back I was considered a genius.

We sat in this artificial dark, awaiting instructions. Herr Sollemach and some of the older boys patrolled in front of us. 'If the Führer asks you to fight for Germany, what do you do?'

Fight! we all yelled.

'If the Führer asks you to die for Germany, what do you do?'

Die!

'What do you fear?'

Nothing!

'Stand up!' The older boys pulled us to our feet, in a line. 'You will be led inside the building to a swimming pool with no water in it, and you will recite the Hitler-Jugend oath and jump off the diving board.' Herr Sollemach paused. 'If the Führer asks you to jump off a cliff, what do you do?'

Jump!

We were blindfolded, so we did not know which of the fifteen of us would be pulled to the diving board first. Until, that is, I felt Franz's hand being torn away from mine.

'Reiner!' he cried.

I suppose at that moment I was thinking of nothing but

my mother, warning me to take care of my younger brother. I stood up and yanked off my blindfold and ran like crazy past the boys who were dragging my brother into the building. '*Ich gelobe meinem Führer Adolf Hitler Treue,*' I cried, streaking past Herr Sollemach. '*Ich verspreche ihm und den Führern, die er mir bestimmt, jederzeit Achtung und Gehorsam entgegen zu bringen . . .*'

I promise to be faithful to my Führer, Adolf Hitler. I promise to him, and to those leaders he has assigned to me, to give them my undivided obedience and respect. In the presence of this blood banner, which represents our Führer, I swear to devote all my energies and my strength to the savior of our country, Adolf Hitler. I am willing and ready to give up my life for him, so help me God.

And without looking, I leaped.

Wrapped in a coarse brown blanket, my clothes still soaking, I told Herr Sollemach that I was jealous of my brother for being chosen first to prove his allegiance and courage. That was why I had cut him in line.

There was water in the pool. Not much, but enough. I knew they could not let us all jump and kill ourselves. But since each of us was being brought into the building individually, we could not hear the splash.

I knew, however, that Franz would, because he was already at the edge of the pool. And that, then, he would be able to jump.

But Herr Sollemach was less convinced. 'It is admirable to love your brother,' he said to me. 'But not more than your Führer.'

I was careful the rest of that day to avoid Franz. Instead I played Trapper and Indian with abandon. We split up into platoons based on the colors of our armbands and hunted down the enemy to rip off their armbands. Often, these games escalated into full-on brawls; they were meant to toughen us up. Instead of protecting my brother, I ignored him. If he was trampled in the dirt, I wasn't going to pick him up. Herr Sollemach was watching too closely.

Franz wound up with a split lip and bruises up and down his left leg, a nasty scrape on his cheek. My mother would hold me accountable, I knew. And still, when we were walking back home at dusk, he bumped his shoulder against mine. I remember the cobblestones on the street were still warm, from the heat of the day; there was a rising full moon that night. 'Reiner,' he said simply. '*Danke.*'

The next Sunday we met at an athletic hall and squared off in boxing matches. The idea was to crown a winner from our group of fifteen boys. Herr Sollemach had brought Inge and her friends to watch, because he knew that boys would show off even more if girls were present. The winner, he said, would get a special medal. 'The Führer says that a physically healthy individual with a sound character is more valuable to the *völkisch* community than an intellectual weakling,' Herr Sollemach said. 'Are you that healthy individual?'

One part of me was healthy, I knew that much. I could feel it every time I looked at Inge Sollemach. Her lips were pink as ribbon candy, and I bet just as sweet. When she sat down on the bleachers, I watched the rise and fall of the buttons on her cardigan. I thought about peeling back those layers to touch skin, how she would be white as milk, soft as—

'Hartmann,' Herr Sollemach barked, and both Franz and I stood. This surprised him for a moment, and then a smile spread across his face. 'Yes, yes, why not?' he muttered. 'Both of you, into the ring.'

I looked at Franz, at his narrow shoulders and his tender belly, at the dreams in his eyes that scattered when he realized what Herr Sollemach wanted us to do. I climbed between the ropes and put on the padded helmet, the boxing gloves. As I passed by my brother, I murmured, *Hit me.*

Inge rang the bell to get us started and then ran back to her girlfriends. One of them pointed at me, and she looked up. For one amazing moment the world stood perfectly still while our eyes met. 'Come on,' Herr Sollemach urged. The rest of the boys were cheering, and still I circled Franz with my hands up.

'Hit me,' I muttered under my breath again.

'I can't.'

'*Schwächling!*' one of the older boys yelled. Stop acting like a girl!

Halfheartedly, I shot out my right fist into my brother's chest. All the air rushed out of his body as he jackknifed. There was a cheer from the boys behind me.

Franz looked up at me in fear. 'Fight back,' I yelled at him. I jabbed with my gloves, pulling my punches before I could make contact with his body again.

'What are you waiting for?' Herr Sollemach screamed.

So I punched Franz, hard, in the back. He fell to one knee, and there was a gasp from the girls in the bleachers. Then he managed to drag himself upright. He pulled back his left fist and threw a punch at my jaw.

I do not know what flipped the switch in me. I suppose it was the fact that I had been struck, and was in pain. Or maybe the girls watching, whom I wanted to impress. Maybe it was just the sound of the other boys egging me on. I started beating

Franz, in the face, the gut, the kidneys. Over and over, rhythmically, until his face was a bloody pulp and spit bubbled out of his mouth as he collapsed on the floor.

One of the older boys jumped into the ring and raised my glove, the conquering champion. Herr Sollemach patted me on the back. 'This,' he told the others, 'is the face of bravery. This is what the future of Germany looks like. Adolf Hitler, *Sieg Heil!*'

I returned the salute. So did all the other boys. Except my brother.

With adrenaline pumping through my veins, I felt invincible. I took on contender after contender, and everyone fell. After years of being punished for letting my temper get the best of me in school, I was being praised for it. No, I was being exalted.

That night, Inge Sollemach gave me a medal, and fifteen minutes later, behind the athletic center, my first real kiss. The next day my father called on Herr Sollemach. He was very disturbed by Franz's injuries.

Your son is gifted, Herr Sollemach explained. *Special.*

Yes, my father responded. *Franz has always been an excellent student.*

I am speaking of *Reiner,* Herr Sollemach said.

Did I know this brutality was wrong? Even that first time, when my brother was the victim? I have asked myself a thousand times, and the answer is always the same: of course. That day was the hardest, because I could have said no. Every time after that, it became easier, because if I didn't do it again, I would be reminded of that first time I did not say no. Repeat the same action over and over again, and eventually it will feel right. Eventually, there isn't even any guilt.

What I mean to tell you, now, is that the same truth holds.

This could be you, too. You think *never*. You think, *not I*. But at any given moment, we are capable of doing what we least expect. I always knew what I was doing, and to whom I was doing it. I knew, very well. Because in those terrible, wonderful moments, I was the person everyone wanted to be.

A leksander had been working for me for a week now. We exchanged pleasantries, but mostly, he arrived to bake just as I was going to sleep; when I woke up to take the loaves to market, he was untying his white apron.

Sometimes, though, he stayed a little later, and I left a little later. He told me that his brother had been born with a caul over his face; that he hadn't had enough air. His parents had died in a plague in Humenne, Slovakia; he'd been taking care of Casimir for a decade now. He explained that Casimir's disorder, as he called it, led him to eat things that he shouldn't – stones, dirt, twigs – which was why he had to be watched all the time he was awake. He told me of the places he had lived, some with stone castles that pierced the clouds and others with bustling cities in which there were horseless carriages that moved as if pulled by ghosts. He did not stay long anywhere, he said, because people felt uneasy around his brother.

Aleks took to the baking like a natural, something that my father had always believed was the mark of a contented soul. You cannot feed others if you are always hungry, *he used to tell me*, and when I said this to Aleksander, he laughed. 'Your father never met me,' he said. He was always modest in his long-sleeved white shirt, no matter how hot it grew in the kitchen, unlike my father, who used to strip down to his

135

undershirt in the sweltering heat. I complimented him on his rhythm. He moved with grace, as if baking were a dance. Aleksander admitted that he had been a baker once before, a lifetime ago.

We spoke, too, of the toll of the dead. Aleks asked me what the villagers were saying, where the new casualties had been found. Recently, the attacks had come within the perimeter of the village walls, not just on its outskirts. One of the ladies of the evening was found with her head nearly torn from her body in front of the doors of the saloon; the remains of a schoolteacher who had been walking to class were left on the steps of the statue of the village founder. It was as if, some people said, the beast responsible was toying with us.

'They are saying,' I told him one day, 'that maybe it's not an animal.'

Aleks looked over his shoulder. He had the peel thrust deep in the belly of the hearth. 'What do you mean? What else could it be?'

I shrugged. 'Some kind of monster.'

Instead of laughing, as I expected, Aleks sat down beside me. He picked at a chink in the wooden table with his thumb. 'Do you believe that?'

'The only monsters I have ever known were men,' I said.

Sage

'Here,' I say, handing Josef a glass of water.

He drinks. After nearly three hours of talking nonstop, his voice is pebbled, hoarse. 'This is very kind of you.'

I don't respond.

Josef looks up at me over the lip of his glass. 'Ah,' he says. 'You are starting to believe me.'

What am I supposed to say? Hearing Josef talk about his childhood – about the Hitler Youth, with a level of detail that could only have been gleaned from someone who lived it – makes me certain that yes, he is telling me the truth. But there is still a substantial disconnect for me, to see the Josef this community knows and loves recounting a time when he was someone completely different. It is as if Mother Teresa confessed that, in her girlhood, she had set cats on fire.

'It's a little convenient, isn't it, to say that the reason you did something horrible was because someone else told you to,' I point out. 'That doesn't make it any less wrong. No matter how many people are telling you to jump off a bridge, you always have the option to turn around and walk away.'

'Why didn't I say no?' Josef mulls. 'Why didn't so many of us? Because we so badly wanted to believe what Hitler told us. That the future would be better than our present.'

'At least you had a future,' I murmur. 'I know of six million people who didn't.' I feel my stomach turn over as I watch Josef in his chair, drinking his water as if he had not just told the beginning of a story of abject horror. How could anyone be that vicious to others, and not have the aftereffects bleed out in tears, in nightmares, in tremors? 'How can you want to die?' I blurt out. 'You say you're religious. Aren't you afraid of being judged?'

Josef shakes his head, lost within himself. 'There was a look in their eyes, sometimes . . . They weren't dreading the trigger being pulled, even if the gun was already pointed at them. It was as if they ran toward it. I could not fathom this, at first. How could you not want to draw breath one more day? How could your own life be such a cheap commodity? But then I started to understand: when your existence is hell, death must be heaven.'

My grandmother, had she been one of those who would walk toward the gun? Was that a mark of weakness, or of courage?

'I am tired,' Josef sighs. 'We will talk more on another day, yes?'

What I want is to wring information out of him, until he is dry and brittle as a bone. I want him to talk until he has blisters in his throat, until his secrets litter the floor around us. But he is an old man, and so instead, I tell him that I will pick him up tomorrow for our grief group.

On the car ride home, I call Leo and tell him everything that Josef just told me.

'Hmm,' he says when I am done. 'That's a start.'

'A start? That's a ton of information to work with.'

'Not necessarily,' Leo says. 'After December 1936, all non-Jewish German kids had to join the Hitler Youth. The information he's given you corroborates other things I've heard from suspects, but it doesn't implicate him.'

'Why not?'

'Because not all members of the Hitler Youth became SS men.'

'Well, what have *you* found out?' I ask.

He laughs. 'It's only been three hours since I talked to you in the bathroom,' Leo says. 'Plus, even if I *did* have detailed information, I couldn't share it with you, as a private citizen.'

'He says he wants me to forgive him before he dies.'

Leo whistles, a low, long note. 'So now you're supposed to be his assassin *and* his priest?'

'I guess in this case he'd prefer a Jew – even a self-renounced Jew – to a priest.'

'It's a nice, macabre touch,' Leo says. 'Asking the descendants of the people you killed to let you off the hook before you shuffle off that mortal coil.' He hesitates. 'You can't, you know. For the record.'

'I know,' I say. There are dozens of reasons why not, starting with the very base fact that I am not the person who was wronged by him.

But.

If you turn the request just slightly, if you let it hit the light of reason from another angle, what Josef has asked isn't the empty plea of a murderer. It's a dying man's wish.

And if I don't grant it, doesn't that make me just as heartless as he is?

'When are you talking to him again?' Leo asks.

'Tomorrow. We're going to grief group.'

'All right,' he says. 'Call me.'

As I hang up I realize I've missed the turnoff to my house. And more to the point, that I already know where I am headed.

* * *

The word *babka* comes from *baba,* which in Yiddish and Polish means 'grandmother.' I cannot think of a single Chanukah celebration that didn't include these sweet loaves. It was an unwritten assumption that my mother would buy a turkey the size of a small child, that my sister Pepper would get to mash the potatoes, and that my nana would bring three loaves of the famous babka. Even as a little girl I remember grating the bittersweet chocolate, terrified I was going to shred my knuckles in the process.

Today, I send Daisy home early. I've told her I am here to bake with my grandmother, but really, I wanted the privacy. My grandmother butters the first loaf pan as I roll out the dough and brush the edges with an egg wash. Then I sprinkle some of the chocolate filling inside, and start to roll the dough tight as a drum. I twist the logs quickly, five full turns, and brush the top with egg again. 'Yeast,' my grandmother says, 'is a miracle. One little pinch, some water, and look at what happens.'

'It's not a miracle, it's chemistry,' I say. 'The real miracle is the moment someone looked at fungus for the first time and said, *Hmm, let's see what happens when we cook with it.*'

My grandmother passes me the loaf pan so that I can put the dough inside and press the streusel topping down. 'My father,' she says, 'used to send messages to my mother through babka.'

I smile at her. 'Really?'

'Yes. If the filling was apple, it was meant to tell her the bakery had had a sweet day, lots of customers. If it was almond, it meant *I miss you bitterly.*'

'And chocolate?'

My nana laughs. 'That he was sorry for whatever had gotten him into trouble with her. Needless to say, we ate a lot of chocolate babka.'

I wipe my hands on a dishcloth. 'Nana,' I ask. 'What was he like? What did he do, when he wasn't working? Did he ever call you a special nickname or take you somewhere unforgettable?'

She purses her lips. 'Ach, again with the biography.'

'I know he died in the war,' I say softly. 'How?'

She makes a big production of furiously buttering the second loaf pan. Then finally, she speaks. 'Every day, after school, I would come to the bakery and there would be a single roll waiting for me. My father called it a *minkele*, and he only made one a day. It had the flakiest crumb to it, and a center of chocolate and cinnamon so warm it slid down your throat, and I know he could have sold hundreds, but no, he said that this was special just for me.'

'He was killed by Nazis, wasn't he?' I ask quietly.

Nana turns away from me. 'My father trusted me with the details of his death. *Minka*, he would say, when my mother read me the story of Snow White, *make a note: I do not want to wind up in a glass case with people looking at me.* Or: *Minka, make a note: I would like fireworks, instead of flowers. Minka, make sure I do not pass in the summertime. Too many flies for the mourners to deal with, don't you think?* It was a game to me, a lark, because my father was never going to die. We all knew he was invincible.' She takes one of her canes from where it is hanging on the counter and walks to the kitchen table, sitting heavily on one of the chairs. 'My father trusted me with the details of his death, but in the end, I couldn't manage a single one.'

I kneel down on the floor in front of her and rest my head in her lap. Her hand, small and birdlike, nests in the crown of my hair. 'You've held this inside you for so long,' I whisper. 'Wouldn't it be better to talk about it?'

She touches the scarred side of my face. 'Would it?' she asks.

I pull back. 'That's different. I can't pretend this never happened, no matter how much I want to. It's written all over me.'

'Exactly,' my grandmother says, and she pushes up the sleeve of her sweater to reveal the numbers on her forearm. 'I talked once about it, when I was much younger, to my doctor, who saw this. He asked if I would come to speak at his wife's class. She was a history professor at a university,' she says. 'The talk went well. I got over my stage fright enough to deliver it without throwing up, anyway. And then the teacher, she asked if there were any questions.

'A boy stood up. Truth be told, I thought it was a girl, there was so much hair, down to here. He stood up and he said, "The Holocaust never happened." I did not know what to do, what to say. I was thinking, *How dare you tell me this, when I lived it? How dare you erase my life just like that?* I was so upset that I could barely see straight. I muttered an apology and I walked right off that stage, out the door, with my hand pressed up against my mouth. I thought if I didn't hold it there, I would start to scream. I went to my car and I sat inside until I knew what I should have said. History tells us that six million Jews disappeared during that war. If there was no Holocaust, where did they go?' She shakes her head. 'All of that, and the world didn't learn anything. Look around. There's still ethnic cleansing. There's discrimination. There are young people like that foolish boy in the history class. I thought for sure that the reason I survived was to make certain something like that would never happen again, but you know, I must have been wrong. Because, Sage, it still happens. Every day.'

'Just because you had some neo-Nazi stand up in that classroom doesn't mean that it's not important for you to tell your story,' I say. 'Tell it to *me*.'

She looks at me for a long moment, then silently stands with her cane and walks out of the kitchen. Across the hall, in the first-floor study she has converted into a bedroom so that she doesn't have to climb stairs, I hear her moving things around, rifling through drawers. I get up, slip the loaves into the oven. Already, they're rising again.

My grandmother is sitting on her bed when I come in. The room smells like her, like powder and roses. She is holding a small leather-bound notebook with a cracked binding.

'I was a writer,' she says. 'A child who believed in fairy tales. Not the silly Disney ones your mother read to you, but the ones with blood and thorns, with girls who knew that love could kill you just as often as it could set you free. I believed in the curses of witches and the madness of werewolves. But I also mistakenly believed that the scariest stories came from imagination, not real life.' She smooths her hand over the cover. 'I started writing this when I was thirteen. It is what I did when other girls were fixing their hair and trying to flirt with boys. Instead, I would dream up characters and dialogue. I would write a chapter and give it to my best friend, Darija, to read, to see what she thought. We had a plan: I would become a bestselling author and she would be my editor and we would move to London and drink sloe gin fizzes. Ach, we didn't even know what sloe gin was back then. But this is what I was doing, when the war came. And I did not stop.' She hands the volume to me. 'It is not the original, of course. I don't have that anymore. But as soon as I could, I rewrote from memory. I *had* to.'

I open the front cover. Inside, in small, tight cursive, words crawl across the page, packed end to end without any white space, as if that were a luxury. Maybe, back then, it was. 'This is my story,' my grandmother continues. 'It's not the one you're looking for, about what happened during the war. That's not nearly as important.' She meets my gaze. 'Because *this* story, it's the one that kept me alive.'

My grandmother, she could have given Stephen King a run for his money.

Her story is supernatural, about an *upiór* – the Polish version of a vampire. But what makes it so terrifying is not the monster, who's a known quantity, but the ordinary men who turn out to be monsters, too. It is as if she knew, even at that young age, that you cannot separate good and evil cleanly, that they are conjoined twins sharing a single heart. If words had flavors, hers would be bitter almonds and coffee grounds. There are times when I'm reading her story that I forget she was the one to write it – that's how good it is.

I read the notebook in its entirety, and then I reread it, wondering if I have missed a single word. I try to absorb the story, to the point where it is one I can play back to myself syllable by syllable, the way my grandmother must have done. I find myself reciting paragraphs when I am showering, washing the dishes, taking out the trash.

My grandmother's story is a mystery, but not in the way she intended. I try to pull apart the characters and their dialogue to see the skeleton beneath that must have been her real life. All writers start with a layer of truth, don't they? If not, their stories would be nothing but spools of cotton candy, a fleeting taste wrapped around nothing but air.

I read about Ania, the narrator, and her father and hear my grandmother's voice; I imagine my great-grandfather's face.

When she describes the cottage on the outskirts of Łódź, the town square crossed by horse-drawn carts, the forest where Ania would walk with moss sinking beneath her boots, I can smell the peat burning and taste the ash on the bottom of their bread. I can hear the footsteps of children striking the cobblestones as they chase each other, long before they ever had anything or anyone to really run from.

I am so engrossed in the story that I am late to pick Josef up for grief group. 'You slept well?' he asks, and I tell him yes. As he sits down in the car, I think of the parallels between my grandmother's story – the monster that hunts villagers and kills Ania's father – and the SS, who came into my grandmother's life unannounced and destroyed her family. My grandmother's childhood – those little rolls baked just for her, the long, lazy afternoons when she and her best friend dreamed of their future, even the walls of her family's apartment – unfolds in a parallel line beside Josef's tale of the Hitler Youth. Yet they are inching closer; I know that they are destined to cross.

That makes me hate Josef, right now.

I bite my tongue, though, because Josef does not even know I have a grandmother, much less one who survived the genocide in which he was involved. I am not sure why I want to guard this information from him. Maybe because he'd be thrilled to hear he was one step closer to finding the right person to forgive him. Maybe because I think he doesn't deserve to know.

Maybe because I do not like the idea of my grandmother and someone like Josef still coexisting in this world.

'You are very quiet today,' Josef muses.

'Just thinking.'

'About me?'

'Don't flatter yourself,' I say.

Because I was late picking Josef up, we are the last ones to arrive at grief group. Stuart immediately approaches, looking for my ever-present bag of baked goods – but I don't have anything today. I was too busy reading my grandmother's journal to bake. 'I'm really sorry,' I tell him. 'I came empty-handed.'

'If only Stuart could say the same,' Jocelyn murmurs, and I realize he's brought his wife's death mask in again.

Minka, make a note, I think, remembering my greatgrandfather. *When I die, no mask, okay?*

Marge rings the little bell that always makes me think we are at a yoga class, instead of a grief therapy group. 'Shall we get started?' she asks.

I don't know what it is about death that makes it so hard. I suppose it's the one-sided communication; the fact that we never get to ask our loved one if she suffered, if she is happy wherever she is now . . . if she *is* somewhere. It's the question mark that comes with death that we can't face, not the period.

All of a sudden I realize there is one empty chair. Ethel is missing. I know, even before Marge tells us the news, that her husband, Bernie, has died.

'It happened on Monday,' Mrs. Dombrowski says. 'I got the call from Ethel's oldest daughter. Bernie's in a better place now.'

I look over at Josef, who is picking at a thread on his pants, undisturbed.

'Do you think she'll come back here?' Shayla asks. 'Ethel?'

'I hope so,' Marge says. 'I think if any of you would like to reach out to her, she'd appreciate it.'

'I want to send flowers or something,' Stuart says. 'Bernie had to be a pretty good guy, to have a lady like that who took care of him for so long.'

'You don't know that,' I say slowly, and everyone turns to me, shocked. 'None of us ever met the man. He could have beat her every day for all we know.'

'Sage!' Shayla gasps.

'I don't mean to speak ill of the dead,' I add quickly, ducking my head. 'I imagine Bernie was a great guy who used to go bowling every week and who loaded the dishes into the dishwasher after every meal Ethel cooked. But do you think that only good guys wind up with people like us, left behind? Even Jeffrey Dahmer had a mother.'

'That's an interesting point,' Marge says. 'Do we grieve because the person we lost was such a light in the world? Or do we grieve because of who he was to us?'

'Maybe a little of both,' Stuart says, his hand running over the contours of his wife's death mask as if he were blind and learning her features for the first time.

'So does that mean we shouldn't feel bad when someone horrible dies?' I ask.

I can feel Josef's gaze boring into my temple.

'There are definitely people who make this earth better by leaving it,' Jocelyn muses. 'Bin Laden. Charlie Manson.'

'Hitler,' I say innocently.

'Yeah, I read this book once about a woman who was his personal secretary and she made him out to be like any other boss. Said he used to gossip about the secretaries' boyfriends with them,' Shayla says.

'If they didn't regret killing people, why should anyone regret when *they* die?' Stuart says.

'So you think once a Nazi, always a Nazi?' I ask.

Beside me, Josef coughs.

'I hope there's a special place in Hell for people like that,' Shayla says primly.

Marge recommends a five-minute breather. While she talks quietly to Shayla and Stuart, Josef taps my shoulder. 'May I speak to you privately?'

I follow him into the hallway and fold my arms. 'How dare you?' he hisses, stepping so close to me that I retreat a step. 'What I told you was in confidence. If I wanted the world to know what I used to be, I could have turned myself in to authorities years ago.'

'So you want absolution without any of the punishment,' I say.

His eyes flash, the blue nearly obliterated by the black of his pupils. 'You will not speak of this in public anymore,' he orders, so loudly that several others in the adjacent room turn toward us.

His anger rushes at me, a rogue wave. Even though my scar is on fire, even though I feel as if I have been caught by the teacher passing a note in class, I force myself to look him in the eye. I stand rigid, nothing but breath between us, an empty truce.

'Don't you ever speak to me that way again,' I whisper. 'I am *not* one of your victims.'

Then I turn on my heel and walk away. For just a moment, when Josef let his own death mask slip, I could see the man he used to be: the one buried beneath the kindly exterior for so many decades, like a root growing slow beneath pavement, still capable of cracking concrete.

I cannot leave grief group early without drawing attention to myself, and since I brought Josef to the meeting, I have to take him home or else face Marge's inquiry. But I don't speak to him, not when we are saying our good-byes to the others or walking to the parking lot. 'I am sorry,' Josef says, five minutes into our drive.

We are stopped at a red light. 'Well. That's a loaded statement.'

He continues to stare straight out the window. 'I mean about what I said to you. During the break.'

I don't respond. I don't want him thinking he is off the hook. And no matter what he said to me, I can't just drop him off at the curb and walk away forever. I owe it to my grandmother. Plus, I promised Leo I wouldn't. If anything, hearing Josef snap like that makes me even more determined to get enough evidence to have him prosecuted. This is a man, clearly, who at one point in his life could do whatever he wanted without fear of retribution. In a way, by asking me to kill him, he's just doing more of the same.

I think it's about time he got what he really deserves.

'I am nervous, I suppose,' Josef continues.

'About what?' I ask, feeling my scalp prickle. Is he onto me? Does he know that I plan to string him along, and then turn him in?

'That you will listen to all I have to say to you and still not do what I've asked.'

I face him. 'With or without me, Josef, you're going to die.'

He meets my gaze. 'Do you know of *Der Ewige Jude*? The Wandering Jew?'

The word *Jew* makes me shudder, as if such a term should not even be allowed to take up passing residence on his lips. I shake my head.

'It is an old European story. A Jew, Ahasuerus, taunted Jesus as he stopped to rest while carrying his cross. When the Jew told Jesus he should move quicker, Jesus cursed him to walk the earth until the Second Coming. For hundreds of years there have been sightings of Ahasuerus, who cannot die, no matter how much he wants to.'

'You do realize the great irony here in comparing yourself to a Jew,' I say.

He shrugs. 'Say what you will about them, but they thrive, in spite of' – he glances at my face – 'everything. I should have died, several times now. I have had cancer and car accidents. I am the only elderly man I know who has been hospitalized for pneumonia and still survived. You believe what you like, Sage, but I know the reason I am still alive. Like Ahasuerus – every day I am here is another day to relive my mistakes.'

The light has turned green, and there are cars behind me honking, but I haven't put my foot on the accelerator. Josef seems to retreat into himself, lost in thought. 'Herr Sollemach, from the Hitler-Jugend, used to tell us Jews were like weeds. Pull out one and two more grow in their place . . .'

I press down on the gas, and we jolt forward. I'm disgusted with Josef, for being exactly who he professed to be. I'm disgusted with myself for not believing him, at first; for being fooled into thinking that this man was a grandfatherly Good Samaritan, like everyone else in this town.

'. . . but I used to think,' Josef says quietly, 'that there are some weeds that are just as beautiful as flowers.'

*T*here was something behind me. It was a sixth sense, a chill on the back of my neck. I had turned around a dozen times since entering the woods, but saw only the bare trees standing like sentries.

Still, my heart was racing. I walked a little faster toward the cottage, clutching my bread basket, wondering if I was close enough for Aleks to hear me if I screamed.

Then I heard it. The crunch of a twig, a break in the surface of the snow.

I could run.

If I ran, whatever was behind me would chase me.

Once again, I picked up my pace. Tears leaked from the corners of my eyes, and I blinked them back. Abruptly I ducked behind a tree wide enough to conceal me. I held my breath, counting as the footfalls came closer.

A doe walked into the clearing, swiveling its head to stare at me before nibbling at the bark on a birch a few feet away.

Relief turned my legs to jelly. I leaned against the trunk of the tree, still trembling. This was what happened when you let the idle prattle of the villagers seep into your mind like poison. You saw shadows when there were none; you heard a mouse and imagined a lion. Shaking my head at my own *stupidity, I stepped away from the tree and started toward home again.*

It attacked me from behind, covering my head with something hot and dank, some sort of fabric or sack that kept me blind. I was pinned by my wrists, with weight on the small of my back so I could not stand up. My face was shoved into the ground. I tried to yell, but whatever was behind me pushed my head down so that my mouth filled with snow instead. I felt heat and blades and claws and teeth, oh, the teeth, sinking into a half-moon on my throat and stinging like a thousand needles, like a swarm of bees.

I heard hoofbeats, and then felt the cold air on the back of my neck, felt the absence of pressure and pain. Like a great, winged bird, something swooped down from above and called my name. That was the last thing I remembered, because when I opened my eyes, I was in Damian's arms, and he was carrying me home.

The door opened, and Aleks stood inside. 'What happened?' he asked, his eyes flying to mine.

'She was attacked,' Damian answered. 'She needs a surgeon.'

'She needs me,' Aleks said, and he took me from Damian's arms into his own. I cried out as I was jostled between them, as Aleks slammed the door closed with his boot.

He carried me into my bedroom. As he lay me down, I saw all the blood on his shirt, and my head began to swim. 'Ssh,' he soothed, turning my head so that he could see the wound.

I thought he was going to faint. 'Is it bad?'

'No,' he said, but I knew he was lying. 'I just can't bear the sight of blood.'

He left me for a few minutes, promising to return, and when he did, he had a bowl of warm water, a cloth, and a bottle of whiskey. The last he held up to my lips. 'Drink,' he commanded, and I tried, but found myself coughing violently. 'More,' he said.

Eventually, when the fire in my throat had turned into a glow in my belly, he began to wash my neck and then spilled whiskey over the open gash. I nearly came out of my skin. 'Let go,' he said. 'It will be better that way.'

I did not understand what he meant until I saw him threading the needle and realized what he was going to do. As he pierced the hollow of my throat, I blacked out.

It was late in the afternoon when I awakened again. Aleks sat in the chair beside my bed, his hands steepled before him, as if in prayer. When he saw me stirring, a visible relief washed over his features.

His hand on my forehead was warm. He stroked my cheek, my hair. 'If you wanted my attention,' Aleks said, 'all you had to do was ask.'

Josef

My brother used to beg for a dog, when we were little. Our neighbors had one – some sort of retriever – and he would spend hours in their yard teaching it to roll over, to sit, to speak. But my father was bothered by pet dander, and because of this, I knew that no matter how hard Franz pleaded, he wasn't going to get his wish.

One autumn night when I was maybe ten years old and asleep in the room I shared with Franz, I heard whispering. I woke to find my brother sitting up in bed, with a small hunk of cheese on the covers between his legs. Nibbling on the cheese was a tiny field mouse, and as I watched, my brother stroked the fur on its back.

Now mind you, my mother did not keep the kind of house that attracts vermin. She was always scrubbing the floor or dusting or what have you. The next day, I found my mother stripping the sheets off our beds, even though it was not laundry day. 'Those filthy, dirty mice – as soon as it gets cold outside, they try to find a way in. I found droppings,' she told me, shuddering. 'Tomorrow on your way home from school, you will buy some traps.'

I thought of Franz. 'You want to kill them?'

My mother looked at me strangely. 'What else should we do with pests?'

That night before we went to sleep, Franz took another sliver of cheese he had stolen from the kitchen and put it down beside him on the bed. 'I am going to name him Ernst,' Franz told me.

'How do you know he's not an Erma?'

But Franz didn't answer, and before long, he was asleep.

On the other hand, I stayed awake. I listened carefully till I heard the scratch of tiny claws on the wood floor and watched, in the moonlight, as the mouse scrambled up the blanket to get the cheese Franz had left. Before it could succeed, however, I grabbed the mouse and smacked it against the wall in one quick motion.

The noise woke up Franz, who started crying when he saw his pet dead on the floor.

I am sure the mouse didn't feel anything. After all, it was only a mouse. Plus my mother had made it very clear what should be done with such a creature.

I was just doing what she would have, eventually.

I was only following orders.

I don't know if I can explain how it felt to suddenly be the golden child. It is true, my parents didn't have much to say about Hitler and the politics of Germany, but they were proud when Herr Sollemach held me up as the benchmark for all other boys in our little *Kameradschaft*. They didn't complain about my marks as much, because instead I would come home every weekend with winners' ribbons and praise from Herr Sollemach.

To be honest, I do not know if my parents believed in the Nazi philosophy. My father could not have fought for Germany even if he wanted; he had a gammy leg from a sledding injury when he was a child. And if my parents had their doubts about

Hitler's vision for Germany, they appreciated his optimism and the hope that our country could regain its greatness. Still, having me as Herr Sollemach's favorite did nothing but help their status in the community. They were the fine Germans who had produced a boy like me. No nosy neighbor was going to comment on the fact that my father had not enlisted, not with me as the star representative of the local HJ.

Every Friday night, I ate dinner at Herr Sollemach's house. I brought flowers for his daughter, and one summer evening when I was sixteen, I lost my virginity to her on an old horse blanket in a cornfield. Herr Sollemach took to calling me *Sohn*, as if I were already a member of his family. And shortly before my seventeenth birthday, he recommended me for the HJ-Streifendienst. These were patrol force units within the Hitler-Jugend. Our job was to keep order at meetings, to report disloyalty, and to denounce anyone who spoke ill of Hitler – even, in some cases, our own parents. I had heard of a boy, Walter Hess, who turned his own father in to the Gestapo.

It is funny, the Nazis did not like religion, but that is the closest analogy I can use to describe the indoctrination we had as children. Organized religion, to the Third Reich, was in direct competition with serving Germany, for who could pledge an equal allegiance to both the Führer *and* God? Instead of celebrating Christmas, for example, they celebrated the Winter Solstice. However, no child really chooses his religion; it is just the luck of the draw which blanket of beliefs you are wrapped in. When you are too young to think for yourself, you are baptized and taken to church and droned at by a priest and told that Jesus died for your sins, and since your parents nod and say this is true, why should you not believe them? Much the same was the message we were given by Herr Sollemach and the others who taught us. *What is bad is harmful*, we were told. *What is good is useful*. It truly was that simple. When our teachers would put a caricature of a Jew on the board for us to see, pointing at the traits that were associated with inferior species, we trusted them. They were our elders, surely they knew best? Which child does not want his country to be the best, the biggest, the strongest in the world?

One day Herr Sollemach took our *Kameradschaft* on a special trip. Instead of marching out of town, like we did on many of our hikes, Herr Sollemach walked us up the short road that led to Wewelsburg Castle, the one that Heinrich Himmler himself had requisitioned for SS ceremonial headquarters.

We all knew the castle, of course, we'd grown up with it. Its three towers shielded a triangular courtyard, perched high on a rock above the Alme valley; it was part of our local history lessons. But none of us had been inside since the SS began its reconstruction. Now, it was no longer a place to play football in the courtyard; it was for the elite.

'Who can tell me why this castle is so important?' Herr Sollemach asked, as we trudged up the hill.

My brother, the scholar, answered first. 'It's got historic relevance, since it's near the site of an earlier German victory – where Hermann der Cherusker defeated the Romans in A.D. nine.'

The other boys snickered. Unlike in *Gymnasium*, Franz wasn't going to get any points for knowing his history textbook here. 'But why is it important to *us*?' Herr Sollemach demanded.

A boy named Lukas, who was a member of the HJ-Streifendienst like me, raised his hand. 'It now belongs to the Reichsführer-SS,' he said.

Himmler, who as chief of the SS, had taken over the German police and the concentration camps, had visited the castle in 1933 and had leased it that same day for a hundred years, planning to restore it for the SS. In 1938, the north tower was still under construction – we could see this as we approached.

'Himmler says the *Obergruppenführersaal* will be the center of the world, after the final victory,' Herr Sollemach announced. 'He has deepened the moats already and is trying to spruce up the interior. Rumor has it he will be here today to check on its progress. Do you hear that, boys? The Reichsführer-SS himself, right in Wewelsburg!'

I did not see how Herr Sollemach would gain entrance to the castle, since it was guarded, and not even the leader of the local *Kameradschaft* was in the habit of mingling with the highest echelon of officers in the National Socialist Party. But as we approached Herr Sollemach heiled and the guard heiled back. 'Werner,' Herr Sollemach said. 'Quite an exciting day, no?'

'You're right on time,' the soldier said. 'Tell me, how is Mary? And the girls?'

I should have realized that Herr Sollemach would leave nothing to chance.

My brother pulled me by the arm to draw my attention to the man in the center of the courtyard, addressing a clot of officers.

'Blood tells,' the man said. 'The laws of Aryan selection favor those who are stronger, smarter, and more righteous in character than their inferior counterparts. Loyalty. Obedience. Truth. Duty. Comradeship. These are the cornerstones of the knighthood of old, and the future of the Schutzstaffel.'

I did not understand what he was saying, really, but I knew from the respect he was getting from the crowd that this must be Himmler himself. Yet this slight, stuffy man looked more like a bank teller than the head of the German police.

Then I realized he was pointing at me. 'You, boy,' he said, and he gestured.

I stepped forward and saluted the way we had been taught at our HJ meetings.

'You are from around here?'

'Yes, Reichsführer,' I said. 'I am a member of the HJ-Streifendienst.'

'So tell me, boy. Why would a country looking toward racial purity and the future of a new world choose a decrepit castle as a training center?'

This was a trick question. Clearly, a man as important as Himmler would not have made a mistake in choosing a place like Wewelsburg. My mouth went dry.

My brother, standing beside me, coughed. *Hartmann*, he whispered.

I didn't know what he was trying to say by speaking our last name. Maybe he thought I should introduce myself. That way Himmler would know exactly who was the idiot standing in front of him.

Then I realized my brother had not said *Hartmann*. He'd said *Hermann*.

'Because,' I replied, 'it's not a decrepit castle.'

Himmler smiled slowly. 'Go on.'

'It is the same place Hermann der Cherusker fought the Romans and won. So even though other cultures wound up becoming part of the Roman Empire, the German identity stayed intact. Just like we will again, now, when we win the war.'

Himmler narrowed his eyes. 'What is your name, boy?'

'*Kameradschaftsführer* Hartmann,' I said.

He walked through the crowd and put his hand on my shoulder. 'A warrior, a scholar, and a leader – all in one. *This* is the future of Germany.' As the crowd erupted in cheers, he pushed me forward. 'You will come with me,' Himmler said.

He led me down a set of stairs toward *die Gruft*, the vault. In the basement of the tower that was still under construction was a round room. At its center, buried in the floor, was a gas pipe. Around the edges of the room were twelve niches, each with its own pedestal. 'This is where it will all end,' Himmler said, his voice hollow in the small chamber. 'Ashes to ashes, dust to dust.'

'Reichsführer?'

'This is where I will be, long after the final victory. This will be the final resting place of the top twelve SS generals.' He turned to me. 'Perhaps there is time for a bright young man like you to reach that potential.'

It was at that moment I decided to enlist.

As proud as Herr Sollemach was about my enlistment as an SS-*Sturmmann*, my mother was equally devastated. She was worried for me, as the war escalated. But she was equally worried for my brother, who – at eighteen – still lived with his head in a book, and who would be losing the protection I provided.

She and my father held a little social gathering on the eve before I was to report to the concentration camp Sachsenhausen, as part of the SS-Totenkopfverbände, the Death's Head Unit. Our friends and neighbors came. One of them, Herr Schefft, who worked for the local newspaper, took a photograph of me blowing out the candles on the chocolate cake my mother made – you can see it here; I still have the clipping she mailed me afterward. I have looked at that picture often. You see how happy I am in it? Not just because I am holding my fork over the plate, waiting to eat something delicious. Not just because I was drinking beer like a man, instead of a boy. Because everything is still possible, for me. It is the last photograph I have of myself where my eyes aren't full of knowledge, of understanding.

One of my father's friends began to sing to me: '*Hoch soll er leben, hoch soll er leben, dreimal hoch.*' *Long may he live, long may he live, three cheers*. Suddenly, the door burst open, and my friend Lukas's little brother ran in, wild and quivering with excitement. 'Herr Sollemach says we must come right away,' he said. 'And we shouldn't wear our uniforms.'

Now, this was curious; we always wore our uniforms with great pride. And my mother was not terribly inclined to let us out at midnight. But the other members of the HJ – including Franz – and I followed. We ran to the community center, where we held our meetings, and found Herr Sollemach dressed, like us, in street clothes. Parked in front was a truck, the kind used by the military, with an open back and benches for us to sit on. We piled in, and from the snippets of information I received from other boys, learned that some German official named Vom Rath had been assassinated by a Polish Jew, that the Führer himself had said spontaneous retaliations by the German people would not be stopped. By the time the truck pulled up in Paderborn, just a few miles away from Wewelsburg, the streets were filled with people armed with sledgehammers and axes. 'This is where Artur lives,' Franz murmured to me, speaking of his former friend from school. This didn't surprise me. The last time I'd been to Paderborn was a year ago, when my father had gone to buy my mother a fancy pair of leather boots for Christmas, handmade by a Jewish cobbler.

We were given instructions:

1. Do not endanger non-Jewish German life or property.
2. Do not loot the Jewish businesses or homes, just destroy them.
3. Foreigners – even Jewish ones – were not to be the subjects of violence.

Herr Sollemach pressed a heavy shovel into my hand. 'Go, Reiner,' he said. 'Show these swine the punishment they deserve.'

There were torches, the only way we could see in the dark of the night. The air was filled with screams and smoke. The sound of shattering glass was a constant rain, and the shards crunched beneath our boots as we ran through the town, yelling at the tops of our lungs and smashing the storefront windows. We were wild boys, frenzied, our sweat and our fear drying on our skin. Even Franz, who did not strike a single business storefront that I saw, was running with his cheeks flushed and his hair matted down with perspiration, caught in the vortex of a mob mentality.

It was strange, being told to cause destruction. We were good German boys, who behaved well and who were repri- manded by our mothers for breaking a lamp or a china teacup. We had grown up poor enough to recognize the value of one's belongings. Yet this world, full of fire and mayhem, was the final proof that we had fallen through Alice's Looking Glass. Nothing was as it had been; nothing was as it seemed to be. The proof lay broken and glittering at our feet.

Finally we reached the store I had visited with my father,

the cobbler's tiny shop. I leaped up and grabbed the bottom of his swinging sign, yanking it from its moorings so that it hung drunkenly by a single chain. I hurled the bowl of my shovel into the showcase window and reached between the jagged edges of glass to pull out shoes, a dozen pairs of boots and pumps and loafers, sweeping them into the puddles of the street. SA Stormtroopers were kicking in the doors of homes and dragging the residents, in their nightclothes, into the center of town. They cowered in small knots, huddled over their children. One father was made to strip down to his underclothes and dance for the soldiers. *Kann ich jetzt gehen?* the man begged, as he twirled in a circle. Now may I go?

I do not know what made me do it, but I approached the man's family. His wife, maybe seeing my smooth cheeks and my young face, grabbed onto my boot. *Bitte – die sollen aufhören*, she pleaded. Please make them stop.

She was sobbing, tearing at my trousers, grabbing for my hand. I didn't want her snot on me, her saliva. Her hot breath and those empty words falling into the cup of my palm.

I did what came naturally. I kicked her away from me.

As the Reichsführer-SS had said at Wewelsburg that day: *Blood tells.* It was not that I wanted to hurt this Jewish woman. I wasn't really thinking of her, at all. I was protecting myself.

In that instant I realized what this night had been all about. Not violence, not riots, not public humiliation. These measures were a message, to let the Jews know they had no hold over us ethnic Germans – not economically or socially or politically, not even after that assassination.

It was nearly dawn by the time the convoy headed back to Wewelsburg. The boys dozed on each other's shoulders, their clothes glittering with the pixie dust of broken glass. Herr Sollemach was snoring. Only Franz and I were awake.

'Did you see him?' I asked.

'Artur?' Franz shook his head.

'Maybe he's gone already. I hear a lot of them have left the country.'

Franz stared at Herr Sollemach. His blond hair fell over one eye as he shook his head. 'I hate that man.'

'Shh,' I warned. 'I think he can hear through his pores.'

'*Arschloch*.'

'He probably hears through that, too.'

My brother smiled a little. 'Are you nervous?' he asked. 'About going away?'

I was, but I would never admit that. It wasn't officer-like to be afraid. 'It will be fine,' I said, hoping I could convince myself, too. I shoved against him with my elbow. 'Don't get into trouble while I'm gone.'

'Don't forget where you came from,' Franz said.

He talked like that, sometimes. Like he was a wizened old man in the body of an eighteen-year-old. 'What's that supposed to mean?'

Franz shrugged. 'That you don't have to listen to what they say. Well, maybe that's not true. But you don't have to believe it.'

'The thing is, Franz, I *do*.' If I could explain to him how I felt, maybe then he wouldn't stick out like such a sore thumb at the HJ meetings when I was not around. And God knows the less he stuck out, the less likely he was to be bullied. 'Tonight wasn't about hurting Jews. They were collateral damage. It was about keeping *us* safe. Us Germans.'

'Power isn't doing something terrible to someone who's weaker than you, Reiner. It's having the strength to do something terrible, and choosing not to.' He turned to me. 'Do you remember that mouse in our bedroom, years ago?'

'What?'

Franz met my gaze. 'You know. The one you killed,' he said. 'I forgive you.'

'I didn't ask for your forgiveness,' I told him.

My brother shrugged. 'That doesn't mean you didn't want it.'

The first person I ever shot was running away from me.

I was no longer working at a concentration camp. In August 1939, we had been mobilized from Sachsenhausen and sent to follow the German troops as part of the SS-Totenkopfstandarte. It was now September 20. I remember this, because it was Franz's birthday and I did not have the time or the resources to write to him that day. We had crossed into Poland seven days earlier, trailing behind the army. Our route was from Ostrowo, through Kalisch, Turek, Żuki, Krosniewice, Kladava, Przedecz, Włocławek, Dembrice, Bydgoszcz, Wirsitz, Zarnikau, and finally Chodziez. We were to annihilate any form of resistance we found.

On that particular day, we were doing what we'd been dispatched to do – conducting house searches, rounding up insurgents, and arresting those who were suspicious: Jews, Poles, activists. Another soldier, Urbrecht – a boy with a face like risen dough and a sensitive stomach – had accompanied me to this enclave of homes. It was a miserable, rainy day. We did a lot of shouting; my voice was stripped raw from telling the stupid Poles, who did not understand my German, to get out and join the others. There was a mother, a girl of about ten, and a teenage boy. We were looking for the father, who was one of the leaders of the local Jewish community. But there was no one else in the house, or so Urbrecht said, after canvassing it. I screamed in the face of the woman, asking her where her husband was, but she would not answer. As the rain drenched her, she fell to her knees and started sobbing and pointing back to the house. It was giving me a headache like no other.

Nothing the son said could soothe her. I poked her in the back with my rifle, indicating where they should march, but the woman remained kneeling in a muddy puddle. As Urbrecht hauled her upright, the teenage boy started to run back to the house.

Now, I had no idea what he was after. For all I knew, it was a weapon that Urbrecht had overlooked. I did what I had been told to do: I shot.

The boy was running, and the next instant, he wasn't. The sound of the bullet was deafening, hollow. At first, I couldn't hear anything because of it. And then, I did.

The cries were soft and hitched together like train cars. I stepped over the broken body of the boy and walked into the kitchen. I have no idea how that idiot Urbrecht might have missed the baby who had been lying in the laundry basket, the one who was now wide awake and shrieking her head off.

Say what you will about the inhumanity of the SS-TV during the invasion of Poland, but I gave that woman her baby before we marched her off.

We started with the synagogues.

Our commander, *Standartenführer* Nostitz, explained the *Judenaktion* we would be undertaking in Włocławek. It was much like what we had done with Herr Sollemach in Paderborn almost a year earlier, but on a bigger scale. We rounded up Jewish leaders and forced them to clean lavatories with their prayer shawls; we made them dig ditches in pools of water. Some of the soldiers beat the old men who couldn't work fast enough, or bayoneted them, and others took pictures.

We made religious leaders shave off their beards, and throw their holy books into the mud. We had dynamite, and we used it to blow up the synagogues and set them on fire. We broke the windows of Jewish shops and rounded up masses of Jews to be arrested. Leaders of the Jewish community were lined up in the street and executed. The scene was chaos, with glass raining through the air and burst pipes spilling water onto the street, horses rearing back from the carts they pulled; blood turning the cobblestones red. The Polish civilians cheered us on. They didn't want the Jews here any more than we Germans did.

Two days into the *Aktion,* the *Standartenführer* ordered two *Sturmbanne* within the battalion to splinter off and perform a special task. There were lists of names recorded by the SD and the police, names of intellectuals and resistance leaders in Poznań and Pomerania. We were to find and eliminate these people.

It was an honor to be chosen. But it wasn't until we reached Bydgoszcz that I came to understand the scope of this exercise. The 'death list' wasn't a sheet of names. It was eight hundred people. A tome.

True, they were easy to find. They were Polish teachers, priests, leaders of nationalist organizations. Some were Jews; many were not. They were rounded up and gathered. A small group was singled out to dig a ditch – they believed it was an antitank trench they were creating. But then the first group of prisoners was led up to the ditch and it was our job to shoot them. There were six of us trusted with this task. Three were to aim at the head, three at the heart. I picked the heart. Our shots rang out, and there was a fireworks display of blood, of brains. Then the next group of prisoners stepped up to the edge of the ditch.

The ones at the end of the line, they saw what was happening. They must have understood as they turned toward us soldiers that they were facing their death. And yet for the most part they did not run, they did not try to escape. I do not know if this meant they were very, very stupid or very, very brave.

One teenage boy stared at me as I lifted the rifle to my shoulder. He lifted his hand and pointed to himself. In perfect German, he said, *neunzehn*. Nineteen.

After the first fifty, I stopped looking at their faces.

My fortitude in Poland got me sent to SS-Junkerschule Bad Tölz, an officers' training school. Before shipping out, I was given three weeks' leave, and I went back home.

Only a year had passed, but I was markedly different. When I left, I was still a child; now I was a man. I had pulled a screaming baby out of the arms of its mother. I had killed boys and girls my own age – and much younger, too. I had gotten used to taking what I wanted, when I wanted it. Being in the home of my parents chafed; I felt too big for the space, too full of electricity.

My brother, on the other hand, saw our little home in Wewelsburg as a haven. He was at the top of his class at *Gymnasium*, expecting to head to university. He wanted to become a writer, still, and failing that, a professor. He did not seem to understand the simplest logistical fact: Germany was at war; nothing was as it had been. Any childhood dreams we had had were long gone, sacrificed to the greater good of our country.

Franz had received a document stating that he needed to report to recruitment headquarters, but he had thrown it into the fire. As if that might be enough to keep the SS from finding him and forcing him to do it.

'They don't need people like me,' he had said at dinner.

'They need every able-bodied man,' I had told him.

My mother feared Franz being singled out as a political opponent of the Reich, instead of being recognized as indifferent. I did not blame her. I knew what happened to those who were political opponents of the Reich. They disappeared.

The first day after I came home, I woke to find sunlight streaming through the windows and my mother sitting on the edge of my narrow bed. Franz was already gone to *Gymnasium*; I had slept till nearly noon.

I drew the covers up to my chin. 'Is something the matter?'

My mother tilted her head. 'I used to watch you sleep when you were a newborn,' she told me. 'Your father thought I was crazy. But I believed that if I turned away, you might forget to take the next breath.'

'I'm not a baby anymore,' I said.

'No,' my mother agreed. 'You're not. But that doesn't mean I don't worry about you.' She bit her lip. 'They are treating you well?'

How could I explain to my own mother the things I had done? The Jews whose doors I had kicked in, so that we could seize radios, appliances, valuables, and anything else that might help the war effort? The elderly rabbi I had beaten for staying out to pray after curfew? The men, women, and children we herded up in the middle of the night and killed?

How could I explain how I drank to drive away the images I had seen all day? That I would be so drunk that sometimes, the morning after, my hangover would be so violent I couldn't stand. How I would sit on the edge of the pit with my legs dangling, my shoulder sore from the recoil of the gun, between groups. I'd smoke a cigarette and I'd wave the nose of the gun to direct the next line of victims so they knew where to lie down.

Then I'd shoot. Precision wasn't necessary, although we learned to be economical. Two bullets to the head was too much. The sheer force would almost tear it from the body.

'What if you get hurt in Poland?' she asked.

'I could get hurt in Germany,' I reminded her. 'I'm careful, Mother.'

She touched my arm. 'I don't want any Hartmann blood spilled.'

I could tell, from the look on her face, that she was thinking about Franz. 'He will be all right, too,' I told her. 'There are special forces groups headed by men with doctorates. There's room for scholars in the SS, too.'

This made my mother brighten. 'Maybe you can tell that to him.'

She left, promising to make me a lunch fit for a king, since I had slept through breakfast. I showered and dressed in my civilian clothes, aware that even the way I carried myself now made me look like a soldier. By the time I was finished with the plate of food my mother had prepared for me, the house was quiet. My father was at work, my mother at her church volunteer group. Franz was in classes until two o'clock. I could have walked into town, but I didn't feel like being sociable. So instead, I went back to the bedroom I had shared with my brother.

On his desk was a small block of wood, roughly fashioned like a werewolf. Lined up along the blotter were two more, in various stages of precision. There was also a vampire, with its arms crossed and its head thrown back. In my absence my little brother had become quite the craftsman.

I picked up the vampire and was testing the points of its sharp teeth against the ball of my thumb when I heard Franz's voice. 'What are you doing?'

I whirled around to find him staring down at me. 'Nothing.'

'That's mine,' he snapped, grabbing the carving from my hand.

'Since when did you take up whittling?'

'Since I decided I wanted to make a chess set,' Franz said. He turned away and began to search his bookshelves. Franz collected books the way some people collect coins or stamps. They overran his desk and his shelves; they were piled up beneath his bed. He never donated a book to a church rummage sale because he said he never knew if he'd want to read it again. I watched him pull a stack of horror stories from the narrow space between his desk and the wall, and I scanned the titles. *The Wolf of Crimea. Blood Lust. The Haunting.*

'Why do you read that stuff?' I asked.

'Why is it any of your business?' Franz emptied his book bag on the bed and replaced his school textbooks with the novels. 'I'll be back later. I have to walk Otto. The Muellers' dog.'

It didn't surprise me to hear that Franz had taken on this odd job, just that the Muellers' dog was still alive after all this time. 'Are you planning on reading to him, too?'

Franz didn't reply, just hurried out of the house again. Shrugging, I settled on my narrow mattress with one of his books and cracked the spine. I read the same sentence three times before I heard the front door close, and then I went to the window and watched my brother cross the street.

He strode right past the Muellers' house.

I walked downstairs and slipped outside, using my tactical military training to follow Franz for several minutes to a house I did not recognize. I didn't know the residents, but it looked as if nobody was home. The shutters were drawn, the house in a state of disrepair. Yet when Franz knocked, the door opened to admit him.

I waited for about fifteen minutes, hiding behind a hedge, until my brother reappeared, his book bag slack and empty against his hip.

I stepped out from behind the shrubbery. 'What are you up to, Franz?'

He pushed past me. 'I'm bringing books to a friend. As far as I know that's not a crime.'

'Then why would you tell me you're walking a dog?'

My brother didn't say a word, but two bright spots of color appeared on his cheeks.

'Who lives here that you don't want me to know you are visiting?' I raised my brows, grinning, suddenly wondering if my little brother had become a ladies' man in my absence. 'Is it a girl? Has something other than poetic meter finally got you twitching?' Playfully, I cuffed him on the shoulder, and he ducked away from me.

'Stop it,' he muttered.

'Ah, poor Franz. If you'd asked me I would have told you to bring her chocolates, not books—'

'It's not a girl,' Franz blurted out. 'It's Artur Goldman. That's who lives here.'

It took me a moment to place the name. The Jew from Franz's class at *Gymnasium*.

Most of the Jews in our town had left. I didn't know where they'd gone – to the big cities, maybe Berlin. I had not given any thought to it, really. But obviously, my brother had. 'Jesus. Is this why you won't join the SS? Because you're a Jew-lover?'

'Don't be an idiot—'

'I'm not the idiot here, Franz,' I said. 'I'm not the one fraternizing with enemies of the Reich.'

'He's my friend. He misses school. So I bring him books. That's it.'

'You have a brother who is an SS officer candidate,' I said quietly. 'You will stop fraternizing with a Jew.'

'No,' my brother replied.

No.

No.

I could not remember the last time someone had told me that.

I grabbed him by the throat. 'How do you imagine it will look when the Gestapo finds out? You would ruin my career for this, after all I've done to protect you?' I released my hold on his neck, and he choked and jackknifed, coughing. 'Be a man, Franz. For once in your miserable life, be a fucking man.'

He stumbled away from me. 'Who the hell have you turned into, Reiner?'

I fumbled a cigarette out of my pocket and lit it, took a drag. 'Perhaps I came on too strong,' I admitted, softening my voice. 'Perhaps all you really need to hear from me is this.' I blew a ring of smoke. 'Tell Artur you can no longer visit him. Or else I will make sure no one is there for you to visit.'

The composure on my brother's face cracked; he turned to me with an expression I had seen so often this past year I had grown cold to it. 'Please,' Franz said. 'You wouldn't.'

'If you really want to save your friend,' I told him, 'then stay away from him.'

Two nights later I was awakened by my brother's arm, pressing hard on my windpipe. 'You lied,' he hissed. 'You said you wouldn't do anything to Artur.'

'And *you* lied,' I said. 'Or you wouldn't have known that they left.'

It had not been difficult to sew the seeds of intolerance, to let the family know they were not welcome here. I didn't make them leave town, really. That was pure instinct:

self-preservation, on their part. I had done it because I knew I was strong where my brother was weak, that he would continue to visit Artur – and here was the proof that I had been right to take action. If it was books today, tomorrow it would be food. Money. Shelter. That, I could not let happen.

'I did you a favor,' I gritted out.

My brother released the pressure on my throat. In the moonlight I saw an expression on his face I had never seen before. His eyes were black and flat; his jaw wired with rage. He looked like he was capable, in that instant, of killing me.

I knew then my mother could stop worrying. Even if Franz were dragged to the recruitment center; even if he never set foot in university and was shipped off, like me, to officer training; even if he had to fight on the front lines – he would be able to survive this war.

We never spoke of Artur Goldman again.

In the months I spent at *Junkerschule*, I studied *Mein Kampf*, I played war strategy games in sandboxes, and I took endless exams, which weeded one out of every three cadets from the program. We had classes in tactics, terrain and map reading, combat training, current events, weapons training. We studied weapons technology, went to the shooting range, and learned about the administration of the SS and the police. We were taught how to maneuver a tank, how to survive in the wild, and how to fix a broken vehicle. We were groomed into soldiers who were above average in knowledge, determination, and endurance. I graduated in 1940 with a commission as a second lieutenant in the Waffen-SS, an *Untersturmführer*. I was posted to the Government General in Poland, until April 24, 1941, when the 1.SS Infantry Brigade was formed.

We were a special Waffen-SS unit, part of the *Kommandostab* of the Reichsführer-SS, and we were deployed in shooting situations against civilians. As an *Untersturmführer*, I led one of the fifteen companies that made up the 8th SS Infantry Regiment, which fell under the umbrella of the brigade. We moved through northern Ukraine, from Dubno to Równo to Zhytomyr. What we did was just what I had done years earlier in Poland – except there were fewer Jewish leaders and political prisoners left.

My supervisor, Hauptsturmführer Voelkel, had given us our orders: round up all political undesirables, and all racial inferiors – Gypsies, for example, and all Jews – men, women, and children. We were to collect their valuables and clothes, to march them to open fields and ravines on the outskirts of towns and cities that had been conquered, and to kill them.

The *Reinigungsaktionen* went as such: we would require the Jews to report at a given site – school or prison or factory – and then take them to a place that had been prearranged. Some of these places were natural ravines, some were dugouts built by the prisoners themselves. After they'd given up their clothing and valuables, we would drive them into the pit and make them lie facedown. Then, as the commanding officer of the regiment, I would give the order. The NCOs and volunteers, Waffen-SS men, would lift their Karabiner 98ks and shoot the prisoners in the back of the neck. Then some soldiers would haul in a load of dirt or lime before the next group was driven into the pit.

I would walk among the bodies, find the ones that were still moving, and deliver the coup de grâce with my pistol.

I did not think about what I was doing. How could I? To be stripped naked, shouted at to move faster and faster toward the pit with your children running beside you. To look down and see your friends and your relatives, dying an instant before you. To take your place between the twitching limbs of the wounded, and wait for your moment. To feel the blast of the bullet, and then the heaviness of a stranger falling on top of you. To think like this was to think that we were killing other humans, and to us, they could not be humans. Because then what did that say about *us*?

And so, after each *Aktion*, we got drunk. So incredibly drunk that we drove from our nightmares that unholy image of the ground bleeding, the red runoff swelling like a geyser after all the bodies were in the pit. We drank until we could no longer smell the shit that coated the corpses. Until we did not see, printed on the backs of our eyelids, the occasional child who clawed his way to the top of the tangle of limbs, shot but not dead, and who ran around the pit bleating for his mother or father until I put us out of our misery and killed him with a single bullet.

Some of the officers went crazy. I feared I might, too. There was another second lieutenant who had one of his men get up in the middle of the night, walk out of camp, and shoot himself in the head. The next day the second lieutenant refused – simply refused – to shoot anyone. Voelkel had him transferred to the front lines.

In July, Voelkel told us there would be an *Aktion* on the road between Równo and Zhytomyr. Eight hundred Jews had been rounded up.

Although I had given the men explicit orders about how they were to conduct themselves and when to shoot, when the third group of prisoners stood naked at the edge of the pit, shaking and weeping, one of my enlisted men began to fall apart. Schultz put aside his rifle and sank to the ground.

I ordered him to stand down and picked up his weapon. 'What are you waiting for?' I barked at the soldiers who were responsible for bringing the next group of prisoners forward. This time, I was the first to fire my weapon. I would set the example. I did this for the next three sets of prisoners, and as blood and gray matter sprayed onto my uniform, I set my jaw and ignored it. As for Schultz, he would be posted behind the front. The SS did not want anyone on the front lines who might not be able to shoot.

That night, my men went carousing at the local tavern. I sat outside under the stars and listened to the glorious silence. No crackerjack of bullet shots, no screams, no cries. I had a bottle of whiskey that was nearly empty after two hours of nursing it. I did not go into the tavern until my men left, staggering down the street and balanced precariously on each other like a child's wooden blocks. At this hour, I expected the tavern to be unoccupied; but instead, there were a half dozen officers gathered, and in a corner, Voelkel stood in front of one of the tables. Seated before him was Annika Belzer, the support staff who traveled with the Hauptsturmführer. An executive secretary, she was much younger than either Voelkel or his wife back home. She was also an abysmal typist. Everyone in the 8th SS Infantry Regiment knew exactly why she'd been hired, and why the Hauptsturmführer needed secretarial support even when his unit was mobile. Annika had hair that was an unearthly platinum blond, wore too much makeup, and was currently sobbing. As I watched, Voelkel jammed the barrel of his handgun into her mouth.

The others in the bar were not paying attention, or at least they were pretending not to, because you didn't mess with the leader of the infantry brigade.

'Well then,' Voelkel said, cocking the trigger. 'Can you make *this* come?'

'What are you doing?' I blurted out.

Voelkel looked over his shoulder. 'Ah, Hartmann. So you think just because you got an enlisted man to listen to you, you can boss me around?'

'You can't get it up, so you're going to shoot *her*?'

He turned to me, his lips curling upward. 'Why should *you* have all the fun?'

It was different. A Jew was one thing, but this girl, she was German. 'If you pull that trigger,' I said calmly, although my heart was hammering so loud I could feel it move the heavy wool of my uniform jacket, 'the Obersturmbannführer will hear about it.'

'If the Obersturmbannführer hears about it,' Voelkel said, 'I will know who to blame, hmm?'

He removed the gun from Annika's mouth and smacked her across the cheek with it. She fell to her knees, then scrambled upright and ran out. Voelkel strode toward a group of SS officers and began to drink shots with them.

Suddenly I had a headache. I didn't want to be here; I didn't want to be in the Ukraine at all. I was twenty-three. I wanted to be sitting at my mother's kitchen table, eating her homemade ham soup; I wanted to be watching pretty girls walk down the street in high heels; I wanted to kiss one of them in the brick alley behind the butcher's shop.

I wanted to be a young man with his life ahead of him, not a soldier who walked through death every waking day, and scraped its entrails from his uniform each night.

I staggered out of the tavern and saw a flash of something bright from the corner of my eye. It was the secretary, her hair catching the light of a streetlamp.

'My knight in shining armor,' she said, holding out a cigarette.

I lit it for her. 'Did he hurt you?'

'No worse than usual,' she said, shrugging. As if she'd

conjured it, the door to the tavern opened, and Voelkel stepped into the cold. He gripped her chin and kissed her hard on the mouth. 'Come, my dear,' he said, smooth and charming. 'You aren't going to be angry with me the whole night, are you?'

'Never,' she replied. 'Just let me finish my cigarette.'

His glance flickered over me, and then he disappeared back into the tavern.

'He's not a bad man,' Annika insisted.

'Then why do you let him treat you that way?'

Annika looked me in the eye. 'I could ask you the same,' she said.

The next day, it was as if our altercation had never happened. By the time we had arrived in Zwiahel, we were no longer using rifles but rather machine guns for our *Aktion*. Soldiers funneled the Jews in an endless stream into the trenches. There were so many of them, this time. Two thousand. It took two days to kill them all.

There was no point in spreading sand between the layers of the bodies; instead, others in the regiment simply herded the Jews on top of their relatives and friends, some of whom were still in the throes of dying. I could hear them whispering against each other's necks, soothing, in the seconds before they were shot themselves.

One of the last groups had a mother and a child. This was not extraordinary; I had seen thousands of them. But this mother, she carried the little girl, and told her not to look, to keep her eyes closed. She placed her toddler between two fallen bodies as if she were tucking her in for the night. And then she began to sing.

I didn't know the words, but I knew the melody. It was a lullaby that my mother had sung to my brother and me when we were little, albeit in a different language. The little girl sang, too. *'Nite farhaltn,'* the Jewess sang. Don't stop.

I gave the command, and the machine guns chattered to life and shook the ground upon which I was standing. Only after the soldiers were finished did my ears stop ringing.

That's when I heard the little girl, still singing.

She was slick with blood and her voice was not much more than a whisper, but the notes rose like soap bubbles. I walked through the pit and pointed my gun at her. Her face was still buried in her mother's shoulder, but when she sensed me looming over her, she looked up.

I fired my weapon into her dead mother's body.

Then the crack of a pistol shot rang out and there was no more music.

Beside me, Voelkel holstered his gun. 'Aim better,' he said.

I had spent three months with the 1.SS Infantry Brigade, haunted by my nightmares. I would sit down for breakfast and see the ghost of a dead man standing across the room. I would look at my laundered uniforms, spotless, and still see the places where blood had seeped into the wool. I would drink at night so that I blacked out, because the space between wakefulness and sleep was the most dangerous one to tread.

But even after the last Jew in Zwiahel had been shot, even after Voelkel commended us on a job well done, I could still hear that toddler singing. She was long gone, buried beneath countless layers of her townsfolk, yet the breeze would draw a violin bow across the branches of a tree and I would again hear her lullaby. I would listen to the chime of coins being counted, and I would imagine her laughter. Her voice was caught in the shell of my ear, as if it were the ocean.

I started drinking early that night, skipping dinner entirely.

The tavern bar was swimming in front of me, untethered; I had to imagine each shot that passed through my lips rooting me to the stool upon which I was seated. I thought maybe I could just pass out right there on the gummy tables that were never wiped clean enough.

I don't know how long I'd been sitting there when she showed up. Annika. When I opened my eyes, my cheek pressed against the wood of the table, she was sideways and staring at me. 'Are you okay?' she asked, and I lifted my head, which was the size of the world, and watched her spin upright.

'Looks like you need a hand getting home,' she said.

Then she was hauling me to my feet, although I didn't want to go. She was talking a million miles a minute and dragging me out of the bar, to a place where I would be alone with my memories. I struggled against her, which wasn't hard, because she was a tiny thing and I was considerably bigger. She immediately cringed, expecting to be hit.

She thought I was like Voelkel.

That, if nothing else, broke through the haze of my head. 'I don't want to go home,' I said.

I do not remember how we got to her quarters. There were stairs, and I was in no condition to navigate them. I have no idea whose idea it was to take off our clothes. I have no idea what happened, which let me tell you, is a great regret for me.

Here is what I *do* recall, with perfect clarity: waking up to the cold kiss of a pistol against my forehead, and Voelkel looming over me, telling me that my career as an officer was over.

'*I* *have a surprise for you,' Aleks said, when I wandered into the kitchen. 'Sit down.'*

I climbed onto a stool and watched the muscles in his back flex as he opened the door to the brick oven and pulled something from inside. 'Close your eyes,' he said. 'Don't peek.'

'If it's a new recipe then I certainly hope you've still made the rest of the usual order—'

'All right,' Aleks interrupted, so near that I could feel the heat of his skin close to mine. 'You can look now.'

I opened my eyes. Aleks was holding out his palm. In its center was a roll that looked just like the one my father used to make for me, and this alone made me feel like crying.

I could already smell the cinnamon and the chocolate. 'How did you know?' I asked.

'The night I had to suture your neck. You talk a lot when you're three sheets to the wind.' He grinned. 'Promise me you'll eat the whole thing.'

I broke it open. Steam rose between us in the shape of a secret. The crumb inside was slightly pink, warm, like flesh. 'I promise,' I said, and I took the first bite.

Sage

Can you blame the creationist who doesn't believe in evolution, if he has been fed that alleged truth his whole life, and swallowed it hook, line, and sinker?

Maybe not.

Can you blame the Nazi who was born into an anti-Semitic country and given an anti-Semitic education, who then grows up and slaughters five thousand Jews?

Yes. Yes, you can.

The reason I am still sitting at Josef's kitchen table is the same reason traffic slows after a car wreck – you want to see the damage; you can't let yourself pass without that mental snapshot. We are drawn to horror even as we recoil from it.

Spread before me on the table are pictures – the photo he showed me days ago of himself as a soldier in a camp; and the photo clipped from the newspaper taken on Kristallnacht, with Josef – *Reiner* – grinning and eating his mother's home-made cake.

How could someone who murdered innocent people look so . . . so . . . ordinary?

'I just don't understand how you did it,' I say, into the silence. 'How you lived a normal life, and pretended none of this ever happened.'

'It is amazing, what you can make yourself believe, when

you have to,' Josef says. 'If you keep telling yourself you are a certain kind of person, eventually you *will* become that person. That's what the Final Solution was all about, really. First I convinced myself that I was of pure race, Aryan. That I deserved things others did not, simply by the accident of my birth. Think about that – that *hubris*, that arrogance. By comparison, convincing myself and others that I was a good man, an honest man, a humble teacher was easy.'

'I don't know how you sleep at night,' I reply.

'Who says that I do?' Josef answers. 'Surely you see now that I did horrible things. That I deserve to die.'

'Yes,' I reply bluntly. 'You do. But if I kill you, I'm no better than you were.'

Josef considers this. 'The first time you make a decision like that, a decision which rubs against all your morals, is the hardest. The second time, though, is not so hard. And that makes you feel a fraction better about the first time. And so on. But you can keep dividing and dividing and you'll never entirely get rid of the sourness in your stomach that you taste when you think back to the moment you could have said *no*.'

'If you are trying to get me to help you die, you're doing a lousy job.'

'Ah, yes, but there is a difference between what I did and what I am asking *you* to do. I *want* to die.'

I think of those poor Jews, stripped and humiliated, clinging to their children as they marched into a pit filled with bodies. Maybe they wanted to die, too, at that moment. Better that, than live in a world where this sort of hell could happen.

I think of my grandmother, who – like Josef – refused to speak of this for so long. Was it because she thought that if she didn't talk about it, she wouldn't have to relive it? Or was it because even a single word of memory was like opening

Pandora's box, and might let evil seep like poison into the world again?

I think, too, of the monsters she wrote about in her story. Did they hide in the shadows from others? Or from themselves?

And I think of Leo. I wonder how he subjects himself to these sorts of stories, willingly, every day. Maybe it's not so much about catching the perpetrators, after sixty-five years. Maybe it's just so that he knows someone is still listening, for the sake of the victims.

I force my attention back to Josef. 'So what happened? After Voelkel caught you in bed with his girlfriend?'

'He did not kill me, obviously,' Josef says. 'But he made sure I would not work within his regiment anymore.' He hesitates. 'At the time I did not know if that was a blessing or a curse.'

He reaches for the photo he showed me, the one of himself in the camp, holding a pistol. 'Those who did not want to do their job in a shooting brigade were not punished or forced to do it. It was still their choice. They were just transferred instead.

'After the disciplinary hearing, I was sent to the Eastern Front. A *Bewährungseinheit* – a penal company. Now, I was a lieutenant under recall. I'd been demoted to sergeant and I had to prove myself or lose my rank.' Josef unbuttons his shirt and shrugs his left arm from the sleeve. There is a small circular burn mark on the underarm, at the armpit. 'They gave me a *Blutgruppe* tattoo, applied to the members of the Waffen-SS. We were all supposed to have one, although it did not always work out that way. One small letter in black ink. If I needed a blood transfusion or I was unconscious, or my *Erkennungsmarke* had gone missing, the doctor would know my blood type and could take care of me first. And as it turned out, that saved my life.'

'There's nothing there but a scar.'

'That's because I cut it away with a Swiss Army knife when I moved to Canada. Too many people knew that SS had them; they were hunting down war criminals. I did what I had to do.'

'So you were shot,' I say.

He nods. 'We had no food and the weather was brutal, and the Red Army ambushed our platoon one night. I took a bullet meant for my commanding officer. Lost a great deal of blood and almost died. The Reich, they saw it as an act of heroism. At the time, I had only been hoping for suicide.' He shakes his head. 'It was enough, though, to redeem myself. I had irreparable nerve damage in my right arm; I would never hold a rifle steady again. But by now, in late 1942, they needed me somewhere else anyway. Somewhere not the front line. And you did not have to hold a gun steady against an unarmed prisoner.' Josef looks up at me. 'I had previous experience in the concentration camps; it was where I started my SS career. So after nine months in the hospital, I was sent back to one. This time, as the *Schutzhaftlagerführer* of the women's camp. I was responsible for the prisoners whenever they were present. Anus Mundi, that is what the prisoners called the camp. I remember stepping off the transport and looking at those iron gates, the words twisted between the parallel lines of metal. *Arbeit macht frei.* Work will set you free. And then I heard someone call my name.' Josef looks up at me. 'It was my brother, Franz. After all that resistance to supporting the Reich, he was now a *Hauptscharführer* – a sergeant – working at the same camp, in administrative duties.'

'This Anus Mundi,' I say. 'I've never heard of it.'

Josef laughed. 'That was just a nickname. You speak some Latin, yes? It means "Asshole of the World." But you,' he said. 'You probably know it as Auschwitz.'

*H*e could hear every beat of her heart. It was almost in time with her boots, as she ran. She should have known better, he told himself. This was all her fault.

When she rounded the corner, he hit her from behind. She landed hard on the stones as he reached for the neck of her dress, tearing it halfway down her body while he rolled her onto her back. One arm pressed against her collarbone was all he needed to keep her steady. She begged, they always did, but he did not listen. Her heart was racing now, and it was driving him mad.

The first bite was the most gratifying, like a blade cutting through clay. Her pulse fluttered like an aspen leaf in the hollow of her throat. The skin was soft; it took only a gentle tug to peel it back so that he could see the exposed muscle, the veins throbbing. He could hear the blood, too, rushing like a swollen river, and it made saliva pool in his mouth. With years of dexterity he carved through the muscle, snapping sinew and tendon like bowstrings as he shredded the flesh, dissecting until the sweet copper blood burst from the artery onto his tongue. It dripped down his chin like the juice of a melon as she went limp beneath him, as her skin shriveled. When his teeth struck her spine, he knew she was of no more use. Her head, connected only by a strip of ligament, rolled a short distance away.

He wiped his mouth clean. And wept.

Sage

E ven though Josef has spoken so much of death that it darkens his lips like a berry stain; even though I cannot get the images out of my head of a little girl singing and a young man pointing to himself and reciting his age, what I find myself thinking about are the others. The ones Josef hasn't told me about. The ones who didn't even leave a mark on his memory, which is infinitely more horrible.

He was at Auschwitz, and so was my grandmother. Did she know him? Did they cross paths? Did he threaten her, beat her? Did she lie awake at night in her fetid bunk and redraw the monster in her story with features that matched his?

I have not mentioned Josef to my grandmother for good reason. She has spent over six decades keeping her memories bottled up. But as I leave Josef's house, I cannot help but wonder if my grandmother is one of the ones he doesn't recall. And if *he* is one of the ones she has worked so hard to forget. The inequity there makes me sick to my stomach.

It is pitch dark and raining when I leave Josef's house, shaking beneath the responsibility of his confessions. What I want is someone I can run to, someone who will hold me tight and tell me that I'm going to be okay, someone who will hold my hand until I fall asleep tonight. My mother would have done that, but she's not here anymore. My grandmother might, but she would want to know what has upset me so deeply.

So I drive to Adam's house, even though I have told him I don't want to see him, even though it is nighttime – the portion of the pie chart of his life that belongs to someone other than me. I park at the curb and look in the fishbowl window of the living room. There is a boy watching television, *Jeopardy!* And beyond the couch a girl sits at the kitchen table reading. Buttery light spills over her shoulders like a cape. The kitchen sink faucet is running, and Adam's wife is washing dishes. While I watch, he appears with a fresh dish towel and takes a salad bowl from her soapy hands. He dries it, sets it on the counter, and then wraps his arms around Shannon from behind.

The sky opens overhead, which is surely a metaphor and not just a low-pressure system. I start to run and make it to my car just as the night is cleaved by a violet streak of lightning. I peel away from the curb, from this happy family, and drive too fast to the divided highway. The puddles on the asphalt are vast and black. I think of Josef's image, the ground welling up with blood, and I am so distracted that at first I do not see the doe fly from the woods at the edge of the road to leap in front of my car. I veer sharply, struggling to control the wheel, and hit the guardrail, smacking my head against the window. The car comes to a stop with a hiss.

For a moment, I black out.

When I open my eyes, my face is wet. I think I might be crying, but then I touch my cheek and my hand comes away bloody.

For one horrible, heart-stopping moment, I relive my past.

I look at the empty passenger seat, and then peer through the shattered windshield, and remember where I am and what has happened.

The deer is lying in the road, screened by the white veil of the headlights. I stumble out of the car. In the pouring rain, I kneel down and touch its face, its neck, and I start to sob.

I am so distraught that it takes me a moment to realize that there is another car illuminating the night, a hand gentle on my shoulder. 'Miss,' the policeman asks, 'are you all right?'

As if that were an easy answer. As if I could reply with a single word.

After the cops call Mary, she insists on getting me checked out at a hospital. When the doctor puts a butterfly bandage on my forehead and tells her I ought to be watched for signs of concussion, she announces I will be staying overnight at her house, and does not allow me to argue. By then my head hurts so much I am in no condition to put up a fight, which is how I wind up in Mary's kitchen drinking tea.

Mary's hands are covered with dried purple paint – she'd been working on a mural when she was contacted by the police. The painting surrounds me, on the walls of the breakfast nook: a half-finished dreamscape of the apocalypse. Jesus – I'm guessing it's Jesus, anyway, because he's got the long hair and the beard but his face looks suspiciously like Bradley Cooper's – is holding out his hand to those tumbling toward Mephistopheles – who is female, and resembles Michele Bachmann. The poor souls who are falling are in various states of undress, and some are still just roughly sketched, but I can make out the features of Snooki, Donald Trump, Joe Paterno. I touch my finger to a spot on the mural just behind my back. 'Elmo?' I say. 'Really?'

'How long has he been a toddler?' Mary asks, shrugging as she passes me the sugar. 'He never gets old. Clearly he made a deal with the Devil.' She holds my hand across the table. 'It means a lot to me, you know. That you called me.'

I choose not to point out that the police were the ones who called.

'I thought you were angry at me, because I told you to take time off. But really, it's for your own good, Sage.' She smiles a little. 'Sister Immaculata used to say that to me all the time when I was a kindergartner in parochial school. I never stopped talking. So one day she put me in the trash can. I was short enough that I fit. Every time I complained, she kicked the can.'

'I'm supposed to be grateful that you didn't throw me in the Dumpster?'

'No, you're supposed to be grateful that someone cares enough about you to help you get back on track again. You know it's what your mother would have wanted.'

My mother. The reason I had gone to grief group in the first place. If she hadn't died, I might never have cultivated a friendship with Josef Weber.

'So what happened tonight?' Mary asks.

Well, that's a loaded question. 'You know. I hit a deer, and my car swerved into the guardrail.'

'Where were you headed? The weather was *awful*.'

'Home,' I say, because that isn't a lie.

I would like to tell her all about Josef, but she already dismissed me once when I tried to confide in her. It is like he said: we believe what we want to, what we need to. The corollary is that we choose not to see what we'd rather pretend doesn't exist. Mary can't accept the thought that Josef Weber might be a monster, because that implies that she was duped by him.

'Were you with him?' Mary asks tightly.

At first I think she is talking about Josef, but then I realize she means Adam. 'Actually I told Adam I didn't want to see him for a while.'

Mary's jaw drops. 'Amen!'

'But then I drove to his house.' When Mary buries her face in her hands, I grimace. 'I wasn't going to go inside. I swear it.'

'Hello? Why didn't you come here?' Mary asks. 'I have enough herbal tea and Häagen-Dazs to compensate for any breakup, and I'm more emotionally available than Adam ever was.'

I nod. 'You're right. I should have called you. But instead, I saw him with his wife and kids. I got . . . rattled, I guess. And I was distracted, which is why I hit the deer.'

I realize that I've crafted this entire story without even mentioning Josef's name. I have more in common with my grandmother than I originally thought.

'Nice try,' Mary says. 'But you're lying.'

I blink at her, my breath caught in my throat.

'I know you. You were driving to see him because you wanted to tell him you'd made a mistake. If you hadn't Peeping Tommed the whole happy family scene, you probably would have climbed a trellis and thrown pebbles at the window until he came outside to talk to you.'

I scowl at her. 'You make me sound like such a loser.'

Mary shrugs. 'Look, all I'm saying is that it wouldn't hurt you to hold a grudge longer than a single breath.'

'Isn't that a little Old Testament for a nun?'

'Ex-nun. And let me tell you, that serenity crap from *The Sound of Music*? Bullshit. Inside the cloister, the sisters are just as petty as people on the outside. There are some you love and some you hate. I did my share of spitting in the Holy Water font before another nun used it. It was totally worth the twenty rosaries I said for penance.'

I rub my left temple, which is throbbing. 'Can you get me my phone?'

She gets up and rummages through my purse to find it for me. 'Who are you calling?'

'Pepper.'

'Liar. The last time you talked to your sister she hung up on you because you said tutoring a four-year-old to get into an exclusive preschool made as much sense as hiring a swim coach for a guppy. You wouldn't call Pepper if you were trapped in the car and it was about to catch fire—'

'Just let me check my messages, will you?'

Mary thrusts the phone at me. 'Go ahead. Text him. By tomorrow morning, you're going to be begging him to forgive you anyway. It's your M.O.'

I scan my contacts for Leo's number. 'Not this time,' I promise.

Apparently even Nazi hunters take a breather. Although I leave three voice mails for Leo that night and the next morning, he does not answer, and he does not call me back. I fall into a fitful sleep in Mary's guest bedroom, where an elaborate carving of Jesus carrying his cross hangs over my head. I dream that I have to drag a crucifix up a Sisyphean hill, and look down from its peak to see the bodies of thousands of naked men, women, children.

Mary drives me home on her way to the bakery, even though I insist that it would just be better for me to join her there. Once I'm back in my house, though, I am restless. I don't think I can handle another session with Josef today; I don't want to talk to him until I have connected with Leo, anyway.

I want to get my mind off Josef, so I decide to bake something that requires my undivided attention: brioche. It's a bread that is an anomaly – 50 percent of it is butter, yet instead of being a brick of a loaf, it is melt-in-your-mouth, sweet, airy. To make it on a hot, humid day like this is an added challenge, because it requires all ingredients to be cold. I even refrigerate the mixing bowl and the dough hook.

I begin by beating the butter with a rolling pin while the dough is mixing. Then I add it, in small portions, to the mixer. This is my favorite part about brioche. The dough doesn't quite know what to do with all that butter, and begins to come apart. But with enough time, it manages to bring itself back to center, to a satin consistency.

I turn off the mixer and rip off a hunk of dough the size of a plum. Holding it between my hands, I pull it slowly to see if it sheets – growing transparent as it stretches. I set the dough into a container and cover it tightly with plastic wrap, then place it on my counter and begin to clean up the kitchen.

The doorbell rings.

The sound startles me. I'm not home during the day, usually, and no one ever rings the doorbell at night. Even Adam, when he comes, has his own key.

I am expecting the mail lady or the UPS guy, but the man standing on my porch is not in uniform. He's wearing a rumpled suit jacket and a tie, even though it's easily eighty-five degrees out. He has black hair and beard stubble and eyes the color of polished walnut. And he's easily six foot three. 'Sage Singer?' he says, when I open the door. 'I'm Leo Stein.'

He is not what I anticipated, in more ways than one. Immediately, I shake my bangs forward to cover my face, but I can tell I'm too late. Leo is staring at me, as if he can see through the screen of hair. 'How did you know where I live?' I ask.

'Are you kidding? We're the Department of Justice. I know what you had for breakfast this morning.'

'Really?'

'No.' He grins, and it takes me by surprise. I would think a person like him doesn't smile very often. I would think, given all he's heard, that he's forgotten how. 'Could I come in?'

I don't know if there's a protocol here. If I'm even allowed to turn him away. I wonder if I've done something terribly wrong; if there have been hidden cameras focused on me and Josef; if I am in trouble.

'Okay, the first thing you have to do is breathe,' Leo says. 'I'm here to help you, not arrest you.'

I turn in profile, so that he can't see the bad side of my face.

'Um,' he says. 'Is something wrong?'

'No. Why?'

'Because you're twisted the way I was when I fell asleep at my desk last month. I couldn't straighten my neck for a week.'

I take a deep breath and meet his gaze, challenging him to look at me.

'Oh,' he says softly. 'Well, that's not what I expected.'

I don't know why I feel like I've been slapped. Most polite people do not say anything at all when they see my scars. If Leo had done that, at least I could have pretended he didn't notice.

'It's silly, but I pictured you with brown eyes. Not blue,' he says.

My mouth drops open.

'I like the blue, though,' Leo adds. 'It suits you.'

'That's all you have to say?' I reply. 'Really?'

He shrugs. 'If you were thinking I'd run away screaming

because you have a few silver cyborg lines on your face, I'm sorry to disappoint you.'

'Cyborg?'

'Look, I don't know you very well, but you seem a *little* fixated on physical appearance. That's far less interesting to me than the fact that you brought Josef Weber to my attention.'

At the mention of Josef's name, I shake my head to clear it. 'I talked to him yesterday. He's done so many horrible things.'

Leo reaches into a battered briefcase and takes out a file. 'I know,' he says. 'That's why I thought it was time for us to meet each other.'

'But you said I would have to talk to one of your historians.'

A flush works its way up his neck. 'I was in the neighborhood,' he says.

'You were in New Hampshire for something else?'

'Philly,' he replies. 'Close enough.'

Philly is eight hours away by car. I step back, holding the door. 'Well, then,' I reply. 'You must be hungry.'

Leo Stein cannot stop eating the brioche. The first batch has come out of the oven, impossibly light. I serve it warm, with jam and tea. 'Mmm,' he rhapsodizes, his eyes closing in delight. 'I've never tasted anything like this.'

'They don't have bakeries in Washington?'

'I wouldn't know. My sustenance consists of really bad coffee and sandwiches that come out of a vending machine.'

I have spent the past two hours telling Leo everything Josef told me. In between, I have shaped the brioche into a traditional tête, brushed it with an egg wash, and baked it.

It's easier for me to talk when my hands are busy. With each word that passes my lips, I feel less heavy. It is as if I am giving him sentences made of stones, and the more I relay, the more of the burden he is carrying. He takes notes and writes on his legal pad. He scrutinizes the clipping I slipped into my pocket before I left Josef, the one of him eating his mother's cake that ran in the local paper in Wewelsburg.

And he doesn't even do a double take when he looks at me.

'Are you going to talk to him directly?' I ask.

Leo looks up at me. 'Not yet. You've developed a good rapport. He trusts you.'

'He trusts me to forgive him,' I say. 'Not to turn him in.'

'Forgiveness is spiritual. Punishment is legal,' Leo says. 'They're not mutually exclusive.'

'So you'd forgive him?'

'I didn't say that. It's not my place, or yours, if you ask me. Forgiveness is the imitation of God.'

'So's punishment,' I point out.

He raises his brows and smiles. 'The difference is that God never hates.'

'I'm surprised you can believe in God, after meeting so many evil people.'

'How could I not,' Leo asks, 'after meeting so many survivors?' He wipes his mouth with his napkin. 'So you saw his tattoo,' he clarifies.

'I saw a mark that could have been a tattoo.'

'Where?' Leo holds up his arm. 'Show me.'

I touch his left biceps muscle, below the armpit. I can feel the heat of his skin through the cotton of his shirt. 'Here. It looked like a cigarette burn.'

'That's consistent with Waffen-SS *Blutgruppe* tattoos,' Leo says. 'And with the file we've got so far. As is his claim that he was with the 1.SS Infantry Brigade in 1941, and that he worked at Auschwitz Two after 1943.' He opens the folder on the table between us. I see a grainy photograph of a young man in a Nazi uniform with skulls on the lapels of his coat. It could be Josef, I suppose, but I can't tell. HARTMANN, REINER, I read, peeking as he slips the photograph from its paper clip. There is an address in spiky handwriting I cannot read, and the letters AB, which must be his blood type. Leo closes the folder quickly – classified information, I suppose – and sets the photo beside the newspaper clipping. 'The question is: Are these the same guy?'

In the first, Josef is a young boy; in the second, he's a man. The quality of both photos is shoddy at best. 'I can't tell. But does it really matter? I mean, if all the other stuff he's said fits?'

'Well,' Leo answers, 'that depends. In 1981 the Supreme Court concluded that anyone who was a guard at a Nazi concentration camp took part in supporting the activities that occurred there – including murder, if we're talking about Auschwitz Two. The court's analysis was reminiscent of a trial in Germany years earlier in which a suspect said that if German authorities prosecuted him, they should prosecute everyone at the camp, because the camp operated as a chain of functions and everyone in that chain had to perform his function, or the whole apparatus of annihilation would have ground to a halt. So everyone from the guards to the bean counters at Auschwitz is culpable for what happened there, simply because they were aware of what was going on inside its fences, and performed their duties. Think about it like this – let's say you and your boyfriend decide to kill me in my office. The deal is that your boyfriend is going to chase me around the room with a knife while you stand outside holding the door closed so I can't escape. Both of you are going down for Murder One. It's just a division of labor about how you each participated.'

'I don't have a boyfriend,' I blurt out. It turns out that it is easier to say aloud than I would have expected, and instead of feeling as if my heart has been ripped out of my chest, it seems as if I am made of helium. 'I mean, I did, but things aren't . . .' I shrug. 'Anyway. He won't be killing you in your office anytime soon.'

Leo blushes. 'Guess that means I'll be able to sleep well tonight.'

I clear my throat. 'So all we have to do is prove that Josef worked at Auschwitz,' I say. 'If he's confessed to that, isn't it enough?'

'That depends on how trustworthy his confession is.'

'Why would any court think he'd lie about that?'

'Why does anyone lie?' Leo says. 'He's old. He's got mental issues. He's a masochist. Who knows? For all we know, he wasn't even there. He could have read a book and regurgitated that history to you; that doesn't mean it's his own.'

'Even though you have a file with his name on it?'

'He's already given you one false name,' Leo points out. 'This could be another.'

'So how do we make sure he's really Reiner?'

'There are two ways,' Leo says. 'Either he has to keep talking to you and eventually spill information that's inside this file – up-close SS information that isn't the kind of stuff you can glean from watching the History Channel 24/7. Or we need an eyewitness who remembers him from the camp.' He touches the newspaper clipping and the Nazi Party registration photo. 'Someone who *could* say that these two men are one and the same.'

I look at the loaf of brioche, no longer steaming but fragrant and warm. The jam, staining the maple table. My grandmother told me that her father used to ask her a riddle: *What must you break apart in order to bring a family close together?*

Bread, of course.

I think of this, and even though I am not religious, I pray that she will forgive me.

'I think I know someone who can help,' I say.

'*S*ay what you want,' Damian argued. 'I am only trying to keep you safe.'

I had opened the door, expecting Aleks, only to find the captain of the guard instead. I had told him I was busy, and this was true. This week, business had grown stronger. We could not produce enough baguettes to feed demand. The loaves, like my rolls, were sweeter than anything my father had ever baked. Aleks joked with me, and said he had a secret ingredient, but he would not tell me what it was. Then it would only be an ingredient, he said.

Now, I listened to Damian as he lectured me in my kitchen. 'An upiór?' I said. 'Those are folktales.'

'There's a reason tales get told. What else makes sense? The livestock was one thing, Ania. But this . . . this beast is going after humans.'

I had heard of them, of course. Of the undead who rose from their coffins, unsatisfied, and gorged themselves on the blood of others. An upiór would eat its own flesh, if it had to.

Old Sal, who sold baskets in the village square, was superstitious. She never walked near a black cat; she threw salt over her shoulder; she wore her clothes inside out the night of the full moon. She was the one who buzzed about this upiór that was terrorizing our village, whispering every time we set up

201

shop beside each other at market. You can spot them in a crowd, *she had said.* They live among us, with their ruddy cheeks and their red lips. And after their death, they complete their transformation. If that's already happened, it's too late. The only way to kill an *upiór* is to cut off its head, or cleave open its heart. And the only way to protect yourself from one is to swallow its blood.

I had dismissed Old Sal's stories, and now, I would dismiss Damian's. I folded my arms. 'What is it you want me to do, then?'

'It's said that you can catch an upiór *if you can distract it,'* he explained. *'Once it sees a knot, it has to untie it. If there's a pile of seeds, it has to count them.' Damian reached above my head, took a bag of barley grain, and dumped it on the counter.*

'And why would the upiór *happen to wander into my bakery?'*

'It's possible,' Damian said, 'that he's already here.'

It took me a moment to understand. And then, I was furious. 'So because he's an outsider, he's the easy target? Because he didn't go to school with you like all your soldier friends, or because he has a different way of pronouncing words? He's not a monster, Damian. He's just different.'

'Do you really know that?' he challenged, backing me up against the wall of the brick oven. 'His arrival coincided with the killings.'

'He's here all night, and at home with his brother all day. When would he even have time to do the things you claim?'

'Are you with him, while he's working, watching him? Or are you asleep?'

I opened my mouth. The truth was, I had been spending more and more time in the kitchen with Aleks. I told him about my father, and about Baruch Beiler. He told me about how he'd wanted to be an architect, designing buildings so tall that you became dizzy standing on the top floors. Occasionally I fell asleep curled at the table, but when I did I always awakened to find that Aleks had carried me to my bed.

Sometimes I thought that I liked staying up late with him because I knew he'd do that.

I started to sweep the barley up with my hands, but Damian caught my wrist. 'If you are so sure, then why not leave it and see what happens?'

I thought of Aleks, running with his brother from town to town. I thought of his hands at my throat, sewing me whole again. I met Damian's eyes. 'All right,' I said.

That night, I did not meet Aleks in the kitchen. I was not even there when he let himself inside. Instead, when he knocked softly on my bedroom door, I told him I was feeling ill and wanted to rest.

But I didn't. I imagined him distracted by the barley, sorting it into piles. I imagined blood on his hands and pooling in his mouth.

When I couldn't sleep, I lit a candle and crept down the hall to the kitchen.

I felt the heat through the wooden door, radiant from the oven. If I stood on my toes, I could peer through a chink in the wood. I would not have a panoramic view of the kitchen, but maybe I could see Aleks working as he usually did, allaying my worst fears.

I had a perfect view of the butcher-block table, with the bag of barley still spilled on its side.

But the pile of grains had been organized, seed by seed, into military formation.

The door swung open so suddenly I fell inside, landing on all fours. The candle I was carrying rolled out of its holder and skittered across the stone floor. As I reached for it, Aleks's boot stepped down, extinguishing the flame. 'Spying on me?'

I scrambled to my feet and shook my head. My gaze was drawn to the barley, in neat rows.

'I'm a little behind in my baking,' Aleks said. 'I had a mess to clean up when I arrived.'

I realized that he was bleeding. A bandage was wrapped around his forearm. 'You're hurt.'

'It's nothing.'

He looked like the man I had laughed with yesterday, when he did his impression of the town drunk. He looked like the man who had lifted me into his arms when I saw a mouse skitter across the floor and refused to walk in the kitchen until I was sure it had been caught.

He was so close, now, that I could smell peppermint on his breath; I could see the flecks of green in the molten gold of his eyes. I swallowed. 'Are you what I think you are?'

Aleks did not blink. 'Would it matter?'

When he kissed me, I felt like I was being consumed. I was rising, expanding from the inside, frustrated that there was skin between us, that I could not get closer. I clawed at the small of his back, my fingers slipping beneath his shirt. He held my head in the cradle of his hands, and gently, so gently that I did not even feel it, he bit my lip.

There was blood in my mouth and on his. It tasted like metal, like pain. I pulled away from him, drinking the taste of myself for the first time.

In retrospect I could only think that he was as shaken by the moment as I was. Or surely he would have heard the approach of Damian, who flung open the door with his soldiers, their bayonets trained on us.

Leo

The reason that we go to meet the people who bring us plausible tips about potential Nazis is so that we can make sure they aren't nuts. You can usually get a good reading in a few moments about whether your informant is balanced and sane, or whether she is acting on a grudge, is paranoid, or is just plain crazy.

Within moments of meeting Sage Singer I know this: she isn't trying to frame this Josef Weber guy; she has nothing to gain from turning him in.

She's incredibly sensitive because she has a scar that ripples from her left eyebrow down her cheek.

Also: because of said scar, she has no idea that she's incredibly hot.

I get it, really I do. When I was thirteen I had the worst case of acne – I swear my pimples gave birth to smaller pimples. I got called 'Pepperoni Face,' or Luigi, because that was the name of the guy who owned the pizzeria in my hometown. On school picture day I was so nervous about having my image captured for eternity that I actually willed myself into throwing up so I could stay home. My mother told me that when I was older, I'd teach people to never judge a book by its cover, and that's pretty much exactly what my job entails. But sometimes, when I glance in the mirror, even now, I feel like I'm still staring at that kid.

I bet whatever Sage is picturing, when she looks at her reflection, is a lot worse than what the rest of us actually see.

Genevra is the one who is dispatched to vet most of the cold callers who reach our department; I've only met two or three. They were all in their eighties, Jews who still saw the faces of their captors superimposed on everyone they happened to meet. In none of those cases did the allegation pan out to be correct.

Sage Singer is not eighty years old. And she's not lying, either.

'Your grandmother,' I repeat. 'She's a survivor?'

Sage nods.

'And somehow, in the past four conversations I've had with you . . . that never came up?'

I am still trying to figure out if this is a very good thing, or a very bad thing. If Sage's grandmother is willing and able to identify Reiner Hartmann as an officer at Auschwitz-Birkenau, that would be a direct link between the file Genevra's amassed and the information Sage has culled from the suspect. But if Sage has predisposed her grandmother in any way to the suspect – by saying for example that she has been talking to him – then any eyewitness testimony given is prejudicial.

'I didn't want you to think that was why I called you. It had nothing to do with my grandmother. She never talks about her experience, ever.'

I lean forward, clasping my hands. 'So you haven't told her about your meetings with Josef Weber?'

'No,' Sage says. 'She doesn't even know he exists.'

'And she's never discussed her time at Auschwitz with you?'

Sage shakes her head. 'Even when I've asked her, specifically, she won't talk about it.' She looks up at me. 'Is that normal?'

'I don't know that there's anything normal about being a survivor,' I say. 'Some feel that because they lived, it's their responsibility to tell the world what happened, so it won't happen again, and so people won't forget. Others believe that the only way to go on with the rest of their lives is to act as if it never happened.' I sweep my crumbs into my napkin and carry my plate to the sink. 'Well,' I say, thinking out loud. 'I can give my historian a call. She can get a photo array cobbled together in a few hours and then . . .'

'She won't talk to *you*, either,' Sage says.

I smile. 'Grandmothers find me especially charming.'

She folds her arms. 'If you hurt her I'll—'

'Note to self: don't threaten a federal agent. And second note to self: don't worry. I give you my word, I won't push her if she isn't able to open up about it.'

'And if she does? Then what? You arrest Josef?'

I shake my head. 'We don't have any criminal jurisdiction over Nazis,' I explain. 'We can't incarcerate your man, or set him free. The crimes took place outside the United States long before we had extraterritorial jurisdiction statutes. It wasn't until 2007 that the U.S. Genocide Statute was amended to cover more than genocides perpetrated by non-Americans outside the United States. Prior to that, it basically covered U.S. citizens other than General Custer's actions against the Native Americans. All we can do is try to catch him on immigration charges, and get him deported. And even then, I've been trying for years to get Europeans to develop a moral backbone and take Nazis back and prosecute, and it hardly ever happens.'

'So we're doing all this for nothing?' Sage asks.

'We're doing all this because your grandmother made her home in the United States, and we owe her peace of mind.'

Sage looks at me for a long moment. 'Okay,' she says. 'I'll take you to her condo.'

There are things in Reiner Hartmann's file that Sage Singer doesn't know about.

It's my job to tell her as little as possible, to instead coax out of her what she can tell me. And even then, I cannot be sure that a court will be able to connect the dots and prosecute him. I cannot be sure that Hartmann will survive long enough to receive his comeuppance.

So far, what Sage has relayed to me is information that could be gleaned from the U.S. Holocaust Memorial Museum archives, or from poring through a book. Military actions and dates; company units, career trajectories. Even the blood group tattoos are something you'd know about, if you study Third Reich history. As untenable as it seems that someone is making up a false guilty identity, stranger things have happened.

But in this file, there are specifics about Reiner Hartmann that only Reiner Hartmann – and his superiors, and maybe his closest confidants – should know.

None of which Sage Singer has said yet.

Which could mean that Josef Weber hasn't gotten around to telling her those stories. Or that Josef Weber isn't Reiner Hartmann.

At any rate, getting an ID from Sage's grandmother Minka is just one more piece of the puzzle. Which is how I find myself driving back toward Boston – on the exact same route I just traveled from Logan Airport to New Hampshire – with Sage sitting beside me in the car.

'That's a new one,' I say. 'No one in my department has ever been so upset by a testimony that they went out and hit a deer with their car.'

'It wasn't intentional,' Sage mutters.

'*A bi gezunt.*'

'I beg your pardon?'

I turn to her. 'It means "so long as you're healthy." You don't speak Yiddish, I guess.'

'I'm not Jewish. I told you that.'

Actually, she had asked me if it mattered. 'Oh,' I say. 'I just assumed . . .'

'Morality has nothing to do with religion,' she says. 'You can do the right thing and not believe in God at all.'

'So you're an atheist?'

'I don't like labels.'

'I imagine you wouldn't, growing up here. Doesn't exactly look like a diverse religious community.'

'That's probably why it took Josef so long to find someone from a Jewish family,' Sage says.

'Well, it doesn't really matter, since you're not going to forgive him.'

She is silent.

'You're *not*,' I repeat, my jaw dropping. '*Are* you?'

'I don't want to. But there's a part of me that says he's just an old, frail man.'

'One who possibly committed crimes against humanity,' I reply. 'And even becoming Mother Teresa wouldn't erase that. He waited over half a century to confess? That's not inherent goodness. It's procrastination.'

'So you believe people can't change? That once you do a bad thing, you're a bad person?'

'I don't know,' I admit. 'But I do think some stains never wash out.' I glance at her. 'Other people in town, they knew your family was Jewish?'

'Yes.'

'And Josef picked you to confess to. You aren't an individual to him any more now than a Jew was over sixty-five years ago.'

'Or maybe he picked me because he thinks of me as his friend.'

'Do you really believe that?' I ask, and Sage doesn't reply. 'To be forgiven, the person has to be sorry. In Judaism, that's called *teshuvah*. It means "turning away from evil." It's not a one-time deal, either. It's a course of action. A single act of repentance is something that makes the person who committed the evil feel better, but not the person against whom evil was committed.' I shrug. 'That's why Jews don't just go to Confession, and say the rosary.'

'Josef says he's already made his peace with God.'

I shake my head. 'You don't make peace only with God. You make it with people. Sin isn't global. It's personal. If you do wrong to someone, the only way to fix that is to go to that same person and do right by him. Which is why murder, to a Jew, is unforgivable.'

She is quiet for a moment. 'Have you ever had someone walk into your office and confess to you?'

'No.'

'Then maybe Josef is different,' Sage says.

'Did he come to you because he wants to make himself feel better? Or because he wants to make his victims feel better?'

'Obviously that's not possible,' she replies.

'And that makes you feel badly for him?'

'I don't know. Maybe.'

I focus my attention on the road. 'The German people have paid billions of dollars of reparations. To individuals. To Israel. But you know what? It's been nearly seventy years and they've never held a public forum to apologize to Jews for the crimes of the Holocaust. It's happened elsewhere – South Africa, for example. But the Germans? They had to be dragged by the Allies into the Nuremberg Trials. Officials who had helped build the Third Reich stayed on in government after the war, just by denying they were ever Nazis, and the German people accepted it. Young people today in Germany who are taught about the Holocaust brush it off, saying it's ancient history. So, no, I don't think you can forgive Josef Weber. I don't think you can forgive anyone who was involved. I think you can only hold them accountable, and try to look their children and grandchildren in the eye without blaming them for what their ancestors did.'

Sage shakes her head. 'Surely there were some Germans who were better than others, some who didn't want to go along with what Hitler said. If you can't see them as individuals – if you can't forgive the ones who ask for it – doesn't that make you just as bad as any Nazi?'

'No,' I admit. 'It makes me human.'

Minka Singer is a tiny woman with the same snapping blue eyes as her granddaughter. She lives in a small assisted-living condo and has a part-time caretaker who moves like a shadow around her employer, handing her reading glasses and her cane and a sweater before she can seemingly even think to ask for them. Contrary to what Sage indicated, she is absolutely *thrilled* to be introduced to me.

'So tell me again,' she says, as we settle on the couch in her living room. 'Where did you meet my granddaughter?'

'Through work,' I answer carefully.

'Then you know how she bakes, yes? A person could get used to that kind of food all the time.'

'You'd have to have a lifetime deal with Jenny Craig,' I reply, and then I realize why Minka has been so happy to meet me. She wants me to date her granddaughter.

I'm not gonna lie: the thought of that makes me feel like I've been zapped by a bolt of electricity.

'Grandma,' Sage interrupts. 'Leo didn't come all this way to talk about my bread.'

'You know what my father used to say? True love is like bread. It needs the right ingredients, a little heat, and some magic to rise.'

Sage turns beet red. I cough into my hand. 'Ms. Singer, I've come here today because I'm hoping you'll tell me your story.'

'Ach, Sage, that was meant for your eyes only! The silly fairy tale of a young girl, that's all.'

I have no idea what she's talking about.

'I work for the United States government, ma'am. I track down perpetrators of war crimes.'

The light goes out of Minka Singer's eyes. 'I have nothing to say. Daisy?' she calls out. 'Daisy, I'm very tired. I'd like to lie down—'

'I told you so,' Sage murmurs.

From the corner of my eye, I see the caretaker approaching.

'Sage is lucky,' I say. 'My grandparents aren't alive anymore. My grandpa, he came here from Austria. Every year he held a big backyard party on July twenty-second. He'd have beer for the grown-ups and an inflatable pool for us kids, and the biggest cake my grandmother could make. I always assumed it was his birthday. It wasn't until I was fifteen that I learned he had been born in December. July twenty-second, that was the day he became a U.S. citizen.'

By now Daisy has reached Minka's side and has her hand beneath the woman's frail arm to help her stand. Minka rises and takes two shuffling steps away from me.

'My grandfather fought in World War Two,' I continue, getting to my feet. 'Like you, he never talked about anything he'd seen. But when I graduated from high school, he took me to Europe as a graduation gift. We visited the Colosseum in Rome, and the Louvre in Paris, and we hiked in the Swiss Alps. The last country we visited was Germany. He took me to Dachau. We saw the barracks, and the crematoria, where the bodies of prisoners who had died were burned. I remember a wall with a ditch below it, angled away, to catch the blood of prisoners who were shot. My grandfather told me that immediately after visiting the concentration camp, we would be leaving the country. Because I was going to want to kill the first German I saw.'

Minka Singer looks back over her shoulder. There are tears in her eyes. 'My father promised me I would die with a bullet to the heart.'

Sage gasps, stricken.

Her grandmother's eyes flicker toward her. 'There were dead people everywhere. You had to walk on them, sometimes, to get away. So we saw things. A bullet in the head, there were always brains coming out, and it scared me. But a bullet in the heart, that didn't seem so bad by comparison. So that was the deal my father made me.'

I realize in that instant the reason Minka has never spoken of her experience during the war is not that she has forgotten the details. It's *because* she remembers every last one, and wants to make sure that her children and grandchildren do not have to suffer the same curse.

She sits back down on the couch. 'I don't know what you want me to say.'

I lean forward and take her hand. It is cool and dry, like tissue paper. 'Tell me more about your father,' I suggest.

Part Two

When I reach the age of Twenty
I will explore this world of plenty
In a motorized bird myself I will sit
And soar into space oh! so brightly lit
I will float, I will fly to the world so lovely, so far
I will float, I will fly above rivers and sea
The cloud is my sister, the wind a brother to me.

– from 'A Dream,' written by Avraham (Abramek) Koplowicz,
b. 1930. He was a child in the Łódź ghetto. He was taken
from the ghetto on the final transport to Auschwitz-Birkenau
in 1944 and was murdered there at age fourteen. This poem
has been translated from the original Polish by
Ida Meretyk-Spinka, 2012.

*W*hat they had told me of the upiór could not be true. The whip wielded by Damian had lashed open Aleks's back, so that his skin hung in ribbons, and he was bleeding. How could a monster with no blood of his own do that?

Not that it mattered. The crowd had turned out to watch the punishment, to revel in the pain of the creature that had caused them so much misery. In the moonlight, sweat gleamed on Aleks's body, twisting in agony as he strained against his bonds. The villagers threw water in his face, vinegar and salt in his wounds. A light snow fell, blanketing the square – a bucolic picture postcard, except for the brutality at its center.

'Please,' I begged, breaking free from the soldiers who were restraining the onlookers, so that I could grab Damian's arm. 'You have to stop.'

'Why? He wouldn't have. Thirteen people have died. Thirteen.' He jerked his head at a soldier, who caught me around the waist and held me back. Damian lifted the whip again and sent it whizzing through the air, cracking against Aleks's flesh.

It did not matter, I realized, if Aleks was even to blame. Damian knew the village simply needed a scapegoat.

The cat's-eye tail had opened a gash along Aleks's cheek. His face was unrecognizable. His shirt hung in shreds at his *waist as he sagged to his knees. 'Ania,' he gasped. 'Go . . . away . . .'*

'You bastard!' Damian shouted. He hit Aleks so hard in the face that blood sprayed like a fountain from his nose, that his head snapped back on the stalk of his neck. 'You could have hurt her!'

'Stop!' I shrieked. I stomped as hard as I could on the foot of the soldier who was restraining me, and threw myself on top of Aleks. 'You'll kill him,' I sobbed.

Aleks was limp in my arms. A muscle jumped along Damian's jaw as he watched me try to bear the weight. 'You can't kill something,' he said coldly, 'that's already dead.'

Suddenly a soldier burst through the seam of the crowd, skidding in the snow to salute Damian. 'Captain? There's been another murder.'

The villagers parted, and two soldiers stepped forward, carrying the body of Baruch Beiler's wife. Her throat had been torn out. Her eyes were still open. 'The tax man, he's missing,' one soldier said.

I stepped forward as Damian knelt beside the victim. The woman's body was still warm, the blood still steaming. This had happened moments ago. While Aleks was here, being beaten.

I turned back, but the ropes that had held him a moment ago were slack, curled on the snow like vipers. In the blink of an eye, all the time it took the murmuring crowd to realize that a man was wrongly accused, Aleks had managed to escape.

Minka

My father trusted me with the details of his death. 'Minka,' he would say, in the hot summer, 'make sure there is lemonade at my funeral. Fresh lemonade for all!' When he dressed up in a borrowed suit for my sister's wedding, my father said, 'Minka, at my funeral, you must be sure I look as dapper as I do today.' This upset my mother to no end. 'Abram Lewin,' she would say, 'you're going to give the girl nightmares.' But my father, he would just wink at me and say, 'She is absolutely right, Minka. And for the record, no opera at my funeral. I hate opera. But dancing, now, that would be nice.'

I was not traumatized by these conversations, as my mother thought. How could I be, knowing my father? He owned a very successful bakery, and I had grown up watching him load loaves into a brick oven in his undershirt, his muscles flexing. He was tall and strong and invincible. The real joke behind the joke was that my father was too full of life to ever die.

After school, I would sit in the shop and do my homework while my older sister, Basia, sold the bread. My father didn't let me work at the cash register, because school was more important to him. He called me his little professor, because I was so smart – I had skipped two grades, and passed a three-day exam last year to get into *Gymnasium*. It had been a shock to find out that even though I qualified, I was not accepted to the school. They only took two Jews that year. My sister, who had always been a little jealous of the premium placed on my intelligence, pretended to be upset, but I knew deep down she was happy that finally I would have to work a trade, just like her. However, one of my father's customers intervened. My father was such an accomplished baker that beyond the challah and the rye and the loaves that every Jewish housewife bought daily, he had special clients who were Christian, who came in for his babka and his poppy-seed cake and mazurek. It was one of these clients, an accountant, who intervened so that I could attend the Catholic high school. During religious hour, I would be excused from class to do my homework in the hall, with the other Jewish girl who attended. Then after school, I would walk to my father's bakery in Łódź . When the shop closed, Basia would go home to her newlywed husband, Rubin, and my father and I would walk through the streets to our house, in a neighborhood mixed with Christians and Jews.

One evening, as we were walking, a phalanx of soldiers marched past us. My father pushed me into the hollow made by a doorframe to let them pass. I did not know if they were SS, or Wehrmacht, or Gestapo; I was a silly girl of fourteen who didn't pay attention to that. All I knew was that they never smiled, and they moved only at right angles. My father started to shield his eyes from the setting sun, and then realized that his gesture looked like a *Heil*, their greeting, so he pulled his arm down to his side. 'At my funeral, Minka,' he said, without a hint of laughter in his voice, 'no parades.'

I was spoiled. My mother, Hana, cleaned my room and did all the cooking. When she wasn't fussing over me, she was needling Basia to make her a grandmother already, even though my sister had only been married for six months to the boy she'd been in love with since she was my age.

I had friends in my neighborhood – one girl, Greta, even went to my school. Sometimes she invited me to her home to play records or listen to the radio, and she was perfectly nice, but in school, if we passed in the hall, she never made eye contact with me. That's just the way it was; Polish Christians did not like Jews, at least not in public. The Szymanskis, who lived in the other half of our building and invited us for Christmas and Easter (when I would stuff myself with non-kosher food), never looked down on us because of our religion, but my mother said that's because Mrs. Szymanski was not a typical Pole, but rather was born in Russia.

My best friend was Darija Horowicz. We had been in school together until I passed the entrance exams, but Darija and I still managed to see each other most every day and fill in all the details we'd missed about each other's lives. Darija's father owned a factory outside the city, and sometimes we would take a horse and buggy out there to have picnics by the lake. There were always boys buzzing around Darija. She was beautiful – a tall and graceful ballet dancer, with long, dark eyelashes and a little bow of a mouth. I was nowhere near as pretty as she was, but I figured the boys who buzzed around Darija couldn't all have her as their girlfriend. There would be some heartbroken fellow left over for me, and maybe he would be so taken with my wit that he wouldn't notice my crooked front tooth or the way my belly pooched out a tiny bit in the front of my skirt.

One day, Darija and I were in my bedroom, working. We had a Grand Plan, and it involved the book that I was writing. Darija was reading it, chapter by chapter, and making corrections with a red pen, which was what we thought an editor would do. We were going to move together to London and live in a flat, and Darija would work at a publishing house and I would write novels. We'd have fancy cocktails and dance with handsome men. 'In our world,' Darija said, throwing aside the chapter she was marking up, 'there will be no semicolons.'

It was one of our favorite pastimes: reimagining a world run by Darija and myself that was perfect – a place where you could eat as many kaiser rolls as you wanted without getting fat; a place where no one took mathematics in school; a place where grammar was an afterthought instead of a necessity. I looked up from the notebook in which I was scribbling. 'Seems indecisive, doesn't it? Either be a period or be a comma, but make up your mind.' The chapter I had been working on for the past hour was only a few sentences long. Nothing was coming to me, and I knew why. I was too tired to be creative. My parents had been fighting last night, and woke me up. I could not hear all of their argument, but it was about Mrs. Szymanski. She had offered to hide my mother and me, if need be, but couldn't take all of us. I didn't understand why my father was so upset. It wasn't as if my mother and I would ever think of leaving him.

'In our world,' I said, 'everyone will have an automobile with a radio.'

Darija flipped onto her belly, her eyes lighting up. 'Don't remind me.' Last week we had seen an automobile pull up to Wodospad, a fancy restaurant where once I had seen a movie star. When the driver got out of the car, we could hear music wafting from the inside, seeping into the air and lingering like perfume. It was a wonder to think about having music with you as you traveled.

On that day I had also noticed a new sign on the restaurant: *Psy i Żydzi nie pozwolone.*

No dogs or Jews allowed.

We had heard stories of Kristallnacht. My mother had a cousin whose shop had been burned to the ground in Germany. One of our neighbors had adopted a boy whose parents had been killed in a pogrom. Rubin kept begging my sister to go to America, but Basia wouldn't leave my parents behind. When she told them that we should move into the Jewish area of the city before things got worse, my father said she was too excitable. My mother pointed to the beautiful wooden buffet table, which must have weighed three hundred pounds and which had belonged to my great-grandmother. 'How can you grab a suitcase and pack up your life?' she asked my sister. 'You'd leave all your memories behind.'

I know Darija was remembering that sign on the restaurant, too, because she said, 'In our world, there will be no Germans.' Then she laughed. 'Ah, poor Minka. You look like you're going to be sick at the very thought. But then, a world without Germans is a world without Herr Bauer.'

I put aside the notebook and inched closer to Darija. 'Today, he called on me three times. I'm the only one he picked more than once to answer a question.'

'That's probably because you raised your hand every time.'

That was true. German was my best subject in school. We had a choice of taking French or German. The French teacher, Madame Genierre, was an old nun with a giant wart on her chin that had hairs growing out of it. On the other hand, the German teacher, Herr Bauer, was a young man who looked a little like the actor Leon Liebgold if you squinted or just daydreamed excessively, as I was wont to do. Sometimes when he leaned over my shoulder to correct gender agreement on my paper, I would fantasize how he might take me in his arms and kiss me and tell me we should run away together. As if that would ever happen between a teacher and a student, or a Christian and a Jew! But he was easy on the eyes, at the very least, and I wanted him to notice me, so I took every class he offered: German Grammar, Conversation, Literature. I was his star pupil. I met with him during lunch, just to practice. *Glauben Sie, dass es regnen wird, Fräulein Lewin?* he would ask. Do you think it's going to rain?

Ach ja, ich denke wir sollten mit schlechtem Wetter rechnen. Oh yes, I think we should expect bad weather.

Sometimes, he would even share a private joke with me in German. *Noch eine weitere langweilige Besprechung!* Yet another boring meeting, he would say in passing, smiling pleasantly, as he marched beside Father Jankowiak down the hall, knowing that the priest could not understand a word he was saying, but that I did.

'Today I made him blush,' I confided, smiling. 'I told him I was writing a poem and asked him how you might say, in German, "He took her in his arms and kissed her breath away." I was hoping maybe he'd *show* me, instead of *tell* me.'

'Ugh.' Darija shuddered. 'The thought of a German kissing me makes my skin crawl.'

'You can't say that. Herr Bauer, he's different. He never talks about the war. He's far too much of a scholar for that. Besides, if you lump them all together because they're German, how does that make you any different from the way they lump us all together just because we're Jews?'

Darija picked up a book from my nightstand. 'Oh, Herr Bauer,' she cooed. 'I'll follow you to the ends of the earth. To Berlin. Oh wait, that's the same thing, isn't it?' She mashed the book up against her face and pretended to kiss it.

I felt a flash of annoyance. Dariya was lovely, with her long neck and her dancer's body. I didn't make fun of her when she strung along several boys at once, who'd flock around her at parties and vie for the honor of getting her some punch or a sweet.

'It's just as well,' she said, tossing the book aside. 'If you start running around with the German professor, you're going to break Josek's heart.'

Now it was my turn to blush. Josek Szapiro was the one boy who didn't look twice at Darija. He'd never asked me to take a walk with him or complimented me on a sweater or how I fixed my hair, but the last time we had gone on a picnic to the lake near the factory, he had spent a whole hour talking to me about my book. He had recently been hired by the *Chronicle* to write and was almost three years older than I was, but he didn't seem to think it was foolish to believe I could one day be published.

'You know,' Darija said, pointing to the pages she had been reading, 'this is really just a love story.'

'So what's wrong with that?'

'Well, a love story, that's no story at all. People don't want a happy ending. They want conflict. They want the heroine to fall for the man she can never have.' She grinned at me. 'I'm just saying that Ania's boring.'

At that, I burst out laughing. 'She's based on you and me!'

'Then maybe *we're* boring.' Darija sat up, crossing her legs. 'Maybe we need to make ourselves more cosmopolitan. After all, I could be the kind of lady who'd drive to a restaurant in a car with a radio.'

I rolled my eyes. 'Right. And I'm the queen of England.'

Darija grabbed my hand. 'Let's do something shocking.'

'Fine,' I replied. 'I won't hand in my German homework tomorrow.'

'No, no. Something *worldly*.' She smiled. 'We could have schnapps at the Grand Hotel.'

I snorted. 'Who is going to serve two little girls?'

'We won't *look* like little girls. Can't you steal something from your mother's closet?'

My mother would kill me if she found out.

'I won't tell her if you don't,' Darija said, reading my mind.

'I won't *have* to tell her.' My mother had a sixth sense. I swear, she must have had eyes in the back of her head, to be able to catch me sneaking a taste of the stew from the pot before dinner was served, or to know when I was working on my story in my bedroom instead of doing my homework. 'When she has nothing else to worry about, she worries about me.'

Suddenly, from the living room, there was a shriek. I scrambled to my feet and ran, Darija at my heels. My father was clapping Rubin on the back, and my mother was embracing Basia. 'Hana!' my father crowed to her. 'This calls for some wine!'

'Minusia,' my mother said, using her pet name for me. She looked happier than I had ever seen her. 'Your sister is having a baby!'

It had been strange when my sister moved out after her wedding, so that I had my own room. It was stranger now to think of her as somebody's mother. I hugged Basia and kissed her on the cheek.

'Oh, there's so much to do!' my mother said.

Basia laughed. 'You have some time, Mama.'

'You can never be too prepared. We'll go out shopping tomorrow for yarn. We must start knitting! Abram, you'll make do without her at the cash register. Which, you know, is not a good job for a woman who's expecting. Standing there all day long with her back hurting and her feet swollen—'

My father exchanged a look with Rubin. 'This could be a vacation,' he joked. 'Maybe for the next five months, she'll be too busy to bother complaining about me . . .'

I glanced at Darija. Who smiled, and raised her brows.

We looked like two children playing dress-up. I was wearing one of my mother's silk dresses and a pair of Darija's mother's pumps, and the kitten heels kept getting stuck between the cobblestones on the street. Darija had done up my face with makeup, which was supposed to make us look older but which made me feel like a painted clown.

The Grand Hotel rose above us like a wedding cake, with tiers upon tiers of windows. I imagined the stories going on behind each one. The two people in silhouette on the second floor were newlyweds. The woman staring out from the third-floor corner suite was remembering her lost love, whom she would meet for coffee later that afternoon, for the first time in twenty years . . .

'So?' Darija asked. 'Aren't we going in?'

As it turned out, it was even more difficult to actually go into the hotel pretending to be someone else than it was to gather enough bravery to walk there in our fancy clothes. 'What if we see someone we know?'

'Who are we going to see?' Darija scoffed. 'The fathers are all getting ready to go for evening prayers. The mothers are home getting dinner ready.'

I glanced at her. 'You first.'

My mother thought I was at Darija's, and Darija's mother thought she was at my house. We could easily get caught, but we were hoping our adventure would compensate for whatever punishment we might incur. As I hesitated, a woman swept up the stairs of the hotel past me. She smelled strongly of perfume and had nails and lips painted fire-engine red. Her clothes were not as fine as those of the clientele of the hotel – or the man she was with, for that matter. She was one of Those Women, the ones my mother pulled me away from. Women of the night were more common in Bałuty, the poorer section of the city – women who looked like they never slept, their shawls wrapped around their bare shoulders as they peeked from their windows. But that didn't mean there was a lack of loose women here. The man walking behind this one had a tiny mustache, like Charlie Chaplin, and a walking cane. As she sailed through the hotel doorway, he cupped his hand on her bottom.

'That's disgusting,' Darija whispered.

'That's what people are going to think we are if we go inside!' I hissed.

Darija pouted. 'If you weren't going to go through with this in the first place, Minka, I don't know why you said—'

'I never said anything! *You* said that you wanted—'

'Minka?' At the sound of my name, I froze. The only thing worse than my mother discovering I was not at Darija's house was someone recognizing me and running back to tell my mother.

Grimacing, I turned around to see Josek, dapper in his coat and tie. 'It *is* you,' he said, smiling, and he didn't even steal a glance at Darija. 'I didn't realize you came here.'

'What's that supposed to mean?' I asked, guarded.

Darija elbowed me. 'Of course we come here. Doesn't everyone?'

Josek laughed. 'Well, I don't know about everyone. The coffee's better elsewhere.'

'What are you doing here?' I asked.

He lifted a notebook. 'An interview. A human interest piece. That's all they let me do, so far. My editor says I have to earn breaking news.' He looked at my dress, pinned in the back because it was too big, and the borrowed shoes on my feet. 'Are you going to a funeral?'

So much for looking sophisticated.

'We're headed out on a double date,' Darija said.

'Really!' Josek replied, surprised. 'I didn't think—' Abruptly, he stopped speaking.

'You didn't think what?'

'That your father would let you go out with a boy,' Josek said.

'Clearly that's not the case.' Darija tossed her hair. 'We're not babies, Josek.'

He grinned at me. 'Then maybe you'd like to come out with *me* sometime, Minka. I'll prove to you that the coffee at Astoria puts the Grand Hotel to shame.'

'Tomorrow at four,' Darija announced, as if she was suddenly my social secretary. 'She'll be there.'

As Josek said his good-byes and walked off, Darija looped her arm through mine. 'I'm going to kill you,' I said.

'Why? Because I got you a date with a handsome boy? For goodness' sake, Minka, if I can't have fun, at least let me live vicariously through you.'

'I don't want to go out with Josek.'

'But Ania needs you to go out with him,' Darija said.

Ania, my character, who was too boring. Too safe.

'You can thank me later,' she said, patting my hand.

Astoria Café was a well-known hangout on Piotrkowska Street. At any given moment, you might find Jewish intellectuals, playwrights, composers arguing the finer points of artistic merit over smoky tables and bitter coffee; or opera divas sipping tea with lemon. Even though I was dressed in the same borrowed outfit I'd worn the day before, being in close quarters with these people made my head swim, as if I might become enlightened simply by breathing the same air.

We were sitting near the swinging doors of the kitchen, and every time they opened, a delicious smell would waft over us. Josek and I were sharing a platter of pierogi, and drinking coffee, which was – as he had promised – heavenly. *'Upiory,'* he said, shaking his head. 'That's not what I expected.'

I had been telling him – shyly – of the plot for my story: of Ania, and her father the baker; of the monster who invades their town by masquerading as a common man. 'My grandmother used to talk about them when she was still alive,' I explained. 'At night, she would leave grain on the wooden table at the bakery, so that if an *upiór* came, he would be forced to count it until the sunrise. If I didn't go to bed when I was supposed to, my grandmother said the *upiór* would come for me and drink my blood.'

'Pretty grisly,' Josek said.

'The thing is, it didn't scare me. I used to feel bad for the *upiór*. I mean, it wasn't *his* fault he was undead. But good luck getting someone to believe that, when there were people like my grandmother running around saying otherwise.' I looked up at Josek. 'So I started to daydream a story about an *upiór*, who may not be as evil as everyone thinks. At least not compared to the human who's trying to destroy him. And certainly not in the eyes of the girl who's starting to fall for him . . . until she realizes he may have killed her own father.'

'Wow,' Josek said, impressed.

I laughed. 'You were expecting a romance, maybe?'

'More than I was expecting a horror story,' he admitted.

'Darija says that I have to tone it down, or no one will ever want to read it.'

'But you don't believe that . . .?'

'No,' I said. 'People have to experience things that terrify them. If they don't, how will they ever come to appreciate safety?'

A slow smile spread across Josek's face. In that moment, he looked handsome. At least as handsome as Herr Bauer, if not more. 'I didn't realize Łódź had the next Janusz Korczak in its midst.'

I fidgeted with my teaspoon. 'So you don't think it's crazy? For a girl to write something like this?'

Josek leaned closer. 'I think it's brilliant. I see what you're doing. It's not just a fairy tale, it's an allegory, right? The *upiory*, they are like Jews. To the general population, they are bloodsuckers, a dark and frightening tribe. They are to be feared and battled with weapons and crosses and Holy Water. And the Reich, which puts itself on the side of God, has commissioned itself to rid the world of monsters. But the *upiory*, they are timeless. No matter what they try to do to us, we Jews have been around too long to be forgotten, or to be vanquished.'

Once, in Herr Bauer's class, I had made an error during an essay and substituted one German word for another. I was writing about the merits of a parochial education, and meant to say *Achtung*, which meant 'attention, respect.' Instead, I used *Ächtung*, which meant 'ostracism.' As you can imagine, it completely changed the point of my essay. Herr Bauer asked me to stay after class to have a discussion about the separation of church and state, and what it was like to be a Jew in a Catholic high school. I wasn't embarrassed at the time, because mostly I didn't even pay attention to what made me different from the other students – and because I got to spend a half hour alone with Herr Bauer, talking as if we were equals. And of course it was a mistake, not a stroke of brilliance, that had led me to make the observation in my paper that Herr Bauer thought was so insightful . . . but I wasn't about to admit to that.

Just like I'm not going to admit to Josek, now, that when I was writing my story I never in a million years was thinking of it as a political statement. In fact, when I imagined Ania and her father, they were Jewish, like me.

'Well,' I said, trying to make light of Josek's explanation. 'Guess I can't put anything past you.'

'You're something else, Minka Lewin,' he said. 'I've never met another girl like you.' He threaded his fingers through mine. Then he lifted my hand and pressed his lips to it, suddenly a courtier.

It was old-world and chivalrous and made me shiver. I tried to remember every sensation, from the way all the colors in the café suddenly seemed brighter to the electric current that danced over my palm like lightning in a summertime field. I wanted to be able to tell Darija every last detail. I wanted to write them into my story.

Before I could finish my mental catalog, though, Josek wrapped his hand around the back of my head, drew me closer, and kissed me.

It was my first kiss. I could feel the pressure of Josek's fingers on my scalp, and the scratchy wool of his sweater under my palm. My heart felt like fireworks must, when after finally being lit, all that gunpowder has somewhere to go.

'So,' Josek said after a moment.

I cleared my throat and looked around at the other patrons.

I expected them all to be staring at us, but no, they were tangled in their own conversations, punctuating the air with gestures that cut through the haze of the cigarette smoke.

I had a brief flashing image of myself and Josek, living abroad, and working together at our kitchen table. There he was, his white shirtsleeves rolled up to the elbows as he furiously typed a story on deadline. There I was, chewing the top end of a pencil as I added the final touches to my first novel.

'Josek Szapiro,' I said, drawing back. 'What's gotten into you?'

He laughed. 'Must be all this talk of monsters and the ladies who love them.'

Darija would tell me to play hard to get. To walk out and make Josek come after me. To Darija, every relationship was a game. Me, I got tired of figuring out all the rules.

Before I could answer, though, the doors of the café burst open and a swarm of SS soldiers exploded into the room. They began to smack the patrons with their truncheons, to overturn chairs with people still in them. Old men who fell to the floor were trampled or kicked; women were thrown against the walls.

I was frozen in place. I had been near SS soldiers when they passed, but never in the middle of an action like this one. The men all seemed to be over six feet tall, hulking brutes in heavy green wool uniforms. They had clenched fists and pale silver eyes that glittered the way mica did. They smelled like hatred.

Josek grabbed me and shoved me behind him through the swinging kitchen doors. 'Run, Minka,' he whispered. 'Run!'

I did not want to leave Josek behind. I grabbed on to his sleeve, trying to pull him with me, but as I did a soldier yanked on his other arm. The last thing I saw, before I turned and sprinted, was the blow that spun Josek in a slow pirouette, the blood running from his temple and broken nose.

The soldiers were dragging out the café patrons and loading them into trucks when I climbed through the window of the kitchen and walked as normally as I could in the opposite direction. When I felt I was a safe distance away, I started to run. I twisted my ankle in the kitten heels, so I kicked them off and kept going barefoot, even though it was October and the soles of my feet were freezing.

I did not stop running, not when I got a stitch in my side or when I had to scatter a group of little beggar children like pigeons; especially not when a woman pushing a cart of vegetables grabbed my arm to ask if I was all right. I ran for a half hour, until I was at my father's bakery. Basia was not at the cash register – shopping with Mama, I assumed – but the bell that hung over the door rang, so that my father would know someone had entered.

He came out from the kitchen, his broad face glistening with sweat from the heat of the brick ovens, his beard dusted with flour. His delight at seeing me faded as he noticed my face – makeup streaked with tears – my bare feet, my hair tumbling out of its pins.

'Minusia,' he cried out. 'What happened?'

Yet I, who fancied myself a writer, couldn't find a single word to describe not only what I had seen but how everything had changed, as if the earth had tilted slightly on its axis, ashamed of the sun, so that now we would have to learn to live in the dark.

With a sob, I threw myself into his arms. I had tried so hard to be a cosmopolitan woman; as it turned out, all I wanted was to stay a little girl.

But I had grown up in an instant.

If the world hadn't been turned inside out that afternoon, I would have been punished. I would have been sent to my room without dinner and barred from seeing Darija or doing anything but my schoolwork for at least a week. Instead, when my mother heard what had happened, she held me tightly and would not let me out of her sight.

Before we walked home, my father's arm tightly anchored around me and his eyes darting around the street as if he expected a threat to leap out of an alley at any minute (and why should he think any differently, after what I had relayed to him?), we went to the office where Josek's father worked as an accountant. My father knew his father from *shul*. 'Chaim,' he said gravely. 'We have news.'

He asked me to tell Josek's father everything – from the time we arrived at the café to the moment I saw a soldier hitting Josek with an iron rod. I watched the blood drain from his father's face, saw his eyes fill with tears. 'They took people away in trucks,' I said. 'I don't know where.'

An internal battle played over the older man's face, as hope struggled with reason. 'You'll see,' my father said gently. 'He'll come back.'

'Yes.' Chaim nodded as if he needed to convince himself. He looked up then, as if he was surprised to see us still standing there. 'I have to go. I must tell my wife.'

When Darija came after dinnertime to find out about my date with Josek, I told my mother to make an excuse and say I wasn't feeling well. It was the truth, after all. That date seemed unrecognizable now, so badly tarnished by the firestorm of events that I couldn't remember what it used to look like.

My father, who picked at the food on his plate that night, went out after the dishes were cleared. I was sitting on my bed, my eyes squeezed shut, conjugating German verbs. *Ich habe Angst. Du hast Angst. Er hat Angst. Wir haben Angst.*

We are afraid. *Wir haben Angst.*

My mother came into my bedroom and sat down beside me. 'Do you think he's alive?' I asked, the one question that no one had spoken out loud.

'Ach, Minusia,' my mother said. 'That imagination of yours.' But her hands were shaking, and she hid this by reaching for the brush on my nightstand. She turned me, gently, so that I was sitting with my back to her, and she began to brush out my hair in long, sweeping strokes, the way she used to when I was little.

What we learned, from information that leaked through the community in tiny staccato bursts, like rapid gunfire, was that the SS had rounded up 150 people from the Astoria that afternoon. They had taken them to headquarters and had interrogated the men and women individually, beating them with iron bars, with rubber clubs. They broke arms and fingers and demanded ransom payments of several hundred marks. Those who didn't have the money with them had to give the names of family members who might. Forty-six people were shot to death by the SS, fifty were freed after payment, and the rest were taken off to a prison in Radogoszcz.

Josek had been one of the lucky ones. Although I hadn't seen him since that afternoon, my father told me he was back home with his family. Chaim, who like my father had Christian clients as well as Jews, had somehow made the arrangements for money to be brought to SS headquarters in exchange for his son's freedom. He told everyone who would listen that if not for the bravery of Minka Lewin, they might not have had such a happy ending.

I had been thinking a lot about happy endings. I had been

thinking about what Josek and I were speaking of, moments before Everything Happened. Of villains, and of heroes. The *upiór* in my story, was he the one who terrorized others? Or was he the one being persecuted?

I was sitting on the steps that led to the second floor of the school building one afternoon while the rest of the students had Religious Studies. Although I was supposed to be crafting an essay, I was writing my story instead. I had just started a scene where an angry mob beats at Ania's door. My pencil could not keep up with my thoughts. I could feel my heart start to pound as I imagined the knock, the splinter of the wood against the weapons the townspeople had brought for the lynching. I could feel sweat breaking out along Ania's spine. I could hear their German accents through the thick cottage door—

But the German accent I heard was actually Herr Bauer's. He sank down beside me on the step, our shoulders nearly bumping. My tongue swelled to four times its normal size; I could not have spoken aloud if my life depended on it. 'Fräulein Lewin,' he said. 'I wanted you to hear the news from me.'

The news? What news?

'Today is my last day here,' he confessed, in German. 'I will be going back to Stuttgart.'

'But . . . why?' I stammered. 'We need you here.'

He smiled, that beautiful smile. 'My country apparently needs me, too.'

'Who will teach us?'

He shrugged. 'Father Czerniski will take over.'

Father Czerniski was a drunk, and I had no doubt the only German he knew was the word *Lager*. But I didn't need to say this out loud, Herr Bauer was thinking the same thing.

'You will continue to study on your own,' he insisted fiercely. 'You will continue to excel.' Then Herr Bauer met my gaze, and for the first time in our acquaintance, he spoke Polish to me. 'It has been an honor and a privilege to teach you,' he said.

After he walked downstairs, I ran to the girls' bathroom and burst into tears. I cried for Herr Bauer, and for Josek, and for me. I cried because I would not be able to lose myself daydreaming about Herr Bauer anymore, which meant more time would be spent in reality. I cried because when I remembered my first kiss, I felt sick to my stomach. I cried because my world had become a raging ocean and I was drowning. Even after I splashed my face with cold water, my eyes were still red and puffy. When Father Jarmyk asked if I was all right during math, I told him that we had received sad news the previous night about a cousin in Kraków.

These days, no one would question that kind of response.

When I left school that afternoon, headed directly to the bakery as usual, I thought I was seeing an apparition. Leaning on a lamppost across the street was Josek Szapiro. I gasped, and ran to him. When I got closer, I could see the skin around his eyes was yellow and purple, all the jewel tones of a fading bruise; that he had a healing cut through the middle of his left eyebrow. I reached up to touch his face, but he caught my hand. One of his fingers was splinted. 'Careful,' he said. 'It's still tender.'

'What did they do to you?'

He pulled my hand down. 'Not here,' he warned, looking around at the busy pedestrians.

Still holding my hand, he tugged me away from the school. To anyone passing by, we might have looked like an ordinary couple. But I knew from the way Josek was holding on to me – tightly, as if he were drowning in quicksand and needed to be rescued – that this wasn't the case.

I followed him blindly through a street market, past the fishmonger and the vegetable cart, into a narrow alley that ran between two buildings. When I slipped on cabbage rinds, he anchored me to his side. I could feel the heat of his arm around me. It felt like hope.

He didn't stop until we had navigated a rabbit warren of cobbled pathways, until we were behind the service entrance of a building I did not even recognize. Whatever Josek wanted to say to me, I hoped that it didn't involve leaving me here alone to find my way back.

'I was so worried about you,' he said finally. 'I didn't know if you'd gotten away.'

'I'm much tougher than I look,' I replied, raising my chin.

'And as it turns out,' Josek said quietly, 'I'm *not*. They beat me, Minka. They broke my finger to get me to tell them who my father was. I didn't want them to know. I thought they would go after him, and hurt him, too. But instead they took his money.'

'Why?' I asked. 'What did you ever do to them?'

Josek looked down at me. 'I *exist*,' he said softly.

I bit my lip. I felt like crying again, but I didn't want to do it in front of Josek. 'I'm so sorry this happened to you.'

'I came to give you something,' Josek said. 'My family leaves for St. Petersburg next week. My mother has an aunt who lives there.'

'But . . .' I said stupidly, wanting only to unhear the words he had just spoken. 'What about your job?'

'There are newspapers in Russia.' He smiled, just a little bit. 'Maybe one day I will even be reading your *upiór* story in one.' He reached into his pocket. 'Things are going to get worse here before they get better. My father, he has business acquaintances. Friends who are willing to do favors for him. We are traveling to St. Petersburg with Christian papers.'

My eyes flew to his face. If you had Christian papers, you could go anywhere. You had the so-called proper documents to prove that you were Aryan. This meant a free pass from all restrictions, roundups, deportations.

If Josek had had those papers a week ago, he would never have been beaten by the SS. Then again, he would never have been at Astoria Café, either.

'My father wanted to make sure that what happened to me never will happen again.' Solemnly, Josek unfolded the documents. They were, I realized, not for a boy his age. They were instead for a teenage girl. 'You saved my life. Now it's my turn to save yours.'

I backed away from the papers, as if they might burst into flame.

'He couldn't get enough for your whole family,' Josek explained. 'But, Minka . . . you could come with us. We would say you're my cousin. My parents will take care of you.'

I shook my head. 'How could I become part of *your* family, knowing I had left mine behind?'

Josek nodded. 'I thought you would say that. But take them. One day, you may change your mind.'

He pressed the papers into my hand, and closed my fingers around them. Then he pulled me into his arms. The papers were caught between our bodies, a wedge to drive us apart, like any other lie. 'Be well, Minka,' Josek said, and he kissed me again. This time, his mouth was angry against mine, as if he were communicating in a language I hadn't learned.

* * *

An hour later, I was in the steamy belly of my father's bakery, eating the roll he made for me every day, with the special twisted crown on the top and a center of chocolate and cinnamon. At this time of day, we were alone; his employees came in before dawn to bake and left at midday. My legs were hooked around the stool where I sat, watching my father shape loaves. He set them to proof inside the floured folds of a baker's couche, patting the round, dimpled rise of each one, supple as a baby's bottom. Inside my brassiere, the edges of my Christian papers seared my skin. I imagined getting undressed that night, finding the name of some *goyishe* girl tattooed over my breast.

'Josek's family is leaving,' I announced.

My father's hands, which were always moving, stilled over the dough. 'When did you see him?'

'Today. After school. He wanted to say good-bye.'

My father nodded and pulled another clot of dough into a small rectangle.

'Are we going to leave town?' I asked.

'If we did, Minusia,' my father said, 'who would feed everyone else?'

'It's more important that we're safe. Especially with Basia having a baby.'

My father slammed his hand down on the butcher block, creating a small storm of flour. 'Do you think I cannot keep my own family safe?' he bellowed. 'Do you think that's not important to me?'

'No, Papa,' I whispered.

He walked around the counter and gripped my shoulders. 'Listen to me,' he said. 'Family is everything to me. *You* are everything to me. I would tear this bakery down brick by brick with my own hands if it meant you wouldn't be harmed.'

I had never seen him like this. My father, who was always so sure of himself, always ready with a joke to diffuse the most difficult situation, was barely holding himself together. 'Your name, Minka. Short for Wilhelmina. You know what it means? *Chosen protection*. I will *always* choose to protect *you*.' He looked at me for a long moment, and then sighed. 'I was going to save these for a Chanukah gift, but I'm thinking maybe now is the time for a present.'

I sat while he disappeared into the back room where he kept the records of shipments of grain and salt and butter. He returned with a burlap sack, its drawstring pulled tight as a spinster's mouth. '*A Freilichen Chanukah*,' he said. 'A couple of months early, anyway.'

With impatient hands I yanked at the knots to untie the package. The burlap pooled around a shiny pair of black boots.

They were new, which was a big deal. But they were nothing fancy, nothing that would make a girl rhapsodize over their fashionable stitching or style. 'Thank you,' I said, forcing a smile and hugging my father around the neck.

'These are one of a kind. No one else has a pair like them. You must promise me to wear these boots at all times. Even when you are sleeping. You understand, Minka?' He took one from my lap and reached for the knife he used to hack off bits of dough from the massive amoeba on the counter. Inserting the tip into a groove at the heel, he twisted, and the bottom of the sole snapped off. At first, I could not understand why he was ruining my new present; then I realized that inside this hidden compartment were several gold coins. A fortune.

'No one knows they are in there,' my father said, 'except you and me.'

I thought of Josek's broken hand, of the SS soldiers

demanding money from him. This was my father's insurance policy.

He showed me how both heels opened, then fitted each back to the boot and whacked them a few times on the counter. 'Good as new,' he said, and he handed the boots to me again. 'And I mean it – I want you to wear them everywhere. Every day. When it's cold, when it's hot. When you're going to the market or when you're going dancing.' He grinned at me. 'Minka, make a note: I want to see you wearing them at my funeral.'

I smiled back, relieved to be settled on familiar ground. 'That may be a little tricky for you, don't you think?'

He laughed, then, the big belly laugh that I always thought of when I thought of my father. With my new boots cradled in my lap, I considered the secret we now shared, and the one we didn't. I never told my father about my Christian papers; not then, not ever. Mostly because I knew he would force me to use them.

As I finished the roll my father had baked just for me, I looked down at my blue sweater. On my shoulders, there was a dusting of flour that he had left behind when he grabbed me. I tried to brush it off, but it was no use. No matter what, I could see the faint handprints, as if I had been warned by a ghost.

In November, there were changes. My father came home one day with yellow stars, which we were to wear on our clothing at all times. Łódź, our town, was being called Litzmannstadt by the German soldiers who overran it. More and more Jewish families were moving into the Old Town, or Bałuty, some by choice, and some because the authorities had decided that the apartments and houses they had owned or rented for years should now be reserved for ethnic Germans. There were streets in town that we could no longer walk down but instead had to take circuitous routes or bridges. We were not allowed to use public transportation or to leave home after dark. My sister's pregnancy became visible. Darija went on a few dates with a boy named Dawid, and all of a sudden she thought she knew everything there was to know about love stories.

'If you don't like what I'm writing,' I said one day, 'then why don't you stop reading it?'

'It's not that I don't like it,' Darija replied. 'I'm just trying to help you with realism.'

Realism, to Dariya, meant reliving her moments of passion with Dawid so that my character, Ania, could have just as romantic a kiss. From the way Darija talked, you'd think Dawid was a combination of the *Green Fields* actor Michael Goldstein and the Messiah.

'Have you heard from Josek?' she asked.

She wasn't saying it to be mean, but Darija must have realized that the odds of me getting mail were very slim. The post did not come and go with any regularity anymore. I preferred to think that Josek had written me often, maybe even two or three times a day, and that these missives were piling up somewhere at a dead letter office.

'Well,' she said when I shook my head. 'I'm sure he's just really busy.'

We were at the studio where Darija practiced ballet three times a week. She was good – at least as proficient in her craft as I was in my writing. She used to talk about joining a dance company, but these days, no one talked about the future. I watched her pull on her jacket with its yellow star on the front shoulder and back, and wrap a scarf around her neck. 'The bit you wrote about consuming an *upiór's* blood,' she said. 'Did you make that up?'

I shook my head. 'My grandmother used to tell me that.'

Darija shuddered. 'It's creepy.'

'Good creepy or bad creepy?'

She linked her arm through mine. 'Good creepy,' she said. 'People-will-want-to-read-it creepy.'

I smiled. This was the Darija I knew, the Darija I missed because she was usually too busy fawning over her new boyfriend. 'Maybe tonight we can stay over together at my place,' I suggested as we walked out of the building, knowing that she was probably planning to go on a date with Dawid. There was a barrage of soldiers passing as we exited, and instinctively we ducked our heads. Once, when soldiers passed, I used to feel a cold ache in the pit of my stomach. Now, it was so commonplace I didn't even notice.

There was a buzz in the street; from a distance we could hear screams. 'What's happening?' I asked, but Darija was already moving in that direction.

In one of the squares three men were hanging from gallows so new I could still smell the sap of the trees their timber had come from. A group of people had gathered; at the front of the crowd, a woman was weeping and trying to get to one of the dead men, but the soldiers wouldn't let her. 'What did they do?' Darija asked.

An elderly lady beside her replied. 'Criticized Germans here in the city.'

The soldiers began to move through the crowd, telling people to go home. Somehow, Darija got separated from me. I heard her calling my name, but I worked my way forward until I was standing at the edge of the gallows. The soldiers didn't pay attention to me; they were too busy dragging away the family of the deceased.

This was the closest I had ever come to someone dead. At my grandmother's funeral, I was little, and all I remember is the coffin. The man who was now twisting like a leaf on an autumn tree looked like he was asleep. His neck was snapped at a strange angle, and his eyes were closed. His tongue protruded a little. There was a dark shadow in his pants, where he must have urinated. *Before or after?* I wondered.

I thought of all the blood and guts in the horror story I was writing, of the *upiór* eating the heart of a victim, and realized that none of it mattered. The shock value was not in the gore. It was in the fact that a minute ago, this man was alive, and now, he wasn't.

That afternoon when my father and I walked past the gallows, he tried to distract me with conversation about our neighbors, about the bakery, about the weather, as if I did not notice the stiff forms of the men behind me.

My parents argued that night. My mother said I should not be walking around town anymore. My father said that was impossible; how would I go to school? I fell asleep to their angry voices and had a nightmare. Darija and I were at the hanging, but this time, when I got closer to the body and it slowly rotated toward me so that I could see the face, it was Josek's.

The next morning I ran to Darija's home. When her mother let me in, I was dumbfounded – the house, which was usually neat as a pin, was in total disarray. 'It's time,' Darija's mother told me. 'We're going to the Old Town, where it's safer.'

I did not believe it was safer in the Old Town. I didn't think it would be safer until the British started winning the war.

After all, they'd never lost one, so I knew it would only be a matter of time before Hitler and his Third Reich were conquered. 'She is very upset, Minka,' Darija's mother confided. 'Maybe you will be able to cheer her up.'

Music from Tchaikovsky's *Sleeping Beauty* seeped from beneath the closed door of Darija's room. When I walked inside, I saw that her rug had been rolled up, the way she sometimes did when she danced. But she wasn't dancing. She was sitting on the floor cross-legged, crying.

I cleared my throat. 'I need your help. I'm totally stuck on page fifty-six.'

Darija didn't even look at me.

'It's this part where Ania goes to Aleksander's home,' I said, frantically making it up as I went. 'Something has to upset her. I just don't know what it is.' I glanced at Darija. 'At first I thought it was Aleksander with another woman, but I don't think that's it at all.'

I did not think Darija was listening, but then she sighed. 'Read it to me.'

So I did. Although there was nothing written on the page, I pulled word after word from my core, like silk for a spider's web, spinning a make-believe life. That's why we read fiction, isn't it? To remind us that whatever we suffer, we're not the only ones?

'Death,' Darija said when I was finished, when the last sentence hovered like a cliff. 'She needs to see someone die.'

'Why?'

'Because what else would scare her more?' Darija asked, and I knew she wasn't talking about my story any longer.

I took a pencil out of my pocket and made notes. 'Death,' I repeated. I smiled at my best friend. 'What would I do without you?'

That, I realized too late, was exactly the wrong thing to say. Darija burst into tears. 'I don't want to leave.'

I sat down beside her and hugged her tight. 'I don't *want* you to leave,' I agreed.

'I'll never get to see Dawid,' she sobbed. 'Or you.'

She was so upset, I didn't even get jealous about being the second party in that sentence. 'You're just going across town. Not to Siberia.'

But I knew that meant nothing. Every day, a new wall appeared, a fence, a detour. Every day the buffer zone between the Germans in this city and the Jews grew thicker and thicker. Eventually, it would force us into the Old Town, like Darija's family, or it would shove us out of Łódź completely.

'This isn't the way it was supposed to happen,' Darija said. 'We were supposed to go to university and then move to London.'

'Maybe we will one day,' I replied.

'And maybe we'll be hanged like those men.'

'Darija! Don't say that!'

'You can't tell me you haven't thought about it,' she accused, and she was right, of course. Why them, when everyone had spoken badly of the Germans? Were they louder than the rest of us? Or were they just picked at random to make a point?

On Darija's bed were two boxes, a ball of twine, and a knife for cutting it. I grabbed the knife and sliced the fleshy center of my palm. 'Best friends forever,' I vowed, and I handed her the knife.

Without hesitation, she cut her own palm. 'Best friends,' she said. We pressed our hands together, a promise sealed in blood. I knew it didn't work this way, because I had studied biology at *Gymnasium*, but I liked the thought of Darija's blood running through my veins. It made it easier to believe I was keeping a piece of her with me.

Two days later, Darija's family joined the long line of Jewish families snaking out of this part of town toward Bałuty with as many possessions as they could haul. On that same day, the men who had been hanged were finally allowed to be cut down. This was clearly meant as an insult, since burial in our religion was meant to happen as quickly as possible. During that forty-eight-hour stretch, I passed the gallows six times – going to the bakery, to Darija's, to school. After the first two times, I stopped noticing. It was as if death had become part of the landscape.

My nephew, Majer Kaminski, was a *shayna punim*. It was March 1940, and he was six weeks old, and already he smiled back if you smiled at him; he could hold up the weight of his own head. He had blue eyes and jet hair and a gummy grin that, my father used to say, could melt even Hitler's black heart.

Never had a baby been so beloved – by Basia and Rubin, who gazed at him like he was a miracle every time they passed by his bassinet; and by my father, who was already trying to teach him recipes; and by myself, who made up nonsense lyrics to lullabies for him. Only my mother was distant. Sure, she *kvelled* about her grandson and she cooed at him when Basia and Rubin brought him to visit, but she rarely held Majer. If Basia passed him into her arms, my mother would find an excuse to put him down, or to shuffle him to me or my father instead.

It didn't make any sense to me. She had wanted to be a grandmother forever, and now that she was one, she couldn't even bear to cuddle her grandchild?

My mother always saved the best food for Friday nights, because my sister and Rubin came for Shabbat dinner. There were usually potatoes and root vegetables in our rations, but tonight, somehow, my mother had purchased a chicken – a food we had not seen in months, since Germany occupied the country. There were black markets all over the town where you could get just about anything, for a price; the question was, what had she traded in return for this feast?

I was salivating so badly, though, I almost didn't care. I fidgeted during the prayer over the candles and the Kiddush over the wine and the *Ha-motzi* over my father's delicious challah, and then finally it was time to sit down and eat. 'Hana,' my father sighed, biting into the first bite of the chicken, 'you are truly a marvel.'

At first none of us spoke, we were that occupied with the delicious food. But then, Rubin interrupted the silence. 'Herschel Berkowicz, who works with me? He was ordered to leave his home last week.'

'Did he go?' my mother asked.

'No . . .'

'And?' my father said, his fork paused en route to his mouth.

Rubin shrugged. 'Nothing so far.'

'You see? Hana, I was right. I'm always right. You refuse to move, and the sky doesn't fall on your head. Nothing happens.' On February 8, the chief of police had listed streets where Jews were allowed to live and posted a calendar citing when the rest were supposed to leave. Although at this point, everyone knew a family that had gone east to Russia or into the area of the town allotted for Jews, others – like my father – were resistant to leave. 'What can they do?' he said, shrugging. 'Kick us *all* out?' He patted his mouth with his napkin. 'Now. I will not let this glorious meal be ruined with talk of politics. Minka, tell Rubin what you were telling me about mustard gas the other day . . .'

It was something I had learned in chemistry class. The reason mustard gas worked was that it was made in part of chlorine, which had such a tight atomic structure that it sucked electrons in from whatever it came in contact with. Including human lungs. It literally ripped apart the cells of your body.

'This is what passes for dinner conversation now?' my mother sighed. She turned to Basia, who was cradling Majer in her left arm. 'How's my angel sleeping? Through the night yet?'

Suddenly there was a pounding at the door. 'You're expecting someone?' my mother asked, looking at my father as she went to answer it. Before she could reach the door, however, it flew open and three soldiers burst into the parlor. 'Get out,' one of the officers said in German. 'You have five minutes!'

'Minka,' my mother cried. 'What do they want?'

So I translated, my heart pounding. Basia was hiding in the corner, trying to make the baby invisible. They were Wehrmacht soldiers. One of them swept the crystal off my great-grandmother's oak server, so that it shattered on the floor. Another overturned the table, with all our food on it, the candles still burning. Rubin stamped out the flames before they could spread.

'Go!' the officer shouted. 'What are you waiting for?'

My father, my brave, strong father, cowered with his hands over his head.

'Outside in five minutes. Or we come back in and start to shoot,' the officer said, and he and his comrades stormed out of our apartment.

I didn't translate that part.

My mother was the one who moved first. 'Abram, get your

mother's silver from the server. Minka, you take pillowcases and go around and collect anything that has value. Basia, Rubin, how fast can you go home and gather your things? I'll stay with the baby until you get back.'

It was the call to action that we needed. My father began rummaging through the drawers of the server, and then he started to move books from shelves and reach into jars in the kitchen cabinets, collecting money that I had not known was hidden there. My mother settled Majer in his bassinet although he was screaming, and began to collect winter coats and woolen scarves, hats, and mittens, warm clothing. I flew into my parents' bedroom and took my mother's jewelry, my father's tefillin and tallith. In my own room, I looked around. What would you grab, if you had to pack up your life in only minutes? I took the newest dress I owned and its matching coat, the one I had worn for the High Holy Days last fall. I took several changes of underwear and a toothbrush. I took my notebook, of course, and a stash of pencils and pens. I took a copy of *The Diary of a Lost Girl* by Margarete Böhme, in its original German – a novel I had found at a secondhand store and had hidden from my parents because of its racy subject matter. I took an exam upon which Herr Bauer had written 'Exceptional Student' in German.

I took the Christian papers Josek had given me, hidden inside the boots my father had made me promise to wear at all times.

I found my mother standing in the center of the dining room, surrounded by the broken crystal. She was holding Majer in her arms and whispering to him. 'I prayed you'd be a girl,' she said.

'Mama?' I murmured.

When she looked up at me, she was crying. 'Mrs. Szymanski, she would have raised a little girl like her own.'

I felt like my mind was filled with mud. She wanted to give Majer, *our* Majer, away to be raised by someone other than Basia and Rubin? Was that why she'd agreed to watch the baby while they ran home to pack? Yes, I realized, in a moment of painful clarity – because it was the way to keep him safe. It was why families had shipped their children to England and the United States. It was why Josek's family thought I should go with them to St. Petersburg. With survival comes sacrifice.

I looked down at Majer's tiny face, his waving hands. 'Then give him to her, right now,' I urged. 'I won't tell Basia.'

She shook her head. 'Minka, he's a boy.'

For a moment I just blinked at her, and then I realized what my mother was talking about. Majer, of course, had had his *bris*. He was circumcised. If the Szymanskis told authorities their little girl was Christian, there would be no way to prove otherwise. But a little boy – well, all you had to do was open his diaper.

I realized, too, why my mother had not wanted to cuddle her grandson. Deep down she knew she should not become attached, in case she lost him.

My father appeared, a rucksack on his back and pillowcases stuffed to the breaking point in each hand. 'We must go,' he said, but my mother did not budge.

I could hear screams as the soldiers worked their way through the homes of our neighbors. My mother flinched. 'Let's wait downstairs for Basia,' I suggested. Only then did I notice her watch was missing. It was what she had traded for the chicken, I guessed – the chicken, which now lay unfinished on the floor of the dining room; the meal she had cooked to give the rest of her family the illusion that everything was going to be just fine. 'Mama,' I said gently. 'Come with me.'

It was the first time I remember acting like the grown-up, being the one to take my mother's hand, instead of the other way around.

My father had a cousin who lived in Bałuty, and in this we were lucky. People who were evicted and who knew no one had to get assigned a room by the authorities. The authorities, in the case of the Jewish ghetto, were the *Judenrat*, which was headed by one man – Chaim Rumkowski, the Chairman, the Eldest of the Jews. My mother had never liked my father's cousins; they were poor and lower-class, and in this they were an embarrassment to her. When they came to our home for my sister's wedding dinner, my cousin Rivka kept holding things up to the light as if she were an appraiser, saying, *And how much do you think* this *cost?* My mother had huffed and muttered and made my father swear that she would not have to suffer their company again in her own home. It was ironic, then, to find ourselves on their doorstep in the position of beggars; to see my mother with her mouth pinched shut, at the mercy of their good graces.

In the four square kilometers that the Germans had decreed to be the Jewish part of town there were 160,000 people. Four or five families crowded into apartments meant for one. One-half of these homes had a bathroom. We were in one of them, and for this, I gave thanks every day.

The ghetto was surrounded by a fence made of wood and barbed wire. A month after we arrived, it was completely sealed off from the rest of Łódź . There were *Fabriken*, factories – some in warehouses but many in bedrooms and basements – where people worked, making boots, uniforms, gloves, textiles, furs. It had been Chairman Rumkowski's idea to become indispensable to the Germans – to be such a useful group of workers that they would come to see how badly they needed us. In return for our making what they needed for the war effort, they would pay us in food.

My father got a job baking bread for the ghetto. Mordechai Lajzerowicz was the head of the ghetto bakeries, and he reported to Chairman Rumkowski. There were times when no flour or grains came in a shipment, and there weren't enough ingredients to bake. My father didn't hire his own bakers; they were assigned by Rumkowski. The loudspeakers that blared all day in German in the squares would tell people who needed work to assemble every morning, and they would be directed to this *Fabrik* or another. My mother, who had not worked while I was growing up, now got a job as a seamstress in a fur shop. Until then, I hadn't even known that she could hem – we'd taken our clothes to a tailor in the past. In only a few weeks' time, my mother had calluses on her fingers from needle sticks, and she started to squint from the poor light in the factory. We split the food she received in payment with Basia and Rubin, because Basia had to stay home with the baby.

Except for the fact that my mother, father, and I all shared a tiny room now, I did not mind living in the ghetto. I had more time to write my story. I got to go to school with Darija again, at least at first, until they closed all the schools. In the afternoons we would go to the apartment she shared with two other families, none of whom had children, and we'd play card games. Often, because of the curfew, I would stay over at Darija's. Being in the ghetto sometimes felt like we were living in a cage, but it was a wonderful cage, if you were fifteen years old. My friends and family surrounded me. It felt safe.

I believed that if I stayed where I was supposed to be, I'd be protected.

In the late summer, when there was no bread in the ghetto because no flour had been brought in, my father became frantic – he considered it his personal responsibility to feed his neighbors. Thousands of people marched in the streets while my father pulled the shades down at the bakery and hid in the back, afraid of the mob. *We are hungry!* The chant swelled in the heat, like dough rising. The German police shot into the air to disperse everyone.

There was more and more shooting as people kept pouring into the ghetto, but its boundaries remained fixed. Where were they all supposed to go? What were they supposed to eat? Although by the winter there was full-scale rationing, there was never enough. Every two weeks, we each got 100 grams of potatoes, 350 grams of beets, 300 grams of rye flour, 60 grams of peas, 100 grams of rye flakes, 150 grams of sugar, 200 grams of marmalade, 150 grams of butter, and 2500 grams of rye bread. Working in a bakery, my father got an extra portion of bread during the day, which he always saved for me.

Of course, he could no longer bake me my special roll.

In the winter, the bakery closed down again. This time, it wasn't because they ran out of flour but because there was no fuel. No wood had been supplied to the ghetto, and only a little coal. My father and his cousin and Rubin took apart fences and ruined buildings and carried the wood back home so that we would have something to burn. One morning, I found my cousin Rivka tearing up floorboards in a closet. 'Who needs a floor in a pantry,' she said, when she saw me watching.

Yet even with all these extreme measures, people were

freezing to death at night in their homes. The *Chronicle*, the newspaper that detailed everything that happened in the ghetto, reported on the casualties every day.

Suddenly being here didn't seem so safe anymore.

One afternoon Darija and I were walking to her home from school. It was frigid, and a wind whipped out of the north that made it even colder than the thermometer suggested. We huddled with our arms linked as we crossed the bridge at Zgierska Street, which Jews were not allowed to walk down anymore. A trolley was passing, and standing on the platform of the car was a woman in a long fur coat, her legs in silk stockings. 'Who would be stupid enough to wear silk stockings on a day like today?' I murmured, thankful for the woolen leggings I had on, double layers. When we had scrambled to leave our home, I had taken silly things like party dresses and colored pencils, but my parents had had the foresight to take our winter coats and sweaters. Unlike some of the others in the ghetto, we at least had warm clothing to weather this horrible winter.

Darija didn't answer; I saw her staring at the woman as the trolley passed. 'If I had them,' she said, 'I'd wear them. Just because.'

I squeezed her arm. 'Someday we'll both wear silk stockings.'

When we reached Darija's apartment, it was empty; everyone else was still at work. 'It's freezing in here,' Darija said, rubbing her hands together. Neither of us bothered to take off our coats.

'I know,' I said. 'I can't feel my toes.'

'I have an idea to warm us up.' Darija dumped her book bag on the floor and turned on the record player. Instead of putting on popular music, though, she found one of her old classical records. She started to dance, slowly at first, so that I could follow along. I laughed as I tried; I was clumsy on a good day, and here I was trying to be graceful in my winter coat and many layers? Impossible. Eventually I collapsed to the floor. 'I'll leave the dancing to you,' I told Darija, but it had worked; I was winded and my cheeks were pink and warm. Instead, I took out my notebook and read over the pages I had written last night.

My book was taking a turn, now that I had been relocated to the ghetto. Suddenly, the charming little village I had created was more sinister – a prison. I had lost sight of who was a hero and who was a villain; the dire circumstances in which I had set my story made everyone a little bit of both. The most detailed descriptions were of the smell of the bread in Ania's father's bakery. Sometimes when I wrote about smearing a slice with fresh butter, I found myself salivating. I could not conjure food for myself, and had not had anything but watery soup for months – but I could imagine so vividly what I was missing that my belly ached.

The other thing I could write about now was blood. God knows I had seen enough of it. In the few months I had been here, I had seen three people shot by German soldiers. One was standing too close to the ghetto fence, so a guard shot him. Two were women, fighting noisily over a loaf of bread. The officer who approached to stop the argument shot them both, took the bread, and threw it into a puddle of mud.

Here's what I now knew about blood: it was brighter than you would imagine, the color of the deepest rubies, until it dried sticky and black.

It smelled like sugar and metal.

It was impossible to get out of your clothes.

I had come to see, too, that all my characters and I were

motivated by the same inspiration. Whether it was power they sought, or revenge, or love – well, those were all just different forms of hunger. The bigger the hole inside you, the more desperate you became to fill it.

As I wrote, Darija kept dancing. Turning, whipping her head at the last possible moment, in a circle of *chaînés* and *piqué* turns. She looked like she might be able to bore a hole through the floor with the chisel made by her feet. As she moved with dizzying speed, I put down my notebook and started to clap. That was when I noticed the policeman peering through the window.

'Darija!' I hissed, slipping my notebook underneath my sweater. I jerked my head in the direction of the window, and her eyes grew wide.

'What should we do?' she asked.

There were two police forces in the ghetto – one made of Jews, who wore the Star of David like the rest of us, and the German police. Although they both enforced the rules, which was a challenge because the rules changed daily, there were significant differences between them. When we passed German policemen on the street, we would bow our heads; and boys would remove their hats. Otherwise, we had no contact with them.

'Maybe he'll go away,' I said, averting my eyes, but the German rapped on the windowpane and pointed to the door.

I opened it, my heart pounding so loud that I thought for certain he could hear it.

The officer was young and slight like Herr Bauer, and if not for the fact that he was wearing a dark uniform I had learned to be terrified of, Darija and I might even have giggled behind our hands about how handsome he was. 'What are you doing in here?' he demanded.

I answered him in German. 'My friend is a dancer.'

He raised his eyebrows, surprised to hear me speaking his language. 'I can see that.'

I didn't know if there was maybe a new law that we couldn't dance here in the ghetto. Or if Darija had unwittingly offended the soldier by playing the music loud enough to be heard through the windows, or because he didn't like ballet. Or if he was just in the mood to hurt someone. I had seen soldiers kick elderly men on the street as they passed, simply because they could. In that moment I wished desperately for my father, who always had a ready smile and something new from his oven that he could use to distract the soldiers who sometimes came into the bakery to ask too many questions.

The soldier reached into his pocket, and I screamed. I threw my arms around Darija and pulled her down to the floor with me. I knew he was reaching for his gun, and I was going to die.

Without ever having fallen in love, or finished my book, or studied at university, or held my own baby in my arms.

But there was no gunshot; instead the soldier cleared his throat. When I was brave enough to squint up at him, I saw that he was holding out a business card. Tiny and cream-colored, it said: ERICH SCHÄFER, STUTTGART BALLET. 'I was the artistic director there before the occupation,' he said. 'If your friend would like to come to me for pointers, I would be happy to provide some.' He inclined his head and left, closing the door behind him.

Darija, who hadn't understood a word he'd said in German, took the card from my hand. 'What did he want from me?'

'To give you dance lessons.'

Her eyes widened. 'You're kidding me.'

'No. He used to work for the Stuttgart Ballet.'

Darija leaped to her feet and did a turn around the room, smiling so wide that I fell into the chasm of her happiness. But then, just as quickly, the light in her eyes burned hotter, angrier. 'So I am good enough for lessons, but not good enough to walk down Zgierska Street?'

She ripped the business card in half and tossed it into the belly of the woodstove. 'At least it is something to burn,' Darija said.

In retrospect, it's amazing that Majer – my little nephew – did not get sick before. With my sister and Rubin and six other couples in a tiny apartment, there was always someone coughing or sneezing or running a fever. Majer, though, had been sturdy and adaptable, happy to be carried by Basia or, when he was old enough, to be in a day-care center while she worked in a textile factory. This week, though, Basia had come to my mother, frantic. Majer was coughing. He was running a fever. Last night, he had not been able to catch his breath, and his lips had turned blue.

It was late February 1941. My mother and Basia had stayed up all night with Majer, taking turns holding him. They both had to go to work, though, or risk losing their jobs. With hundreds of people streaming into the ghetto daily from other countries, a worker was easily replaceable. Some people were being sent to work outside the ghetto. We didn't want to risk breaking our family apart.

Because Majer was sick, my father planned to send Rubin home from the bakery early. This was a big deal for several reasons – the most important ones being that my father did not really have the authority to do that; and that it meant one less man to transport the loaded bread cart to the distribution point storehouse at 4 Jakuba Street. 'Minka,' my father announced that morning. 'You will come at noon, and you will take Rubin's place.'

There were no schools anymore, so I had a job, too, as a delivery girl for a leather goods factory that produced and repaired shoes, boots, belts, and holsters. Darija worked there with me; we were sent all over the ghetto on various errands or to make deliveries. It was believed that perhaps I might not be missed if I slipped away, or that if I was, Darija could cover for me for the afternoon. Secretly, I knew my father was thrilled to have me in his bakery. Rubin was not a baker by trade; he had been assigned to work with my father simply because they had been standing in line together to seek employment. Although it did not take an advanced university degree to bake bread, there was definitely an art to it – one that my father used to say I had in spades. I knew instinctively how much bread to pinch from the amorphous mass of dough in order to make a batard that was exactly thirteen inches long. I could braid six strands of challah in my sleep. But Rubin, he was constantly messing up – mixing a dough that was too wet or too dry, daydreaming when he should have been using the peel to move the loaves in the brick oven before the bottom crusts burned.

After running a midday errand, I slipped off to the bakery instead of returning to the shoe factory. I happened to catch sight of myself in the plate-glass window of a *Fabrik* where textiles were manufactured. At first I averted my eyes – that's what I did when I passed people on the street, mostly. It was just too sad to look at others, to see your own pain written across their faces. But then I realized that it was just my reflection – and yet, oddly unfamiliar. The chubby cheeks and baby fat I'd carried around last year were gone. My cheekbones were sharp and angular, my eyes huge in my face. My hair, which had once been my pride and joy – long and thick – was matted and dry, hidden underneath my wool cap. I was skinny enough to be a ballerina, like Darija.

I wondered how I hadn't noticed the weight slipping off me or for that matter, anyone else in my family. We were all starving, all the time. Even with our extra bread ration, there was never enough food, and what there was was spoiled, rotten, or rancid. As I walked into the bakery I spied my father, stripped to his undershirt in front of the brick ovens, sweating in the blistering heat. His muscles were no longer beefy, just striated like rope. His belly was flat, his cheeks hollow. And yet, to me, he still seemed a commanding presence in the room as he shouted directions to his workers and simultaneously shaped dough to rest on a plank. 'Minusia,' he said, his voice ringing out across the floured table. 'Come help me over here.'

Rubin nodded at me and slipped off his apron. He had arranged with my father to leave through the back door of the bakery, but he wasn't going to announce his departure, lest someone else see it as a special favor. I stepped up beside my father and began to expertly rip pieces of dough and shape them into batards. 'How was work today?' he asked.

I shrugged. 'The same. What news have you had about Majer?'

My father shook his head. 'Nothing. But no news is good news.'

And that was all we said. Even talking took too much energy when we had a set number of loaves to produce before the transport to the warehouse. I thought instead of what it used to be like inside my father's own bakery, how sometimes he would sing in a scratchy baritone and how Basia, at the register, would say he was scaring away customers.

I remembered the way the light would slant inside at about four thirty in the summer, when the sun was beginning to slip behind the buildings across the street; how I would curl up in the padded window seat with one of my schoolbooks and doze off, my stomach full from the roll my father had made me, cinnamon sugar dusting my skirt like glitter. How he would shake me awake, asking what he'd done to deserve such a lazy girl, smiling the whole time so that I knew he meant the exact opposite.

And I thought of Majer, who had just learned to say my name.

When it was nearly time for us to load the loaves into baskets and transport them to Jakuba Street, the door opened, letting in a flickering tongue of cold air. Rubin walked back into the bakery, his hands buried in his pockets, his chin ducked into the scarf wrapped around his neck. 'Rubin?' I said, my stomach flipping. If he was here, it could only be to tell us something awful.

He shook his head. 'Nothing's changed,' Rubin said. 'Basia and your mother are home now with Majer.' He turned to my father and shrugged. 'It was doing me no good to sit around there.'

'Then grab a basket,' my father said, squeezing Rubin's shoulder.

Rubin and I and the other bakery employees began to load up the bread from the wire racks where it cooled. It was backbreaking work – loaves weigh more than you'd think when packed tightly together. I ferried baskets from the bakery into the cart that was pulled up to the front door. Three little boys gathered on the stoop across the street. They were shivering, but they stood in the snow, stamping their feet, for as long as we were out there. They could smell the steam and the flour, which was the next best thing to eating the bread itself.

When it was full, my father walked behind the cart and pushed, while two of the stronger employees grabbed the yoke in the front to tug. He motioned to me to walk beside him, because I hadn't the strength to pull. 'Oh!' I cried out, remembering that I'd left my scarf wrapped around the neck of a chair inside. 'I'll be right back.' I ran into the bakery again to find Rubin still inside. He had unbuttoned his coat partway and was slipping a loaf beneath his clothing.

Our eyes met.

Bread smuggling was a crime. So was any speculation on the black market for foodstuffs. But occasionally people would sell their rations on the black market, usually because something tragic made it necessary.

'Minka,' Rubin said evenly. 'You saw nothing.'

I nodded. I had to. Because if I turned Rubin in to my father, he would look the other way. And if Rubin was caught trading that bread for something else and it was discovered that my father had been in on the theft, he could be punished, too.

As the cart creaked toward Jakuba Street, with a plume of steam rising from the bread and teasing our nostrils, Rubin disappeared. One minute he was walking behind me; the next, he was gone. My father did not comment, which made me wonder if maybe he already knew what I was trying so hard not to tell him.

I lied to my father and told him I had to give Darija a book I had borrowed and would meet him at our house before curfew. Instead, I went to the spot in town where I had seen the deals happening between smugglers and thieves, hoping to catch

Rubin before he did something stupid. At nightfall, when the sky was gray and blending with the cobblestones and you could not be sure if what you were seeing was real, those who were desperate moved through the shadows, willing to trade their food, their jewels, their souls.

It was easy to find Basia's husband, with his red beard and the loaf of bread wrapped in brown paper. 'Rubin!' I cried out. 'Wait!' He looked up at me, as did the man with the hollow black eyes who was taking the package from him.

One moment the parcel was there, and the next it was hidden, slipped somewhere in the ratty folds of the other man's coat.

'Whatever you're doing,' I begged, grabbing Rubin's arm, 'don't. Basia wouldn't want you to.'

Rubin shrugged me off. 'You're a child, Minka. You don't know anything.'

But I wasn't a child. There were none left in this ghetto, really. We had all grown up by default. Even a baby like Majer was not a child, because he would have no memory of a life that wasn't like this one.

'Get rid of the girl,' the man hissed. 'Or the deal's off.'

I ignored him. 'What could possibly be worth your own life?'

Rubin, who had kissed me on the forehead the night he got engaged to Basia and told me he had always wanted a little sister; who had found me a copy of *Grimms' Fairy Tales* written in German for my last birthday; who had promised me he would interview any boy who dared to ask me out on a date – Rubin shoved me away so hard that I fell down.

My woolen stockings tore. Sitting up, I rubbed my knee where I had scraped it on the cobblestones. I watched the man press a small brown packet into Rubin's palm.

At the very same instant, there was a shout, and a whistle, and suddenly Rubin and the other man were surrounded by three soldiers. 'Minka!' Rubin shouted, and he threw the bag at me.

I caught it just as he was shoved to the ground. The butt of a rifle was smacked into the side of Rubin's head, and I started to run.

I did not stop – not when I reached the bridge over Zgierska Street, not even when I knew that none of the soldiers was pursuing me. Instead, I flew back home, burst through the doors, and collapsed into my mother's arms. Sobbing, I told her about Rubin. Basia, who was standing in the doorway with a wailing Majer, started to scream.

It was then that I remembered the package I was still clutching. I held out my hand, and my fingers opened like the petals of a rose.

My mother cut the twine with a kitchen knife. The paper, waxy and mottled, fell away to reveal a tiny vial of medicine.

What could possibly be worth your own life? I had pleaded.

His son's.

Information in the ghetto traveled now like a wisteria vine: twisted, convoluted, and blooming from time to time with unlikely bursts of color. It was through this network that we learned Rubin had been put in prison. Yet even though Basia went daily to see him, she was not allowed in.

My father tried to use every business connection he had outside the ghetto to find information about Rubin, or better yet, to bring him home. But the connections that had gotten me into Catholic school back then were meaningless now. Unless my father happened to be friends with an SS officer, Rubin was going to remain in jail.

It made me think of Darija's policeman, the one from the Stuttgart Ballet. There was no guarantee that he would be in a position to help, and yet, he had been a name in a sea of German uniforms. But Darija had burned his card, and so even that tiny spark of possibility was lost to me.

We did not know what would happen to Rubin, yet earlier that month, Chairman Rumkowski had issued a statement: thieves and criminals would be sent to do manual labor in Germany. It was the Eldest's way of removing the riffraff from our community. And yet, who would ever have thought of Rubin as riffraff? I wondered how many people in prison were actually criminals at all.

The thought of Rubin being shipped away left Basia inconsolable, even though she had Majer – who had improved quickly once he'd started taking the medicine – to think of. One night she slipped into my room. It was just after 3:00 a.m., and I immediately assumed something was wrong with the baby. 'What is it?'

'I need your help,' Basia said.

'Why?'

'Because you're smart.'

It was rare for Basia to admit she needed anything from me, much less my intelligence. I sat up in bed. 'You're thinking of doing something stupid,' I guessed.

'Not stupid. Necessary.'

That reminded me of Rubin, selling the bread. Angry, I stared at her. 'Do either of you even *care* that you have a little boy who depends on you? What if you wind up being arrested, too?'

'That's why I'm asking *you* for help,' Basia said. 'Please, Minka.'

'You're Rubin's wife. If *you* can't get into the prison to see him, there's nothing *I'll* be able to do.'

'I know,' Basia said softly. 'But that's not who I'm going to see.'

Chaim Rumkowski's reputation in the ghetto sat squarely on the fine line between love and hate. You had to publicly admire the chairman or your life could be hell, since he was the one who granted favors, housing, and food. But you also had to wonder about a man who had willingly agreed to deal with the Germans, to starve his own people, and to explain away the horrible conditions we were living in by saying at least we were alive.

There were rumors, too, that Rumkowski had a weakness for pretty girls. Which was exactly what Basia and I were counting on.

It hadn't been hard to get my mother to watch Majer by explaining that Basia was once again going to try to get into the prison to see her husband. It made sense, too, that she would want to dress in her best outfit and style her hair to look as pretty as she could for her husband. I didn't lie to my mother; I just neglected to mention that our destination was not the prison but instead Chairman Rumkowski's office.

There was nothing I could say that my sister could not have said herself to talk her way into a private audience with the Eldest of the Jews, but I understood why she wanted me there. For courage, going in; and for support, going out.

His office looked palatial compared to the cramped quarters of our apartment or the bakery. He had staff, of course. His secretary – a woman who smelled of perfume, instead of grime and smoke, like us – took one look at me and flicked a glance at a Jewish policeman standing like a sentry in front of a closed door. 'The chairman isn't in,' she said.

Rumkowski spent a lot of time traveling around the

ghetto – having schoolchildren paraded around in front of him, giving speeches, officiating at wedding ceremonies, or visiting the *Fabriken* that he thought would make us indispensable to the Germans. So it was not impossible that he would not be present when Basia and I came to his headquarters. But we had been sitting in the cold for hours, and had seen the chairman enter the building surrounded by an entourage no more than fifteen minutes ago.

He was easily recognizable, with his shock of white hair and his round black glasses, his heavy wool coat with its yellow star on the sleeve. It was that emblem that had made me grab Basia's hand outside when she shivered as he passed. 'You see,' I whispered. 'In the end he's no different than you or me.'

So I looked the secretary in the eye and said, 'You're lying.'

Her eyebrows rose. 'The chairman isn't in,' she repeated. 'And if he were, he would not see you without an appointment. And he does not have any openings for the next month.'

I knew this, too, was a lie, because I had heard her on the telephone arrange a meeting with the head of the Provisioning Department tomorrow morning at nine. I opened my mouth to say so, but Basia elbowed me in the ribs. 'I'm sorry,' she said, stepping forward and averting her gaze. 'I think you may have dropped these?'

She held out a pair of earrings. I knew that the secretary had not dropped these. They had, in fact, been screwed into my sister's ears when she dressed for our outing. They were a beautiful pair of pearls that had been a wedding gift from Rubin. 'Basia!' I gasped. 'You can't!'

She smiled at the secretary and spoke through her teeth to me. 'Shut *up*, Minka.'

The woman pursed her lips, then plucked the earrings out of my sister's hand. 'No promises,' she said.

The secretary walked toward the closed office door. She was wearing silk stockings, which amazed me. I couldn't wait to tell Darija that I had seen a Jew looking just as fine as any German lady. She knocked, and a moment later we heard a deep voice rumbling through the door, telling her to enter.

With a glance back at us, she slipped inside.

'What are you going to say to him?' Basia whispered.

We had decided that I would do all the talking. Basia was there as a pretty distraction, as the dutiful wife – but she was afraid that she would grow tongue-tied if she tried to explain why we were there.

'I don't even know if we'll get in,' I replied.

I had a plan. I was going to ask the chairman to set Rubin free in time for his wedding anniversary, next week, so that he could celebrate with his wife. That way he would be seen as an advocate of true love, and if Chaim Rumkowski loved anything, it was his own image in the eyes of his people.

The door swung open, and the secretary walked toward us. 'You have five minutes,' she announced.

We started forward, holding hands, but the secretary grasped my upper arm. '*She* can go in,' the woman said. 'Not *you.*'

'But—' Basia looked wildly over her shoulder at me.

'Beg him,' I urged. 'Get down on your knees.'

Lifting her chin, Basia nodded and walked through the door.

As the secretary sat down again and began to type, I stood nervously in the center of the anteroom. The policeman caught my eye and immediately looked away.

Twenty-two minutes after my sister had entered the private office of the Eldest of the Jews, she stepped outside. Her blouse was untucked in the back. Her red lipstick, which I had borrowed from Darija, was gone except for a smear in the left corner.

'What did he say?' I burst out, but Basia linked her arm through mine and hurriedly dragged me out of Rumkowski's office.

As soon as we were on the street again, with a bitter wind blowing our hair into a frenzy around our faces, I asked her again. Basia let go of my arm and leaned over in the street, vomiting onto the cobblestones.

I held her hair back from her face. I assumed this meant that she had failed to rescue Rubin. Which was why I was surprised when she turned to me a moment later, her face still white and pinched, and her eyes blazing. 'He won't have to go to Germany,' she said. 'The chairman is going to send him to a work camp here in Poland instead.' Basia grabbed my hand and squeezed. 'I saved him, Minka. I saved my husband.'

I hugged her, and she hugged me back, and then she held me at arm's length. 'You cannot tell Mama or Papa we came here,' Basia said. 'Promise me.'

'But they'll want to know how—'

'They'll assume that Rubin made a deal on his own,' she insisted. 'They would not want to know that we owe the chairman a debt.'

This was true. I had heard my father grousing about Rumkowski enough to know that he would not want to be beholden to the man.

Later that night, with Majer asleep between us in the bed, I could hear my sister quietly crying. 'What's the matter?'

'Nothing. I'm fine.'

'You should be happy. Rubin's going to be all right.'

Basia nodded. I could see her profile, silvered by the moon, as if she were a statue. She looked down at Majer then, and touched her finger to his lips, as if she was keeping him quiet, or pressing him a kiss.

'Basia?' I whispered. 'How did you convince the chairman?'

'Just like you told me.' A tear slipped down her cheek to land on the sheets between us. 'I got down on my knees.'

When Rubin had been sent off to a work camp, Basia and the baby had moved in with us. It was like old times, my sister sleeping in my bed, but now my nephew was caught between us like a secret. Majer was learning his colors, and the sounds made by farm animals he had only seen in pictures. We all talked about what a prodigy he was, how proud Rubin would be of his son when he came home. We talked as if this moment was coming any day now.

Rubin didn't write, and we all made excuses for him. He was too tired; he was too busy. He didn't have access to paper and pencil. The postal service was virtually nonexistent. Only Darija was brave enough to say what we were all thinking: that maybe the reason Rubin had not written was that he was already dead.

In October 1941, Darija and I both got food poisoning. It was not remarkable that this happened, given the quality of the food, only that it had not happened before, and that we were both still strong enough to drag ourselves out of our sickbeds after two days of incessant vomiting. But by then, our delivery jobs had been given away.

We reported to Lutomierska Street to be assigned new positions. Standing in line with us was a boy who had gone to our school. His name was Aron, and he used to unconsciously whistle in class while doing his exams, which always got him in trouble. He had a gap between his front teeth and was so tall that he stood with his shoulders hunched, a human question mark. 'I hope they put me anywhere but a bakery,' Aron said.

I bristled. 'What's wrong with a bakery?' I asked, thinking of my father.

'Nothing, it's just too good to be true. Like purgatory. Too much heat in the winter, and food all around you that you aren't allowed to eat.'

I shook my head, smiling. I liked Aron. He wasn't much to look at, but he made me laugh. Darija, who knew such things, said he fancied me; that's why he'd always happened to be the one holding the door of the school building for me as I was walking out; or accompanied me as far as he could in the ghetto before he had to turn off on the street that led to his own home. Once he had even given me a bit of his bread ration during lunch at school, which Darija said was virtually a proposal of marriage in these times.

Aron was no Herr Bauer. Or Josek, for that matter. But sometimes when I was lying next to Basia and Majer at night, and they had fallen asleep, I pressed the back of my hand against my lips and wondered what it would be like to kiss him. I was not smitten with him, really, only with the idea that someone might look at a girl with worn clothing and clunky boots and dull ropes of hair and see instead a thing of beauty.

There were children as young as ten in the square, waiting; and elderly people who could not stand without leaning on the person beside them. My parents had coached me on what to say, in the hope that I would be routed into my father's bakery or my mother's tailoring *Fabrik*. Sometimes the officials placing you took into consideration your talents or previous experience. Sometimes they just assigned you at random.

Darija grabbed my arm. 'We could say we're sisters. Then maybe they'll put us together again.'

I didn't think it would make a difference. Besides, it was already Aron's turn. I peered around his skinny frame as the official at the table scrawled something down on a piece of paper and handed it to him. When he turned, he was smiling. 'Textiles,' he said.

'You know how to sew?' Darija asked.

Aron shrugged. 'No, but apparently I'm going to learn.'

'Next.'

The voice cut through our conversation. I stepped forward, dragging Darija with me. 'One at a time,' the man before us said.

So I stepped in front of Darija. 'My sister and I, we both know how to bake. And sew . . .'

He was staring at Darija. Then again, everyone stared at Darija; she was that pretty. The man pointed to a truck at the corner of the square. 'You'll be on that transport.'

I started to panic. The people who left the ghetto, like Rubin, did not come back. 'Please,' I begged. 'A bakery . . . the saddle shop.' I thought of the job no one else wanted to do. 'I'll dig graves, even. Just please don't send me out of the ghetto.'

The man looked past me. 'Next,' he called.

Darija started to cry. 'I'm so sorry, Minka,' she sobbed. 'If we hadn't tried to stay together—'

Before I could answer, a soldier grabbed her by the shoulder and pushed her into the flatbed of the truck. I climbed in after Darija. The other girls were about our age; some I recognized from school. Some seemed panicked, others almost bored. No one spoke; I knew better than to ask where we were headed. Maybe I did not want to hear the answer.

A moment later we were driving through the gates of the ghetto – a place I had not left in over a year and a half.

I felt it, viscerally, as the gates were closed behind us again. The air was easier to breathe, out here. The colors were brighter. The temperature a tiny bit warmer. It was an alternate reality, and it stunned all ten of us girls into silence as we bounced and jostled away from our families.

I wondered who would tell my parents that I was gone. I wondered if Aron would miss me. If Majer would know me, if he ever saw me again. I grabbed Darija's hand and squeezed. 'If we have to die,' I said, 'at least we'll be together.'

At that, the girl sitting next to Darija laughed. 'Die? You stupid cow. You're not going to die. I've been on this truck every day for a week. You're just going to the officers' headquarters.'

I thought about how the man had been staring at Darija, and wondered what it was, exactly, we were supposed to do for the officers.

We drove through the streets of the city where I had grown up, but something was different. The details I remembered from my childhood – the boy selling newspapers, the fishmonger with her oversize hat, the tailor coming outside for a smoke and squinting into the sunlight – all those familiar faces were gone. Even the gallows, which had been built by the German soldiers in the square, had been dismantled. It reminded me of a story I had written once about a girl who woke up and found every trace of herself erased from the world as she knew it: a family that didn't know her; a school that had no record of her; a history that had never happened. It was as if I had only dreamed the life I used to lead.

Fifteen minutes later, we pulled through another gate that locked behind us. The barracks of the German soldiers were former government buildings in Łódź . We were shuttled out of the truck and turned over to a broad-shouldered woman with chapped red hands. She spoke in German, but it was clear that some of the other girls already knew the routine because they had been assigned this work detail before. We were each given a bucket and rags and some ammonia and told to follow her. From time to time she would stop and direct a girl into a building. Darija and the girl who had called me a cow were sent into a big stone hall with a giant Nazi flag draped from its roof.

I followed the woman through several passageways until we reached a residential area, with small apartments wedged together like clenched teeth. 'You,' she said in German. 'You will do all the windows.'

I nodded and turned the doorknob. This must have been where the German officers lived, because it was not like any other military barracks I had ever seen. There were no bunks or footlockers, but beautifully carved wooden bureaus and a single bed, its covers still messy. Dishes were stacked neatly in a drying rack beside the sink. On the table was a single plate with a bright purple bloom of jam painting its surface.

I started to salivate. I had not had jam in . . . forever.

For all I knew, though, someone was watching me through a chink in the wall. Pushing all thoughts of food out of my mind, I picked up the rag in my bucket and the ammonia and walked toward one of the eight windows in the apartment.

I had never cleaned anything in my life. My mother cooked and cleaned and organized and picked up after me. Even now, Basia was the one who pulled the blanket up on our bed and made tight little corners every morning.

I looked at the bottle of ammonia and uncorked its cap, gagging at the smell. Immediately, I closed it, my eyes tearing. I sat down at the kitchen table and found myself face-to-face with that breakfast plate.

Very quickly I touched my forefinger to the spot of jam and stuck it in my mouth.

Oh, God. My eyes began to tear again, for a very different reason. Every bit of my brain had begun firing in memory. Of eating my father's rolls, slathered with fresh butter and strawberry preserves that my mother had made. Of picking blueberries in the country where Darija's father's factory had been. Of lying on my back and imagining that the clouds in the sky were a scooter, a parrot, a tortoise. Of having nothing to do, because that's the occupation of a child.

That jam tasted like a lazy summer day. Like freedom.

I was so lost in my senses that I didn't hear the footsteps heralding the approach of the officer who, a second later, turned the doorknob and entered his residence. I leaped up, grabbing my bucket so fast that the ammonia tumbled out onto the floor. 'Oh!' I cried, falling to my knees to mop up the mess with the rag.

He was about my father's age, with silver hair that matched the buttons of his uniform. When he saw me his eyes flicked over my huddled body. 'Finish your work quickly,' he said in German, and then, because he didn't expect me to understand, he pointed at the window.

I nodded and turned away. I could hear the creak of the chair as he sat down at a desk and began to leaf through papers. With a shaking hand, I uncorked the ammonia bottle again, plugged my nose, and tried to twist the rag into its narrow neck so that I could soak up some of the cleaning fluid. I was able to get just the corner wet. Gingerly, I pressed it up against the window at the dirtiest part, as if I were dabbing at a wound.

The officer looked up after a few moments. '*Schneller*,' he said tightly. Faster.

I turned around, my heart pounding. 'I'm sorry,' I replied, babbling in his own language to keep him from getting even angrier than he already was. 'I've never done this before.'

His eyebrows raised. 'You speak German.'

I nodded. 'It was my best subject.'

The officer got out of his chair and walked toward me. By now I was frantic, trembling so hard my knees were knocking. I lifted my hand over my head to ward off the blow that I knew was coming, but instead, the soldier plucked the rag from my clenched fist. He poured some ammonia into the rag and wiped the window with long, smooth strokes. The rag came away filthy and black, so he folded it over to a fresh white spot and poured more ammonia onto it. He continued to clean his own window, and when he finished he picked up a newspaper and began to rub it over the panes of glass. 'This dries it without leaving streaks,' he explained.

'*Danke*,' I murmured, holding out my hand for the rag and the bottle of ammonia, but he just shook his head. He proceeded to finish the other windows until they were spotless; until it seemed as if there was no barrier between the inside of this apartment, where we had entered a strange truce, and the outside world, where I could take nothing for granted.

Then he looked at me. 'Repeat everything you learned.'

I rattled off every step of the window-washing process as if my life depended on it – which, maybe, it did. Flawlessly, in his mother tongue. When I was finished, the officer was staring at me as if I were a museum specimen he'd never encountered before. 'If I were not staring right at you,' he said, 'I wouldn't know you were not *völkisch*. You speak like a native.'

I thanked him, thinking of all those afternoons I'd spent

in conversation with Herr Bauer, and silently winging my gratitude to my former teacher, wherever he was now. I reached for the bucket, intent on finishing the rest of my job in other officers' apartments before the head cleaning woman came back to collect me, but the soldier shook his head and set it on the floor between us. 'Tell me,' he said. 'Can you type?'

With one note from the officer who had taught me to wash windows, I was reassigned to a workshop run by Herr Fassbinder, an ethnic German man who was just over five feet tall and who employed a great number of young girls, many younger than myself. He called us *'meine Kleiner'* – my little ones. The children were responsible for stitching the emblems that were sewed onto German uniforms. If, that first day, I shuddered to see ten-year-olds fashioning swastika patches, it became common enough.

I was not one of the sewers. Instead, I had been sent to work in Herr Fassbinder's office. My job was to process the orders, to answer the telephones, and to give out the candy that he brought in every Friday for the children.

At first, Herr Fassbinder spoke to me only when he needed information from the files, or when he had to dictate a letter and have it typed. But then one day, Aron showed up with a few other boys, hauling bolts of cloth that would be cut and stitched according to the orders that had been placed. I think Aron was as surprised to see me as I was to see him. 'Minka!' he said, as I directed his co-workers to the storage rooms. 'You work here?'

'In the office,' I told him.

'Ooh,' he teased. 'A posh job.'

I looked down at the skirt I was wearing, which was

threadbare at the knees after so much use. 'Oh yes,' I joked. 'I'm practically royalty.'

But we both knew how lucky I was – unlike my mother, who had lost most of her eyesight from sewing in the near dark; or pretty Darija, who was still cleaning at the officers' headquarters and whose graceful dancer's hands were now cracked and bleeding from lye and soap. In comparison, twelve hours at a typewriter in a warm office was a walk in the park.

Just then Herr Fassbinder passed by. He looked from me to Aron and back to me again. Then he shooed me into the office and instructed the little ones to return to work. I had sat down at my desk to type requisition forms when I realized Herr Fassbinder was standing in front of me. 'So?' he said, smiling broadly. 'You have a boyfriend.'

I shook my head. 'He's not my boyfriend.'

'Like I am not your boss.'

'He is just a school friend.' I was nervous, wondering if Aron could somehow get in trouble with his employer for talking to me at my own job.

Herr Fassbinder sighed heavily. 'Well, then, that is a shame,' he said. 'Because he is very much taken with you. Ah, look, I have made you blush. You should give the young man a chance.'

After that, whenever we needed textile supplies, Herr Fassbinder would specifically request that Aron be the one to deliver them. And he would conveniently assign me to unlock the storeroom for him, although there were others at the factory who were more suited to that job than a secretary. Afterward, Herr Fassbinder would come to my desk and pepper me for details. He was, I realized, just a matchmaker at heart.

Gradually, as we sat together in the little office, he began to confide in me. He told me of his wife, Liesl, who was so beautiful that the clouds would part when she stepped outside. She could have had her pick of any man, he told me, but she chose him because he knew how to make her laugh. His greatest regret was that they had not had a baby before she died – of tuberculosis, six years ago. I came to see that all of us in the factory, from the littlest girls to me, were his children.

One day, Herr Fassbinder and I were alone in the office. Work for the embroiderers was halted from time to time because various raw materials had not been delivered; this time, it was thread that had not arrived. Herr Fassbinder went out for a little while, and when he came back, he was flustered. 'We need more workers,' he barked, more upset than I had ever seen him. I was scared of him for the first time, because I didn't know what we would do with more workers when we couldn't even occupy the girls we already had.

The next day, in addition to our usual 150 employees, Herr Fassbinder had recruited 50 mothers with young children. The children were too young to do anything of value in an embroidery shop, so he had them sorting the threads by color. Aron came by with bolts of white fabric. The textile divisions had been employed to make fifty-six thousand camouflage suits for the Eastern Front in the summer; we would be stitching the insignia to match.

I knew, because I processed all the orders, that we hadn't been contracted to do this, and that we had just turned into a glorified day-care center. 'That's not your problem,' Herr Fassbinder snapped when I asked him about it.

That week the announcement was made: twenty thousand Jews were to be deported from the ghetto. Chairman Rumkowski had negotiated the number down by half, but lists of the ten thousand who would be leaving were made by ghetto officials. The Roma, who lived in a separate part of the ghetto, were the first. Criminals came second. Then those who didn't have jobs.

Such as the fifty mothers who had just recently arrived.

Something told me that if Herr Fassbinder had been able to take all ten thousand people on that list into his little *Fabrik*, he would have.

The first week of January, all the people who had been put on those lists had received their summonses – wedding invitations, we called them, with irony: a party no one wanted to attend. A thousand people were taken each day to the trains that led out of the ghetto. By then, our shipment of thread had arrived. By then, our new employees had settled in and were embroidering insignia as if they'd been born to it.

One night as I was covering my typewriter with its dust cover, Herr Fassbinder asked if my family was all right. It was the first time he had ever spoken of me having a life outside these walls, and I was startled. 'Yes,' I said.

'None were on the lists?' he asked bluntly.

I realized then that he knew far more about me than I knew about him. For also on these lists were the *relatives* of those who were Roma, who had no jobs, or who were criminals. Such as Rubin.

Whatever deal Basia had made with the chairman had been a thorough one. She did not know where her husband was, or if he was still alive, but she had not been recommended for deportation because of his crime.

Herr Fassbinder turned out the light, so that I could just discern his profile in the moonlight that spilled through the small window of the office. 'Do you know where they are being taken?' I blurted, suddenly brave in the darkness.

'To work on Polish farms,' he said.

Our eyes met in silence. That was what we had been told about Rubin, months ago. Herr Fassbinder had to know, from my expression, that I did not believe him.

'This war.' He sighed heavily. 'There is no escaping it.'

'Would you say that to someone with papers?' I whispered. 'Christian ones?'

I have no idea what made me tell him – a German – my biggest secret, the one I had never even told my parents. But something about this man, and the lengths he had gone to to protect children who weren't even his, made me think he could be trusted.

'If someone had Christian papers,' he said after a long moment, 'I would tell that person to go to Russia, until the war ends.'

As I left work that night, I started to cry. Not because I knew Herr Fassbinder was right or because I knew that I would still never go as long as it meant leaving my family behind.

But because when we were locking up the factory office in the dark, where no one else could see us, Herr Fassbinder had held the door open for me, as if I was still a young lady, and not just a Jew.

Although we all had believed that the lists created in January would be a single horrible moment in the history of the war, and although the chairman's speeches reminded us and the Germans how indispensable we were as a workforce, only two weeks later the Germans demanded more deportees. By now, rumors were running as fast as fire through the factories, nearly paralyzing production, because no one ever heard again from a person who had left on one of the transports. It was hard to believe that someone who had been resettled wouldn't try to get word to his family.

'I heard,' Darija said one morning when we were waiting at one of the soup kitchens for our rations, 'that they're being killed.'

My mother was too tired these days to stand for hours in the massive crowds that lined up for food. It sometimes seemed it took more time to get our rations than it did to consume them. My father was still at the bakery, and Basia was picking up the baby from his day care – they had officially been disbanded but still operated illegally at many of the *Fabriken*, including Basia's textile factory. That left me with the job of getting the rations and bringing them back home. At least I had Darija with me to pass the time. 'How could they possibly kill a thousand people a day?' I scoffed. 'And why would they, if we're working for them for free?'

Darija leaned closer to me. 'Gas chambers,' she whispered.

I rolled my eyes. 'I thought I was the fiction writer.'

But even though I believed Darija was telling the wildest tales, there were parts of her story that rang true. Like the fact that now the officials were asking for volunteers and promising a free meal if you went on one of the transports. At the same time, food rations were being cut – as if to persuade anyone who was on the fence about the decision. After all, if you took what Rumkowski said at face value and could get out of this hellhole *and* fill your belly while doing it, who *wouldn't* step up?

But then there was the new law that made it a crime to hide someone who was on the list for deportation. Or the case of Rabbi Weisz, who had been given the responsibility of finding three hundred people in his congregation for the most recent transport. He had refused to give a single name, and when the soldiers came to arrest him, they found him and his wife lying dead on their bed, their hands linked tightly.

My mother said it was a blessing that they went at the same time. I couldn't believe she thought I was stupid enough to believe that.

By late March 1942, everyone knew someone who had been deported. My cousin Rivka, Darija's aunt, both of Rubin's parents, my former doctor. It was the season of Passover, and this was our plague, but no amount of lambs' blood would save a household from tragedy. It seemed the only blood that satisfied was that of the families inside.

My parents tried to protect me by giving me only limited information about the *Aussiedlungen*, the roundups. *Be a mensch*, my mother told me, no matter what situation you're in. Be kind to others before you take care of yourself; make whoever you're with feel like they matter. My father told me to sleep in my boots.

It was several hours before I collected the meager store of food that was meant to last us for the next two weeks. By then my feet were frozen and my eyelashes were stuck together. Darija blew into her mittens to warm her hands. 'At least it's not summer,' she said. 'Less of a chance that the milk is already spoiled.'

I walked with her as far as I could until she had to turn down a different street to her apartment. 'What should we do tomorrow?' I asked.

'Oh, I don't know,' Darija said. 'Maybe go shopping?'

'Only if we can stop for high tea.'

Darija grinned. 'Honestly, Minka. Do you ever stop thinking about food?'

I laughed and turned the corner. Alone, I walked faster, averting my eyes from soldiers I passed and even the residents I knew. It was too hard to look at people these days. They seemed so hollow, sometimes, I worried that I might fall right inside those empty stares and never be able to claw my way out.

When I reached the apartment, I climbed over the missing wooden stoop step – Darija's family had burned it in December for firewood – and immediately noticed that nobody was home. Or at least, there was no light, no sound, no life.

'Hello?' I called out, as I walked inside and set the canvas sack with our rations on the kitchen table.

My father was sitting on a chair, holding his head in his hands. Blood seeped between his fingers from a wide cut on his forehead. 'Papa?' I cried, running to him and pulling his hand away so that I could see the wound. 'What happened?'

He looked at me, his eyes unfocused for a moment. 'They took her,' he said, his voice breaking. 'They took your mother.'

It seemed that you didn't even have to be on a list to fill up the necessary quotas for deportation. Or maybe my mother had gotten her 'wedding invitation' and had chosen not to tell us, so we wouldn't worry. We didn't have the whole story; all we knew was that my father had returned from *shul* to find the SS in his living room, screaming at my mother and my uncle. Fortunately, Basia had taken Majer out for some fresh air and wasn't home. When my mother tried to run to my father, he was knocked unconscious with the butt end of a rifle. By the time he came to, she was gone.

He told me all this as I cleaned and dressed the cut on his forehead. Then he sat me down on a chair and knelt at my feet. I could feel him unlacing my boots. He slipped the left one from my foot and smacked the heel against the floor until it wiggled loose, then pulled it apart so that the little compartment with the stash of gold coins was revealed. He reached inside and took out the money. 'You will still have the rest in the other boot,' he said, as if he were trying to convince himself that he was doing the right thing.

After he put my boot back together again, he took my hand and led me outside. For hours we walked the streets, trying to ask anyone we saw if they knew where those who had been rounded up had gone. People shied away from us, as if misery was contagious; the sun sank lower and lower, until it broke like a yolk over the rooftops. 'Papa,' I told him, 'it's nearly curfew,' but he didn't seem to hear me. I was terrified; I thought this was surely a death wish. If he couldn't find my mother, he didn't want to be here anymore. It didn't take long for us to be confronted by two SS soldiers who were patrolling. One of them pointed at my father and started yelling, 'Get off the street!' When my father kept walking toward him, holding out the coins in his hand, the soldier pointed his gun.

I threw myself in front of my father. 'Please,' I begged in German. 'He isn't thinking clearly.'

The second soldier stepped forward and put his hand on his comrade's arm, lowering the gun. I started to breathe again. *'Was ist los?'* he asked. What's the matter?

My father looked at me, his expression so raw that it hurt to stare into his eyes. 'Ask them where they took her.'

So I did. I explained that my mother and my uncle had been collected from our home by soldiers, and that we were trying to find them. Then my father spoke in a universal language, pressing the gold coins into the gloved hand of the soldier.

In the light from the streetlamp, the soldier's response had a shape. The words swelled in the space between us. *'Verschwenden Sie nicht Ihr Geld,'* he said, dropping the coins onto the pavement. He jerked his head toward our apartment, a reminder again that we were breaking curfew.

'My gold is as good as anyone else's!' my father called after them angrily as the soldiers moved down the street. 'We will find someone else, Minka,' he promised. 'There has to be a soldier in the ghetto who is willing to be paid for information.'

I knelt, picking up the coins that winked against the cobblestones. 'Yes, Papa,' I said, but I knew this wasn't true, because I understood what the soldier had said.

Don't waste your money.

The day after my mother disappeared, I went to work. There were several girls missing; others cried as they embroidered. I sat at my typewriter, trying to lose myself in requisition forms but failing miserably. When I had messed up for the fifth time in a row, I finally banged my fist on the keys so that they all flew up at once, printing a line of nonsense, as if the whole world had started to speak in tongues.

Herr Fassbinder came out of his inner office to find me sobbing. 'You are upsetting the other girls,' he said, and sure enough, I could see some of them staring at me through the window that separated my desk from the factory floor. 'Come here.' I followed him into his office and sat down the way I did when I took dictation.

He did not pretend that he didn't know about the *Aussiedlung* of the previous evening. And he did not tell me to stop crying. Instead, he gave me his handkerchief. 'Today, you will work in here,' he announced, and he left me, closing the door behind him.

For five days, I moved like a zombie at work and then like a ghost at home, silently picking up after my father, who had stopped eating and speaking. Basia fed him spoonfuls of broth the way she fed Majer. I had no idea how he made it through his bakery shift, but I assumed his men were covering whatever labor he could not do on his own. I was not sure what was worse: having my mother vanish in an instant, or losing my father by degrees.

One night as I walked home from the *Fabrik* I could feel a shadow behind me, breathing on my neck like a dragon. Every time I turned around, though, I saw nothing but haggard neighbors trying to get home and close their doors before any misery could slip over the threshold. Still, I could not shake the feeling that I was being followed, and the fear rose, doubling, quadrupling, filling every last space in my mind the way my father's dough swelled if given enough time. My heart was pounding by the time I burst through the door of the apartment, which felt wrong now that both of my cousins were gone, as if we were squatters instead of guests. 'Basia?' I yelled out. 'Papa?' But it was just my dumb luck: I was alone.

I unwound my scarf and unbuttoned my coat but left them on because there was no heat in the apartment. Then I slipped a paring knife into my sleeve, just in case.

I heard something break in another room.

The noise had come from the only bedroom in the apartment – the one that had been occupied by my cousins when we first moved in. I crept down the hallway as quietly as I could in my heavy boots and peered through the doorway. One of the windowpanes had been broken. I looked around to see if a rock had been thrown, but there was nothing on the floor but glass. Kneeling, I began to sweep it up carefully with my palms, using my skirt as a dustpan.

There. I hadn't imagined it, that shadow that flickered at the corner of my eye.

Leaping to my feet so that the glass spilled back onto the floor, I yanked aside the bedroom door to find the tall, thin boy who had broken the window to hide inside. Brandishing the knife from my sleeve, I held him at bay. 'We have nothing for you,' I cried. 'No food. No money. Go away.'

His eyes were wide, his clothes torn and ragged. Unlike the rest of us, who were starving, he had visible muscles bulging beneath his shirt. He took a step forward.

'Stop, or I'll kill you,' I yelled, and in that moment, I believed that I could.

'I know what happened to your mother,' he said.

I, who had dreamed up a novel about an undead *upiór* who fell in love with a human girl, could not believe the fantasy this boy spun with words. His name was Hersz, and he had been with my mother on the freight train that left the ghetto. The train had traveled forty-four miles from Łódź to Koło. Then, everyone was taken to another train, this one running on a narrow-gauge track to Powiercie. By the time they arrived it was late in the day, and they spent the night a few kilometers away in an abandoned mill.

It was there that Hersz met my mother. She said that she had a daughter about the same age he was, and she worried about me. She hoped that there would be a way to get word back to the ghetto. She asked Hersz if he had family there, too. 'She reminded me of my mother,' Hersz said. 'My parents both went with the second roundup. I thought that maybe we were being taken to the same place to work, that I would get to see them again.'

We were sitting down now, with Basia and my father, who were hanging on every word Hersz spoke. After all, if *he* was here, didn't that mean my mother might soon follow? 'Go on,' my father urged.

Hersz picked at a scab on his hand. His lips were trembling. 'The next morning, we were divided into small groups by the soldiers. Your mother went with one group into a truck, and I went with another that held ten young men, all tall and strong. We drove up to a big stone mansion. We were brought to the basement of the manor house. There were signatures all over the walls, and one sentence written in Yiddish: *He who comes here, does not walk away alive.* There was a window, too, nailed shut with boards.' Hersz swallowed hard. 'I could hear through it, though. Another truck pulled up, and this time one of the Germans told the people who had been transported that they were to be sent east to work. All they had to do was take a shower first, and put on clean clothes that were disinfected. The people in the truck, they started clapping their hands, and then a little while later, we heard bare feet shuffling by the basement window.'

'So she is all right,' my father breathed.

Hersz looked down at his lap. 'The next morning I was taken to work in the woods, with the others who had spent the night in the basement. As I left, I noticed a big van parked up against the house. The door of the van was open and there was a ramp to get inside. There was a wooden grate on the floor, like the kind you might see in a community bathhouse,' he said. 'But we didn't get into this van. Instead, we went in a truck that had tarpaulin on its sides. About thirty SS men came with us. There was a huge pit that had been dug. I was given a shovel and told to make it bigger. Just after eight in the morning, the first van arrived. It looked like the one I had seen at the manor. Some of the Germans opened the doors and then ran quickly away from it, while gray smoke poured out. After about five minutes, the soldiers directed three of us inside. I was one of them.' He sucked in his breath, as if it were coming through a straw. 'The people inside, they had died from the gas. Some were still holding each other. They were wearing their underwear, but nothing else. And their skin was still warm. Some were still alive, and when that was the case, one of the SS men would shoot them. After the bodies were taken out, they were searched for gold and jewelry and money. Then they were buried in the pit, and the towels and bars of soap they had been given for their *shower* were gathered to be brought back to the manor house for the next transport.'

As I stared at Hersz, my jaw dropped. This made no sense. Why would you go to so much trouble to kill people – people who had been manufacturing items needed for the war effort? And then I began to do the arithmetic. Hersz was here, my mother was not. Hersz had seen the bodies being unloaded from the vans. 'You're lying,' I spat.

'I wish I were,' he whispered. 'Your mother, she was on the third truck of the day.'

My father put his head down on the table and started to weep.

'Six of the boys who had been picked to work in the woods were killed that day, shot because they weren't doing their job fast enough. I survived but didn't want to. I was going to hang myself that night, in the basement. Then I remembered that even if I didn't have family left, your mother did. And that maybe I could find you. The next day on the transport to the woods, I asked for a cigarette. The SS man gave me one, and suddenly everyone in the truck was asking for a smoke. While he was being swarmed, I took a pen from my pocket and used it to poke a hole in the tarpaulin, and tear a long rip. Then I jumped out of the truck. They started shooting, but didn't hit me, and I managed to run through the woods until I found a barn, where I hid underneath the hay in the loft. I stayed there for two days, and then sneaked out and came back here.'

I listened to Hersz's story, although I wanted to tell him he was a fool, trying to break *into* the ghetto when all of us wanted to get out. But then again, if getting out meant dying in a van full of gas, maybe Hersz was the smart one. There was a part of me that still could not believe what he said, and continued to dismiss it. But my father, he immediately covered the only mirror in the house. He sat on the floor, instead of in a chair. He tore his shirt. Basia and I followed his example, mourning our mother the way our religion told us to.

That night when I heard my father crying, I sat down on the edge of the mattress he had shared with my mother. We, who had been so crowded in this apartment, now had more room than we needed. 'Minka,' my father said, his voice so soft I may have imagined it. 'At my funeral, make sure . . . make sure . . .' He broke off, unable to tell me what he wanted me to remember.

Overnight, his hair went snow white. Had I not seen it with my own eyes, I would not have believed it possible.

It is probably the hardest thing to understand: how even horror can become commonplace. I used to have to imagine how you might look at an *upiór* sucking the blood from the neck of a freshly killed human and not have to turn away. Now I knew from personal experience: you could see an old woman shot in the head and sigh because her blood spattered onto your coat. You could hear a barrage of gunfire and not even blink. You could stop expecting the most awful thing to happen, because it already had.

Or so I thought.

The first day of September, military trucks pulled up to the hospitals in the ghetto, and the patients were dragged out by

SS soldiers. Darija told me that at the children's hospital, people reported seeing babies tossed from the windows. I think that was when I realized Hersz could not have been lying. These men and women hobbling in their hospital gowns, some too weak or too old to stand on their own, could not have been going to work in the east. The next afternoon, the chairman gave a speech. I stood with my sister in the square, bouncing Majer between the two of us. He had another cough and was fussy. My father, who had become a shadow of his former self, was at home. He dragged himself to the bakery and back, but he did not go out in public otherwise. In a way, my little nephew could take better care of himself than my father could.

Chairman Rumkowski's voice crackled over the loud-speakers that had been erected at the corners of the square. 'A severe blow has befallen the ghetto,' he said. 'They are asking for the best it possesses – children and old people. I have not had the privilege to have a child of my own, and therefore I devoted the best of my years to children. I lived and breathed together with the children. I never imagined that my own hands would have to deliver the sacrifice to the altar. In my old age, I must stretch out my hands and beg . . . Brothers and sisters, give them to me! Fathers and mothers, give me your children.'

There were gasps and shrieks, shouts from the crowd around us. Majer was in my arms at that point; I pulled him tighter against me, but Basia ripped him from my grasp and buried her face in his hair. Red hair, like Rubin's.

The chairman went on to talk about how twenty thousand people had to be deported. How the sick and the elderly would only tally thirteen thousand. Beside me someone shouted, 'We'll all go!' Another woman cried out her suggestion, that no parents lose an only child, that those with children to spare be the ones to give them up.

'No,' Basia whispered, her eyes full of tears. 'I won't let him be taken.'

She hugged Majer so close that he started to cry. The chairman was saying, now, that this was the only way to appease the Germans. That he understood the horror of his request. That he had convinced the Germans to take only children who were under ten years old, because they would not know what was happening to them.

Basia leaned over and vomited on the ground. Then she pushed through the crowd, away from the chairman's podium, still holding Majer. 'I understand what it means to tear a limb from the body,' Rumkowski was saying, trying to plead his case.

So did I.

It meant that you bled out.

At the end of the workday, Herr Fassbinder did not let us leave the factory, not even to go home and tell our parents we would be staying late. He told the officers who demanded an explanation that he had emergency deadlines and was requiring all of us to sew through the night. He barricaded the doors, and he stood at the entrance with a gun I had never seen him carry before. I think that if a soldier had come to take away the little ones he employed, he would have fought his own country. This was, I knew, for our own protection. A curfew had been imposed keeping everyone in their homes, as the SS and the police searched house by house to select the children who would be deported.

When we started hearing shots and screams, Herr Fassbinder told everyone to remain quiet. The young mothers, on the knife edge of hysteria, rocked their children. Herr Fassbinder handed out candy for them to suck on and let them play with empty spools, stacking them like blocks.

By the next morning, I was frantic. I couldn't bear thinking of Basia and Majer, wondering who would protect them with my father still an empty shell. 'Herr Fassbinder,' I begged. 'Please let me go home. I am eighteen. Too old to be considered a child.'

'You are *meine Kleine*,' Herr Fassbinder replied.

I did something incredibly bold then. I touched his hand. As nice as Herr Fassbinder had been to me, I never allowed myself to think that I was his equal. 'If I go home tomorrow, or the next day, and find that someone else has been taken away from me while I was gone, I don't think I'll be able to live with myself.'

He looked at me for a long moment, and then directed me to the door. Walking outside the factory with me, he flagged a young German policeman. 'This girl must get to her apartment safely,' he said. 'This is a priority and I will hold you responsible if it does not happen. Do you understand?'

The policeman could not have been much older than I was. He nodded, terrified by Herr Fassbinder's promise of retribution. He walked briskly with me to my apartment, stopping when we reached the front steps of the building.

I thanked him under my breath in German and flew inside. The lights were off, but I knew that wouldn't stop the German soldiers from coming inside and looking for Majer. My father was on his feet the moment he heard me enter. He folded me into his arms, stroking my hair. 'Minusia,' he said. 'I thought you were lost to me.'

'Where's Basia?' I asked, and he led me to the pantry, the one whose flooring my poor cousin Rivka had ripped up over two years ago. A small mat made of newspapers was covering the hole that revealed the crawl space beneath. I pulled it aside and saw the gleam of Basia's eyes looking up at me in panic. I heard the soft pop of Majer's thumb in his mouth.

'Good,' I said. 'This is very good. Let's make it better.' Searching frantically around the apartment, I laid eyes on the barrel that my father had brought home from the bakery. Once full of flour, it now served as our kitchen table, since we had burned the original one for fuel. I hauled it onto its side and rolled it into the pantry, then balanced it over the hole in the floor. It would not look strange to keep a flour barrel in the pantry, and it was one more obstacle to any soldier realizing there was a hidey-hole beneath it.

We knew they were getting closer because we could hear people in apartments nearby – both those who were taken from their families and those who were left behind – screaming. It was another three hours, though, before they came into our home, slamming the door back on its hinges and demanding to know where Majer was. 'I don't know,' my father said. 'My daughter hasn't been home since the curfew started.'

One of the SS men turned to me. 'Tell us the truth.'

'My father *is* telling the truth,' I said.

Then I heard it. The cough; and a tiny wail.

Immediately I covered my mouth with my hand. 'You are ill?' the soldier asked.

I couldn't say yes, because that qualified me as one of the sick to be transported. 'Just a sip of water that went down the wrong pipe,' I said, beating my chest with my fist to prove a point, until the noise disappeared.

The soldiers ignored me after that. They began to open cabinets and drawers, places small enough to hide a child. They ripped their bayonets into the straw mattresses we slept on, in case Majer was tucked inside. They looked inside the belly of the woodstove. When they reached the pantry, I stood very still while the soldier swept his gun along the shelves, tumbling our meager rations to the floor, and into the empty barrel. He looked down into its gaping mouth.

The SS man turned around and stared at me without emotion. 'If we find her hiding with the child, we will kill her,' he said, and he kicked the barrel.

It did not tip over. It didn't wobble. It just shifted the tiniest bit to the right, pulling the newspaper along with it, and revealing the tiniest black crack along the edge that was a hint of the gaping hole it covered.

I held my breath, certain he would see this, but the soldier was already calling the others to move on to the next apartment.

My father and I watched the SS men leave. 'Not yet,' my father whispered, when I made a move toward the pantry. He pointed furtively to the window, from which we could still see our neighbors being dragged onto the street, marched away, shot. After ten minutes, when the soldiers had left the street and the only sounds were the wails of other mothers, my father ran to the kitchen and pulled the barrel aside.

'Basia,' I cried. 'It's over.' She was sobbing and smiling through her tears. She sat up, still clutching Majer as my father helped her out of the narrow space. 'I thought they would hear the coughing,' I said, hugging her tightly.

'I thought so, too,' Basia confessed. 'But he was such a good boy. Weren't you, my little man?'

We both looked down, to where Majer's face was pressed tightly against his mother's neck, the only way she had been able to quiet him. Majer wasn't coughing anymore. He wasn't screaming.

But my sister, looking down at her son's blue lips and empty eyes, was.

The children were driven in wagons through the ghetto gate. Some of them were dressed in their fanciest clothing, whatever was left of it at this point. They were crying at the tops of their lungs, calling for their mothers. These mothers were expected to go to their factories to work as if nothing out of the ordinary had happened.

The ghetto was a ghost town. We were a beaten, gray stream of workers who did not want to remember our past and did not think we had a future. There was no laughter, no hopscotch remaining. No hair ribbons or giggles. No color or beauty left behind.

Which is why, they said, her death was so lovely. Like a bird, she flew from the bridge across Lutomierska Street into the road where Jews were not allowed. They said Basia's unbound hair fluttered behind her, like wings; and her skirts became the fan of a tail. They said that the bullets, as they hit her in midair, gave her bright crimson plumage, like a phoenix that was meant to rise again.

I *n the dark, there was a soft growl, almost a purr. The rasp* *of a match. A scent of sulfur. The torch blazed to life again.* *Crouched before me in a pool of blood was a man with wild* *eyes and knotted hair. More blood dripped from his mouth* *and covered his hands, which held a haunch of meat. I fell* *back, struggling to find air. This was the cave in the side of* *the cliff where Aleks had told me he made his modest home; I* *had come here hoping to find him, after he escaped from the* *village square. But this – this was not Aleks.*

The man – could I even call him such? – took a step closer. *That haunch of meat he was devouring had a hand, fingers.* *They were still clutching the top of a gilded cane I could not* *have forgotten if I tried. Baruch Beiler was no longer missing.*

I felt my vision fading, my head spinning. 'It wasn't a wild *animal,' I forced out. 'It was you.'*

The cannibal smiled, his teeth slick and stained crimson. *'Wild animal . . . upiór. Why split hairs?'*

'You killed Baruch Beiler.'

'Hypocrite. Can you honestly say you didn't wish him dead?'

I considered all the times the man had come to the cottage, *demanding tax money we did not have, extorting deals from* *my father that only dragged us deeper and deeper into debt.* *I looked at this beast, and suddenly felt like I was going to be* sick. 'My father,' I whispered. 'You killed him, too?' When the upiór *did not answer, I flew at him, using my nails and my fury as weapons. I raked at his flesh and kicked and swung. Either I would avenge my father's death or I would die trying.*

Suddenly, I felt an arm around my waist, yanking me backward.

'Stop,' Aleksander *cried, his full weight pinning me to the ground. From this angle, I could see the chains that encircled the* upiór's *bare, filthy feet, the pile of bleached bones beside him. I could see, too, the ragged cuffs of Aleksander's shirt, drenched with blood. Whatever he'd done to free himself from the ropes Damian had trapped him in, it must have been painful.*

'Leave me alone,' *I shouted. I did not want Aleks to save me, not this time, not if it meant I could not avenge my father's death.*

'Stop,' *Aleks begged, and I realized I was not the one he was trying to protect.* 'Please. He is my brother.'

I stopped fighting. This was Casimir? The feebleminded boy Aleks had to stay with during the day, and lock up at night, so that he would not eat what he shouldn't? True, I had never seen his face without the leather mask. And Aleks had said he consumed things like stones and twigs and dirt, not humans. If that had been a lie, how could I trust anything Aleks had told me?

I shook my head, trying to understand. Aleks had protected me. He had saved my life when I was hurt – by his own brother. And yet, he had the same unearthly amber eyes as this creature beside me; he had the same blood beating through his veins. 'He is your brother,' *I repeated, my voice breaking.* 'But I no longer have a father.' *I tore away from Aleks and faced Casimir.* 'Because you killed him! Say it!' *I was shaking so hard I could barely stand upright. But Casimir wouldn't speak, wouldn't give me the satisfaction.*

I began to run blindly in the direction from which I'd come, striking against sharp corners, tripping over rocks and ruts in the cavern floor, landing hard on my hands and knees. As I struggled to my feet, Aleksander's arms closed around me. I stiffened, remembering that indirectly, he was the cause of all my pain. 'You could have stopped him,' I sobbed. 'He murdered the only person who ever loved me.'

'Your father is not the only person to ever love you,' Aleks confessed. 'And you cannot blame Casimir for his death.' He turned away so that his face was in shadow. 'Because I am the one who killed him.'

Minka

For a while, people disappeared from the ghetto like finger-prints on a pane of glass – ghosting into vision one moment, and the next, gone as if they'd never been there. Death walked next to me as I trudged down the street, whis-pered into my ear as I washed my face, embraced me as I shivered in bed. Herr Fassbinder was no longer my boss; instead of working in an office, I was reassigned to a factory that made leather boots. My hands shook even when I wasn't sewing; that's how hard it was to force the needle through the tough hides. We lived expecting to be deported at any minute. Some ladies in the factory had the diamonds from their wedding rings implanted as fillings by the dentist. Others smuggled small pouches of coins in their vaginas, and came to work this way, in case the roundups happened there. And still, we went on living. We worked and we ate and we cele-brated birthdays and gossiped and read and wrote and prayed and we woke up each morning to do it all over again.

One day in July 1944 when I went to collect Darija to stand in line for rations, she was gone. I hardly had time to grieve, though. By then, it was almost expected to lose the people who meant the most to you. And besides, three days later, my father and I found ourselves on the list for deportation.

It was hot, the kind of heat that made it impossible to

believe that months ago we could not get warm no matter how hard we tried. The *Fabrik* had been blistering, windows closed, the air so thick it felt like a sponge in your throat. Walking outside for the first time in twelve hours, I was grateful for the fresh air, and in no great hurry to go home, where my father and I would sit up the whole night wondering what would happen the next morning, when we were to assemble in the town square.

Instead, I found myself picking a convoluted path through the narrow streets and twisted alleys of the ghetto. I knew Aron lived somewhere around here, but I had not seen him in several weeks. It was possible that he, like Darija, had already been deported.

I stopped a man on the street and asked if he knew Aron, but the man just shook his head and moved on. I was doing the unthinkable. We didn't talk of those who had been taken from us; it was like those cultures who don't name the dead, for fear that they will haunt us forever. 'Aron,' I asked an old woman. 'Aron Sendyk. Have you seen him?'

She looked at me. I realized, with a shock, that she was not much older than I was, but her hair was white and there were bare patches on her scalp; her skin draped from her bones like fabric too heavy for its hanger. 'He lives there,' she said, and she pointed to a door further down the street.

Aron answered the door with terror on his face, and why wouldn't he? When we heard a knock, it usually was followed by a soldier barging in. Upon his seeing me, though, his features softened. 'Minka.' He reached out his hand to me, to pull me inside. It was like an oven in there.

'Is anyone here?'

He shook his head. He was wearing an undershirt and trousers, which had been pinned to keep from falling off his skinny hips. His shoulders were slick with sweat, shiny, like the knobs of a brass flagpole.

I reached up on my tiptoes and kissed him.

He tasted of cigarettes, and the hair at the nape of his neck was damp. I pressed my body along the length of his and kissed him even harder, as if I had been dreaming of this moment for years. I suppose I had been, too. Just not with Aron.

Eventually Aron must have realized he was not hallucinating, because his arms caught me around the waist and he started to kiss me back, tentatively at first, and then wildly, like a starving man given access to a banquet.

I stepped away from him, and looking him straight in the eye, unbuttoned my blouse. Let it hang open.

I was nothing to look at. My ribs were more prominent than my breasts. There were circles under my eyes that never went away. My hair was dull and tangled, but it was still long at least.

It took me a moment to recognize the look in Aron's eyes. Pity. 'Minka, what are you doing?' he whispered.

Suddenly embarrassed, I pulled the edges of my blouse together to cover myself. I was too ugly, even, to get this boy who had once been interested in me to take the bait. 'If you can't figure that out, I'm doing a very bad job,' I said. 'I'm sorry I disturbed you—'

I turned my back, hurrying to the door as I fastened my buttons, but was stopped by Aron's hand on my arm. 'Don't go,' he said quietly. 'Please.'

When he kissed me again, I thought that if I'd had the time, and maybe a different life, I could have fallen in love with him after all.

He laid me down on the mat where he slept, which was in the center of the one-room apartment. There was no need to ask why now, why him. I didn't want to give the answer and he wouldn't have wanted to hear it. Instead, he just sat down beside me and held my hand. 'You're sure about this?' Aron asked.

When I nodded, he peeled the clothes from my body and let the sweat dry on my skin. Then he pulled off his undershirt and shucked off his pants and covered me.

It hurt, when he moved between my legs. When he pushed inside of me. I didn't understand what all the fuss was about, why the poets wrote sonnets about this moment, why Penelope had waited for Odysseus, why knights rode off to battle with ribbons from their lovers wrapped around the hilts of their swords. And then, I understood. My heart, batting like a moth under my rib cage, slowed to match the beat of his. I could sense the blood in his veins moving with mine, like the inevitable chorus of a song. I was different, with him, transformed from ugly duckling to snowy swan. I was, for a minute, the girl of someone's dreams. I was a reason to stay alive.

Afterward, when I was dressed again, Aron insisted on walking me back home, as if he were a real boyfriend. We stopped outside my apartment. My father was in there, I knew, packing for our deportation in the single suitcase each of us was allowed. He would wonder where I'd been. Aron leaned down, right there in public, with neighbors passing on the street, and kissed me. He seemed so happy that I thought I owed him a grain of truth. 'I wanted to know what it was like,' I whispered. *Because this may be my last chance.*

'And?'

I looked up at him. 'Thank you very much.'

Aron laughed. 'That seems a little formal.' He bowed, an exaggeration of manners. 'Miss Lewin, may I call for you tomorrow?'

If I had any love for him, I owed him more than that grain of truth. I owed him the comfort of a lie.

I curtsied and forced a smile, as if I would be here tomorrow to be courted. 'Of course, kind sir,' I said.

That was the last time we ever spoke.

If you had to pack your whole life into a suitcase – not just the practical things, like clothing, but the memories of the people you had lost and the girl you had once been – what would you take? The last photograph you had of your mother? A birthday gift from your best friend – a bookmark embroidered by her? A ticket stub from the traveling circus that had come through town two years ago, where you and your father held your breath as jeweled ladies flew through the air, and a brave man stuck his head in the mouth of a lion? Would you take them to make wherever you were going feel like home, or because you needed to remember where you had come from?

In the end I took all of these things, and the copy of *The Diary of a Lost Girl*, and Majer's baby shoes, and Basia's wedding veil. And, of course, my writing. It filled four notebooks now. I tucked three of them inside my case and carried the other in a satchel. Into my boots, I wedged my Christian papers, beside the gold coins. My father was silent as he held the door to the apartment that was not ours open for the last time.

It was summertime, but we were wearing our heavy coats. This is how you know that even then, even in spite of the rumors we had heard, we were still hopeful. Or stupid. Because we continued to imagine a future.

We were not put into wagons. Maybe there were too many of us – it seemed like hundreds. As we marched, soldiers rode alongside on horseback, their guns glinting in the sunlight.

My father moved slowly. He had never gone back to being

himself after my mother was taken, and losing Majer and Basia left its mark as well. He could not follow a whole conversation without his eyes going distant; his muscles had atrophied; he shuffled instead of striding from place to place. It was as if he had been bleached of color by some chronic harsh exposure, and although you could discern the outline of the man he'd been, he was no more substantial than a ghost.

The soldiers wanted us to walk at a steady clip, and I worried that my father would not make it. I was weak and dehydrated, and the road we were traveling on seemed to ripple before my eyes – but I was stronger than my father. 'The train station isn't too far,' I urged him. 'You can make it, Papa.' I reached over and took his suitcase in my free hand, so that he wouldn't have to carry the weight.

When the girl in front of me tripped and fell, I stopped. My father stopped, too. It caused a swell, like a tide butting up against a dam. *'Was ist los?'* the soldier closest to us asked. He kicked at the girl, who was lying on her side. Then he bent down and picked up a stick from the side of the road. He poked her and told her to get up.

When she didn't, he took the stick and tangled it into her hair. He tugged, then harder. He yelled at her to get up, and when she didn't he started to twist, until she began to scream and her scalp tore like a hem.

Another soldier approached, leveled his pistol, and shot the girl in the head.

It was suddenly quiet again.

I started to cry. I couldn't catch my breath. This girl whose name I did not know, her brains were on my boot.

I had seen dozens of people shot in front of me, to the point where it was hardly shocking anymore. The ones who were shot in the chest, they dropped like stones, cleanly. The ones who were shot in the head left behind a mess, runnels of gray matter and foamy pink tissue, and now it was on my boot, caught in the treads, and I wondered what part of her mind that was – the power of language? Of movement? The memory of her first kiss or her favorite pet or the day she moved to the ghetto?

I felt my father's hand close around my arm with a strength I did not realize he still possessed. 'Minusia,' he whispered, 'look at me.' He waited until I was staring into his eyes, until my panicked breathing slowed. 'If you die, it will be with a bullet to the heart, not the head. I promise.'

It was, I realized, a macabre version of the game we had once played, planning for his death. Except this time, he was planning for mine.

My father did not speak again until we had boarded the trains. Our suitcases had been taken elsewhere, and we were packed into the freight cars like cattle. My father sat down and put his arm around me, the way he had done when I was little. 'You and I,' he said softly, 'will have another bakery, where we're going. And people will come from miles around to eat the bread we bake. And every day, I'll bake you your own roll, with the cinnamon and chocolate inside, the way you like. Oh, it will smell like heaven, when it comes out of the oven . . .'

I realized that the car had gone quiet, that everyone was listening to my father's fantasies.

'They can take away my home,' he said. 'And my money, and my wife and my child. They can take away my livelihood and my food and' – here his voice hitched – 'my grandson. But they can't take away my dreams.'

His words were a net, drawing everyone into a chorus of agreement. 'I dream,' said a man across the railcar. 'Of doing to them what they've done to us.'

There was a smack on the wooden wall of the railway car, startling us.

Us, them.

But not all Jews were victims – look at Chairman Rumkowski, who sat safe with his new wife in his cushy home making lists, with the blood of my family on his hands. And not all Germans were murderers. Look at Herr Fassbinder, who had saved so many children on the night that children were taken away.

Another sharp rap on the car, this right behind where my head rested on the splintered wood. 'Get out,' a voice whispered, through the narrow slats, from the outside. 'Escape if you can. Your train is going to Auschwitz.'

It was chaos.

The ramp where we disembarked was a sea of humanity. We were numb, stiff, suffocating from the heat, gasping for fresh air. Everyone was screaming – attempting to locate family members, trying to be heard over the soldiers who were stationed every few feet with guns pointed at us, and who yelled for the men to go to one side, and the women to go to the other. In the distance was a long line of people who had arrived before us. I could see a brick building with chimneys.

Several men in striped clothing were trying to sort us. They looked like the pods of a milkweed, plants that might have once had color and animation but that now had dried up, and were waiting to blow away on a breath. They told us, in Polish, to leave our belongings on the ramp. I grabbed the sleeve of one man. 'Is this a factory?' I asked, pointing toward the building with the smokestacks.

'Yes,' he said, his lips pulling away from his yellow teeth. 'It's a factory where they kill people.'

In that instant I remembered the boy who had told me what happened to my mother, how I had thought he was lying or crazy.

My father began to move to the left, with the other men. 'Papa!' I screamed, running toward him.

As the butt of a gun crashed down on my temple, I saw stars. Everything went white, and when I blinked again, my father was moving further down the men's line of the ramp. I was, to my surprise, being dragged forward by a woman who had worked with me at Herr Fassbinder's embroidery *Fabrik*. I turned around and craned my neck just in time to see my father standing in front of the soldier at the head of the line, who stood with his finger on his pursed lips, assessing each man as he stepped forward. *Links,* he would mutter. *Rechts.*

I saw my father heading to the left, moving with the longer line of people. 'Where are they taking him?' I asked wildly.

But no one answered my question.

I was pushed and shuffled and yanked forward until I stood in front of one of the guards. He was standing beside a man in a white coat, who was the one directing us. The soldier was tall and had blond hair; he was holding a pistol. I looked away, trying to find my father in the moving mass of people. The man in the white coat grasped my chin in his hand, and it was all I could do not to spit at him. He looked at the bruise already forming on my head and murmured, '*Links,*' then gestured to the left.

I was euphoric. I was headed in the same direction as my father, which meant surely we would be reunited. '*Danke,*' I murmured, out of habit. But the soldier, the blond one, had heard what I said under my breath. '*Sprichst du deutsch?*' he asked.

'*J-ja, fließend,*' I stammered. I am fluent.

The soldier leaned toward the man in the white coat and murmured something. White Coat shrugged. '*Rechts*,' he pronounced, and I panicked.

My father had been sent to the left, and now I was being sent to the right, because I had been stupid enough to speak German. Maybe I had offended them; maybe I was not supposed to talk back, much less in their native tongue. But I was clearly in the minority. Other women, including the one who had worked with me at Herr Fassbinder's, were being sent to the left. I started to shake my head to protest, to beg to go left, but one of the Polish men in the stripes pushed me to the right.

I have thought about it many times, you know. About what would have happened if I'd gone to the left, which every muscle in my body was pulling me toward. But nobody likes a story without a happy ending, and I knew that I had to do whatever they said, if I were to have any chance of seeing my father again.

As I passed the soldier who had spoken to me, I realized his right hand – the one that was holding his pistol – was twitching. Almost like a tremor. I was afraid he'd shoot me by accident, if not on purpose. So I hurried by him and stood with a smaller group of women, until another soldier marched us to a red-brick building, shaped like the letter I. Across the road, I could see people milling in a grove, sitting quietly in front of the big building with the smokestacks. I wondered if my father was with them, if he could see me standing here.

We were herded into the building and told to undress. Everything off – clothes, shoes, stockings, underwear, hairpins. I looked around, embarrassed to see strangers naked in front of me, and even more embarrassed when I realized that the male soldiers who were guarding us did not plan to leave us in privacy. But they did not even look at our bodies; they seemed indifferent. I moved slowly, as if I were peeling off layers of skin and not just fabric. With one hand, I tried to cover myself. The other held on to my boots, like my father had told me.

One of the guards walked up to me. His eyes slid over me like a frost, settling on my boots. 'These are fine boots,' he said, and I tightened my arms around them.

He reached down and plucked them from my grasp, giving me a pair of wooden clogs instead. 'Too fine for you,' he pronounced.

With those boots went any chance I had of bribing my way out of here or getting information about my father. With those boots went the Christian papers that Josek had gotten me.

We were moved to a table where Jewish women in striped clothing held electric razors. As I got closer, I saw how they were shaving women's heads. Some got away with short hair; others were not as lucky.

I was not a vain girl. I had not grown up pretty; I was always in the shadow of Darija or even Basia. Until we moved to the ghetto, I had baby fat, a round face, thighs that rubbed when I walked. Starving had made me skinny, but it hadn't made me any prettier.

The only saving grace I had was my hair. Yes, it was dull and matted now, but it was also every color of brown, from chestnut to mahogany to teak. It had a natural wave and a curl at the end. Even when I braided it in a rope down my back, that plait was thick as a fist.

'Please,' I said. 'Don't cut off my hair.'

'Maybe you have something to persuade me to give you just a trim.' She leaned closer. 'You look like the kind of person who would smuggle something through.'

I thought of my boots, in that German soldier's hands.

I thought of this woman, who had presumably once been in line like us. If these Germans wanted to turn us into animals, then by all accounts, they had succeeded. 'Even if I did,' I whispered back, 'you'd be the last person on earth I'd ever give it to.'

She looked at me, raised her razor, and buzzed my hair off at the scalp.

It was at that moment I realized I wasn't Minka anymore. I was some other creature, something inhuman. Shivering, sobbing, I followed orders and hurried blindly into the shower room. All I could think of was my mother, and the false bath-house that the boy had told me about; those trucks full of gas that were emptied of bodies in the woods. I stared up at the showerheads, wondering if they would spray water or poison; wondering if I was the only person who had heard these rumors and whose heart was threatening to burst from her chest.

Then, a hiss. I closed my eyes, and tried to picture all the people I had loved in my short life. My parents, Basia, Darija. Rubin and Majer, Josek, Herr Bauer. Even Aron. I wanted to die with their names on my tongue.

I felt a trickle. Water. It was cold and sporadic. The shower-heads turned on and off before I managed to turn in a full circle. *No gas, no gas,* I thought, a litany. Maybe that boy had been wrong. Maybe what happened here was not the same as what had happened in Chełmno. Maybe this was what the soldiers had told us: a work camp.

There it was again: that mewling cry of hope.

'*Raus!*' a guard yelled. Dripping, I shuffled quickly out of the shower room and was given clothing. A work dress, a head covering, a jacket with blue and gray stripes. No socks or underwear.

I dressed fast. I wanted to cover up the shame of being

naked, indistinguishable from the other women around me. I was still buttoning my jacket when a guard grabbed me and dragged me toward a table. There, a man rubbed alcohol on my left forearm and another man began to write on me. I didn't understand what he was doing at first – it burned, and I could smell the sear of flesh. I looked down: A14660. I had been branded, like cattle. I had no name anymore.

We were pushed into a hut with no light, and as my eyes adjusted, I could see bunks, three tiers high, with straw laid on each tier as if this were a stable. There were no windows. The building reeked, and packed inside were several hundred women.

I thought of the railcar, how we had been stuffed inside and had gone for days without seeing the sun or stopping to stretch or go to the bathroom. I did not want to go through all that hell again just to die. *Better now,* I thought.

And before I realized what I was doing, my feet were turning away from the entrance to the hut and I was running with all the strength I could muster, flying across the dirt as best I could in my wooden shoes, toward the electric fence.

I knew, if I got close enough, that I would be free. That Aron and Darija and (please God) my father would remember me as Minka, not as this bald animal, not as a number. My arms stretched outward, as if I were racing toward a lover.

A woman's voice started to yell. I could hear the angry shouts of a guard, who a moment later collided with me, shoving me down on the ground and landing with his full weight on top of me. He dragged me upright by the collar of my dress and threw me into the barracks, so that I landed sprawled on my face on the concrete floor.

The door was slammed shut. I pushed myself to my knees, only to find someone reaching out a hand to me. 'What were you thinking!' a girl said. 'You would have died, Minka!'

I squinted. One moment I could not see past the low light and the shorn head and the bruises on her face. And then the next, I recognized Darija.

Just like that, I became human again.

Darija had been here two days longer than I had, and knew the routine. The *Aufseherin* oversaw the women's blocks. She reported to the *Schutzhaftlagerführer*, the male commandant of the women's camp. On her first day, Darija had seen him beat to death a woman who stumbled out of her straight line during roll call. Inside the huts were the *Stubenältesten* and the *Blockältesten*, who were Jews in charge of the individual rooms of the barrack and the entire barracks, respectively, and who were worse sometimes than the German guards. Our *Blockälteste* was a Hungarian called Borbala, who reminded me of a giant squid. She stayed in a separate room in the hut, and had a chin that ran right into the fleshy sleeve of her neck and eyes that glinted like chips of coal. Her voice was as deep as a man's, and she would scream at us in the morning, at 4:00, to rise. It was Darija who told me to sleep with my shoes on, lest another prisoner steal them, and to tuck my bowl inside my shirt as I slept for the same reason. She explained the *Bettenbau*, the military bed we were expected to fashion out of the straw mattress and the thin blanket. It was, of course, impossible to make straw look as precise as a real mattress. This was just an excuse for Borbala to make someone an example for the rest of us. Darija was the one who told me to run to the toilets, because there were only a limited number for hundreds of us, and we had only a few moments before roll call. Being late was, once again, grounds for a beating. Darija touched her head as she told me this, her temple still blooming with a mottled purple bruise. She had learned the hard way.

At *Appell*, we were counted, sometimes for hours. We were to stand at attention as Borbala called our numbers. If someone was missing, everything stopped while that person was located – usually sick or dead in the hut. She would be dragged into position, and the count would start over again. We were forced to do 'sport' – running in place for hours at a time, then dropping to the ground when Borbala commanded us to do frog leaps. Only after that were rations given: dark water that passed for coffee, a slice of brown bread. 'Save half,' Darija told me that first day, and I thought she was joking, but she wasn't. It was the only solid food we got. There would be a watery broth with rotten vegetables for lunch, maybe a broth with rancid meat for supper. It was better, Darija assured me, to go to bed on a full stomach.

Sometimes there were exercises, even though there wasn't enough food to keep us strong. Sometimes we had to learn German songs and phrases, including basic commands.

All of this was done in the shadow of that long, low building I had seen when we first got off the train, the place with the smokestacks that burned day and night. From those who had been in quarantine longer than we had, we learned that they were crematoria. That Jews had built them. That the only way out of this hellhole was as ash through those chimneys.

Five days after I arrived, and after we had finished the morning *Appell*, Borbala ordered us all to strip naked. We stood in a line in the courtyard while the man in the white coat I remembered from the ramp paraded by us. With him was the same SS officer whose hand shook – the one I now knew to be the *Schutzhaftlagerführer*. I wondered if he would recognize me, try to speak in German. He did not even flick his glance over me, however, and why would he have recognized me? I was just another skinny, shaved prisoner. I knew better than to speak or to move, especially with an SS man present. If we made Borbala look bad, we would pay for it later.

The man in the white coat picked eight girls, who were immediately taken from the hut and sent to Block 10, the medical facility. Anyone else who had a scrape or a cut or a burn or a blister was weeded out as well. His eyes passed over Darija, and then settled on my face. I felt the touch of his stare sliding from my forehead to my chin to my breastbone. My teeth started to chatter, in spite of the heat.

He flicked his glance past me, and I heard Darija exhale heavily through her nostrils.

After an hour, those of us who remained were told to dress and to get our bowls. We would be moved out of quarantine, Borbala told us, after we had our morning meal. A girl named Ylonka volunteered to carry the giant pot of coffee because with the task came an extra bread ration. 'Look at that,' I murmured to Darija, as we stood in line with our bowls. 'The pot is bigger than she is.'

It was true, Ylonka was a tiny thing, but there she was carrying the giant steel tub as if it were filled with manna from Heaven instead of swill. She set it down gently, so not a single drop sloshed over the edge.

Borbala, however, was not as careful. When it came to my turn, nearly half of the coffee spilled onto the ground. I looked at the puddle the *Blockälteste* had made, which was just enough time for her to notice the disappointment on my face. 'So sorry,' she said, in a way that let me know she was not sorry at all, and she held out my slice of bread. Except instead of handing it to me, she dropped it into the mud puddle made by my coffee.

I fell to my knees to grab the bread because even mucked in dirt, it was better than losing an entire ration for the day. But before my fingers could close around it, a boot crushed down on the slice, pushing it deeper into the mud, and hesitating long enough for me to understand the action was deliberate. I squinted into the sunlight and saw the black silhouette of a German officer. I rocked back on my heels, waiting for him to pass.

When he did, I grabbed the bread from the mud and tried to press it against my dress, to get rid of the worst of the filth. I could not see the officer's face anymore, but I knew who it was. As he walked away from me, his right hand was still twitching.

Darija and I shared a bunk with five other women. The hut where we lived was no different from quarantine, except there were more of us – about four hundred crammed into the block. The smells were indescribable – unwashed bodies, sweat, festering sores, rotting teeth, and always in the air around us the sweet, charred, sickly scent of flesh burning. What was new, though, was the condition of these other women. Some had been here for months, and they were no more than skeletons, their skin drawn over their cheekbones and ribs and hips, their eyes sunken and dark. At night, the sleeping quarters were so tight that I could feel the hip bones of the woman behind me, pushed like twin daggers into the small of my back. When one of us rolled over in our sleep the rest of us had to do the same.

I had spent the week trying to get word of my father. Was he in a different part of the camp, working, like I was? Was he wondering if I was alive, too? It was Agnat, a woman who shared the bunk with us, who bluntly told me my father was gone, that he had been gassed that very first day. 'What do you think is the business of this camp?' she chided. 'Death.'

Agnat had been here for a month and had a mouth on her. She would talk back to the *Blockälteste* – a woman we called the Beast – and get beaten with a truncheon; she would spit at a guard and get whipped. But she had also fought off a prisoner who tried to steal my jacket in the middle of the night when I was sleeping fitfully. For this small loyalty, I was grateful to her.

Two days ago, there had been an inspection in the hut. We had lined up while the *Blockälteste* and a guard tossed aside the neat covers we had made on our beds and pulled the bunks away from the wall to see what was being hidden. I knew that prisoners had items stashed – I had seen women with a deck of cards, money, cigarettes. I had seen one girl too sick to eat her midday soup carefully hide it underneath the straw that made up her mattress, so that she could save it for later, even though having any food in the barracks was a serious infraction.

When the guard came to our bunk, he began pulling aside the covers and found, to my surprise, a book by Maria Dąbrowska. 'What is this?'

He smacked one of our bunkmates, a girl who was only fifteen, across the face. Her cheek started to bleed where his gold ring had cut into the skin.

'It's mine,' Agnat said, stepping forward.

I wasn't convinced that the book was hers. Agnat had come from a small village in Poland and could barely read signs, much less a novel. But she stood proudly in front of the guard, claiming the book, until she was dragged outside and whipped unconscious. I thought of my mother's advice to me, when the *Aussiedlung* had begun: *Be a mensch*. Agnat was this, and more.

Darija and I, along with Helena, the fifteen-year-old, were the ones who picked Agnat up and carried her back into the hut. We gave her some of our evening meal when she was unable to stand to get her own. Another woman, who had been a nurse in her former life, did the best she could to clean the open sores made by the lashes and to bandage them.

We lived with lice and rats. We barely had water for washing. Agnat's cuts grew red and fierce, swollen with pus. At night, she could not get comfortable. 'Tomorrow,' Darija told her, 'we will take you to the hospital.'

'No,' Agnat insisted. 'If I go, I won't come back.' The hospital was next to the crematoria. It was called the waiting room because of this.

As I lay in the dark beside Agnat, I could feel the heat of the fever in her body. She grabbed my sleeve. 'Promise me,' she said, but she did not finish her sentence, or maybe she did, and I had already fallen asleep.

The next morning when the Beast came in screaming at us, Darija and I ran to the toilets as usual and then lined up for *Appell*. Agnat, however, was missing. The Beast called her number, twice, and then pointed at us. 'Find her,' she demanded, and Darija and I went back into the hut. 'Maybe she is too sick to stand,' Darija whispered, when we saw the outline of Agnat's form beneath the thin blanket.

'Agnat,' I whispered, shaking her shoulder. 'You have to get up.'

She didn't move.

'Darija,' I said. 'I think . . . I think she's . . .'

I couldn't say it, because saying it would make it real. It was one thing to see the distant, putrid smoke and guess at what was happening in those buildings. It was another to know that a dead woman had been pressed up against me the entire night.

Darija leaned over and closed Agnat's eyes. Then she grabbed her arm, which was already stiffening. 'Don't just stand there,' Darija muttered, and I leaned over the bunk and took Agnat's other arm. It was not hard to maneuver her down; she weighed next to nothing. We put her arms around our necks, as if we were school chums posing for a photograph. Then we dragged Agnat's upright body between us to the courtyard, so that it could still be counted, because if the number was off even by one prisoner they would start over again. We held her upright for the two and a half hours of *Appell*, as flies buzzed around her eyes and mouth.

'Why is God doing this to us?' I murmured.

'God's not doing anything to us,' Darija said. 'It's the Germans.'

When the count was finished, we loaded Agnat's body into a cart with ten other women who had died during the night in our block. I wondered what had become of the Dąbrowska book. If some German soldier had confiscated and destroyed it. Or if there was still room for beauty like that in a world that had come to this.

Nothing grew in Auschwitz. No grass, no mushrooms, no weeds, no buttercups. The landscape was dusty and gray, a wasteland.

I thought this every morning as I was marched to work, past the shacks that were the men's barracks and past the incessant operation of the crematoria. Darija and I were lucky, because we had been assigned to Kanada. It was an area where the belongings that had come in on the trains were sorted. The valuables were tallied and given to the guards, who brought them to the SS officer in charge of getting them to Berlin. The clothing went somewhere else. And then there were the items that no one needed: eyeglasses, prosthetic limbs, photographs. These were to be destroyed. The reason it was nicknamed Kanada was that we all imagined that country as the land of plenty, and certainly that was what we saw every day as the suitcases piled up in the sheds with every new transport. In Kanada, too, if a guard was looking the other way, it was possible to steal an extra pair of gloves, underwear, a hat. I hadn't been brave enough to do it, yet, but the nights were turning cooler. It would be worth the risk of punishment, knowing I had a warm layer under this work dress.

But that punishment, it was real, and it was serious. It was bad enough to have guards that watched over us, telling us to work faster and waving their guns. But the SS officer who was in charge of Kanada also spent a portion of the day weaving among us as we worked, to make sure we did not steal. He was a slight man, not much taller than I was. I had seen him drag outside a prisoner who had hidden a gold candlestick up the sleeve of her jacket. Although we did not see the beating, we could hear it. The prisoner was left unconscious in front of the barracks; the officer returned to walk through the aisles where we worked, with a nauseated look on his face. It made him seem human, and if he was human, how could he do this to us?

Darija and I had talked about this. 'More likely he was upset he had to get his hands dirty. Besides, what do you care?' she said with a shrug. 'All you need to know is that he is a monster.'

But there were all sorts of monsters. For years I had written of an *upiór*, after all. But *upiory*, they were the undead. There were monsters that took over the living, too. We had a neighbor in Łódź whose husband had been hospitalized, and by the time he came home, had forgotten the name of his wife and where he lived. He kicked the family's cat and swore like a sailor and seemed so radically different from the man she knew and loved that she called in a healer. The old woman who'd come to the house said there was nothing to be done; a *dybbuk* – the soul of someone dead, who would do whatever awful things it could in this new body that it hadn't been given time to do in its old one – had attached itself to the husband while he was at the hospital. He had been possessed, his mind usurped by a spirit with squatter's rights.

Secretly, when the SS officer in charge of Kanada passed by, I thought of him as Herr Dybbuk. A human man too weak to force out the evil that had taken up residence in him.

'You are a silly, stupid girl,' Darija said when I mentioned this to her one night, whispering in the bunk we shared. 'Not everything is fiction, Minka.'

I did not believe her. Because this – this camp, this horror – was exactly the sort of stuff no one would ever believe as fact. Take the Allies, for example. If they had heard of people being gassed, hundreds at a time, wouldn't they have already come to save us?

Today I had been given a pair of scissors to cut up the linings of clothes. There was a pile of fur coats I was working my way through. Inside I sometimes found wedding bands, gold earrings, coins, and as I did I turned them over to the guard. I wondered sometimes who had wound up with my boots, and how long it had been before she found the treasure hidden in the heels.

There was always a little ripple of awareness when Herr Dybbuk arrived or departed, as if his presence was an electric shock. Even though I did not turn around to watch, I could hear him approaching with another SS officer. They were speaking, and I eavesdropped on their German conversation as I ripped open a hem.

So then, the beer hall?

At eight.

You won't tell me you're too busy again. I am beginning to think you're avoiding your own brother.

Over my shoulder, I peeked. It was rare to hear two officers talking in such a friendly manner. Mostly, they just yelled at each other the way they yelled at us. But these two, they were apparently related.

'I'll be there,' Herr Dybbuk vowed, laughing.

He was talking to the SS officer who oversaw *Appell*. The man in charge of the women's camp. The one with the tremor in his hand.

The one who was not inhabited by an evil spirit. He was just evil, period. He had ordered Agnat's beating and ran hot and cold when it came to overseeing *Appell*. Either he seemed bored and the count went quickly, or he was on a rampage and took his fury out on us. Just that morning, he had raised his pistol and shot a girl who was too weak to stand upright. When the girl beside her jumped in response, he shot her, too.

These officers were related?

There was a passing similarity, I supposed. They both had the same jaw, the same sandy hair. And tonight, after they had beaten and starved and demeaned us, they would go share a beer together.

I had paused, thinking about this, and the guard who was watching me sift through the suitcases and satchels shouted at me to get to work. So I reached into the pile that never seemed to get any smaller and pulled out a leather valise. I tossed away a nightgown and some brassieres and underwear, a lace hat. There was a silk roll with a string of pearls. I called to the officer, who was smoking a cigarette and leaning against the wall of the shack, and handed it over to him to record and inventory.

I lugged another piece of luggage out of the heap.

This one, I recognized.

I suppose several people might have had the same overnight case as my father, but how many of those would have had the handle repaired with a length of wire, where it had broken after I used it, years ago, as part of a pretend fort to play in? I fell to my knees, turning my back on the guard, and opened the straps.

Inside were the candlesticks that had come from my grandmother, wrapped carefully in my father's tallith. Beneath that were his socks, his undershorts. A sweater that my mother had knit for him. He'd told me once that he hated it, that the sleeves were too long and the wool too itchy, but she had gone to so much trouble, how could he *not* pretend that he loved it more than anything?

I could not catch my breath, could not move. No matter what Agnat had said, no matter what evidence I was confronted with daily as I marched past the crematoria and the long line of new arrivals waiting blindly to go inside, I had not believed my father was truly dead until I opened this suitcase.

I was an orphan. I had nobody left in the world.

With shaking hands I took the tallith, kissed it, and added it to the pile of trash. I set the candlesticks aside, thinking of my mother saying the prayer over them at Shabbat dinner. Then I lifted the sweater.

My mother's hands had worked the needles, looped the yarn. My father had worn it over his heart.

I couldn't let someone else wear this, someone who didn't know that every inch of it told a tale. This yarn lived up to its second meaning – a tale – with every knit and purl part

of the saga of my family. This sleeve was the one my mother
had been working on when Basia fell down and hit her head
on the corner of the piano bench, and needed stitches at the
hospital. This neckline was so tricky she had asked for help
from our housekeeper, who was a much more accomplished
knitter. This hemline she had measured against my father's
midsection, joking out loud that she had not meant to marry
such a long-waisted gorilla of a man.

There is a reason the word *history* has, at its heart, the
narrative of one's life.

I buried my face in the wool and started to sob, rocking
back and forth, even though I knew I was going to attract the
attention of the guards.

My father had trusted me with the details of his death, and
in the end, I was too late.

Wiping my eyes, I started to pull the hem of the sweater, so
that the weave unraveled. I rolled the yarn up around my arm
like a bandage, a tourniquet for a soul that was bleeding out.

The guard closest to me approached, screaming, jerking
his gun at my face.

Do it, I thought. *Take me, too.*

I kept pulling on the yarn, until it lay in a nest around me,
crimped and rust-colored. Somewhere, Darija was probably
watching me and too afraid for her own welfare to tell me to
stop. But I couldn't. I was unraveling, too.

The commotion attracted some of the other guards, who
came over to see what was happening. When one leaned
down to grab the candlesticks, I snatched them in one hand
and then took the scissors I had used to cut up fur coats and
opened their legs wide, pressing the blade against my throat.

The Ukrainian guard laughed.

Suddenly a quiet voice spoke. 'What is going on here?'

The SS officer in charge of Kanada pushed through the crowd. He towered over me, taking in the scene: the open suitcase, the sweater that I had destroyed, my white knuckles on the necks of the candlesticks.

On his orders, just this morning, I had seen a prisoner hit so hard in the back with a truncheon that she vomited blood. That woman had refused to discard tefillin that were found in a suitcase. What I was doing – destroying property that the Germans believed was theirs – was much worse. I closed my eyes, waiting for the blow, welcoming it.

Instead, I felt the officer pry the candlesticks out of my hands.

When I opened my eyes Herr Dybbuk's face was only inches from mine. I could see the tic of a muscle in his cheek, the blond stubble of his beard. '*Wem gehört dieser Koffer?*' To whom does this suitcase belong?

Meinem Vater, I murmured.

The SS officer's eyes narrowed. He looked at me for a long moment, then turned to the other guards and shouted at them to stop staring. Finally, he glanced back at me. 'Get back to work,' he said, and a moment later, he was gone.

I stopped counting the days. They all ran together, like chalk in the rain: shuffling from one side of the camp to the other, standing in line for a bowl of soup that was nothing more than hot water boiled with a turnip. I thought I had known hunger; I had no idea. Some girls would steal tins of food hidden in the suitcases, but I had not been brave enough yet. I would dream sometimes of the rolls my father made me, the cinnamon bursting on my tongue like gustatory fireworks. I would close my eyes and see a table groaning with the weight of Shabbat dinner; would taste the fatty, crisp skin of the chicken, which I used to peel from the bird when it came from the oven, even though my mother would swat at my hand and tell me to wait till it was on the table. Then in my dreams, I would taste all these things, and they would turn to ash in my mouth – not the ash of coals but the ash that was shoveled from the crematoria day and night.

I learned, too, how to survive. The best position for *Appell*, when we lined up in rows of five, was in the middle, out of reach of SS guns and whips, yet close to other prisoners who could hold you up if you fainted. When lining up for food, halfway through the queue was best. The front of the line got served first, but what they were served was the watery bit that floated on top. If you could hold out to the middle of the line, you were more likely to get something nutritious.

The guards and the kapos were always vigilant to make sure we were not talking as we worked or marched or moved. It was only in the hut, at night, that we could speak freely. But as the days stretched into weeks, I found that it took too much energy to have a conversation, anyway. Besides, what was there to say? If we spoke at all, it was of food – what we missed the most, where in Poland you could find the finest hot chocolate or the sweetest marzipan or the richest petits fours. Sometimes, when I would share a memory of a meal, I noticed the others listening. 'It's because you don't just tell stories,' Darija explained. 'You paint with words.'

Maybe so, but that is the funny thing about paint. At the first cold splash of reality, it washes away, and the surface you were trying to cover is just as ugly as ever. Every morning, being marched to Kanada, I would see Jews waiting in the groves until it was their turn at the crematoria. They were still wearing their clothes, and I wondered how long it might be before I found myself ripping the lining of that wool coat or digging into the pockets of those trousers. As I walked by I kept my gaze trained on the ground. If I had been looking up, they would pity me, with my shaved head and my scarecrow body. If I had been looking up, they would see my face and know that what they were about to be told – that this shower was just a precaution, before they were sent out to work – was a lie. If I had been looking up, I would have been tempted to shout out the truth, to tell them that the smell wasn't from a factory or kitchen but from their own friends and relatives being incinerated. I would have started to scream and maybe I would never have stopped.

Some of the women prayed. I saw no point in that; since if there was a God, He would not have let this happen. Others said that the conditions at Auschwitz were so horrendous God chose not to go there. If I prayed for anything it was to fall asleep quickly without concentrating on my stomach digesting its own lining. So instead I went through the motions: line up for *Appell*, line up for work, line up for food, line up for work, march back to the barrack, line up for *Appell*, line up for food, crawl into my bunk.

The work I did was not hard, not compared to what some of the other women had to do. We got to step inside from the cold, into the sorting sheds. We hauled suitcases and clothing, but not stone. The most difficult part of my job was knowing that I was the last person who would touch the clothes this person had worn, who would see his face in photographs, who would read the love letters his wife had written. The hardest, of course, were the possessions of little boys and little girls – toys, blankets, pretty patent leather shoes. No children survived here; they were the first to be sent to the showers. When I came upon their belongings, I sometimes started to cry. It was devastating to hold a teddy bear, because its owner never would again, before tossing it into a pile to be destroyed.

I began to feel a great responsibility, as if my mind was a

vessel, and I had the duty of keeping a record of those who were gone. We had ample opportunity to steal clothing, but the first thing I stole from Kanada was not a scarf or a pair of warm socks. It was someone else's memories.

I had promised myself that even if it meant getting a clout on the head from a guard, I would take that extra moment to look at the trappings of a life that was about to be obliterated from existence. I would touch the spectacles with reverence; I would tie the pink ribbons on the knit baby booties; I would memorize one of the addresses in a small leather-bound book of business contacts.

The photographs, they were the hardest for me. Because they were the only proof that this person, who had owned these undergarments and carried this suitcase, had been alive. Had been happy. And it was my job to obliterate that evidence.

But one day, I didn't.

I waited for the guard to walk away from the row where I was working, and opened up a photo album. Written carefully beneath each picture was a caption, and a date. In the photos, everyone was smiling. I saw a young woman who must have been the owner of this suitcase, smiling up into the face of a young man. I looked at their wedding picture, and at some vacation abroad, with the girl mugging for the camera. I wondered how many years ago this had been.

Then came a series of photos of a baby, carefully captioned. 'Ania, 3 days.' 'Ania sits up.' 'Ania's first steps.' 'First day of school.' 'First tooth lost!'

And then, the pictures stopped.

This child had the same name as the character in my story, which made her seem even more compelling. I could hear the guard yelling at one of the women behind me. Quickly, I popped one of the photos out of the little corner reinforcements that had held it in place. I slipped it up my sleeve.

I panicked when the guard came back, certain that he had seen what I did. But instead, he just told me to speed up my work.

That first night, I went home with pictures of Ania, of Herschel and Gerda, of a little boy named Haim missing his two front teeth. The next day, I was bold enough to take eight photographs. Then I was put on a different detail, loading clothes into carts and transporting them to sheds. As soon as I was reassigned to sorting the belongings, I went back to tucking various photos up my sleeve and squirreling them in the straw of my bunk.

I didn't see it as stealing. I saw it as archiving. Before I went to sleep I would take out these photos, this growing deck of the dead, and whisper my way through their names. Ania, Herschel, Gerda, Haim. Wolf, Mindla, Dworja, Izrael. Szymon, Elka. Rochl and Chaja, the twins. Eliasz, still wailing after his *bris*. Szandla, on her wedding day.

As long as I remembered them, then they were still here.

Darija was working next to me, and she had a toothache. I could see her shoulders shaking with the effort of not moaning. If you showed illness, you were an even bigger target than usual for the guards, who took a tiny snag of weakness and ripped it wide open.

From the corner of my eye I saw her lift up a small autograph book with a sequined cover. When we were little, Darija had had one just like it. We would stand outside the theater and fancy restaurants sometimes, and wait for glamorous women in white fur coats and silver heels to exit on the arms of their handsome beaux. I have no idea if any of them were actually famous, but they seemed that way to us. Darija glanced furtively toward me and slid the book across the bench. I buried it beneath a coat whose lining I was ripping to shreds.

The book was filled with ticket stubs from films and sketches of buildings; the wrapper from a mint candy; and a little poem that I recognized as a hand-clapping game. A hair ribbon, a swatch of tulle from a fancy dress. A winning ticket from a bakery giveaway. Written inside the back cover were two words: 'NEVER FORGET.' Inside the front cover a photo had been glued, of two girlfriends. 'Gitla & Me,' the caption read. I didn't know who 'Me' was. There was no identifying information, and the handwriting, careful and loopy, belonged to a young girl.

I decided I would call her Darija.

I looked over at my friend and saw her wipe away a tear with her sleeve. She could have been wondering what became of her own sequined autograph book. Or of the happy girl who had once owned it.

If I had not seen the transformation myself, I would not have recognized Darija. The long, lithe dancer's body of which I had been so jealous was now a bag of bones. Beneath her clothing, the knobs of her spine stood out like fence posts. Her eyes were sunken, her lips chapped dry. She now bit her nails to the point where they bled.

I'm pretty sure I looked just as awful to her as she did to me.

I ripped out the page with the photograph and tucked it into my sleeve, a move that I now had down to a science.

Suddenly a hand reached over my shoulder and picked up the autograph book.

Herr Dybbuk stood so close to me that I could smell the pine of his aftershave. I did not turn my head, did not speak or acknowledge him. I heard him rifling through the pages.

Surely he would notice the spot in the front where something had been torn out?

He moved away, throwing the book onto the heap of items to be burned. But for at least another quarter of an hour, I could feel the heat of his stare on the back of my neck, and that day I stole nothing else from Kanada.

At night Darija couldn't sleep, the pain was so bad. 'Minka,' she whispered, shivering against me. 'If I die, you won't have a picture of me to save.'

'I won't need one, because you're not going to die,' I told her.

I knew her tooth was infected. Her breath smelled as if she was rotting from the inside out, and her cheek was swollen to twice its size. If the tooth didn't come out, she wasn't going to survive. I hugged her back to my front, giving her whatever body heat I still had. 'Say them with me,' I begged. 'It will distract you.'

Darija shook her head. 'It hurts . . .'

'Please,' I said. 'Just try.' I did not even need the photos anymore. Ania, Herschel, Gerda, Majer, Wolf. With each name I spoke, I imagined the face in the picture.

Then the thinnest thread of Darija's voice responded. 'Mindla?'

'That's right. Dworja, Izrael.'

'Szymon,' Darija added. 'Elka.'

Rochl and Chaja. Eliasz. Fiszel and Liba and Bajla. Lejbus, Mosza, Brajna. Gitla and Darija.

By then she had stopped reciting with me. Her body went lax.

I checked to make sure she was still breathing, and then I let myself fall asleep.

The next day Darija woke with a swollen, red face, her skin on fire. She couldn't drag herself out of bed so I had to do it for her, bearing her weight and hauling her to the toilets and then back to the bunk to make our bed. When the Beast came in, I was waiting to volunteer to get the gruel, because hauling the pot entitled me to an extra ration. I gave it to Darija, who was too weak to even lift the bowl to her mouth. I tried to coax her to open her mouth by singing the way Basia had sung to Majer, when he refused to eat.

'You can't sing,' she croaked, smiling the tiniest bit, and it was just enough for me to get some of the liquid inside.

I hauled her upright during *Appell*, praying that the head officer – the one with the shudder in his arm, whom I thought of now as Herr Tremor – didn't notice she was ailing. Herr Tremor might have had some kind of condition that led him to quiver like that, but it wasn't severe enough to keep him from meting out brutal punishment with his own hands. Last week, when a new girl turned left instead of right at his command, he disciplined the whole block. We had to do calisthenics for two hours in a cold, driving rain. Needless to say, with so many women starving, at least ten collapsed, and when they did, Herr Tremor walked through the mud and kicked them where they lay. But today he seemed in a rush; instead of making an example of us or singling women out for punishment, he hurried through the counting and dismissed the kapos.

I was on a mission. Not only did I have to cover for Darija and do twice the work but I had to find something in particular that I could steal. Something sharp and small, something capable of knocking out a tooth.

I managed to set Darija beside me at the sorting bench and paced myself so that every time she had to bring a valuable to the locked box in the center of the barracks, I had to go, too. By the end of the day, though, I had not found a single item that would work. Three pairs of false teeth, a wedding gown, tubes of lipstick, but nothing pointed and strong.

And then.

In one leather satchel, slipped into a torn silk lining, was a fountain pen.

My hand closed around it with an ache. Holding a pen felt so normal that my past, which I had surgically separated from the current state of my existence, came rushing back. I could see myself curled in the window of my father's bakery, writing my book. I could remember chewing on the tip of a pen as I heard the dialogue of Ania and Aleksander in my head. The story flowed like blood from my hand; sometimes it seemed that I was simply channeling a film that was already playing, that I was only the projector instead of the creator. When I wrote, I felt untethered, impossibly free. And right now, I barely remembered what that was like.

I hadn't realized how much I'd missed writing in the weeks I'd been here. *Real writers can't* not *write*, Herr Bauer had once told me, when we were discussing Goethe. *That is how you know, Fräulein Lewin, if you are destined for the life of a poet.*

My fingers itched, curling around the instrument. I did not even know if there was ink inside. To test it, I pressed the nib against the numbers that had been burned into my left forearm. The ink flowed, a beautiful black Rorschach blot, covering up what they had done to me.

I slipped the pen into my jacket. This was for Darija, I reminded myself. Not for me.

That night I enlisted the help of another girl to prop Darija up at the evening *Appell*. She could barely stand by the time we were sent back to the block, two hours later. She wouldn't let me even touch her cheek, so that I could open her lips and see how bad the infection had become.

Her forehead was so hot it blistered against my hand. 'Darija,' I said, 'you have to trust me.'

She shook her head, near delirium. 'Leave me alone,' she wailed.

'I will. After I knock out that stupid tooth.'

My comment cut through whatever haze she was in. 'Like hell you will.'

'Shut up and open your mouth,' I muttered, but when I went to grab her chin, she reared away.

'Is it going to hurt?' she whimpered.

I nodded, looking her right in the eye. 'Yes. If I had any gas, I'd give it to you.'

Darija started to laugh. Faintly at first, and then a loud bark, one that made the other girls turn around in their bunks. 'Gas,' she wheezed. 'You don't have any gas?'

I realized how silly this was, given the mass extermination that was going on just yards away from our hut. Suddenly I was laughing, too. It was inappropriate and awful gallows humor, and we could not stop. We collapsed against each other, snorting and hooting, until everyone else got disgusted with us and looked away.

When we finally could control ourselves, we had our emaciated arms around each other, the gangly limbs of two tangled praying mantises. 'If you can't anesthetize me,' Darija said, 'then distract me, okay?'

'I could sing,' I suggested.

'You want to cause more pain, or prevent it?' She looked at me, desperate. 'Tell me a story.'

I nodded. I took the pen out of my pocket and tried to clean it as best I could, which wasn't easy given that my clothes were filthy. Then I looked at my best friend, my only friend.

I couldn't tell her a memory from our childhood, because

that would be too upsetting. I couldn't spin a yarn about our future, because we barely had one.

There was really only one story I knew by heart: the one I'd been writing – the one Darija had been *reading* – for years.

'My father trusted me with the details of his death,' I began, the words rising, rote, from some deep cave of my mind. *"Ania," he would say, "no whiskey at my funeral. I want the finest blackberry wine. No weeping, mind you. Just dancing. And when they lower me into the ground, I want a fanfare of trumpets, and white butterflies." A character, that was my father. He was the village baker, and every day, in addition to the loaves he would make for the town, he would create a single roll for me that was as unique as it was delicious: a twist like a princess's crown, dough mixed with sweet cinnamon and the richest chocolate. The secret ingredient, he said, was his love for me, and this made it taste better than anything else I had ever eaten.'*

I opened Darija's mouth gently and positioned the pen at the root of her swollen gum. I lifted a stone I had pried from the latrines. *'We lived on the outskirts of a village so small that everyone knew everyone else by name. Our home was made of river stone, with a thatched roof; the hearth where my father baked heated the entire cottage. I would sit at the kitchen table, shelling peas that I grew in the small garden out back as my father opened the door of the brick oven and slid the peel inside to take out crusty, round loaves of bread. The red embers glowed, outlining the strong muscles of his back as he sweated through his tunic. "I don't want a summer funeral, Ania," he would say. "Make sure instead I die on a cool day, when there's a nice breeze. Before the birds fly south, so that they can sing for me."*

'I would pretend to take note of his requests. I didn't mind the macabre conversation; my father was far too strong for me to believe any of these requests of his would ever come to pass.

Some of the others in the village found it strange, the relationship I had with my father, the fact that we could joke about this, but my mother had died when I was an infant and all we had was each other.'

I looked down to see Darija finally relaxed, caught in the gauze of my words. But I realized, too, that the whole hut had gone quiet; all the women were listening to me.

'*My father trusted me with the details of his death,*' I said, raising the rock directly above the pen. '*But in the end, I was too late.*'

Swiftly I smashed the stone into the pen, a makeshift chisel. The sound that Darija made was unearthly. She reared up as if she'd been run through with a sword. I fell back, horrified by what I'd done, as she clutched her hands to her mouth and rolled away from me.

When she looked up, her eyes were bright red, the blood vessels having burst from the force of her scream. Blood streamed down her chin, too, as if she herself was an *upiór* after a kill. 'I'm so sorry,' I cried. 'I didn't mean to hurt you . . .'

'Minka,' she said, through the blood, through her tears. She grabbed my hand, or at least that's what I thought she was doing, until I realized she was trying to give me something.

In her palm was a broken, rotted tooth.

The next day, Darija's fever had broken. I again carried the breakfast rations from the kitchen, so that I could get an extra helping for Darija to build up her strength. When she smiled at me, I could see the gap where her tooth had been, a black chasm.

A new woman joined us in the block that evening. She was from Radom, and she had given her three-year-old to her elderly mother at the loading ramp, on the whispered advice of one of the men in striped uniforms. She could not stop crying.

'If I'd known,' she sobbed, choking on the truth. 'If I'd known why he said that I never would have done it.'

'Then you would both be dead,' said Ester, the woman who, at age fifty-two, was the oldest one in the block. She worked with us in Kanada and had a steady black market business, trading cigarettes and clothing that were pilfered from the suitcases for extra rations.

This new woman could not stop crying. That was not an unusual phenomenon, but this particular crier, she was a loud one. And we were all exhausted from lack of food and long hours of labor. We were getting upset listening to her. It was worse than the rabbi's daughter from Lublin, who prayed out loud the whole night through.

'Minka,' Ester said finally, when this woman had been wailing for hours, 'do something.'

'What can I do?' I couldn't bring back her child or her mother. I couldn't undo what had happened. To be honest, I was annoyed with the woman; that's how inhuman I had become. We had all suffered losses like she had, after all. What made hers so special that it had to rob us of our precious hours of sleep?

'If we cannot shut her up,' another girl said, 'then maybe we can drown her out.'

There was a chorus of agreement. 'Where were you up to, Minka?' Ester asked.

At first I did not know what she was talking about. But then I realized that these women wanted to hear the story I had written, the one I had used to calm Darija the night before. If it worked as an anesthetic, why wouldn't it numb the pain of hearing this mother weep for her baby?

They sat like reeds on the edge of a pond, fragile and swaying slightly against each other for support. I could see the shine of their eyes in the dark.

'Go on,' Darija said, elbowing me. 'You have a captive audience.'

So I started to speak of Ania, for whom the day had begun like any other. How it was colder than usual for October; how the leaves had blustered off the limbs of the trees into small cyclones that danced like devils around her boots, which was how she knew that something bad was going to happen. Her father had taught her that, as well as everything else she knew: how to tie her shoes, how to navigate by the stars, how to see a monster who was hiding behind the face of a man.

I spoke of the people of the village, who were on edge. Some farm animals had been slaughtered; pet dogs had gone missing. There seemed to be a predator in their midst.

I told them about Damian, the captain of the guard, who wanted Ania to marry him, and wasn't above using force to make that happen. How he told the nervous mob that if they stayed within the walls of the village, they would be safe.

I had written that part just after moving to the ghetto. When I still believed that.

It was quiet in the block. The rabbi's daughter wasn't praying anymore; the new woman's sobs had quieted.

I described Damian taking the last baguette Ania had to sell at market, how he held his coins out of reach until she agreed to kiss him. How she left in a hurry with her empty basket and his eyes boring into her back. 'There was a stream that separated the cottage from the house,' I said, speaking in Ania's narrative voice.

'And my father had placed a wide plank across it so that we could get from one side to the other. But today, when I reached it, I bent to drink, to wash away the bitter taste of Damian that was still on my lips.'

I cupped my hands. *'The water,'* I said, *'ran red. I set down*

*the basket I was carrying and followed the bank upstream . . .
and then I saw it.'*

'Saw what?' Ester murmured.

I remembered, in that minute, what my mother had told me about being a mensch, about putting others' welfare before your own. I looked at the new woman, until she met my gaze.

'You'll have to wait till tomorrow to find out,' I said.

Sometimes all you need to live one more day is a good reason to stick around.

It was Ester who told me to write it down. 'You never know,' she said. 'Maybe one day you will be famous.'

I laughed at that. 'Or more likely the story will die with me.'

But I knew what she was asking. For the narrative to exist, so that it could be read and reread even if I was taken away. Stories outlive their writers all the time. We know plenty about Goethe and Charles Dickens from what tales they chose to tell, even though they have been dead for years.

I think, in the end, that's why I did it. Because there would be no photograph of me for someone to steal or to memorize. There was no family at home anymore to think of me. Maybe I wasn't even remarkable enough to be remembered; looking like I did these days, I was just another prisoner, another number. If I had to die in this hellhole, and the odds were very good that would happen, then maybe someone else would survive and tell their children the story a girl had told at night in the block. Fiction is like that, once it is released into the world: contagious, persistent. Like the contents of Pandora's box, a story that's freely given can't be contained anymore. It becomes infectious, spreading from the person who created it to the person who listens, and passes it on.

Ironically, it was the photographs that made it possible. One day, while reciting my litany, I dropped the deck of faces on the floor. Hurrying to gather them again, I realized that some were facedown. On the white cardboard of one photo I read, 'Mosza, 10 mos.'

Someone had written *that*.

It was a small square, smaller than what I was used to, but it was paper. And I had dozens of them, and a fountain pen.

Having something to live for went both ways. I would play Scheherazade for the block every night, weaving a story of Ania and Aleksander until they lived and breathed the way we did. But then, I would write by the light of the moon for a few hours to the even snores and occasional whimpers of the other women. To safeguard my work, I wrote in German. If these note cards were ever found, I had no doubt the punishment would be severe, but maybe less so if the guards could read the language and recognized it as a story, instead of thinking they were secret notes to be passed between prisoners to incite rebellion. I wrote from memory, adding bits and pieces as I edited my way through the story – always elaborating on scenes where food was described. I described in the greatest detail the crumb of that delicious roll Ania's father bakes for her. The way she could taste the butter in its flaky crust; the heat that stayed trapped on the soft palate; the burst of cinnamon on the tip of her tongue.

I wrote until the fountain pen bled itself dry, until as much of my story as possible was scratched in tiny, careful prose on the backs of over one hundred faces of the dead.

'*Raus!*'

One minute I was asleep, dreaming that I had been brought to a room with a table a kilometer long, on which there were heaps of food, and that I had to eat my way from one end to the other before I would be allowed to leave. The next, the Beast was smacking the straw of the bunk indiscriminately with a metal rod, her blows landing on my back and my thigh before I managed to scramble down from the perch.

Her back was to me, and she was yelling. Several guards filled the block and began to shove women out of the way, yanking the thin blankets off the bunks and sweeping the straw off the wooden planks. They were looking for contraband.

Sometimes we knew about an inspection. I don't know how, but rumors would reach us, so that there was time to hide whatever you had squirreled away in your bunk on your person, instead. Today, though, there had been no warning. I remembered the novel that had been confiscated weeks ago, the one that led to the injuries that caused Agnat's death. In my bunk, buried under the straw where I had lain last night, was the deck of photos with my story written out.

One girl was dragged outside when a guard found a hidden radio. We had been listening to it at night, to Chopin and Liszt and Bach, and once, a Tchaikovsky ballet that Darija had danced to in a recital in Łódź , which made her cry in her sleep. Sometimes, there would be bursts of news in between, and from these I learned that the German offensive was not going well, that they could not reconquer Belgium. I knew that the United States had continued to advance after landing in France this summer. I told myself it was only a matter of time, surely, before this war was over.

If I could survive the moments like this one, anyway.

The Beast stuck her hand into the straw of the bunk below mine and pulled out what looked like a small rock wrapped in paper. She brought it to her mouth, licked it. 'Who sleeps here?' she demanded.

The five girls who crammed into the tiny space stepped forward, holding tightly to each other's hands. 'Who stole this chocolate?' the Beast asked.

The girls looked completely bewildered. It was entirely possible that someone savvier, at the last minute, had shoved her stash of contraband into the straw of their bunk to save herself. At any rate, they stood mute, staring down at the cold dirt floor.

The *Blockälteste* grabbed the hair of one of the girls. Like the rest of us who worked in Kanada, we were allowed to grow ours out. Mine was about an inch long now. It was only one of the many things about that job assignment that made people jealous. The guards there called us fat swine, because we looked healthier than most of the female prisoners, since we could steal bits of food we found in suitcases. 'Is it yours?' the Beast yelled.

The girl shook her head. 'I don't . . . I d-didn't . . .'

'Maybe this will jog your memory,' she said, and she swung her metal rod across the front of all five of their faces, breaking teeth and noses and driving them to their knees.

She kicked between their fallen bodies to search the straw of our bunk. My heart started up like a machine gun; sweat broke out on my temples. I saw her hand close around the deck of photographs, which I had secured with a thread pulled from the hem of my uniform dress.

As the Beast untied the bow, Darija stepped forward. 'They belong to me.'

My jaw dropped. I knew exactly what she was doing: paying me back for saving her life. Before I could speak, another woman stepped forward, too – the one who'd arrived only three nights before, the one who could not stop weeping over the loss of her son and her mother. I still did not even know her name. 'She is lying,' the woman said. 'They're mine.'

'They're both lying.' I looked at the woman, wondering about her motivation. Was she trying to rescue me? Or just die herself? 'She doesn't work in Kanada. And she' – I nodded at Darija – 'does not speak German.'

One moment, I was standing, drenched in bravado, and the next I was being hauled out of the block. It was pouring outside, and the wind raged like a dragon. One of my wooden shoes got stuck in the mud; I had just enough time to grab for it before it got left behind. If you did not have shoes, you would not survive, period.

Standing in the center of the courtyard, rain pelting his wool uniform, was the SS officer I called Herr Tremor. There was no shudder in his grasp as he lifted a whip and brought it down on the back of the girl from my block who had hidden the radio. She lay facedown in a puddle. After each blow he yelled at her to get up, and each time she did, he struck her again.

I would be next.

An uncontrollable shiver ran down the length of me. My teeth were chattering, my nose running. I wondered if he would kill the girl who stole the radio.

Or me, for that matter.

It is a strange thing, to contemplate dying. I found myself thinking of the criteria I had once kept for my father, as an inside joke. I had criteria of my own now:

When I die, please make it fast.

If there is a bullet, aim for my heart, not my head.

It would be good if it did not hurt.

I'd rather die of a sudden blow than an infection. I'd even welcome the gas. Maybe that just felt like going to sleep and never waking up.

I do not know when I started thinking of the mass extermination at this camp as being humane – thinking like the

Germans, I supposed – but if the alternative was to waste away to a corpse, as my mind shut down by degrees due to starvation, well, then, maybe it was best to just get this over with.

As we approached Herr Tremor, he looked up, the rain sleeting across his features. His eyes, I noticed, were like glass. Pale and practically silver, like a mirror. 'I am not done here,' he said in German.

'Should we wait, *Schutzhaftlagerführer*?' asked the guard.

'I have no intention of standing around all day in this pissing rain because some animals cannot follow rules,' he said.

I lifted my chin. Very precisely, in German, I said, '*Ich bin kein Tier.*'

I am not an animal.

His gaze narrowed on mine. I immediately looked down at my feet.

He lifted his right hand, the one holding the whip, and cracked it across my cheekbone so that my head snapped to the side. '*Da irrst du dich.*'

You are mistaken.

I fell to my knees in the mud, holding one hand up to my cheek. The tail of the whip had cut a gash under my eye. Blood mixed with rain, running down my chin. The girl on the ground beside me caught my gaze. Her uniform had been flayed open; the flesh of her back was peeled back like the petals of a rose.

Behind me I could hear conversation; the guards who had brought me here were telling someone else, someone new, what my infraction was. This new officer stepped over me. '*Schutzhaftlagerführer*,' a voice said. 'You are busy here. With your permission perhaps I can help you?'

I could see only the back of his uniform, and his gloved hands, which were clasped behind him. His boots were so shiny that I stared at them, wondering how he could walk through so much mud without getting them filthy.

I could not believe that was what I was thinking about, the minute before I was to be killed.

Herr Tremor shrugged and turned back to the girl on the ground beside me. The other officer walked off. I was hauled upright and taken across the compound, past Kanada, to the administrative building where this officer entered. He shouted an order at the guards, and I was brought downstairs to some kind of cell. I heard a heavy lock being snapped into place after the door was sealed.

There was no light. The walls and the floor were made of stone; it was like an old wine cellar, slightly damp, with moss that made everything slippery. I sat with my back against the wall, sometimes pressing my swollen cheek to the cool stones. The one time I dozed off, I awakened to the feel of a mouse running up my leg beneath my work dress. After that, I stood.

Several hours passed. The cut on my face stopped bleeding. I wondered if the officer had forgotten about me, or if he was just saving me for punishment after the rain stopped, so that Herr Tremor could take his time hurting me. By then my cheek had inflamed so badly that my eye was swollen shut. When I heard the door being opened again, I winced at the beam of light that fell into the cramped space.

I was brought to an office. HAUPTSCHARFÜHRER F. HARTMANN, it said on the door. There was a large wooden desk, and many filing cabinets, and an ornate chair – the kind you always found lawyers sitting in. In that chair was the officer in charge of Kanada.

And spread out in front of him, across the green blotter of his desk and various papers and files, were all of my photographs, flipped onto their bellies to reveal my story.

I knew what Herr Tremor was capable of; I saw it every day at *Appell*. In a way, Herr Dybbuk was more frightening, because I had no idea what to expect from him.

He was in charge of Kanada and I had stolen from him and the evidence was displayed between us.

'Leave us,' he said to the guard who had brought me.

There was a window behind the officer. I watched the rain strike the glass, reveling in the simple fact that I was inside and warm. I was standing in a room where there was faint classical music playing on the radio. If not for the fact that I was probably about to be beaten to death, I would have counted this as the first moment since arriving at the camp that I felt normal.

'So you speak German,' he said, in his native tongue.

I nodded. '*Ja, Herr Hauptscharführer.*'

'And you can apparently write it, too.'

My eyes flickered toward the photographs. 'I studied in school,' I replied.

He passed me a pad of paper and a pen. 'Prove it.' He began to walk around the room, reciting a poem. '*Ich weiß nicht, was soll es bedeuten, / Daß ich so traurig bin, / Ein Märchen aus uralten Zeiten, / Das kommt mir nicht aus dem Sinn.*'

I knew the poem. I had studied it with Herr Bauer and had once taken an examination on this very dictation, for which I received the highest marks. I translated in my head: *I wish I knew the meaning, a sadness has fallen on me. The ghost of an ancient legend, that will not let me be.*

'*Die Luft ist kühl und es dunkelt,*' the *Hauptscharführer* continued. '*Und ruhig fließt der Rhein . . .*'

The air is cool in the twilight and gently flows the Rhine . . .

'*Der Gipfel des Berges funkelt,*' I added under my breath, '*im Abendsonnenschein.*'

He had heard me. He took the pad and checked my transcription. Then he looked up, staring at me as if I were a creature he had never seen before. 'You know this work.'

I nodded. '"The Lorelei," by Heinrich Heine.'

'*Ein unbekannter Verfasser*,' he corrected. Anonymous.

That was when I remembered that Heinrich Heine had been Jewish.

'You realize that you stole material from the Reich,' he murmured.

'Yes, I know,' I burst out. 'I'm sorry. It was a mistake.'

He raised his brows. 'It was a mistake to willfully steal something?'

'No. It was a mistake to think the photographs didn't matter to the Reich.'

He opened his mouth and then snapped it shut. He could not admit that the photographs were valuable, because that was tantamount to admitting that those who were killed had worth; but he couldn't admit that the photos were meaningless, because doing so would dilute his argument for punishing me. 'That is not the point,' he said finally. 'The point is that they do not belong to *you*.'

The officer sank back into his chair, rapping his fingers on his desk. He picked up one of the pictures and flipped it over to the side with writing on it. 'This story. Where is the rest of it?'

I imagined the guards ransacking the block, trying to find more photographs with writing. When they didn't, would they just start hurting people until someone gave them the answer they wanted? 'I haven't written it yet,' I confessed.

This surprised him; I realized he had assumed I was simply recounting a tale I'd read elsewhere. I wasn't supposed to be intelligent enough to create something like this. 'You,' he said. '*You* made up this monster . . . this *upiór*?'

'Yes,' I answered. 'Well, I mean, no. In Poland everyone knows about the *upiór*. But this particular one, he is a figment of my imagination.'

'Most girls write of love. You chose to write about a beast,' he said thoughtfully.

We were speaking in German. We were having a conversation, about writing. As if at any moment he might not take out his pistol and shoot me in the head.

'Your choice of topic reminds me of another mythical beast,' he said. 'The Donestre. You have heard of it?'

Was this a test? A trick? Was it a euphemism for some kind of corporal punishment? Was my treatment dependent on my answer? I knew of *Wodnik* – the water demon – and *Dziwożona* – dryads – but they were Polish legends. What if I lied and said yes? Would I be worse off than if I told the truth and said no?

'The ancient Greeks – which is what *I* studied in school – wrote of the Donestre. It had the head of a lion and the body of a man. It could speak all the languages of the human race, which as you might imagine,' the *Hauptscharführer* said drily, 'came in handy.'

I looked into my lap. I wondered what he would think if he knew my nickname for him, Herr Dybbuk, referred to yet another mythical beast.

'Like your *upiór*, this brute killed freely and devoured its prey. But the Donestre had one peculiar trait. It would save the severed head of its victim, sit beside it, and weep.' He fixed his gaze on me until I glanced up. 'Why do you think that was?'

I swallowed. I had never heard of this Donestre, but I knew the *upiór* Aleksander better than I knew myself. I had lived, breathed, birthed that character. 'Perhaps some monsters,' I said quietly, 'still have a conscience.'

The officer's nostrils flared. He stood up and came around the desk, and I immediately cowered, throwing up my arm to block the blow.

'You realize,' he said, his voice practically a whisper, 'for stealing, I could make an example of you. Publicly flog you, like the prisoner the *Schutzhaftlagerführer* was punishing earlier. Or kill you.'

Tears sprang to my eyes. As it turned out I was not too proud to plead for my meager life. 'Please don't. I'll do anything.'

The *Hauptscharführer* hesitated. 'Then tell me,' he said, 'what happens next?'

To say I was stunned would be an understatement. Not only did the *Hauptscharführer* not lay a hand on me but he kept me in his office for the rest of the day, typing out lists of all the items that had been salvaged in Kanada. These, I would learn, were sent to various places around Europe that were still controlled by the Germans, along with the goods themselves. This, he told me, was my new assignment. I would take dictation, type letters, answer the phone (in German, of course), and take messages for him. When he left to walk through the barracks of Kanada, his usual routine, he did not leave me alone. Instead, he had another officer stand guard inside the office, to make sure I did not do anything suspicious. The whole time I was typing, my fingers shook on the keys. When the *Hauptscharführer* returned, he sat down at his desk without saying a word. He began to punch numbers into an adding machine. Its long white tongue curled over the edge of his desk as he worked his way through a stack of papers.

By late afternoon, my head was swimming. Unlike in Kanada, I had not been given soup at lunch. However limited that sustenance was, it was still food. When the *Hauptscharführer* came back after one of his patrols of Kanada with a muffin and a coffee, my stomach growled so loudly that I knew that in our close quarters, he could hear it.

Shortly afterward there was a knock on the office door, and I jumped in my chair. The *Hauptscharführer* called out for the visitor to enter. I kept my eyes trained on the page in front of me, but immediately recognized the voice of the *Schutzhaftlagerführer*, which sounded like smoke falling over the edge of a blade. 'What a pisshole of a day,' he said, throwing open the door. 'Come, I need to dull my senses at the canteen before I have to suffer through *Appell*.'

The hair on the back of my neck prickled. *He* had to suffer through *Appell*?

His eyes fell on me, head bent, diligently typing. 'Well,' he said. 'What is this?'

'I needed a secretary, Reiner. I told you that a month ago. The amount of paper that gets processed through this office grows bigger every day.'

'And I told you I'd take care of it.'

'It was taking you too long. Write me up, if it makes you feel better.' He shrugged. 'I took matters into my own hands.'

The *Schutzhaftlagerführer* walked around me in a half circle. 'By taking one of my workers?'

'One of *my* workers,' the *Hauptscharführer* said.

'Without my permission.'

'For God's sake, Reiner. You can find another. This one happens to be fluent in German.'

'*Wirklich?*' he said. Really?

He was talking to me, but since I had my back to him, I didn't know he was waiting for a response. Suddenly, something crashed down on the back of my skull. I fell out of my chair onto my knees, reeling. 'You will answer when you are spoken to!' The *Schutzhaftlagerführer* stood over me with his hand raised.

Before he could strike me again, his brother took a firm grasp of his arm. 'I would request that you trust me to discipline my own staff.'

The *Schutzhaftlagerführer*'s eyes glittered. 'You would ask this of your superior, Franz?'

'No,' the *Hauptscharführer* replied. 'I would ask this of my brother.'

The tension dissipated then, like steam through a window. 'So you've decided to adopt a pet.' The *Schutzhaftlagerführer* laughed. 'You would not be the first officer to do so, although I question your judgment when there are fine *volksdeutsche* girls who are ready and willing.'

I dragged myself onto the chair again, running my tongue across my teeth to make sure none had been knocked loose. I wondered if this was what the *Hauptscharführer* planned for me. If I'd been brought here to be his whore.

That was a whole new level of punishment I hadn't considered.

I had not yet heard of a female prisoner being sexually abused by an officer. It was not that they were such gentlemen. But relationships were against the rules, and these officers were big on rules. Plus, we were Jews, and therefore completely undesirable. To lie with one of us was to lie with vermin.

'Let's talk about this in the canteen,' the *Hauptscharführer* suggested. He left the remains of his muffin on his desk. As he passed me, he said, 'You will clean up my desk while I'm gone.'

I nodded, looking away. I could feel the *Schutzhaftlagerführer*'s eyes raking over my face, my knobby body hidden beneath the work dress. 'Just remember, Franz,' he said. 'Stray dogs bite.'

This time the *Hauptscharführer* did not have a junior officer babysit me. Instead, he locked me into the office. This trust unnerved me. The interest in my writing, the news that he was making me his secretary – a job that would allow me to be warm all day long, now that winter was coming, and that could not be considered hard labor by any means. Why show me kindness, if he planned to rape me?

So it's not rape.

The thought fell like a stone into the well of my mind.

It would never happen. I'd slit my throat with a letter opener before I developed any kind of relationship with an SS officer.

I silently sent a thank-you to Aron, who had been my first, so that this German did not have to be.

I crossed to his desk. How long had it been since I had a muffin? My father had baked them, sometimes, with stone-ground cornmeal and the finest white sugar. This one was dark, with currants caught in the cake.

I pressed my fingers to the wax paper, gathering up the crumbs. Half of it I tucked into a little torn corner of the paper, and slipped into my dress, saving it for later. I would share it with Darija. Then I licked my fingers clean. The flavor nearly brought me to my knees. I drank the last sips of coffee, too, before carefully putting the paper into the trash, and drying the cup.

Immediately, I began to panic. What if this was not a show of trust, but another test? What if he came back and checked the garbage can to see if I had stolen his food? I played out the scenarios in my mind. The two brothers would enter, and the *Schutzhaftlagerführer* would say, 'I told you so, Franz.' And then the *Hauptscharführer* would shrug and turn me over to his brother for the whipping I had been expecting this morning. If stealing photographs from the dead was bad, surely taking food that belonged to an officer was much worse.

By the time the *Hauptscharführer* unlocked the office door and entered again – alone – I was so nervous that my teeth were chattering. He frowned at me. 'You are cold?' I could smell beer on his breath.

I nodded, although I had not been this warm for weeks.

He did not look in the trash. He glanced around the room cursorily, then sat down on the corner of his desk and picked up the stack of photographs. 'I must confiscate these. You understand?'

'Yes,' I whispered.

It took me a moment to realize that he was holding something out to me. A small leather journal, and a fountain pen. 'You will take these instead.'

Hesitantly, I took the gifts. The pen was heavy in my hand. It was all I could do to not hold the journal up to my nose, breathe in the scent of the paper and the hide.

'This arrangement,' he said formally. 'It suits you?'

As if I had a choice.

Was I willing to trade my body in order to feed my mind? Because that was the deal he was striking, or so his brother had said. For a price, I could write all I wanted. And I would be assigned to a job anyone else would have killed for.

When I did not answer, he sighed and stood. 'Come,' he said.

I started shaking again, so violently that he stepped away from me. It was time for me to pay up. I crossed my arms, hugging the journal to my chest, wondering where he would take me. To officers' quarters, I supposed.

I could do this. I would go somewhere else, in my mind. I would close my eyes and I would think of Ania and Aleksander and a world I could control. Just as my story had calmed Darija, just as it had soothed the others in my block, I would use it to numb myself.

I clenched my teeth as we walked outside. Although it was no longer raining, there were massive mud puddles. The *Hauptscharführer* strode right through them in his heavy boots, as I struggled to keep up. But instead of turning toward the other side of the camp, where the officers lived, he led me to the entrance to my block. The women had already come back from work and were waiting for *Appell*.

The *Hauptscharführer* called for the *Blockälteste*, who immediately began to ingratiate herself. 'This prisoner will now be working for me,' he announced. 'This book and pen she holds are my possessions. Should they go missing, you will personally answer to me and to the *Schutzhaftlagerführer*. Is that clear?'

The Beast nodded, mute. Behind her, there was a buzz of silence; the curiosity of the other women was palpable. Then the *Hauptscharführer* turned to me. 'By tomorrow? Ten more pages.'

And then, instead of taking me to his quarters and raping me, he left.

The Beast immediately sneered. 'He may be protecting you now, but when he gets tired of what's between your legs he'll find someone else.'

I pushed past her, to where Darija was waiting. 'What did he do to you?' she asked, grabbing on to my forearms. 'I've been worried sick all day.'

I sank down, taking in everything that happened, the strangest turn of events. 'He did absolutely nothing,' I told her. 'No punishment. If anything I got a promotion, because I can speak German. I'm working for an officer who recites poetry and who asked for more of my *upiór* story.'

Darija's brow furrowed. 'What does he want?'

'I don't know,' I answered, amazed. 'He didn't touch me. And look . . .' I took the muffin crumbs from where they were tucked in the waistband of my dress and let her have them. 'He saved this for me.'

'He gave you food?' Darija gasped.

'Well, not exactly. But he left it behind.'

Darija tasted the muffin. Her eyes drifted shut, pure rapture. But a moment later, she fixed her gaze on me. 'You can put a pig in a ball gown, Minka. That doesn't make it a debutante.'

The next morning after *Appell* I presented myself at the *Hauptscharführer*'s office. He was not there, but a junior officer who was waiting unlocked the door for me so that I could go inside. I realized that he was probably at Kanada, patrolling the barracks where Darija and the others worked.

There was a stack of forms to be typed on my makeshift desk beside the typewriter.

Hanging on the back of the chair was a woman's cardigan sweater.

This is how my routine settled: every morning, I would report to the *Hauptscharführer*'s office. There would be work waiting for me while he made his rounds in Kanada. At midday, the *Hauptscharführer* brought lunch from the main camp back to his office. Often he got a second ration of soup or a slice of bread. Yet he never finished either; instead he would leave these in the trash when he left the office, knowing full well I would eat them.

Every day as he ate his lunch, I would read aloud what I had written the night before. And then he would ask me questions: Does Ania know that Damian is trying to frame Aleksander? Will we ever see Casimir committing murder?

But most of his questions were about Aleksander.

Is the love you feel for a brother different from the love you feel for a woman? Would you sacrifice one for the other? What must it cost Aleks to hide who he really is in order to save Ania?

I could not admit this even to Darija, but I began to look forward to going to work – in particular, to lunchtime. It was as if the camp fell away while I was reading to the *Hauptscharführer*. He listened so carefully that it made me forget that outside there were guards abusing prisoners and people being gassed to death and men pulling their bodies from the shower rooms to stack like wood in the crematoria. When I was reading my own work, I got lost in the story, and I could have been anywhere – back in my bedroom in Łódź ; scribbling down ideas in the hallway outside Herr Bauer's classroom; sharing a hot chocolate at a café with Darija; curled in the window seat at my father's bakery. I was not stupid enough to presume that the officer and I were equals, but during those moments, I felt at least as if my voice still mattered.

One day, the *Hauptscharführer* tilted back his chair and propped his boots on his desk as I read to him. I had reached a cliffhanger, the moment where Ania enters the dank cave looking for Aleksander and instead finds his brutal brother. My voice shook as I described her navigating her way in the darkness, her boots crunching on the hard-backed shells of beetles and the tails of rats.

'*A torch flickered on the damp walls of the cave . . .*'

He frowned. 'Torches don't flicker. Firelight does. And even so, that's too clichéd.'

I looked up at him. I never quite knew what to say when he criticized my writing like this. Was I supposed to defend myself? Or was that presuming that I had any say in this strange partnership?

'Firelight dances like a ballerina,' the *Hauptscharführer* said. 'It hovers like a ghost. You see?'

I nodded, making a note in the margin of the book.

'Go on,' he commanded.

'There was a sudden draft, and the torch illuminating my path was extinguished. I stood shivering in the dark, unable to see even a foot in front of myself. Then I heard a rustle, a movement. I spun around. "Aleksander?" I whispered. "Is that you?"'

I looked up to find the *Hauptscharführer* hanging on my words.

'In the dark, there was a soft growl, almost a purr. The rasp of a match. A scent of sulfur. The torch blazed to life again. Crouched before me in a pool of blood was a man with wild eyes and knotted hair. More blood dripped from his mouth and covered his hands, which held a haunch of meat. I fell back, struggling to find air . . . That haunch of meat he was devouring had a hand, fingers. They were still clutching the top of a gilded cane I could not have forgotten if I tried. Baruch Beiler was no longer missing.'

There was a knock at the door; a junior officer stuck his head inside. 'Herr *Hauptscharführer,*' he said. 'It is already two o'clock—'

I snapped the book shut and began to roll a new form into my typewriter.

'I am fully capable of telling time,' the *Hauptscharführer* called out. 'It will be time to go when I *say* it is time to go.' He waited for the door to close. 'You will not start typing yet,' he said. 'Continue.'

I nodded, fumbling with the leather journal again and clearing my throat.

'I felt my vision fading, my head spinning. "It wasn't a wild animal," I forced out. "It was you." The cannibal smiled, his

teeth slick and stained crimson. "Wild animal . . . upiór. Why split hairs?"'

The *Hauptscharführer* laughed.

'"You killed Baruch Beiler."'

'"Hypocrite. Can you honestly say you didn't wish him dead?" I considered all the times the man had come to the cottage, demanding tax money we did not have, extorting deals from my father that only dragged us deeper and deeper into debt. I looked at this beast, and suddenly felt like I was going to be sick. "My father," I whispered. "You killed him, too?" When the* upiór *did not answer, I flew at him, using my nails and my fury as weapons. I raked at his flesh and kicked and swung. Either I would avenge my father's death or I would die trying.'

I continued, describing the arrival of Aleks, the torture of Ania as she tried to reconcile the man she was falling in love with, with a man whose brother was a beast. And what after all did that make *him*?

I spoke of her frantic flight from the cave, of Aleks chasing after her, of her accusation that he'd had the power to keep her father from being murdered, and didn't. '"*Your father is not the only person to ever love you*," I read. "*And you cannot blame Casimir for his death." He turned away so that his face was in shadow. "Because I am the one who killed him."*'

When I finished, my final words remained trapped in the office like the smoke of a rich man's cigar, redolent and sharp. The *Hauptscharführer* clapped: slowly, twice, and then with sustained fervor. 'Brava,' he said. 'I did not see that coming.'

I blushed. 'Thank you.' Folding the journal closed again, I sat with my hands in my lap, waiting to be dismissed.

But instead, the *Hauptscharführer* leaned forward. 'Tell me more about him,' he said. 'Aleksander.'

'But I've read you all I have written up to this point.'

'Yes, but you know more than you've written. Was he born a murderer?'

'That's not how it works with an *upiór*. You have to be the victim of an unnatural death.'

'And yet,' the *Hauptscharführer* pointed out, 'both Aleksander and Casimir suffer the same unfortunate fate. Coincidence? Or just bad luck?'

He was talking about my characters as if they were real. Which, to me, they were.

'Casimir died while avenging Aleksander's murder,' I said. 'Which is why Aleks feels the need to protect him, now. And since Casimir is the younger *upiór*, he's not yet able to control his appetite, the way Aleksander can.'

'So in theory both of these men had normal childhoods. They had parents who loved them, and who took them to church, and celebrated their birthdays. They went to school. They worked as paperboys or laborers or artists. And then one day, due to circumstances, they awakened with a terrible thirst for blood.'

'That's what the legends say.'

'But you, you are the *writer*. You can say anything,' he pointed out. 'Look at Ania. In that one moment, she was ready to kill the man she believed had murdered her father. And yet, she is painted as a heroine.'

I had not thought about this, but it was true. There was no black and white. Someone who had been good her entire life could, in fact, do something evil. Ania was just as capable of committing murder, under the right circumstances, as any monster.

'Was there something in their upbringing, in their history, in their genetics, that made them the way they are now?' the *Hauptscharführer* asked. 'Some fatal, hidden flaw? Surely there are plenty of men who die and who don't suffer the fate of being reborn as an *upiór.*'

'I . . . I don't know,' I admitted. 'Maybe it's the fact that Aleksander doesn't *want* to be an *upiór* that makes him different.'

'You mean, a monster with remorse,' the *Hauptscharführer* mused. Then he stood and took his heavy wool coat from its hanger. On his desk was a second ration of soup he had not touched. 'Tomorrow,' he announced. 'Ten more pages.'

He stepped out of the office, locking the door behind himself. I carefully tied the leather journal again with the ribbon that circled it, and set it beside my typewriter. I crossed to the desk and picked up the soup.

Suddenly I heard the lock turn in the door. I dropped the soup, spilling it on the hardwood beneath the desk. The *Hauptscharführer* was standing there, waiting for me to turn to him.

I trembled, wondering what he would say when he saw the puddle at my feet. But he did not seem to notice. 'What do you think it was like the first time Aleksander bled one of his victims?' he asked. 'Do you think even then he felt shame? Disgust?'

I shook my head. 'He couldn't help himself.'

'Does that make it any less detestable?'

'For the victim?' I asked. 'Or for the *upiór*?'

The officer stared at me, his eyes narrowed. 'Is there a difference?'

I did not answer. Moments later, when the key turned again in the lock, I got down on my hands and knees and lapped up what I could from the floor.

One morning after a storm, when the snow had blanketed the camp, Darija and I stepped outside the block to march to work.

We shuffled behind other women, all wrapped in ragged layers, freezing. The path, which we took every day, marched us along the far side of the fence at the entrance ramp to the camp. Sometimes we would see the new railroad cars arriving; sometimes there was a selection going on as we passed. Sometimes we shuffled past a line of people waiting for the shower they would not survive.

That day as we passed, a new group of prisoners was being belched out of one of the cars. They stood like we had on the platform, carrying their belongings, yelling out names of loved ones.

Suddenly, we saw her.

She was dressed from head to toe in white silk. On her head, a veil streamed out behind her in the cold wind. She was looking around, even as she was herded into line for the selection.

The rest of us women all stopped, riveted by this sight.

It was, unbelievably, not the most depressing thing we had ever seen: a bride, ripped from her own wedding, separated from her groom, and put on a transport to Auschwitz.

On the contrary, it gave us hope.

It meant that no matter what was happening in this camp, no matter how many Jews they managed to round up and kill, there were still more of us out there: living lives, falling in love, getting married, assuming that tomorrow would come.

The main camp of Auschwitz was a village. There was a grocer, a canteen, a cinema, and a theater hall that showcased opera singers and musicians, some of whom were Jews. There was a photography darkroom and a soccer stadium. There was a sporting club that the officers could join, and there were matches: prisoners who had been boxers, for example, pitted against each other while the officers bet on them. There was alcohol, too. The officers were given rations, but from what I saw, occasionally they pooled them to get drunk together.

I knew all this because, as the weeks went by, the *Hauptscharführer* would occasionally send me on an errand for him. I was to pick up cigarettes one day, laundry the next. I became his *Läuferin*, a runner, who would carry messages wherever necessary. He would send me to Kanada from time to time to deliver notes to the junior officers who patrolled when he was in his office. As the winter came, and the temperatures dropped, I would throw caution to the wind and do what I could for Darija and the others. When the *Hauptscharführer* left to go to the Officers' Club for a meal or across the camp for a meeting, and I knew he would be gone for an extended length of time, I would type up a note on his letterhead requesting that prisoner A18557 – Darija – be brought in for questioning. Darija and I would hurry back to the office, where for at least a half hour she could warm herself before having to go back to work in the freezing barracks of Kanada.

There were others like me – privileged prisoners. We would nod to each other as we passed in the village, doing our jobs. We walked the finest of lines: people hated us because we had it easy, but they valued us because we were able to steal things that made their lives better – food they could eat, cigarettes and whiskey they could use to bribe the guards. For a bottle of vodka that Darija took from a suitcase in Kanada, I was able to trade a rind from a squash and some lamp oil from a prisoner working in the Officers' Club. We hollowed out eight thumbprints in the rind, added a wick made of yarn from a sweater, and in this way made candles to celebrate Chanukah. There was a rumor that a Jewish secretary who worked for an officer elsewhere in the camp had managed to swap a pair of reading glasses for a kitten, which was still inexplicably alive in the block where she lived. We were considered untouchable, because of our protectors – some SS men who, for whatever reason, had found us useful. For some, I imagined, that was because of sex. But as the weeks rolled into months, the *Hauptscharführer* still did not lay a hand on me – in anger or in lust. All he wanted, really, was my story.

From time to time he would casually mention something about himself, which was interesting, because I had forgotten that we prisoners were not the only ones who had a life before this one. He had wanted to study at Heidelberg – classics. He had hoped to be a poet himself; or if not, the editor of a literary journal. He had been writing a thesis on the *Iliad* when he was compelled to fight for his country.

He did not like his brother very much.

I knew this, from their interactions. Whenever the *Schutzhaftlagerführer* dropped in to speak with him, I found myself huddling smaller in my chair, as if I could make myself disappear. He did not notice me, most of the time. I was that insignificant to him. The *Schutzhaftlagerführer* drank a lot, and when he did, he got angry. I had seen this, of course, at *Appell*. But sometimes the *Hauptscharführer* would receive a phone call, and he would have to go to the village to bring his brother back to officers' quarters. The next day the *Schutzhaftlagerführer* would come to the office. He would say that the nightmares were what made him do it, that he had to drink to forget what he'd seen in the field. It was as close as he could get to an apology, I supposed. But then, as if this very contrition was distasteful, he would start raging again. The *Schutzhaftlagerführer* would say that *he* was the head of the women's camp and that everyone answered to *him*. Sometimes, to punctuate this, he would sweep his hand across all the papers on the desk or knock over the coatrack or throw the adding machine across the room.

I wondered if the other officers knew that the two men were related. If, like me, they wondered how two such different individuals might have emerged from the same womb.

One of the other perks of my job was knowing when the *Schutzhaftlagerführer* was likely to be on an angry tear, since these tears followed his bouts of private contrition like clockwork.

I was not stupid. I knew that what the *Hauptscharführer* saw in my book was not simply entertainment but an allegory, a way to understand the complicated relationship between himself and his brother, between his past and his present, his conscience and his actions. If one brother was a monster, did it follow that the other had to be one, too?

One day, the *Hauptscharführer* had dispatched me to the village to pick up a bottle of aspirin from the pharmacy. It was snowing hard, and the drifts were so deep that my feet in their wooden clogs were soaked. I wore the coat I had been given, and a pink wool cap and mittens that Darija had stolen from Kanada for me as a Chanukah gift. The trip, which usually took only ten minutes, was twice as long due to the howling wind and the spitting ice.

I picked up the parcel and was headed back to the *Hauptscharführer*'s office, when suddenly the door of the canteen burst open and the *Schutzhaftlagerführer* flew through it, pounding the face of a junior officer.

Believe it or not, there were rules at Auschwitz. An officer could beat any prisoner for no more reason than that the prisoner looked at him funny, but he could not kill without reason, because that meant eliminating a worker from the great cog that was this camp. He could treat a prisoner like pond scum, and could abuse a Ukrainian guard or a Jewish kapo, but he was not allowed to show disrespect to another SS man.

The *Schutzhaftlagerführer* was clearly important, but there had to be someone more important than him, who would get word of this.

I started to run. I raced across the camp, slipping on patches of ice, my cheeks and nose numbed by the cold, until I reached the administration building where the *Hauptscharführer*'s office was.

It was empty.

I hurried outside again, this time to the barracks of Kanada. I found the *Hauptscharführer* talking to several of the guards, pointing out an inaccuracy in their reporting.

'Excuse me, Herr *Hauptscharführer*,' I murmured, as my pulse raced uncontrollably. 'May we speak privately?'

'I am busy,' he said.

I nodded, moving away.

If I said nothing, no one would ever know what I had witnessed.

If I said nothing, the *Schutzhaftlagerführer* would be reprimanded. Maybe even demoted or transferred. Which would certainly be a good thing for all of us.

Well, maybe not for his brother.

I don't know what was more viscerally shocking to me: the fact that I turned around and marched back into the sorting barracks, or the realization that I cared about the *Hauptscharführer*'s welfare. 'I am sorry, Herr *Hauptscharführer*,' I murmured. 'But this is a matter of grave importance.'

He dismissed the officers, and dragged me outside by the arm. The wind and snow howled around us. 'You do not interrupt me in my work, is that clear?'

I nodded.

'Perhaps I have given you the wrong impression. I am the one who orders *you* around, not vice versa. I will not have officers beneath me thinking that I—'

'The *Schutzhaftlagerführer*,' I interrupted. 'He is in a brawl outside the canteen.'

The blood drained from the *Hauptscharführer*'s face. He started to walk briskly in the direction of the camp village, breaking into a run as he turned the corner.

My fingers flexed on the bottle of aspirin, still tucked inside my pink mitten. I walked back to the administration building and let myself into the office. I took off my coat and my hat and mittens, and set them to dry on the radiator. Then I sat down and began to type.

I worked through lunch. This time, there was no reading; there was no extra ration for me. It was not until twilight that the *Hauptscharführer* returned. He dusted the snow off his coat and hung it up with his officer's cap, then dropped down heavily behind his desk, steepling his hands together.

'Do you have a sibling?' he asked.

I faced him. 'I did.'

The *Hauptscharführer* met my gaze and nodded.

He scribbled a message on a piece of stationery and folded it into an envelope. 'Take this to the *Kommandant*'s office,' he said, and I blanched. I had never been there before, although I knew where it was. 'Explain that the *Schutzhaftlagerführer* is indisposed with illness and will not be present at *Appell*.'

I nodded. I pulled on my coat, still wet, and my mittens and my hat. 'Wait.' The *Hauptscharführer*'s voice called me back as I started to turn the doorknob. 'I do not know your name.'

I had been working for him, now, for twelve weeks. 'Minka,' I murmured.

'Minka.' He looked down at the papers on his desk, dismissing me. It was, I realized, the closest he could come to giving me his thanks.

He never called me by name again.

The items that were seized from Kanada were shipped to various places in Europe, along with meticulous lists of what was included in the shipments, which had been typed by me. From time to time, there was a discrepancy. This was usually blamed on a prisoner stealing an item, but more likely, it was an SS officer. Darija said she often saw junior officers slip something into their pockets when they thought no one else was looking.

When the lists did not match the contents, a phone call would be placed to the *Hauptscharführer*. It would be up to him to mete out the necessary punishment, even though it had been weeks since the actual looting.

One afternoon, when Herr *Hauptscharführer* was retrieving his lunch from the village, I answered such a phone call. As always in my precise German, I said, 'Herr *Hauptscharführer* Hartmann, *guten Morgen.*'

The man on the other end of the line introduced himself as Herr Schmidt. 'I'm sorry. Herr *Hauptscharführer* has stepped away from his desk. May I take a message?'

'Yes, you may tell him that the shipment arrived intact. But before I go, I must say, Fräulein . . . I am having the hardest time placing your accent.'

I did not correct him when he called me Fräulein. '*Ich bin Berlinerin,*' I said.

'Really. Because your diction puts mine to shame,' Herr Schmidt replied.

'I attended boarding school in Switzerland,' I lied.

'Ah yes. Perhaps the only place left in Europe that has not been completely ravaged. *Vielen Dank,* Fräulein. *Auf Wiederhören.*'

I placed the receiver in its cradle, feeling as if I'd been through an interrogation. When I turned around, the *Hauptscharführer* was back. 'Who was that?'

'Herr Schmidt. Confirming the shipment.'

'Why did you say you were from Berlin?'

'He asked about my accent.'

'He was suspicious?' the *Hauptscharführer* asked.

If he was, did that mean my time as a secretary had run its course? Would I be sent back to Kanada, or worse, fall prey to another selection?

'I don't think so,' I said, my heart racing. 'He believed me when I said I'd studied abroad.'

The *Hauptscharführer* nodded his agreement. 'Not all would look kindly on your position here.' He sat down, arranging his napkin and slicing into a platter of roast chicken. 'Now. Where did we leave off?'

I turned my wooden chair away from the typewriter to face him and opened the leather journal. I had written my requisite ten pages the night before, but for the first time, I did not think I could share it out loud.

'Go on, go on,' the *Hauptscharführer* urged, waving his fork at me.

I cleared my throat. '*I had never been so aware of my own breathing, or my own pulse.*' That was as far as I got before heat flooded my face and I looked into my lap.

'What is it?' he asked. 'Is it no good?'

I shook my head.

He reached across the desk and grabbed the book from me.

'Of course, there was no heartbeat to hear. Just an emptiness, an understanding that we would never be the same. Did that mean that he had not felt the way I did as he moved between—'

Suddenly, he broke off, blushing just as deeply as I was. 'Oh,' the *Hauptscharführer* said. 'Perhaps this bit is better read silently.'

He kissed me as if he were poisoned, and I was the antidote. Maybe, I thought, that was true. His teeth nipped at my lip, making it bleed again. When he sucked at the wound, I arched in his embrace, imagining him drinking from me.

Afterward, I lay against him, my hand spread across his chest, as if I were measuring the void inside. 'I would do anything to have my heart back,' Aleksander said. 'If only so that I could give it to you.'

'You are perfect like this.'

He buried his face in the curve of my neck. 'Ania,' he said, 'I am far from perfect.'

There is a magic to intimacy, a world built of sighs and skin that is thicker than brick, stronger than iron. There is only you, and him, so impossibly close that nothing can come between. Not the enemy, not your allies. In this safe haven, in this hallowed place and time, I could even ask the questions whose answers I feared. 'Tell me what it was like,' I whispered. 'Your first time.'

He did not pretend to misunderstand. He curled onto his side, his body spooned around mine, so that he would not have to look me in the eye as he spoke. 'It felt as if I had been in a desert for months, and would die if I couldn't drink. But water, it did nothing. I could consume a lake and it would not have been enough. What I craved was what I could smell through the skin, rich as cognac.' He hesitated. 'I had tried to fight the urge. By then, I was so hungry, so faint, that I could barely stand. I crawled into a barn, wishing for death again. She was carrying a bucket of chicken feed, scattering it in the coop, and I could see her from where I crouched in the rafters. I fell like an archangel, covered her scream with the fabric of my cape, and dragged her into the hayloft where I had been hiding.

'She begged me for her life. But mine was more important. So I ripped out her throat. I drank her dry and chewed on her bones and peeled away her flesh until there was nothing left, consumed by my hunger. I was disgusted; I could not believe what I had become. I tried to clean myself, but her blood left a stain on my hands. I stuck my finger down my throat but could not purge. Still, for the first time in a long time, I wasn't hungry; and because of this I could finally sleep. The next morning, when her parents came searching for her, calling her name, I awakened. Beside me was all that was left of her: that head, with the thick blond braid, that round mouth frozen in terror. Those marble eyes, staring back at the monster that was now me. I sat beside her, keeping vigil, and I sobbed.'

The *Hauptscharführer* looked up at me, surprised. 'The Donestre,' he said, and I nodded, pleased that he had caught the reference to the mythical beast he had told me about.

'The second time, it was a prostitute who had stopped to pull up her stockings in an alley. It was easier, or so I told myself, because otherwise, I would have had to admit that what I'd done before was wrong. The third time, my first man: a banker who was locking up at the end of the day. There was a teenage girl once, who was in the wrong place at the wrong time.

And a socialite I heard crying on a hotel balcony. And after that I stopped caring who they had been. It only mattered that they were there, at that moment, when I needed them.'
Aleksander closed his eyes. 'It turns out that the more you repeat the same action, no matter how reprehensible, the more you can make an excuse for it in your own mind.'

I turned in his arms. 'How do I know that one day you won't kill me?'

He stared at me, hesitating. 'You don't.'

That was the end, so far. I had stopped writing at that point so that I could get a few hours of sleep before *Appell*. The *Hauptscharführer* set the journal down on the desk between us. His cheeks were still bright pink. 'Well,' he said.

I could not meet his eye. I had undressed in front of strangers here; I had been stripped in a courtyard by a guard for punishment, and yet I had never felt so exposed.

'It's quite interesting, as all that's really described is a kiss. What makes it graphic is the way you talk of Aleksander's . . . other exploits.' He tilted his head. 'Fascinating, to think of violence being just as intimate as love.'

When he said that, it surprised me. I could not say that I had written this intentionally, but wasn't it the truth? In both relationships, there were only two people: one who gave and one who sacrificed. It made me think of all those hours we had spent at *Gymnasium* analyzing the text of a great author: *But what did Thomas Mann really* mean *here?* Maybe he had meant nothing. Maybe he just wanted to write a story that nobody could put down.

'I take it you have had a beau.'

The *Hauptscharführer*'s voice startled me. I could not manage to stammer a response. Finally, I just shook my head.

'That makes this section even more impressive then,' the *Hauptscharführer* replied. 'If inaccurate.'

My eyes flew to meet his. He abruptly looked away, standing as was his custom after lunch, to leave me the remains while he did a patrol of Kanada.

'Not the . . . mechanics,' he said formally, as he buttoned his overcoat. 'The last bit. When Aleksander says it gets easier, the second time.' The *Hauptscharführer* turned away and settled his cap on his head. 'It never does.'

My typewriter was missing.

I stood in front of the spot that the *Hauptscharführer* had designated as my own little office cubicle, wondering what I had done wrong.

Darija had told me that I should not get used to this treatment, and I had shrugged away her concern. When other women sneered or made sarcastic comments about me and the odd *friendship* I had developed with the *Hauptscharführer*, I brushed them aside. What did I care what people thought of me, as long as I knew the truth? I was delusional enough to convince myself that as long as my story continued, so would my life. Yet even Scheherazade had run out of stories, after 1001 nights. By then, the King who had spared her from execution each dawn so that she could tell him the rest of the tale later that night had been made wiser and kinder by the lessons in her stories.

He made her his queen.

I only wanted the Allies to show up before I ran out of plot twists.

'You no longer work here,' the *Hauptscharführer* said flatly. 'You will report immediately to the hospital.'

I blanched. The hospital was an anteroom for the gas

chamber. We all knew it; it was why, no matter how sick a girl was, she resisted being taken there.

'I am not ill,' I said.

He flicked his glance toward me. 'This is not a negotiation.'

Mentally I recounted my work from yesterday: the requisition forms I had filled out, the messages I had taken. I could find nothing that had been done in error. We had talked for a half hour about my book, too, as usual, and it had spurred the *Hauptscharführer* to tell me of his brief time at university, when he had won an award for his poetry. 'Herr *Hauptscharführer*,' I begged. 'Please, give me another chance. Whatever I did wrong I will fix . . .'

He looked past me toward the open doorway and waved in a young officer, who was to escort me out.

I do not remember much about my arrival at Block 30. My number was entered into the records by a Jewish prisoner who was manning the front desk. I was brought to a room that was small, crowded, and filthy. Patients lay on top of each other on paper pads, their uniforms stained with bloody diarrhea or vomit. Some had long scars that had been rudimentarily stitched. Rats ran over the bodies of those too exhausted to move. Another prisoner, who must have been assigned here as a worker, carried a stack of linen dressing, and followed a nurse as she changed bandages. I tried to get her attention, but she refused to meet my gaze.

Probably out of the fear that she was replaceable, like me.

The girl beside me was missing an eye. She kept clawing at my arm. 'So thirsty,' she said, over and over in Yiddish.

My temperature was taken and recorded. 'I want to see a doctor,' I cried, my voice rising above the moans of the others. 'I am healthy!'

I would tell the doctor that I was fine. That I could go back to work, any kind of work. My worst fear was having to stay here, with these women who looked like broken toys.

A woman shoved aside the skeletal body of the girl with the missing eye and sat down on the pad beside me. 'Shut up,' she hissed. 'Are you an idiot?'

'No, but I need to tell them—'

'If you make enough of a fuss about not being ill, one of the doctors will hear.'

Clearly, this woman was mad. Because wasn't that exactly what I wanted?

'They want the healthy ones,' she continued.

I shook my head, completely confused.

'I came here because I had a rash on my leg. The doctor who saw me decided the rest of me was sound enough.' She pulled up her dress so that I could see the blistered red burns on her abdomen. 'He did this to me with X-rays.'

Shuddering, I started to understand. I had to act ill, at least ill enough to escape the notice of the doctors. But not ill enough to be selected by the guards.

It seemed like an impossible tightrope to walk.

'Some bigwig is coming in from Oranienburg today,' she continued. 'That's what the rumor is. If you know what's good for you, you will not draw attention to yourself. They want to look good for their superiors, if you know what I mean.'

I did. It meant that they needed scapegoats.

I wondered if word would get to Darija that I had been taken here. If she would try to bribe someone with a treasure from Kanada to get me released. If that were even possible.

After a while I lay down on the pad. The girl with the missing eye had a fever; her body was throwing off waves of heat. 'Thirsty?' she kept whispering.

I turned away from her, curling into myself. I slipped the

leather journal from my dress and started to read my story, from the beginning. I used this as an anesthetic, trying to see nothing but the words on the page and the world they created.

I was aware of a stir in the ward as the nurses raced in, tidying up the room and moving prisoners so that we were not lying on top of each other. I slipped my journal inside my dress again, wondering if the doctor was coming.

Instead, a small phalanx of soldiers arrived. They flanked an older man I had never seen before – a highly decorated officer. Judging from the number of underlings surrounding the man and the way the camp officers were practically kissing his boots, he had to be someone very important.

A man in a white coat – the infamous doctor? – was leading what seemed to be a tour. 'We continue to make progress on methods of mass sterilization through radiation,' I translated from the German, as he spoke. I thought of the girl who had warned me to keep my mouth shut, of the burns on her belly.

As the others filed into the small room, I saw the *Schutzhaftlagerführer* standing among them, his hands clasped behind his back.

The high-ranking officer lifted his hand and beckoned him. 'Herr *Oberführer*? You have a question?'

He pointed to the Jew who had been carrying the bandages for the nurse. 'That one.'

The *Schutzhaftlagerführer* in turn jerked his head at one of the guards accompanying the little battalion. The prisoner was taken from the room.

'It is . . .' the *Oberführer* intoned, '. . . adequate.'

The other officers all relaxed infinitesimally.

'Adequate is not impressive,' the *Oberführer* added.

He swept out of the room, and the others followed.

At lunch, I took the broth that I was given. It had a button floating in it, instead of any visible vegetable or meat. I closed my eyes and imagined what the *Hauptscharführer* was eating. Pork roast, I knew, because I had been the one to fetch him the menu earlier this week from the officers' mess. I had eaten pork only once, at the home of the Szymanskis.

I wondered if the Szymanskis were still living in Łódź. If they ever thought of their Jewish friends and what had become of them.

Pork roast, with green beans, and cherry demi-glace; that's what the menu had promised. I did not know what *demi-glace* meant, but I could taste the cherries bursting on my tongue. I remembered taking a wagon out to the country where Darija's father's factory had been, with Josek and the other boys. We had spread a picnic on a checked tablecloth and Josek had played a game, tossing a cherry into the air and then catching it in his mouth. I showed him how I could tie the stem into a knot with my tongue.

I was thinking of this, and of pork roast, and of the picnics we used to have in the summers that were packed by Darija's housekeeper with so much food that we fed the extra to the ducks in the pond – can you *imagine* having extra? I was thinking of this, and trying so hard to remember the flavor of a walnut, and how it differed from a peanut, and considering whether you could lose your sense of taste the way you lost the function of a limb from disuse. I was thinking of this, which was why I did not hear, at first, what was happening at the entrance to the ward.

The *Hauptscharführer* was yelling at one of the nurses. 'Do you think I have time for this incompetence?' he asked. 'Do I need to approach the *Schutzhaftlagerführer* to solve a problem that should be so far beneath him?'

'No, Herr *Hauptscharführer*. I am sure we can locate—'

'Never mind.' Spying me, he strode to the pad where I was lying and grabbed me roughly by the wrist. 'You will report to work immediately. You are no longer sick,' he pronounced, and he pulled me out of the ward, down the front steps of the hospital, and across the courtyard to the administration buildings. I had to run to keep up with him.

When I arrived, my chair and table and typewriter had been set up again in the same spot. The *Hauptscharführer* sat down at his desk. His face was red, and he was sweating, although the outside temperature was below freezing. We did not speak of what had happened until the end of the day. 'Herr *Hauptscharführer*,' I asked hesitantly, 'should I report back here tomorrow morning?'

'Where else would you go?' he asked, and he did not look up from the list of numbers he was adding.

Darija had her own news for me that night. The Beast was dead. The man I'd seen at Block 30 had been the SS-*Oberführer* – Gluecks's deputy at the Inspectorate of Concentration Camps – and he had also come through the barracks to do an inspection. According to one of the women in our block, who was part of the underground resistance movement at the camp, this deputy had a reputation for plucking Jews out of cushy jobs and sending them to the gas chamber. We had a new *Blockälteste*, who attempted to prove herself to the *Aufseherin* by making us do jumping jacks for over an hour, and beating anyone who tripped or fell in exhaustion. But it was not until a week later, when I was running an errand for the *Hauptscharführer*, that I realized it was not just the *Blockälteste* who had been shot. Nearly every other Jew in a job of privilege – from those who worked like me as secretaries to those who served officers' meals at the mess hall to the cellist who played at the theater to the nurse assistant at the hospital – was gone.

The *Hauptscharführer* had not been punishing me by firing me and sending me to the hospital. He had been saving my life.

Two days later, when the camp was thick with snow, we were gathered in the courtyard between the blocks to watch a hanging. Months ago, there had been a revolt by prisoners who worked as *Sonderkommandos* – disposing of the bodies that came out of the gas chambers. We did not see them, as they were kept separate from the rest of us. From what I heard, the men attacked the guards and blew up one of the crematoria. Prisoners escaped, too – though most of them were recaptured and shot. But at the time, it had created quite a buzz. Three officers were killed, including one who had been pushed alive into one of the ovens – which meant that the prisoners had not died in vain.

That had been a bad week for everyone else, as the SS officers took their anger out on every prisoner in the camp. But then it had passed, and we had assumed it was over, until we huddled in the cold with our breath frosting before us and saw the women being led to the gallows.

The gunpowder for the explosions had been traced to four girls who worked at a munitions factory. They would smuggle tiny amounts of powder, wrapped in cloth or paper, and hide it somewhere on their persons. Then it got passed to a girl who worked in the clothing division of our camp, who in turn smuggled it to prisoners who were part of the resistance move-ment, who got it to the *Sonderkommando* leaders in time for the uprising. The girl who worked in the clothing division lived in my block. She was a small, mousy thing who did not give any appearance of being a rebel. *That's why she is a good one,* Darija had pointed out. One day the girl had been dragged away from morning *Appell*. We knew she had been put in the prison cells for a while, and badly tortured, and eventually sent back to live with us – but by then, she was completely broken. She couldn't speak, couldn't look at us. She pulled long strips of skin from her fingers and chewed her nails till they bled. Every night without fail she would scream in her sleep.

Today, she had been left behind in the block, and even now, I could hear her shrieks. Her sister was one of the two girls being hanged.

They were led to the gallows wearing their normal work dresses but no coats. They looked at us, clear-eyed, their heads held high. I could see the family resemblance between one of them and the girl from my block.

The *Schutzhaftlagerführer* stood at the base of the gallows. At his command, another officer tied the girls' hands behind their backs. The first one was pulled up onto the table that stood beneath the gallows, and a noose was slipped around her neck. One moment she was standing, and the next she was pulled upward. The second girl followed. They twisted, fish caught on the line.

All that day, working in the office, I imagined I could hear the screams of the younger sister, whose execution had been delayed. It was impossible, at this distance, but they were etched in my mind, an endless radio loop. It made me think of my own sister. For the first time, I thought that maybe Basia was right, since she had been spared the horrors of a place like this. If you knew you were going to die, wasn't it better to choose the time and place, instead of waiting for fate to drop on you like an anvil? What if Basia's act wasn't one of desperation but a final moment of self-control? The *Hauptscharführer* had chosen to save me last week, but that did not mean the next time he would be as generous. The only person I could truly depend on was myself.

I imagined this was how the younger sister in my block felt when she began routing the gunpowder to the resistance. She wasn't any different from Basia. They both were just looking for a way out.

I was so distracted that the *Hauptscharführer* asked if I had a headache. I did, but I knew it would get worse when I returned to the block at the end of the day.

As it turned out, I needn't have worried. The sister and a fourth girl had been hanged just after the sun set, before *Appell*. I tried not to look as I passed by, but I could hear the creak of the wood as their bodies twirled, macabre ballerinas, with skirts that sang in the bitter wind.

One night it grew so cold that we awakened with frost matting our hair. In the morning, when we were being given our rations, the *Blockälteste* took a tin cup of coffee from one of the women and threw it into the air so that it froze instantly, a great white cloud. The dogs that patrolled with the officers now whined and pawed at the icy ground with their tails between their legs as we stood at *Appell* losing feeling in our extremities. When we walked to work afterward, we had to wrap our scarves around our heads or risk frostbite on any skin that was exposed.

That week the temperatures dipped so low twenty-two women in our block died. Another fourteen who were assigned to outside labor fell to the ground and froze to death. Darija brought me tights and a sweater from Kanada, so that I would have an extra layer. The price of a blanket on the black market at the camp quadrupled.

I was never so grateful for my office job with the *Hauptscharführer*, but I knew that Darija, in the unheated barracks of Kanada, was still in danger of freezing. So as I had done a few times before, when the *Hauptscharführer* left to get his lunch, I hurriedly typed a note on a stolen piece of his letterhead requesting that prisoner A18557 report to his office. Bundling myself into my coat and hat and mittens and scarf, I hurried across the camp to Kanada to deliver the message and bring my best friend out of the cold, if only for a few minutes.

We huddled together, arm in arm, and Darija slipped into my mitten a small piece of chocolate she had squirreled away during her work. We didn't talk; it took too much energy. Even after we had entered the building, we had to keep up the pretense that Darija had been summoned by the *Hauptscharführer*.

We passed SS officers and guards and kept our eyes averted. By this point I was known to them, nothing suspicious. As was my habit, when I reached the office door, I turned the knob first and peeked inside, just in case I had miscalculated and the *Hauptscharführer* had returned.

There was someone in the room.

Behind the *Hauptscharführer*'s desk was a safe. In it was the money that was found at Kanada, which was shipped out daily under lock and key. Each time the *Hauptscharführer* made his rounds of Kanada, he would empty the box that sat in the center of the barracks where valuables were kept. The smaller items, like bills and coins and diamonds, were brought to his office. As far as I knew the only person who had the combination to the safe was the *Hauptscharführer* himself.

But now, as I saw the *Schutzhaftlagerführer* standing in front of its open door, I realized I was wrong.

He was slipping a stack of currency into the inside breast pocket of his coat.

I saw his eyes widen, as he stared at me as if I were a ghost. An *upiór*.

Something that was supposed to be dead.

I realized that he had assumed I was killed last week when the *Oberführer* from Oranienburg had come and systematically liquidated all the Jews working in office jobs.

I started to back out of the room, panicked. I had to get out of there, and I had to get Darija out of there. But even if we were able to break through the fence and escape to Russia it would not have been far enough. As long as I knew that the *Schutzhaftlagerführer* was stealing, and as long as I worked for his brother, I could turn him in. Which meant he'd have to get rid of me.

'Run,' I yelled to Darija as the *Schutzhaftlagerführer*'s hand closed over my wrist. Darija paused, and that was just enough time for the officer to grab her by the hair with his other hand and drag her into the office.

He closed the door behind us. 'What do you think you saw?' he demanded.

I shook my head, looking at the ground.

'Speak!'

'I . . . I saw nothing, Herr *Schutzhaftlagerführer*.'

Beside me, Darija slipped her hand into mine.

The *Schutzhaftlagerführer* saw the slight movement, the rustle between our dresses. I don't know what he thought at that moment. That we were passing a note? That we had some kind of code? Or simply that if he let us go, I would tell my friend what he had done, and then there would be *two* people who knew his secret.

He pulled his pistol out of its holster and shot Darija in the face.

She fell, still holding on to my hand. The plaster wall behind us exploded in a rain of dust. I started to scream. My best friend's blood spattered my face and my dress; I couldn't hear anything after the blast of the gunshot. I fell to my hands and knees, rocking, hugging what was left of Darija, waiting for the bullet that was destined for me.

'Reiner? What are you doing in here, for the love of God?' The *Hauptscharführer*'s voice sounded like it was coming through a tunnel, like I had been wrapped in layers of cotton batting. I looked up at him, still screaming. The *Schutzhaftlagerführer* pulled me upright by the throat. 'I caught these two stealing from you, Franz. It is a good thing I happened to come in when I did.'

He held out the wad of currency that he had been tucking into his coat.

The *Hauptscharführer* set down a tray of food on the desk and looked at me. 'You did this?'

It didn't matter what I said, I realized. Even if the *Hauptscharführer* believed me, his brother would be watching me at every moment, waiting for a chance to do to me what he had done to Darija so that I would not tell the *Hauptscharführer* what I had seen.

Oh, God, Darija.

I shook my head, sobbing. 'No, Herr *Hauptscharführer*.'

The *Schutzhaftlagerführer* laughed. 'What did you think she would say? And why would you even bother to ask?'

A muscle jumped along the *Hauptscharführer*'s jaw. 'You know there are procedures,' he said. 'The prisoner should have been arrested, not shot.'

'What are you going to do? Report me?' When his brother didn't respond, the *Schutzhaftlagerführer*'s face went as red as it did when he was drunk. 'I *make* the procedures. Who would contest what I did? This prisoner was found stealing property from the Reich.'

It was the same infraction that had brought me to this office in the first place.

'I stopped her, in the commission of the crime. The same should be done with her accomplice, even if she is your little whore.' The *Schutzhaftlagerführer* shrugged. 'If you do not punish her, Franz, then I will.' To underscore his point, he cocked the trigger on his pistol again.

I felt something warm run down my leg, and realized to my dismay that I had urinated. A small puddle spread on the floor between my wooden shoes.

The *Hauptscharführer* stepped toward me. 'I did not do what he says,' I whispered.

Tucked inside my dress was the journal with the ten pages I had written last night. Aleksander, locked in a prison cell. Ania, breaking into the jail to see him the morning before his public execution. *Please*, he begged her. *Do one thing for me.*

Anything, Ania promised.

Kill me, he said.

If this had been any ordinary day, the *Hauptscharführer* would be settling down to hear me read that aloud. But this was not any ordinary day.

In the four months I had worked for the *Hauptscharführer*, he had never laid a hand on me. Now, he did. He cupped his hand around my cheek, so gently that it brought tears to my eyes. His thumb stroked my skin the way one would touch a lover, and he met my gaze.

Then he hit me so hard that he broke my jaw.

When I couldn't stand up anymore, when I was spitting bloody saliva into my sleeve to keep from choking, when the *Schutzhaftlagerführer* was satisfied, the *Hauptscharführer* stopped. He stumbled away from me, as if he were coming out of a trance, and looked around his ravaged office. 'Clean up this mess,' he ordered.

He left me under the supervision of another guard, who was ordered to take me to the prison cells as soon as I was finished. I gingerly righted the furniture, wincing when I twisted or moved too quickly. I swept up the plaster dust with my hands. My eyes kept drifting to where Darija lay on the floor, and every time I looked at her I felt like I was going to be sick. So I took off my coat and wrapped her upper body in it. She was already stiffening, her limbs cold and rigid. I started to shake – with cold, with grief, with shock? – and forced myself to go to the janitorial closet and find cleaning supplies, rags, a bucket. I scrubbed the floor. Twice, I passed out from the pain caused by the exertion, and twice the guard poked me with his boot to nudge me back into consciousness.

When the office was clean again, I lifted Darija into my arms. She weighed nothing, but neither did I, and I staggered at the additional burden. With the guard directing me, I carried my best friend – still wrapped in my coat – from the administration building in the frigid cold to a wagon that stood at the outskirts of Kanada. In it were other bodies: people who had died overnight, people who had died during the workday. With all the strength I had I lifted her into the wagon. The only thing that kept me from climbing in there with her was knowing she would hate to see me give up.

The guard grabbed my arm, pulling at me to leave her. I tugged away from him, risking more punishment. I unwrapped the coat from around Darija's torso and slipped into it. There was no body heat left in her to transfer to me. I reached for her hand, flecked with red measles spots of her own blood, and kissed it.

Before she was hanged, the girl who had come back to our block after being imprisoned had whispered wildly of the *Stehzelle*, the starvation cell you had to enter through a tiny door like a dog kennel. The cell was built narrow and tall, so that you could not sit down at all. Instead you had to stand, overnight, with mice running across your feet, until you were released the next morning and expected to carry on through your workday. By the time I was brought to one of these, in a building I had never entered in the months I'd been here, I was numb. The cold had robbed me of feeling in my hands and feet and face, which was good, because it kept my jaw from aching. I could not speak without tearing up from the pain, and that was fine, because I had nothing left to say.

Drifting in and out of consciousness, I imagined that my mother was here. She wrapped her arms around me and kept me warm. She whispered in my ear: *Be a mensch, Minusia.* For the first time I realized what that really meant. As long as you put someone else's welfare in front of your own, it meant you had someone else to live for. Once that was gone, what was the point?

I wondered what would become of me. The *Kommandant* might issue a decree for my punishment: a beating, a whipping, death. But the *Schutzhaftlagerführer* might not even bother to follow rules, and could simply take me out of here himself and shoot me. He might say he caught me escaping, another lie, one impossible to believe with me locked up in this cell, and yet . . . who would stop him? Who would really care if he killed another Jew? Only the *Hauptscharführer*, possibly. Or so I had thought, until today.

I was asleep on my feet, dreaming of Darija. She burst into the office where I was working and told me I had to leave immediately, but I could not make myself stop typing. With every key I struck, another bullet exploded into her chest, her head.

Herr Dybbuk, that was what I had called him before I knew

his rank and name. Someone whose body had been taken over, unwillingly, by a demon.

I could not tell you which man was the real one – the officer who would beat an employee to the point of losing consciousness, or the officer who went out of his way to see a prisoner as a fellow human being. He had tried to tell me during all those lunchtime literary sessions that there is good and evil in all of us. That a monster is just someone for whom the evil has tipped the balance.

And I . . . I had been naïve enough to believe him.

I woke with a start when I felt a hand on my ankle. I gasped, and the hand gripped me tighter, willing me into silence. The grate that opened the cell scraped open, and I lowered myself through it. Standing there was a guard who tied my hands behind my back. I assumed it was morning – I had no idea, as there were no windows in here – and that it was time for him to take me to work.

But where? Was I expected to go back to the *Hauptscharführer*? I did not know if I could stand to be in the same small space as him. It was not the beating I'd received that made me feel this way – after all, I had been hurt by other officers and had continued to see them day after day; it was simply the way of life here. No, it was not the *Hauptscharführer*'s brutality but rather the kindness that had come before it that made it so hard for me to understand.

I started to pray that maybe, instead, I'd be placed on one of the penal gangs that had to work in the brutal cold, moving rocks for the next twelve hours. I could accept the harshness of the elements. Just not that of a German I had been stupid enough to trust.

I was not brought to the administration building. And I

was not brought to the penal gang, either. Instead I was taken to the ramp where the railway cars came into the camp and the selections were made.

There were other prisoners there, being herded into the cars. It made no sense to me, because I knew that the process never worked in reverse. The train cars emptied here, and the people who spilled out of them never left.

The guard pulled me behind the platform and untied my hands. He seemed to have a very hard job of it, taking more time than necessary. Then he shoved me into a line of women who were being loaded into one of the cars. I was lucky; I was still wearing my coat, dried with Darija's blood, and my hat and mittens and scarf; I had the journal with my story tucked into my undergarments. I grabbed on to one of the male prisoners whose job involved herding us inside. 'Where?' I gritted out, my teeth clenched against the pain in my jaw.

'Gross-Rosen,' he muttered.

I knew it was another camp, because I had seen the name on documents. It could not possibly be any worse than it was here.

Inside the train car, I moved to a spot near the window. It would be cold, but there would be fresh air. I slid along the wall to a sitting position, feeling my legs burn after the hours I'd spent standing, and I wondered why I had been brought here.

It was possible this was the punishment that had been handed down from the *Kommandant* for stealing.

Or it was possible that someone had been trying to save me from a worse fate, by making sure I was on a train that would take me far away from the *Schutzhaftlagerführer*.

After what he had done to me, I had no reason to believe that the *Hauptscharführer* was thinking about me at all, or even wondering if I'd survived the night. That was probably a figment of my imagination.

But then again, my imagination was what had kept me alive all these months in this hellhole.

It was not until hours later, when we had arrived at Gross-Rosen to learn that there was not a women's compound and we would be taken on instead to a subcamp called Neusalz, that I took off my mittens to gently test the tenderness of my jaw, and something fell into my lap.

A tiny scroll, a note.

I realized that the guard who had untied my wrists had not been having trouble with the knots. He had slipped this into my mitten.

It was a strip of watermarked paper, the same kind I had rolled into my typewriter every day for the past few months.

'WHAT HAPPENS NEXT,' it read.

I never saw the *Hauptscharführer* again.

At Neusalz, I worked in the Gruschwitz textile factory. My job at first involved making thread – a deep red hue that stained my hands – but because I had worked at an office job and had access to food, I was stronger than most of the other women, and soon I was sent to load train cars with boxes of ammunition. We worked alongside political prisoners – Poles and Russians – who unloaded the supplies that came by rail.

One of the Poles would flirt with me whenever I came close to the tracks. Although we were not supposed to talk to each other, he would pass me notes when the guards were not looking. He called me Pinky, because of my mittens. He would whisper limericks to make me laugh. Some of the other women joked around with me about my boyfriend, and said that he must have a thing for girls who played hard to get. In reality,

I wasn't playing hard to get at all. I didn't speak for fear I'd be punished, and because it still hurt to move my jaw.

I had been at the factory for only two weeks when, one day, he came closer to me than the guards allowed. 'Escape if you can. This camp is going to be evacuated.'

I didn't know what that meant. Would we be taken somewhere and shot? Would we be brought to another camp, a death camp like the one I'd left? Or would I be sent back to Auschwitz, and the *Schutzhaftlagerführer*?

I moved away from the POW as quickly as I could, before he got me into trouble. I didn't tell the other women in my barracks what he had said.

Three days later, instead of being made to report to our work details, the nine hundred women in the camp were assembled and, under guard, marched out of the gates.

We walked about ten miles before dawn. Women who had gathered their meager belongings – blankets and pots and whatever else they had squirreled away at the camp – began to drop them on the sides of the road. We were headed toward Germany, that was all we could surmise. In the front of the convoy, prisoners pulled a wagon that prepared meals for the SS officers. Another wagon at the back of the line held the bodies of those who collapsed from exhaustion and died. The Germans were trying to cover their tracks, I supposed. At least that was the way it worked for the first few days, and then the officers just got lazy, shot those who fell, and left them lying there. The rest of us would simply step around them, like water parted by a stone in a stream.

We hiked through forests. We hiked through fields. We hiked through towns, where people came to stare at us as we passed, some with tears in their eyes, and some spitting at us. When there were Allied warplanes overhead, the officers would slip between us, using us as camouflage. The hunger was worst, but a close second was the condition of my feet. Some of the women were lucky enough to have boots. I was still wearing the wooden clogs that I had been given at Auschwitz. My skin was blistered beneath the multiple stockings I wore; splinters from the wood had rubbed holes in the heels of at least two of the layers. Where snow had seeped into the wool, my skin was nearly frostbitten. And still I did not have it as bad as some of the other girls. One, who had only a single pair of stockings, got such bad frostbite that her little toe snapped off like an icicle from a roof.

This went on for a week. I no longer told myself I had to survive the day, but just one more hour. All this exercise and no food took its toll; I could feel myself wasting away, weakening. I had not believed it was possible to be any hungrier than I already was, but I had not understood what this march would be like. At rest stops, when the officers prepared their own meals, we were left to melt snow so that we would have water to drink. We'd forage through the melting drifts for acorns and bits of moss that we could eat. We never spoke; we were just too weary to muster up the energy. After each of these stops, there were at least a dozen women who could not get to their feet again. Then, the SS executioner – a Ukrainian with a wide, flat nose and a bulbous Adam's apple – would finish them off with a single shot to the back.

Ten days into the march, at one of the rest stops, the officers made a fire. They tossed potatoes into the flames, and dared us to reach in and grab one. There were girls so desperate to get a potato that they set their sleeves on fire, then rolled in the snow to put out the flames, which made the officers laugh. Some who had been successful in getting a potato would eventually die from the burns. After a while, the potatoes charred to ash, because no one else would reach in for them. It was worse, I think, seeing that food go to waste, than simply starving.

That night one woman who had suffered third-degree burns on her hands was screaming from the pain. I was lying beside her and tried to calm her down by packing her arms with fresh snow. 'This will help,' I soothed. 'You just have to stop thrashing.' But she was Hungarian and didn't understand me, and I didn't know how else to help her. After hours of her shrieks, the executioner approached. He stepped over me and shot her, then went back to the spot where the officers were sleeping. I coughed, unable to breathe anything but gunpowder residue, and then wrapped my scarf over my mouth as a filter. The other women around me did not even react.

I reached down and untied the boots that the dead woman was wearing. She would not need them anymore.

They were too big, but they were better than the wooden clogs.

The next morning, before we left the camp the officers had made, I was told to douse the fire. I did, with snow, but noticed the charred remains of the potatoes among the embers. I reached in and picked one up. It crumbled at my touch into a heap of ash, but surely there was still some nutritious value? As quickly as possible, I grabbed handfuls of the ash into my pockets, and for days after that, as I walked, I would stick my fingers into my coat and scoop out bits to eat.

When we had been marching for two weeks, I thought about the POW who had urged me to escape, and now I understood. There were incremental grades of surrender. From the women who kicked off their clogs because the blisters on their feet made it impossible to walk anymore and who then suffered such severe frostbite and gangrene that they died to those who simply lay down and did not get up, knowing they would be dead within minutes – well, it seemed that we were all dying by degrees. Eventually, there would be none of us left.

Which maybe was the point of this march.

And then, it seemed, there was an iota of mercy, in the form of springtime. The days grew warmer; the snow melted in patches. This was a gift in that I knew soon things would begin to grow, and that meant food. But it also depleted our reserve of unlimited water, and created mud bogs we had to slog through. We marched through villages, where we would sleep in the streets while the SS men took turns sleeping inside homes and churches. Then we would wake up and edge into the forests again, where it was harder for the warplanes to spot us.

One afternoon I was assigned to pull the wagon at the front of the convoy when I saw something sticking out of the mud.

An apple core.

Someone must have thrown it away in the woods. A farmer, maybe. A boy, whistling as he ran through the trees.

I looked at the SS officers walking beside the wagon. If I let go for a second, I could run over and pick up the core and slip it into my pocket without them noticing. I was fully aware that in six steps . . . five . . . four . . . we would be past it and it would be too late. I also knew from the charge that ran through our ragged line that I was not the only one to have seen it.

I dropped the handle of the wagon and ran to grab it.

I was not fast enough. An SS man yanked me upright before my fingers could close around the core. He dragged me from my position at the front of the convoy to the rear, where two more officers secured my arms so that I couldn't blend into the line of prisoners. I knew what would happen, because I had seen it before: when we stopped again to rest, the executioner would take me into the woods and would kill me.

My knees were knocking, making it difficult to walk. When the wagon in the front pulled to the side to make the evening meal, the executioner took my arm and led me away from the other women.

I was the only one assigned to be executed that afternoon. By now, it was twilight, the sky was a dusky purple that would have taken my breath away under any other circumstance. The executioner motioned for me to get down on my knees in front of him. I did, but clasped my hands together and started to beg. 'Please. If you spare my life, I'll give you something in return.'

I don't know why I made this promise; I had nothing of value. Everything I'd brought with me from Neusalz I wore on my body.

Then I remembered the leather journal, which I had slipped into the waistband of my dress.

There was nothing about this thuggish man that suggested he was a scholar of literature, or that he even knew how to read. But I lifted my arms in a signal of surrender and then slowly reached beneath my coat for the book in which I had written my story. 'Please,' I repeated. 'Take this.'

He frowned, dismissing the barter at first. But most prisoners did not have a fine leather-bound journal in their possession. I could see him wondering if maybe there was something important written inside.

He reached toward me. As soon as his hand clasped the binding, I took my other hand, now resting on the ground, and grabbed a handful of dirt, which I threw into his eyes.

Then I ran faster than I'd ever run into the night, which bled like a mortal wound between the trees.

* * *

I would not have escaped, if not for several favorable conditions:

1. It was dusk, the most difficult time of the day for my captors to see. Trees became soldiers pointing guns, and the keen eyes of owls could be mistaken for fugitives; boulders resembled enemy tanks, and every animal's footfall made them fear they'd walked into an ambush.
2. The officers had no dogs with them, the march being deemed too grueling for animals, so I couldn't be tracked by my scent.
3. The mud.
4. The fact that the officers were just as weary of this march as I was.

I ran until I collapsed, and by then I could hear the shouts of the SS men who were searching for me. I stumbled, rolling in the near dark down a ravine, landing in a trench at the bottom. I covered my body and my face with the wet mud and drew branches and brush across me. Then I lay as still as I could. At one point, the Germans passed so close that one of the officers stepped on the back of my hand, but I did not make a sound and he did not realize I was hiding beneath his boots.

Eventually, they moved on. I waited a full day before I believed it, and then began to pick my way through the forest. I walked by moonlight, afraid to sleep because of the wild animals that I heard calling to each other. Just when I was certain I would have to lie down and take my chances with the wolves, I saw something in the distance. A looming shadow, a broad-hipped roof, a haystack.

The barn smelled of pigs and chickens. When I slipped inside, the birds were roosting, gossiping to each other like old ladies, too busy to even send up the alarm that I had entered.

I felt my way in the slurry dark, wincing when my foot struck a metal pail. But in spite of the clatter, no one came; no lights in the house down the path flickered on, and so I continued to rummage.

A deep wooden barrel filled with grain squatted just outside the fence of the pigpen.

I dug both hands into the barrel and ate fistfuls of the food, which tasted of sawdust and molasses and oats. I tried hard not to eat too fast, because I knew it would only make me sick. Climbing over the low railing, I pushed two large sows out of the way and dug my hands into a trough. Potato peels. Fruit rinds. The heels of bread.

This was a banquet.

Eventually I lay down with the pigs on either side of me, warmed by their bristled backs and shielded by their bulk. For the first time in five years, I fell asleep so stuffed that even if I had tried, I could not have eaten another bite.

I dreamed that I had been shot by the executioner after all, because surely this was Heaven. Or so I thought, until I woke up to find a pitchfork pointed at my throat.

The woman was about the same age that my mother had been, with a coronet of braids twisted around her head and lines bracketing her mouth. She poked the weapon at my throat and I scrambled backward, as the animals grunted and squealed around me.

I threw up my hands in surrender. '*Bitte*,' I cried, struggling to my feet. I was so weak, I had to grab on to the railing of the pigpen to do it.

She held the pitchfork aloft but then slowly, so incredibly slowly, lowered the tines, holding it instead across her body like a barrier. She tilted her head, staring.

I could only imagine what she was seeing. A skeleton, with mud caking my skin and my hair. My striped prisoner's coat and my filthy pink mittens and hat.

'*Bitte*,' I murmured again.

She put down the pitchfork and ran out of the barn, closing the heavy door behind her.

The pigs were chewing on the laces of my stolen boots. The chickens sitting on the railing between the coop and the pigpen flapped their wings and cackled. I reached over the wooden gate and opened the latch so that I could step outside. The farmer's wife had left because she was terrified, but that didn't mean she wasn't on her way back right now with her husband and a shotgun. Hurriedly I filled my pockets with more of the pig grain I'd eaten last night, because I didn't know when I would have food again. Before I could slip out the door, however, it opened again.

The farmer's wife stood there with a loaf of bread, a jug of milk, and a platter of sausage. She walked toward me. 'You must eat,' she whispered.

I hesitated, wondering if this was a trap. But in the end, I was too hungry to let the chance pass. I grabbed a sausage off the plate and stuffed it into my mouth. I tore off a hunk of bread and tucked it into the side of my cheek, since my jaw was still too sore to chew. I drained the jug of milk, feeling it pour down my chin and neck. How long had it been since I had fresh milk? Then I wiped my hand across my mouth, embarrassed to have acted like such an animal in front of this woman.

'Where did you come from?' she asked.

She spoke German, which meant we must have crossed into Germany by now. Was it possible that there were ordinary citizens who had no idea what was happening in Poland? Had they been lied to by the SS, like we had? Before I could think of what to say, she shook her head. 'It is better if you don't tell me. You stay. It will be safe.'

I had no reason to trust her. It was true that most of the Germans I had met had been brutal terrorists without conscience. But there had also been a Herr Bauer, a Herr Fassbinder, a *Hauptscharführer*.

So I nodded. She motioned to the hayloft. There was a ladder leading up to it, and a shaft of sunlight spilling through a crack in the roof. Still holding the piece of bread she had given me, I began to climb. I lay down on a bed of hay, and I fell asleep before the farmer's wife had even closed the barn door behind her again.

It was hours before I awakened to the sound of footsteps below. I peeked down the ladder to see the farmer's wife lugging a metal pail inside. Draped around her neck was a white towel, and in her free arm was a stack of folded clothing. She motioned, when she saw my face. 'Come,' she said gently.

I crawled down the ladder and shifted uneasily from foot to foot. The woman patted a hay bale, so that I would sit. Then she knelt at my feet. She dipped a washcloth into the water in the pail and leaned forward, carefully wiping my brow, my cheeks, my chin. The washcloth, dark with mud and grime, she rinsed off in the bucket again.

I let her wash my arms and my legs. The water was warm, a luxury. When she began to unbutton my work dress, I pulled away, until she cupped my shoulders in her capable hands. 'Ssh,' she murmured, turning me away from her. I felt the rough fabric being peeled from my body, falling to the floor in a puddle at my feet. I felt the washcloth on every pearl of my spine, on the angular planes of my hip bones, the fortress of my rib cage.

When she turned me to face her, there were tears in her eyes.

I crossed my arms in front of my bare body, ashamed to see myself through her eyes.

After I was dressed in the clean clothing – soft cotton and wool, as if I had been wrapped in a cloud – she brought another bucket of clean water, and a bar of soap, and washed my hair for me. She used her fingers to scrub out the mud, and she cut the mats that could not be worked free. Then she sat behind me, the way my mother used to do, and brushed it.

Sometimes all it takes to become human again is someone who can see you that way, no matter how you present on the surface.

For five days, the farmer's wife came to me with meals. Breakfasts of fresh eggs and rye toast and gooseberry jam, lunches of sliced cheese on thick hanks of bread, suppers of chicken thighs with root vegetables. Slowly, I grew more alert, stronger. The blisters on my feet healed; my jaw stopped aching. I was able to pace myself so that I did not stuff my face with the food as soon as she set it in front of me. We did not speak about where I'd come from, or where I would be going. I tried to convince myself that I could stay here, in the barn, until the war was over.

I was once again at the mercy of a German, but like a dog that has been kicked so often it shies away from any kind hand, I was slowly being coaxed into believing that I might be able to trust.

In return, I tried to show my gratitude. I cleaned out the chicken coop, a job that took me hours, because I had to keep sitting to rest. I collected the eggs, and had them neatly piled in a pail when the farmer's wife arrived each afternoon. I cleaned cobwebs from the rafters and swept the hayloft so that you could see the wooden floor beneath the bales.

One night, the woman did not come.

I felt a pang of hunger, but it was nothing like what I'd experienced in the camp or on the march. I had gone without for so long that missing a single meal now almost didn't register. Maybe she was ill; maybe she had taken a trip. The next morning, when the barn door slid open, I crawled down the ladder quickly, aware that I had missed her company more than I even let myself know.

The farmer's wife stood with the sun silhouetting her, so it took me a moment to realize that her eyes were red and puffy, that she was not alone. A man wearing a flannel shirt and suspenders, who leaned heavily on a cane, stood behind her. With him was a member of the police force.

The light leached from my smile. I was rooted to the barn floor, gripping the ladder so hard the wood bit into the skin beneath my fingernails. 'I'm sorry,' the farmer's wife choked out, but that was all she said, because her husband gave her a firm shake. The police officer bound my hands together, then pulled the barn door wide and led me to a truck that was idling in the driveway.

My mother used to say that sometimes if you turn a tragedy over in your hand, you can see a miracle running through it, like fool's gold in the hardest shard of rock. This was certainly true of the deaths of my family – if only because they did not live to see me in this state, to see the *world* in this state. The murder of another woman had yielded me a pair of sturdy boots. If not for the march from Neusalz, I would never have found this barn and had nearly a week of three square meals in my belly.

And if the farmer had indeed discovered his wife's secret stowaway, and he had called the police to turn me in, at least it meant that I would travel to this next camp in the back of a truck, conserving strength I would never have had if I'd walked the entire distance. Which is why, when we arrived at Flossenbürg on March 11, 1945 – the same day, ironically, as those who had begun the march from Neusalz – more than half of those women were dead, but I was still alive.

A week later we were put onto trains and taken to another camp.

We arrived at Bergen-Belsen the last week of March. In the cars we had been stacked like cans on a grocery shelf, so that shifting even a little meant a foot in your face or a grunt from someone else, and everyone was trying desperately to get away from the overflowing bucket we used as a latrine. When the train stopped, we staggered out, holding on to each other as if we had been drinking heavily. I managed only a few steps before I sank down.

The first thing I noticed was the smell. I couldn't describe it, even if I tried. The burning flesh of Auschwitz was nothing compared to this, the stink of disease and piss and shit and death. It got into your nostrils and throat, and left you breathing shallowly through your mouth. Everywhere, there were stacks of the dead, some haphazard, some neatly arranged like building blocks or a house of cards. Those healthy enough to move were hauling the bodies away.

Everyone at this camp had typhus. How could they not, when there were hundreds of people crammed into barracks meant for fifty, when the latrine facility was a hole outside, when there wasn't enough food or fresh water for the thousands of prisoners who had been trucked in?

We did not work. We rotted. We would curl like snails on the floor of the barracks, because that was the only way we could all fit. Guards would come in to dispose of the dead.

Sometimes they would take the living, too. It was an honest mistake; we didn't always know which was which. All night long there would be soft moans, skin blistering with fever, hallucinations. Then we would shuffle outside in the morning for *Appell*, lining up to be counted for hours.

I became friendly with a woman named Tauba, who, with her daughter Sura, used to live in Hrubieszów. Tauba had a prized possession, one she held on to as fiercely as I had once held on to my leather journal. It was a threadbare, lice-infested blanket. She and Sura had used it on the march that brought them here, braving the snow and the elements and surviving the nights when others died of the cold. Now, Tauba used it to warm Sura, who fell sick just days after arriving at the camp. She would wrap her daughter in the blanket and rock her back and forth, singing lullabies. When it was time for *Appell*, Tauba and I would hold Sura upright between the vise of our bodies.

One night, in her dream-state, Sura begged for food. Tauba held her closer. 'What would you like me to cook for you?' she whispered. 'Maybe a roast chicken. With gravy and candied carrots and whipped potatoes.' Her eyes were bright with tears. 'With butter, a big dollop, like snow on the top of a mountain.' She hugged Sura more tightly, and the girl's head snapped back on its delicate stem. 'In the morning, when you are hungry again, I will bring you my special pancakes, stuffed with cottage cheese, and sprinkled with sugar. Baked beans and eggs and brown bread and fresh blueberries. There will be so much food, Surele, that you will not be able to finish it.'

I knew that some of the stronger women had managed to get to the kitchens and find food in the waste bins. I don't know why they weren't punished – it was either because the guards didn't want to get too close to us and risk illness or because no one cared anymore. But the next morning, after making sure Sura was still breathing, I followed a small contingency to the kitchen. 'What do we do?' I asked, nervous about standing around in broad daylight. But then again, it wasn't as if we were skipping a work detail. There was nothing for us to do at this camp but wait. Did it matter if we were here, underneath a kitchen window, instead of in a barracks?

The window opened, and a sturdy woman tossed a pail of scraps out. Potato peels, ersatz coffee grounds, rinds from sausages and oranges, the bones from a roast. The women fell to the ground like animals, grabbing what they could. In my moment's hesitation, I lost out on the most valuable bits of refuse, but I managed to get a wishbone from a chicken, and a handful of potato peels. I slipped these into my pocket and hurried back to Tauba and Sura.

I handed the potato peels to Tauba, who tried to coax her daughter into sucking on one. But Sura had slipped into unconsciousness. 'Then you eat it,' I urged. 'When she gets better, she'll need your strength.'

Tauba shook her head. 'I wish I could believe that.'

I reached into my pocket for the bone I'd taken. 'When I was little and my sister, Basia, and I both wanted something very badly – like a new wagon or a trip to the country – we would make a deal,' I told Tauba. 'When Mama cooked her Shabbat chicken, and we got the wishbone, we'd wish for the same thing. That way, it couldn't help but come true.' I held up the bone, curling my fingers around one side of its slingshot neck, letting Tauba curl her fingers around the other. 'Ready?' I asked.

The bone broke in her favor. But it would not have mattered either way.

That night, when the kapo came to sort through the dead, Sura's body was the first one taken.

I listened to Tauba keening, turned inside out by loss. She buried her face in the blanket, all she had left of her daughter. But even muffled, her cries turned into shrieks; I covered my ears and still could not block them out. The shrieks became knives, poised like daggers around the crown of my face. I watched with wonder as they pierced my sunken skin, releasing not blood but fire.

Minka. Minka?

Tauba's face swam into my vision, as if I were lying on the bottom of the sea and staring up at the sun. *Minka, you've got the fever.*

I was shaking uncontrollably now, my clothes soaked in sweat. I knew how this would turn out. In a few days' time, I would be dead.

Then Tauba did the most amazing thing. She took that blanket, and she tore it in half. She wrapped part of it around my shoulders.

If I was going to die, I wanted to do it on my own terms. In this, I was like my sister after all. It would not be in a fetid hut, surrounded by the sick. I would not let the last person who made a decision about me be a guard, hauling my corpse somewhere to decompose in the midday sun.

So I staggered outside, where the air was cooler against my skin. I pulled the blanket tight around me, and I collapsed on the ground.

I knew I was saving someone the trouble of carting my body out in the morning. But for now, I shook in the throes of my fever, and I looked up at the night sky.

There had not been many stars in Łódź . It was too big and dynamic a city. But my father had taught me the constellations when I was a girl and we had traveled to the countryside on vacation. There would be just the four of us, staying at a rented cottage by a lake, fishing and reading and hiking and playing backgammon. My mother always beat the rest of us at card games, but my father always caught the biggest fish.

At night, sometimes, my father and I would sleep on the porch, where the air was so fresh that you drank it instead of simply breathing. My father taught me about Leo, the constellation directly overhead. Named for yet another mythical monster, the Nemean Lion, a giant, ferocious beast with skin that couldn't be penetrated by knives or swords. Hercules' first task was to slay it, but he realized quickly that the lion couldn't be shot with arrows. Instead, he chased the monster into a cave, stunned it with a blow to the head, and strangled it. As proof of his victory, he used the lion's own claws to skin its pelt.

You see, Minka, my father would say. *Anything is possible. Even the most terrible beast might one day be a distant memory.* He would hold my hand in his, tracing my finger along the brightest stars in the constellation. *Look,* he would say. *There is the head, and the tail. There's the heart.*

I was dead, and I was looking at the wing of an angel. White and ethereal, it swooped and dove in the corner of my vision.

But if I was dead, why did my head feel as heavy as an anvil? Why could I still smell the horrible stench of this place?

I struggled to sit up and realized that what I had imagined

as a wing was a flag, a strip of cloth fluttering in the wind. It was tied to the guard tower that stood across from the barracks where I'd been housed.

That guard tower was empty.

So was the one behind it.

There were no officers walking around, no Germans, period. It was like a ghost town.

By then, some of the other prisoners had begun to figure out what had happened. 'Get up!' one woman yelled. 'Get up, they are all gone!'

I was swept in a tide of humanity toward the fence. Had they left us here to starve to death? Were any of us strong enough to tear down the barbed wire?

In the distance were trucks with red crosses painted on the sides. At that moment, I knew it didn't matter if we weren't strong enough. There were others, now, who would be strong *for* us.

There is a picture of me from that day. I saw it once on a PBS documentary about April 15, 1945, when the first British tanks approached Bergen-Belsen. I was shocked to see my face on the body of a skeleton. I even bought a copy of the video so that I could play it and stop it at the right moment, and make sure. But yes, that was me, with my pink hat and mittens, and Sura's blanket wrapped around my shoulders.

I've told no one that this was me, in someone's camera footage, until now.

I weighed sixty-seven pounds on the day the British liberated us. A man in a uniform approached me, and I fell into his arms, unable to stand any longer. He swung me up and carried me to a tent that was serving as an infirmary.

You are free, they said over the loudspeakers, in English, in German, in Yiddish, in Polish. *You are free, be calm. Food is coming. Help is on the way.*

You will ask me, after this, why I didn't tell you this before.

It is because I know how powerful a story can be. It can change the course of history. It can save a life. But it can also be a sinkhole, a quicksand in which you become stuck, unable to write yourself free.

You would think bearing witness to something like this would make a difference, and yet this isn't so. In the newspapers I have read about history repeating itself in Cambodia. Rwanda. Sudan.

Truth is so much harder than fiction. Some survivors want to speak only of what happened. They go to schools and museums and temples and give talks. It's the way they can make sense of it, I suppose. I've heard them say they feel it is their responsibility, maybe even the reason they lived.

My husband – your grandfather – used to say, *Minka, you were a writer. Imagine the story you could tell.*

But it is exactly *because* I was a writer that I could never do it.

The weapons an author has at her disposal are flawed. There are words that feel shapeless and overused. *Love*, for example. I could write the word *love* a thousand times and it would mean a thousand different things to different readers.

What is the point of trying to put down on paper emotions that are too complex, too huge, too overwhelming to be confined by an alphabet?

Love isn't the only word that fails.

Hate does, too.

War.

And *hope.* Oh, yes, *hope.*

So you see, this is why I never told my story.

If you lived through it, you already know there are no words that will ever come close to describing it.

And if you didn't, you will never understand.

Part Three

*How wonderful it is that nobody need wait a single
moment before starting to improve the world.*

– Anne Frank, Diary of a Young Girl

*H*e *was faster than me, and stronger. When he finally caught me, he clamped a hand around my mouth so that I could not scream and dragged me into an abandoned barn, where he tossed me down in a dusty bed of hay. I stared up at him, wondering who he really was, how I had not seen it. 'Will you kill me, too?' I challenged.*

'No,' Aleks said quietly. 'I am doing what I can to save you.'

He reached through the broken glass of the window to scoop a handful of snow. Rubbing it into his arms, he then wiped himself dry with the shreds of his shirt.

It was easy to see the fresh wounds on his shoulders and chest and back. But there were at least a dozen others, narrow cuts that ran down the inside of his arm, over his wrist, into his palm. 'After he attacked you, I started doing it,' Aleks said. 'Baking the bread.'

'I don't understand . . .'

In the moonlight, the scars on his arm were a silver ladder. 'I did not ask to be who I am,' he said tightly. 'I try to keep Casimir locked up and hidden. I feed him raw meat, but he's always hungry. I do what I can to keep him from letting his nature win. I try to keep a rein on it myself, too. Most of the time, I can. But one day, he got away when I was out trying to find him food. I tracked him into the woods. He had gone after your father, who was cutting wood for the oven, but your father had the advantage of an ax. When I ran in, trying to distract Casimir, it gave your father a chance to fight back. He managed to land a blow to Casimir's thigh. I went to grab the ax away. I don't know if it was the smell of the blood or the adrenaline in his system . . .' Aleks looked away. 'I don't know why it happened, why I couldn't control myself. He is still my brother. That's my only excuse.' Aleks raked his hand through his hair, making it stand like a rooster's comb. 'I knew if it happened again, even once, it would be too much. I had to find a way to protect others, just in case. So I asked to work for you.'

I looked at his scars, and I thought of the roll he had been baking me each day, the way he begged me to eat it all. I thought of the baguettes that I had sold this week, the customers who told me that the mere taste of them was a religious experience. I thought of Old Sal, saying that the only way to be immune to an upiór *was to consume its blood. I thought of the rosy tint to the dough, and I understood what Aleks was telling me.*

He was literally bleeding himself dry, to save us all from himself.

Sage

My grandmother was a survivor two times over. Long before I knew she had any connection to the Holocaust, she battled cancer.

I was tiny, maybe three or four. My sisters were in school during the day, but my mother took me to Nana's house every morning when my grandfather left for work, so that she would not be alone during her recovery. My grandmother had a radical mastectomy. During her recuperation, she would lie on the couch while I watched *Sesame Street* and colored at the coffee table in front of her, and my mom cleaned and did her dishes and cooked her meals. Every hour, she would do her exercises, which consisted of crawling her fingers up the wall behind the couch and stretching as high as she could – a way to rebuild the muscles damaged by the surgery.

Each morning after we arrived, my mother would help Nana into the bathroom for her shower. She would close the door and unzip my grandmother's housecoat, and then she would let my grandmother rinse herself off under the steaming water. Fifteen minutes later, she would knock softly and enter again, and the two of them would come out: Nana smelling of talcum powder, dressed in a fresh housecoat, the hair at her nape damp but the rest of it mysteriously dry.

One day, after my mother got Nana settled in her shower, she went upstairs with a stack of folded laundry. 'Sage,' she told me, 'stay here till I come back.' I didn't even turn away from the television; Oscar the Grouch was on, and I was scared of Oscar. If I looked away, he could sneak out of his garbage can when I wasn't looking.

But as soon as my mother was out of sight and Oscar was offscreen, I wandered to the bathroom. The door was unlatched, so that my mother would be able to get in. I pushed it open just a crack, and immediately felt my hair curl as the steam surrounded me.

I couldn't see, at first. It was as if I'd walked into a cloud. But then, when my vision cleared, I noticed my grandmother on the other side of the shower glass, sitting on a little plastic stool. She had turned off the water, but on her head was a shower cap that looked like a cartoon mushroom, red with white dots. Draped over her lap was her towel. With her good hand, she was patting powder on her body.

I had never seen her naked. I had never seen my mother naked, for that matter. So I stared, because there were so many differences between her body and mine.

The skin, for one, which sagged at her knees and her elbows and belly, as if there wasn't enough to fill it. The whiteness of her thighs, as if she never ran around outside in shorts, which was probably true.

The number on her arm, which reminded me of the ones that the grocery clerk scanned when we were buying food.

And of course, the scar where her left breast had been.

Still angry and red, the puckered flesh covered a cliff, a sheer wall.

By then my grandmother had seen me. She opened the shower door with her right hand, so that I nearly choked from the smell of talcum. 'Come closer, Sagele,' she said. 'There's nothing about me I want to hide from you.'

I took a step forward, and then I stopped, because the scars on my nana were much scarier, even, than Oscar.

'You notice that something's different about me,' my grandmother said.

I nodded. I did not have the words, at that age, to explain what I wasn't seeing, but I understood that it was not what should have been. I pointed to the wound. 'It's missing,' I said.

My grandmother smiled, and that was all it took for me to stop seeing the scar, and to recognize her again. 'Yes,' she said. 'But see how much of me is left?'

I wait in my nana's room while Daisy gets her ready for bed. With tenderness, her caretaker stacks her pillows the way she likes and tucks her into the covers before retiring for the night. I sit down on the edge of the bed and hold my grandmother's hand, which is cool and dry to the touch. I don't know what to say. I don't know what there is *left* to say.

The skin on my face tingles, as if scars can recognize each other, even though the ones my grandmother has revealed this time have been invisible. I want to thank her for telling me. I want to thank her for surviving, because without her, I wouldn't be here to listen. But like she said, sometimes words are not big enough to contain all the feelings you are trying to pour into them.

My grandmother's free hand dances over the edge of the sheet, pulling it up to her chin. 'When the war ended,' she says, 'this was what took getting used to. The comfort. I couldn't sleep on a mattress, for a long time. I'd take a blanket and sleep on the floor instead.' She looks up at me, and for a second, I can see the girl she used to be. 'It was your grandfather who set me straight. *Minka,* he said. *I love you, but I'm not sleeping on the ground.'*

I remember my grandfather as a soft-spoken man who loved books. His fingers were always stained with ink from receipts he would write customers at his antiquarian bookstore. 'You met in Sweden,' I say, which is the story we had all been told.

She nods. 'After I recovered from typhus, I went there. We survivors could travel anywhere in Europe, then, for free. I went with some other women to a boardinghouse in Stockholm, and every day, I ate breakfast in a restaurant, just because I could. He was a soldier on leave. He said he had never seen a girl eat so many pancakes in his life.' A smile creases her face. 'He came every day to that restaurant and sat next to me at the counter until I agreed to let him take me out to dinner.'

'You swept him off his feet.'

My grandmother laughs. 'Hardly. I was all bones. No breasts, no curves, nothing. I had hair that was only an inch long all over my head – the best style I could fashion after the lice were gone. I barely looked like a girl,' she says. 'On that first date, I asked him what he saw in me. And he said, *My future.'*

Suddenly I remember being young, and taking a walk around the neighborhood with my sisters and my grandmother. I hadn't wanted to go; I was reading a book, and strolling without a destination in mind seemed pointless. But my mother pressured all three of us girls, and so we traipsed at my grandmother's snail pace around the block. She was horrified when we wanted to dart down the middle of the street. 'Why stay in the gutter,' she said, 'when you have this fine sidewalk?' I thought, at the time, she was being overly cautious, worried about cars on a residential street that never saw any traffic. Now, I realize, she could not comprehend why we wouldn't use the sidewalk simply because we *could*.

When a freedom is taken away from you, I suppose, you recognize it as a privilege, not a right.

'When we first got to America, your grandfather suggested I join a group with others who were like me; who'd been, you know, in the camps. I dragged him with me. We went to three meetings. Everyone there talked about what had happened, and how much they hated the Germans. I didn't want that. I was in a beautiful new country. I wanted to talk about movies, and my handsome husband, and my new friends. So I left, and instead I went on with my life.'

'After what the Germans did to you, how could you forgive them?' Saying the word out loud makes me think of Josef.

'Who says that I did?' my grandmother replies, surprised. 'I could never forgive the *Schutzhaftlagerführer* for killing my best friend.'

'I don't blame you.'

'No, Sage. I mean I *couldn't* – literally – because it is not my place to forgive him. That could only be done by Darija, and he made that impossible. But by the same logic, I *should* be able to forgive the *Hauptscharführer*. He broke my jaw, but he also saved my life.' She shakes her head. 'And yet I can't.'

She is quiet for so long that at first I think she has fallen asleep.

'When I was in that starvation cell,' my grandmother says quietly, 'I hated him. Not for fooling me into trusting him, or even for beating me. But because he made me lose the compassion I had for the enemy. I no longer thought of Herr Bauer or Herr Fassbinder; I believed one German was the same as any other, and I hated them all.' She looks at me. 'Which means, for that moment, I was no better than any of them.'

Leo sees me close the bedroom door behind me after my grandmother falls asleep. 'You okay?'

I notice he has cleaned up the kitchen, rinsed out the glasses we used for our tea, swept the table clear of crumbs, washed down the counter. 'She's asleep now,' I reply, not really answering his question. How can I? How could anyone be okay, after hearing what we've heard today? 'And Daisy's here if she needs anything.'

'Look, I know how hard it must be to hear something like that—'

'You don't know,' I interrupt. 'You do this for a living, Leo, but it's not personal for you.'

'Actually, it's very personal,' he says, and immediately I feel guilty. He's dedicated his whole life to finding the people who perpetrated these crimes; I didn't care enough to push my grandmother to open up to me, even as a teenager, when I found out that she was a survivor.

'He's Reiner Hartmann, isn't he?' I ask.

Leo turns off the lights in the kitchen. 'Well,' he says. 'We'll see.'

'What aren't you telling me?'

He smiles faintly. 'I'm a federal agent. If I told you, I'd have to kill you.'

'Really?'

'No.' He holds the door open for me and then makes sure it is locked behind us. 'All we know right now is that your grandmother was at Auschwitz. There were hundreds of SS officers there. She still hasn't identified your Josef as one of them.'

'He's not my Josef,' I say.

Leo opens the passenger door of his rental car for me, then walks around to the driver's side. 'I know you have a vested interest in this, and I know you want it finished yesterday. But in order for my department to follow through, we have to dot all the i's and cross all the t's. While you were in with your grandmother, I called one of my historians in Washington. Genevra's working up an array of photographs and FedExing it to me at the hotel. With any luck tomorrow, if your grandmother's up to it, we could have the proof we need to get this ball rolling.' He pulls out of the driveway.

'But Josef confessed to me,' I argue.

'Exactly. He didn't want to be extradited or prosecuted, or he would have confessed to *me*. We don't know what his agenda is; if this is some delusion he's harboring, if he just has a weird death wish – there are a dozen reasons he might want you to take part in an assisted suicide, and maybe he thinks he has to make himself seem reprehensible before you'll consider it. I don't know.'

'But all those details—'

'He's in his nineties. He could have been watching the History Channel for the past fifty years. There are a lot of experts on World War Two. Details are good, but only if they can be pinned down to a particular individual. Which is why, if we can corroborate his story with an eyewitness who actually saw him at Auschwitz, we suddenly have a case.'

I fold my arms across my chest. 'Things move much quicker on *Law & Order: SVU.*'

'That's because Mariska Hargitay's contract's up for renewal,' Leo says. 'Look, the first time I listened to a survivor's testimony, I felt the same way – and it *wasn't* my own grandmother.

I wanted to kill all the Nazis. Even the ones who are already dead.'

I wipe my eyes, embarrassed to be crying in front of him. 'I can't even imagine some of the things she told us.'

'I've heard them a few hundred times,' Leo says softly, 'and it doesn't get any easier.'

'So we just go home now?'

Leo nods. 'Get a good night's sleep, and wait for my package to get here. Then we can visit your grandmother again, and hope she's up to making an ID.'

And if she does, who are we helping? Not my grandmother, that's for sure. She has spent years reinventing herself so that she isn't a victim anymore; but aren't we redefining her as one if we ask her for that ID? I think of Josef, or Reiner, or whatever his name used to be. Everyone has a story; everyone hides his past as a means of self-preservation. Some just do it better, and more thoroughly, than others.

But how can anyone exist in a world where nobody is who he seems to be?

Silence grows between us, filling all the empty space in the rental car. I jump when the GPS tells us to turn right, onto the highway. Leo fumbles with the radio. 'Maybe we should listen to some music.'

He winces as rock fills the car.

'Too bad we don't have any CDs,' I say.

'I don't know how to work one of those things anyway. I don't have one in my car.'

'A CD player? Are you kidding? What do you drive . . . a Model T?'

'I have a Subaru. It just happens to have an eight-track.'

'They still exist?'

'Don't judge. I'm a vintage kind of guy.'

'So you like oldies,' I say, intrigued. 'The Shirelles, and the Troggs; Jan and Dean . . .'

'Whoa,' Leo says. 'Those aren't oldies. Cab Calloway, Billie Holiday, Peggy Lee . . . Woody Herman . . .'

'I'm about to blow your mind,' I reply, and I tune the radio to a new station. As Rosemary Clooney croons to us, Leo's eyes widen.

'This is incredible,' he says. 'Is it a Boston station?'

'It's SiriusXM. Satellite radio. Pretty nifty technology. In related news, they also now make movies that *talk.*'

Leo smirks. 'I *know* what satellite radio is. I just never—'

'Figured it was worth listening to? Isn't it kind of dangerous to live in the past?'

'No more dangerous than living in the present and realizing nothing's changed,' Leo says.

That makes me think of my grandmother again. 'She said that's why she didn't want to talk about what happened to her. That there didn't seem to be much of a point.'

'I don't entirely believe her,' Leo says. 'Watching history repeat might be self-defeating, but there's usually another reason that survivors keep their experiences to themselves.'

'Like?'

'To protect their families. It's PTSD, really. Someone who's been traumatized like that can't switch off some emotions and leave others intact. Survivors who look perfectly fine on the outside can still be emotionally empty at the core. And because of that, they can't always connect with their kids or their spouses – or they make the conscious decision *not* to connect, so that they don't fail the people they love. They're afraid of passing on the nightmares, or of getting attached and losing someone again. But as a result of that, their kids grow up and model that behavior with their own families.'

I try but can't remember my father being distant. He did, however, keep my grandmother's secrets for her. Had my nana tried to spare him by staying silent, and had he suffered anyway? Did that emotional disconnection skip a generation? I screened my face from people; I found a job that allowed me to work nights, alone; I let myself fall for a man I knew was never going to be mine, because I did not think I'd ever be lucky enough to find someone to love me forever. Had I been hiding because I was a freak, or was I a freak because I'd been hiding? Was my scar only part of it – the trigger for trauma, passed down through the bloodline?

I don't realize I'm sobbing until the car suddenly swerves across three lanes and Leo gets off at an exit. 'I'm sorry,' he says, pulling to the curb. A reflection from the rearview mirror boxes his eyes. 'That was a stupid thing to say. For the record, it doesn't always happen that way. Look at you, you turned out perfectly fine.'

'You don't know me.'

'But I'd like to.'

Leo's answer seems to shock him as much as it shocks me. 'I bet you say that to all the girls who are crying hysterically.'

'Ah, you've figured out my M.O.'

He hands me a handkerchief. Who still carries a handkerchief? A guy who has an eight-track in his car, I suppose. I wipe my eyes and blow my nose, then tuck the little square into my pocket.

'I'm twenty-five years old,' I say. 'I got laid off from my job. My only friend is a former Nazi. My mother died three years ago and it feels like it was yesterday. I have nothing in common with my sisters. The last relationship I had was with a married man. I'm a loner. I'd rather have a root canal than have my photo taken,' I say, crying so hard I am hiccupping. 'I don't even have a pet.'

Leo tilts his head. 'Not even a goldfish?'

I shake my head.

'Well, lots of people lose their jobs,' Leo says. 'Your friend-ship with a Nazi could lead to the deportation or extradition of a war criminal. I'd think that would give you something to chat about with your sisters. And I also bet it would make your mother proud, wherever she is now. Photos are so airbrushed these days you can't trust what you see, anyway. And as for you being a loner,' he adds, 'you seem to have no trouble having a conversation with me.'

I consider this for a moment.

'You know what you need?'

'A reality check?'

Leo puts the car in gear. 'Perspective,' he says. 'The hell with going home. I've got a better idea.'

I remember thinking, as a kid, that churches were so incred-ibly beautiful, with their stained-glass windows and stone altars, their vaulted ceilings and polished pews. In contrast, the temple where I was dragged for my sisters' bat mitzvahs – a full hour's ride away – was downright homely. Its roof came to a massive brown metal point; some sort of abstract ironwork – probably meant to be a burning bush but it looked more like barbed wire – decorated the lobby. The color scheme was aqua, orange, and burnt sienna, as if the 1970s had projectile-vomited all over the walls.

Now, as Leo holds the door open for me so I can walk inside, I decide that either Jews must be universally bad interior decorators or all temples were built in 1972. The doors to the sanctuary are closed, but I can hear music seeping out from beneath them. 'Looks like they've already started,' Leo says, 'but that's okay.'

'You're taking me on a date to Friday night services?'

'This is a date?' Leo replies.

'Are you one of those people who looks up the nearest hospital before you travel, except it's not a hospital you scout out but a temple?'

'No. I was here once before. I had a case once that involved the testimony of a guy who had been part of a *Sonderkommando*. When he died a few years later, a contingent from my office came to the funeral here. I knew we couldn't be too far away.'

'I told you – religion isn't really my thing—'

'Duly noted,' he says, and he grabs my hand, cracks open the sanctuary door, and pulls me inside.

We slip into the last pew on the left. Up on the bema, the rabbi is welcoming the congregation, and telling them how good it is to worship with everyone. He begins to read a prayer, in Hebrew.

I think back to the moment I lobbied my parents to stop going to temple. Sweat breaks out on my forehead. I think I'm having a flashback. Leo's hand closes around mine. 'Just give it a chance,' he whispers.

He doesn't let go.

When you do not understand the language being spoken, you have two options. You can struggle against the isolation, or you can give yourself up to it. I let the prayers roll over me like steam. I watch the congregation when it is their turn for responsive reading, like actors who've memorized their cues. When the cantor steps forward and sings, the music is the melody of sorrow and regret. It suddenly hits me: these words, they are the same words my grandmother grew up with.

These notes, they are the same notes she listened to. And all of these people – the elderly couples and the families with small children; the preteens waiting on their bar and bat mitzvahs and the parents who are so proud of them that they cannot stop touching their hair, their shoulders – they would not be here if things had gone the way Reiner Hartmann and the rest of the Nazi regime had planned.

History isn't about dates and places and wars. It's about the people who fill the spaces between them.

There is a prayer for the sick and the healing, a sermon from the rabbi. There is a blessing over challah and wine.

Then it is time for the *kaddish*. The prayer for loved ones who've died. I feel Leo get to his feet beside me.

Yisgadal v'yiskadash sh'mayh rabo.

Reaching down, Leo pulls me up, too. Immediately I panic, sure that everyone is staring at me, a girl who doesn't know the lines of the play she's been cast in.

'Just repeat after me,' Leo whispers, and so I do, unfamiliar syllables that feel like pebbles I can tuck into the corners of my mouth.

'Amen,' Leo says finally.

I don't believe in God. But sitting there, in a room full of those who feel otherwise, I realize that I *do* believe in people. In their strength to help each other, and to thrive in spite of the odds. I believe that the extraordinary trumps the ordinary, any day. I believe that having something to hope for – even if it's just a better tomorrow – is the most powerful drug on this planet.

The rabbi gives the closing prayer, and when he lifts his face to the congregation, it is clear and renewed: the surface of a lake at dawn. If I'm going to be honest, I feel a little like that myself. Like I've turned the page, found a fresh start.

'*Shabbat shalom,*' the rabbi says.

The woman sitting next to me, who is about the same age as my mother and who sports a gravity-defying spiral of cherry-red hair, smiles so widely I can see her fillings. '*Shabbat shalom,*' she says, clasping my hand tightly, as if she has known me forever. A little boy in front of us, who has been wiggling most of the time, bounces onto his knees and holds out his chubby starfish fingers, a toddler's high five. His father laughs. 'What do you say?' he prompts. '*Shabbat* . . .?' The boy buries his face in his father's sleeve, suddenly shy. 'Next time,' the man says, grinning.

All around us the same words are being spoken, like a ribbon that sews its way through a crowd, a drawstring pulling everyone together. As people begin to drift away, milling into the lobby where Oneg Shabbat – tea and cookies and conversation – has been set up, I stand. Leo, however, doesn't.

He is gazing around the room, with an expression on his face I cannot quite place. Wistfulness, maybe. Pride. Finally, he looks at me. 'This,' he says. 'This is why I do what I do.'

At the Oneg Shabbat, Leo brings me iced tea in a plastic cup and a rugelach that I politely decline, because it's clearly store-bought and I know I could do better. He calls me a pastry snob, and we are still laughing about that when an older couple approaches. I start to turn away, instinctively trying to conceal the bad half of my face, but a sudden thought of my grandmother flashes through my mind, explaining her mastectomy scar years ago and today, her memories of the Holocaust. *But see how much of me is left?*

I lift my chin and directly face the couple, daring them to comment on my rippled skin.

But they don't. They ask us if we're new in town.

'Just passing through,' Leo tells them.

'It's a nice community for settling down,' the woman says. 'So many young families.'

Clearly, they assume we're a couple. 'Oh. We're not – I mean, he isn't—'

'What she's trying to say is that we're not married,' Leo finishes.

'Not for long,' the man says. 'Finishing her sentences, that's the first step.'

Twice more we are approached and asked if we've just moved here. The first time, Leo says that we were going to go to the movies but nothing was playing so we came to temple instead. The second time, he replies that he is a federal agent and I'm helping him crack a case. The man who's been chatting with us laughs. 'Good one,' he says.

'You'd be surprised how hard it is to get people to believe the truth,' Leo tells me later, as we walk across the parking lot.

But I'm not surprised. Look at how hard I fought Josef, when he tried to tell me who he used to be. 'I guess that's because most of the time we don't want to admit it to ourselves.'

'That's true,' Leo says thoughtfully. 'It's amazing what you can convince yourself of, if you buy into the lie.'

You can believe, for example, that a dead-end job is a career. You can blame your ugliness for keeping people at bay, when in reality you're crippled by the thought of letting another person close enough to potentially scar you even more deeply. You can tell yourself that it's safer to love someone who will never really love you back, because you can't lose someone you never had.

Maybe it is because Leo is a professional keeper of secrets; maybe it is because I have been so emotionally bruised today;

maybe it is just because he listens more carefully than anyone else I've ever met – for whatever reason, I find myself telling him things I have never before admitted out loud. As we drive north again, I talk about how I was always an outsider, even in the confines of my family. I tell him that I worry my parents died wondering if I'd ever be able to support myself. I admit that when my sisters come to visit, I tune out their talk of carpools and Moroccanoil treatments and what Dr. Oz has to say about colon health. I tell him that once, I went for a whole week without speaking a word, just to see if I could, and if I would recognize my voice when I finally did. I tell him that the moment bread comes out of the oven, when I hear each loaf crackle and sing as it hits the cool air, is the closest I've come to believing in God.

It is nearly eleven o'clock when we pull into Westerbrook, but I'm not tired. 'Coffee?' I suggest. 'There's a great place in town that stays open till midnight.'

'If I drink coffee now I'll be bouncing off the ceiling till dawn,' Leo says.

I look down at my hands in my lap, feeling impossibly naïve. Someone other than me would have been able to pick up on social cues, would know that this camaraderie between us is forced by the case Leo's investigating, and not an actual friendship.

'But,' he adds, 'maybe they have herbal tea?'

Westerbrook is a sleepy town, so there are only a handful of people in the café, even though it is a Friday night. A girl with purple hair who is absorbed in a volume of Proust looks annoyed when we interrupt her to place an order. 'I'd make a snide comment about the youth of America,' Leo says, after he insists on paying for my latte, 'but I'm too impressed by the fact that she's reading something other than *Fifty Shades of Grey*.'

'Maybe this will be the generation that saves the world,' I say.

'Doesn't every generation think they'll be the one to do it?'

Did mine? Or were we so wrapped up in ourselves that we didn't think to look for answers in the experiences of others? I had known what the Holocaust was, of course, but even after learning my grandmother was a survivor I had studiously avoided asking questions. Was I too apathetic – or too terrified – to think such ancient history had anything to do with my present, or my future?

Did Josef's? By his own account he had believed, as a boy, that a world without Jews would be a better place. So does he see the outcome, now, as a failure? Or as a bullet that was dodged?

'I keep wondering which is the *real* him,' I murmur. 'The man who wrote college recommendations for hundreds of kids and who cheered a baseball team to the state playoffs and who shares his roll with his dog – or the one my grandmother described.'

'It might not be an either-or,' Leo says. 'He could be both.'

'Then did he have to lose his conscience to do what he did in the camps? Or did he never have one?'

'Does it even matter, Sage? He clearly has no sense of right and wrong. If he did, he would have turned down the orders to commit murder. And if he committed murder, he could never develop a conscience afterward, because it would be suspect – like finding God on your hospital deathbed. So what if he was a saint for the past seventy years? That doesn't bring back to life the people he killed. He *knows* that, or he wouldn't have bothered to ask you for forgiveness. He feels like there's still a stain on him.' Leo leans forward. 'You know, in Judaism, there are two wrongs that can't be forgiven. The first is murder, because you have to actually go to the wronged party and plead your case, and obviously you can't if the victim is six feet underground. But the second unforgivable wrong is ruining someone's reputation. Just like a dead person can't forgive the murderer, a good reputation can't ever be reclaimed. During the Holocaust, Jews were killed, *and* their reputation was destroyed. So no matter how much Josef repents for what he did, he's really striking out on two counts.'

'Then why try?' I ask. 'Why would he spend seventy years doing good deeds and giving back to his community?'

'That's easy,' Leo says. 'Guilt.'

'But if you feel guilty, that means you have a conscience,' I point out. 'And you just said that's impossible for Josef.'

Leo's eyes light up at our verbal sparring. 'You are far too smart for me, but only because it's past my bedtime.'

He keeps talking, but I do not hear him. I do not hear anything, because suddenly the door of the café opens and in walks Adam, with his arm around his wife.

Shannon's head is bent close to his, and she is laughing at something he's just said.

One morning, when we were tangled in the sheets of my bed, Adam and I had tried to top each other by telling the worst joke ever.

What's green and has wheels? Grass – I lied about the wheels.

What's red and smells like blue paint? Red paint.

A duck walks into a bar and the bartender asks, What'll it be? The duck doesn't answer because it's a duck.

Have you seen Stevie Wonder's new house? Well, it's really nice.

So . . . a seal walks into a club.

How do you make a clown cry? You kill his family.

What do you call a man with no arms and no legs who is on your doorstep? Whatever his name happens to be.

We had laughed so hard that I started to sob, and I couldn't stop, and I think it had nothing to do with the jokes.

Did he just tell Shannon one of the one-liners? Maybe a joke I'd told him?

This is only the third time I've seen Shannon in person, the first without a great distance or a pane of glass between us. She is one of those effortlessly pretty women, like the Ralph Lauren models, who don't need makeup and who have all the right streaks in their blond hair and who can wear an untucked shirt and have it be a fashion choice instead of sloppiness.

Without really thinking about what I'm doing, I slide my chair closer to Leo's.

'Sage?' Adam says. I don't know how he can speak my name without his face becoming flushed. I wonder if his heart is racing like mine is, and if his wife notices.

'Oh,' I reply, trying to act surprised. 'Hey.'

'Shannon, this is Sage Singer. Her family was one of our clients. Sage, this is my wife.' I feel sick to my stomach at his description of me. But then again, what would I have expected him to say?

Adam's eyes flicker to Leo, waiting for an introduction. I slip my arm through his. To his credit, he doesn't look at me like I've just lost my mind. 'This is Leo Stein.'

Leo holds out his hand to shake Adam's, and then his wife's. 'Pleasure.'

'Just saw the new Tom Cruise film,' Adam says. 'Have you seen it?'

'Not yet,' Leo replies. I have to stifle a smile; Leo probably thinks the 'new' Tom Cruise film is *Risky Business*.

'It was a compromise,' Shannon says. 'Guns and aliens for

him, and Tom Cruise for me. But then again, I would have watched paint dry if it meant getting a sitter and leaving the house.' She is smiling, never breaking eye contact, as if she is trying to prove to both of us that my scar doesn't bother her in the least.

'I don't have kids,' I say. *I never really had your husband, either.*

Leo puts his arm around my shoulders and squeezes. '*Yet.*'

My jaw drops. When I turn to him, a smile twitches at the corners of his mouth. 'How did you say you know Sage, again?' he asks Adam.

'Business,' we say in unison.

'Would you two like to join us?' Leo asks.

'No,' I quickly reply. 'I mean, weren't we just leaving?'

Taking my cue, Leo stands up, grinning. 'You know Sage. She doesn't like to be kept waiting. If you know what I mean.' Putting his arm around my waist, he says his good-byes and leads me out of the café.

As soon as we have turned the corner, I light into him. 'What the *hell* was that?'

'From your reaction, I'm assuming it was the boyfriend you told me you didn't have. And his wife.'

'You made it sound like I'm a sex fiend . . . like we . . . you and me . . .'

'Are sleeping together? Isn't that what you wanted him to think?'

I bury my face in my hands. 'I don't know what I want him to think.'

'Is he a cop? I'm getting that vibe . . .'

'He's a funeral director,' I say. 'I met him when my mother died.'

Leo's brows shoot up to his hairline. 'Wow. My gut instinct

was *way* off there.' I watch the usual interplay of emotions across his face as he connects the dots: this man touches dead bodies; this man touched me.

'It's just a job,' I point out. 'It's not like *you* go and reenact the Allied victory in the bedroom.'

'How would you know? I do a mean Eisenhower impression.' Leo stops walking. 'For what it's worth, I'm sorry. I guess it's a pretty big shock to find out that a guy you were involved with is married.'

'I already knew,' I confess.

Leo shakes his head, as if he can't quite figure out how to say what he needs to. I can tell he's biting his tongue. 'None of my business,' he says finally, walking briskly to the car.

He's right. It's none of his business. He doesn't know what love is like, for someone who looks like me. I have three options: (1) Be sad and lonely. (2) Be the woman who is cheated on. (3) Be the other woman.

'Hey,' I shout, catching up to him. 'You have no right to judge me. You know nothing about me.'

'Actually, I know a lot about you,' Leo counters. 'I know that you're brave – brave enough to call my office and open a can of worms that could have stayed shut your whole life. I know that you love your grandma. I know that your heart is so big you're struggling with whether or not you can forgive a guy who's done something unforgivable. You're pretty remarkable in a lot of ways, Sage, so you'll have to excuse me if I'm a little disappointed to find out that you're not quite as bright and shiny as I thought you were.'

'And you? Have you never done anything wrong in your life?' I argue.

'No, I've done plenty wrong. But I didn't go back and do it again.'

I don't know why seeing Leo disillusioned feels even worse than running into Adam and Shannon. 'We're not together,' I explain. 'It's complicated.'

'Do you still love him?' Leo asks.

I open my mouth, but nothing comes out.

I love feeling loved.

I don't love knowing that I will always come in second place.

I love the fact that at least sometimes when I am in my home, I'm not alone.

I don't love the fact that it's not always.

I love not having to answer to him.

I don't love that he doesn't answer to me.

I love the way I feel when I am with him.

I don't love the way I feel when I'm not.

When I don't respond, Leo turns away. 'Then it's really not complicated,' he says.

That night I sleep like I haven't slept in months. I don't hear my alarm go off, and it isn't until the phone rings that I sit up awake, expecting Leo. After our argument last night, he was polite to me, but the easy camaraderie we'd had had disappeared. When he dropped me off at my place, he talked about business, and what would happen after he received the FedEx delivery of the photo spread.

It is probably better this way – treating him like a colleague and not like a friend. I just don't understand how I can miss something I barely even had.

I think I might have dreamed an apology to him. I can't be sure what I'm apologizing for, though. 'I wanted to talk about last night,' I blurt into the receiver.

'Me, too,' Adam says on the other end of the phone.

'Oh. It's you.'

'You don't sound too thrilled. I've been going crazy all morning trying to find five minutes to call you. Who was that guy?'

'You're kidding, right? You couldn't possibly be complaining because I was out with someone else . . .'

'Look, I know you're angry. And I know you asked for some time apart. But I miss you, Sage. You're the one I want to be with,' Adam promises. 'It's just not as simple as you think.'

Immediately, I think back to my conversation with Leo. 'Actually, it is,' I say.

'If you went out with Lou—'

'Leo.'

'Whatever . . . to get my attention, it worked. When can I see you again?'

'How could I have been trying to get your attention when I didn't even know you and your wife would be having Date Night?' I cannot believe Adam's making this about him. But then again, it's always about him.

There is a beep on the phone, my other line. I recognize Leo's cell number. 'I have to go,' I tell Adam.

'But—'

As I hang up, I realize that I have always been the one calling Adam, instead of the other way around. Have I suddenly become attractive because I'm not available?

And if so, what does that say about my attraction to him?

'Morning,' Leo says.

His voice sounds rough around the edges, like he needs a cup of coffee. 'How did you sleep?' I ask.

'About as well as can be expected when the hotel is filled with preteen girls who are here for a soccer tournament. I have some impressive dark circles under my eyes. But on the bright side, I now know all the words to the new Justin Bieber single.'

'I can only imagine that will come in handy in your line of work.'

'If me singing that stuff doesn't make former war criminals confess, I have no idea what will.'

He sounds . . . well, like the way he sounded before we ran into Adam last night. The fact that this makes me unaccountably happy is something I don't understand, and don't really want to question.

'So according to the desk clerk here at the luxurious Courtyard by Marriott, who I think may be violating child labor laws, the FedEx truck shows up shortly before eleven,' Leo says.

'What should I do in the meantime?'

'I don't know,' Leo replies. 'Take a shower, paint your nails, read *People* magazine, rent a chick flick. That's what I'm going to do.'

'My tax dollars are being put to *such* good use in your salary . . .'

'Okay, fine, I'll read *Us Weekly* instead.'

I laugh. 'I'm serious.'

'Call your grandma and make sure she's still feeling up to a visit from us. And then – well, if you really want to do something, you could go visit Josef Weber.'

I feel my breath catch in my throat. 'Alone?'

'Don't you usually visit him alone?'

'Yes but—'

'It's going to take time to build our case, Sage. Which means that during the process Josef has to believe you're still considering doing what he asked you to do. If I hadn't been here today, would you have seen him?'

'Probably,' I admit. 'But that was before . . .' My voice trails off.

'Before you knew he was a Nazi? Or before you understood what that really meant?' His voice is sober now, no more joking. 'If anything, that's exactly why you should keep up pretenses. You know now what's at stake.'

'What am I supposed to say to him?' I ask.

'Nothing,' Leo advises. 'Let him talk to you. See if he says something detailed either that matches what your nana told us or that we can ask her about.'

It isn't until I've hung up and am standing in the shower with the hot water streaming down my back that I realize I have no transportation. My car is still at the service station waiting to be fixed after the accident. It's too far to walk to Josef's house. I towel off and dry my hair and throw on a pair of shorts and a tank top, even though I would bet a hundred dollars that Leo will again be wearing a suit when he shows up. But if, as he said, appearances are part of this game, then I have to wear what I've worn in the past to Josef's house.

In my garage I find the bike I last used when I was in college. Its tires are flat, but I unearth a hand pump to get them reasonably inflated. Then I quickly whip up a batter in the kitchen and bake streusel muffins. They are still steaming when I wrap them in foil, stick them gently in my backpack, and start pedaling to Josef's house.

As I bike up these New England hills, as my heart races, I think about what my grandmother told me yesterday. I remember the story of Josef's childhood. They are two speeding trains coming at each other, destined to crash. I am helpless to stop it, yet I cannot turn away.

By the time I reach Josef's house I am breathing hard

and sweating. When he sees me, he frowns, concerned. 'You are all right?'

That's a loaded question. 'I rode my bike here. My car's in the shop.'

'Well,' he says. 'I am glad to see you.'

I wish I could say the same. But now, when I see the lines in Josef's face, they smooth before my eyes into the stern jaw of the *Schutzhaftlagerführer* who stole, lied, and murdered. I realize, ironically, that he has gotten what he hoped for: I believe his story. I believe it so much I can barely stand here without being sick.

Eva darts out the door and dances around my feet. 'I brought you something,' I say. Reaching into my backpack, I pull out the package of freshly baked muffins.

'I think that being your friend is very bad for my waistline,' Josef says.

He invites me into the house. I take my usual seat across from him at the chessboard. He puts up the kettle and returns with coffee for both of us. 'Truthfully I was not sure you would come back,' he says. 'What I told you last time . . . it was a lot to take in.'

You have no idea, I think.

'A lot of people, they hear Auschwitz and they immediately assume you are a monster.'

His words bring to mind my grandmother's *upiór*. 'I thought that was what you wanted me to think.'

Josef winces. 'I wanted you to hate me enough to want to kill me. But I didn't realize how that would make me feel.'

'You called it the Asshole of the World.'

Josef takes a shallow breath. 'It is my turn, yes?' He leans forward and knocks away one of my pawns with a Pegasus knight. He moves slowly, carefully, an old man. Harmless.

I remember my grandmother talking about how his hand shook, and I watch as he lifts my pawn from the inlaid wooden chessboard, but his movements are too unsteady in general for me to be able to tell if he has a particular lasting injury.

He waits until my concentration is focused on the board before he begins to speak. 'In spite of the reputation Auschwitz has now, I found it was a good assignment. I was safe; I wouldn't be shot by a Russian. There was even a little village in the camp where we could go for our meals and drinks and even concerts. When we were relaxing there, it was almost possible to believe there wasn't a war going on.'

'We?'

'My brother, the one who worked in Section Four – administration. He was an accountant who added numbers and sent the tallies to the *Kommandant*. My rank was much higher than his.' Josef brushes the crumbs from his napkin onto his plate. 'He reported to me.'

I touch my finger to a dragon-bishop, and Josef makes a sound low in his throat. 'No?' I ask.

He shakes his head. Instead, I place my hand on the broad back of a centaur, the only rook I have left. 'So you were the head of administration?'

'No. I was in Section Three. I was SS-*Schutzhaftlagerführer* of the women's camp.'

'You were the head honcho at a death factory,' I said flatly.

'Not the boss,' Josef said. 'But high in the chain of command. And besides, I did not know what was happening at the camp when I first arrived in 1943.'

'You expect me to believe that?'

'I can only tell you what I know. My job wasn't at the gas chambers. I oversaw the prisoners who were kept alive.'

'Did you get to pick and choose?'

'No. I was present when the trains arrived, but that task fell to the camp doctors. Mostly I just walked around. I was an overseer. A presence.'

'A supervisor,' I say, the word bitter in my mouth. A manager, for the unmanageable.

'Precisely.'

'I thought you were injured on the front line.'

'I was – but not so badly that I couldn't do this.'

'So you were in charge of the female prisoners.'

'That was left to my subordinate, the SS-*Aufseherin*. Twice a day, she oversaw roll call.'

Instead of moving my rook, I reach for my white queen, the exquisitely carved mermaid. I know enough about chess to realize that what I am about to do defies the odds, that of all the pieces to sacrifice the valuable queen is the last one I should consider.

I slide the mermaid to an empty square, knowing full well that it stands in the path of Josef's Pegasus knight.

He looks up at me. 'You do not want to do this.'

I meet his gaze. 'Guess I figure I'll learn from my mistakes.'

Josef captures my queen, as I'm expecting.

'What did *you* do?' I ask. 'At Auschwitz?'

'I told you.'

'Not really,' I say. 'You told me what you *didn't* do.'

Eva lies down at Josef's feet. 'You don't need to hear me say it.'

I just stare at him.

'I punished those who could not do their work.'

'Because they were starving to death.'

'I did not create the system,' Josef says.

'You did nothing to stop it, either,' I point out.

'What do you want me to tell you? That I am sorry?'

'How am I supposed to forgive you if you're not?' I realize I am shouting. 'I can't do this, Josef. Find someone else.'

Josef's fist crashes down on the table, making the chess pieces jump. 'I killed them. Yes. Is that what you want to hear? That with my own two hands, I murdered? There. That is all you need to know. I was a murderer, and for this, I deserve to die.'

I take a deep breath. Leo will be angry at me, but he of all people should understand how I feel right now, listening to Josef talk about the joy of officers' meals and cello concerts when my grandmother, at the same time, was licking the ground where soup had spilled. 'You do *not* deserve to die,' I say tightly. 'Not on your own terms, anyway, since you didn't give that luxury to anyone else. I hope you die a slow, painful death. No, actually, I hope you live forever, so that what you did eats away at you for a long, long time.'

I slide my bishop across the board into the position no longer protected by Josef's knight. 'Checkmate,' I say, and I stand up to leave.

Outside, I straddle my bike and turn back to see him standing at the open door. 'Sage. Please, don't—'

'How many times did *you* hear those words, Josef?' I ask. 'And how many times did *you* listen?'

It isn't until I see Rocco at the espresso machine that I realize how much I've missed working at Our Daily Bread. 'Do my eyes deceive?' he says. 'Look at what the cat dragged in. / One long-lost baker.' He comes around the counter to give me a hug and without even asking, starts to make me a cinnamon latte with soy.

It is busier than I remember it being, but then again, at this time of the day, I'm usually on my way home to go to bed.

The Storyteller

There are mothers in jogging clothes, young men typing furiously on their laptops, a cluster of Red Hat ladies sharing a single chocolate croissant. That makes me glance at the wall behind the counter, the baskets filled with expertly browned baguettes, buttery brioche, semolina loaves. Is this newfound popularity due to the baker who took over for me?

Rocco can read my mind, because he nods in the direction of a plastic banner hanging on the wall behind me: HOME OF THE JESUS LOAF. 'We get foot traffic / But just because you're holy / Don't mean you're hungry,' he says. 'All I pray for now / Is that you'll come back, or else / Mary gets raptured.'

I laugh. 'I miss you, too, Rocco. Where is the blessed boss, anyway?'

'Somewhere in the shrine. / Crying 'cause Miracle-Gro / Isn't Heaven-sent.'

I pour my latte into a takeaway cup and cut through the kitchen on my way to the shrine. The kitchen is spotless. The containers of poolish and other pre-ferments are organized neatly by date; different tubs of grains and flours are labeled and arranged alphabetically. The wooden counter where I shape the dough has been wiped down; the bulk mixer rests like a sleeping dragon in the corner. Whatever Clark has been doing here, he has been doing well.

It makes me feel like even more of a loser.

If I'd been naïve enough to think that Our Daily Bread was nothing without me and my recipes, I now realize that this isn't true. It may be different, but ultimately, I'm replaceable. This has always been Mary's dream; I'm just living on the fringes.

I walk up the Holy Stairs to find her kneeling in the monkshood. She is weeding, wearing rubber gloves pulled high up her arms. 'I'm glad you came by. I've been thinking about you.

How's your head?' She glances at the bruise from the car accident, which I've covered with my bangs.

'I'm fine,' I tell her. 'Rocco says the Jesus Loaf is still getting you business.'

'In iambic pentameter, I'm sure . . .'

'And it seems like Clark's got the baking under control.'

'He does,' Mary says bluntly. 'But like I said the other night: he isn't you.' She gets to her feet and gives me a big hug. 'You sure you're all right?'

'Physically, yes. Emotionally? I don't know,' I admit. 'There's been a little drama with my grandmother.'

'Oh, Sage, I'm sorry . . . Is there anything I can do?'

Although the thought of an ex-nun getting involved with a Holocaust survivor and a former Nazi sounds like the punch line to a joke, it is actually what drew me to the bakery today. 'As a matter of fact, that's why I'm here.'

'Anything,' Mary promises. 'I'll start to say a rosary for your grandma today.'

'That's okay – I mean, you *can* if you want to – but I was hoping to borrow the kitchen for about an hour?'

Mary puts her hands on my shoulders. 'Sage,' she says. 'It's *your* kitchen.'

Ten minutes later, I have an oven warming, an apron wrapped around my waist, and I am up to my elbows in flour. I could have baked at home, true, but the ingredients I needed were here; the sourdough itself would have taken days to prepare.

It feels strange to be working with such a tiny amount of dough. It feels even stranger to hear, just outside, the cacophony of the lunchtime crowd coming in. I move around the kitchen, weaving from cabinet to shelf to pantry. I chop and mix bittersweet chocolate and ground cinnamon; I add a hint of vanilla. I create a small cavern as deep as my thumb in the knot of dough, and twist its limbs into an ornate crown. I let it proof, and in the meantime, instead of hiding in the back room, I go into the café and talk to Rocco. I work the cash register. I chat with customers about the heat and the Red Sox, about how pretty Westerbrook is in the summer, not once trying to cover my face with my bangs. And I marvel at how all these people can go about their lives as if they are not sitting on a powder keg; as if they don't know that when you pull back the curtain of an ordinary life, there might be something terrible hidden behind it.

'*The second time,*' Aleks told me, as I lay beside him after we made love, '*it was a prostitute, who had stopped to pull up her stockings in an alley. It was easier, or so I told myself, because otherwise, I would have had to admit that what I'd done before was wrong. The third time, my first man: a banker who was locking up at the end of the day. There was a teenage girl once, who was in the wrong place at the wrong time. And a socialite I heard crying on a hotel balcony. And after that I stopped caring who they had been. It only mattered that they were there, at that moment, when I needed them.*' Aleksander closed his eyes. '*It turns out that the more you repeat the same action, no matter how reprehensible, the more you can make an excuse for it in your own mind.*'

I turned in his arms. '*How do I know that one day you won't kill me?*'

He stared at me, hesitating. '*You don't,*' he said.

We did not speak after that. We did not know that someone was outside listening to everything we had said, and to the symphony of our bodies. So while Damian slipped away from where he was eavesdropping and went to the cave to capture a frantic, frightened Casimir, I rose over Aleks like a phoenix. I felt him move within me, and I thought of not death, but only resurrection.

Leo

My cell phone rings when I have just spread the photo array from Genevra across the expanse of the hotel bed. 'Leo,' my mother says, 'I had a dream about you last night.'

'Really,' I say, squinting at Reiner Hartmann. Genevra used the photograph from his SS file, which is now propped up against a pillow that was decidedly uncomfortable and that has left me with a crick in my neck. I look at the first page of the file, with his personal information and the snapshot in uniform, trying to compare this picture with the one I am planning to present to Minka.

HARTMANN, REINER
Westfalenstrasse 1818
33142 Büren-Wewelsburg
DOB 18 / 04 / 20
Blutgruppe AB

You can't see his eyes very well in the photograph; there is a strange shadow in the grain. But the reproduction in the suspect array isn't shoddy, as I had first thought; it's just that the original isn't in the best shape.

'I was with your son and we were playing at the beach. He kept telling me, "Grandma, you have to bury your feet or nothing will grow." So I figured, he wants to play a game, fine. And I let him pile the sand up to my ankles and pour water over them from a bucket. And then guess what?'

'What.'

'When I shook off the sand there were tiny roots growing out of the bottoms of my feet.'

I wonder if Minka will not be able to make an ID because of the quality of the photograph.

'That's fascinating,' I say absently.

'Leo, you're not listening to me.'

'I am. You had a dream about me that I wasn't in.'

'Your *son* was in it.'

'I don't have a son—'

'You have to remind me?' my mother sighs. 'What do you think it means?'

'That I'm not married?'

'No, the dream. The roots growing out of the soles of my feet.'

'I don't know, Ma. That you're deciduous?'

'Everything's a joke to you,' my mother says, miffed. I can sense that if I don't take a few minutes to focus on her, I'm going to have to field a call from my sister, too, telling me that my mom is angry. I push the photographs away.

'Maybe that's because what I do for a living is so hard to understand, I need a way to let it go at the end of the day,' I tell her, and I realize that this is true.

'You know I'm proud of you, Leo. Of what you do.'

'Thanks.'

'And you know I worry about you.'

'Believe me, you make that patently clear.'

'Which is why I think it's important for you to take a little time to yourself.'

I don't like where this is going.

'I'm working.'

'You're in New Hampshire.'

I scowl at the phone. 'I swear to God, I'm hiring you. I think you're a better tracker than anyone I've got in the office—'

'You called to ask your sister for a hotel recommendation and she told me you were on the road for business.'

'Nothing's sacred.'

'Anyway, maybe you want to get a massage when you're back at the hotel at the end of the day—'

'Who is she?' I ask wearily.

'Rachel Zweig. Lily Zweig's daughter. She's getting a degree in massage therapy in Nashua—'

'You know, the cell phone service really stinks up here,' I say, holding the phone away from me at arm's length. 'I'm losing you.'

'Not only can I track you, I can tell when you're feeding me a load of BS, Leo.'

'I love you, Ma,' I laugh.

'I loved you first,' she says.

As I gather the photo spread together into its file, I wonder what my mother would make of Sage Singer. She'd love the fact that Sage could keep me well fed, since always I look too skinny to my mother. She would look at her scar and think of her as a survivor. She would appreciate the way Sage still grieves for her own mom, and her close attachment to her grandmother – since to my mother, family is the carbon atom at the base of all life-forms. On the other hand, my mother has always wanted me to marry someone who is Jewish, and Sage – a self-professed atheist – doesn't qualify. Then again she has a grandmother who survived the Holocaust, which has to earn her a few points—

I break off in my thoughts, wondering why I'm thinking of

marrying a woman I met yesterday – one who is simply a means to a witness for me, and one who clearly, as evidenced by last night, is in love with someone else.

Adam.

A guy who stood about six four and had shoulders you could use as a Thanksgiving banquet table. *Goyishe*, my mother would call him, with his sandy hair and aw-shucks smile. Seeing him last night, and watching Sage react as if she'd been electrocuted, brought back every acne-riddled middle school post-traumatic flashback – from the cheerleader who told me I wasn't really her type after I published a sonnet to her in the school literary magazine, to my junior prom date, who started dancing with a soccer jock when I was getting her a cup of punch, and wound up going home with him.

I've got nothing against Adam, and what Sage wants to do to screw up her life is her own business. I also know that it takes two to make a mistake of that magnitude. But . . . Adam has a *wife*. The expression on Sage's face when she saw the woman made me want to put my arm around her and tell her she could do so much better than this guy.

Like, maybe, me.

Fine, okay, I have a little bit of a crush on her. Or maybe her baking. Or her husky, raspy, incredibly sexy voice, which she doesn't even realize is sexy.

This feeling takes me by surprise. I spend my life hunting down people who want to stay lost, but I have had considerably less luck finding someone I'd like to keep around for a while.

Stuffing the file into my briefcase, I shake these thoughts off. Maybe my mother is right and I *do* need a massage, or whatever form of relaxation it will take to get me back to separating my work life from my private life.

All of my best-laid plans, however, go out the window as soon as I arrive at her place and find her waiting for me. She's wearing jean shorts, cutoffs, like Daisy Mae. Her legs are long and tan and muscular, and I can't stop staring at them. 'What?' she says, glancing down at her calves. 'Did I cut myself shaving?'

'No. You're perfect. I mean, you *look* perfect. I mean . . .' I shake my head. 'Did you talk to your grandmother this morning?'

'Yeah.' Sage leads me into her home. 'She's a little scared, but she's expecting us.'

Last night, before we left, Minka had agreed to look at a photo spread. 'I'll make her as comfortable as I can,' I promise.

Sage's house is the visual representation of that favorite sweatshirt you own, the one that you search through your drawer for, because it's so comfortable. The couch is over-stuffed, the light creamy and soft. There's always something baking. It is the kind of place you could settle down for a few moments and wake up, years later, because you never left.

It's completely orthogonal to my apartment in Washington, which is full of black leather and chrome and right angles.

'I like your place,' I blurt out.

She glances at me oddly. 'You were here yesterday.'

'I know. It's just . . . very cozy.'

Sage looks around. 'My mother was good at that. At drawing people in.' She opens up her mouth and then shuts it again abruptly.

'You were going to say that you're not,' I guess.

She shrugs. 'I'm good at pushing people away.'

'Not *all* people,' I say, and we both know I'm talking about last night.

Sage hesitates, as if she is about to tell me something, but then turns and walks into the kitchen. 'So what color did you decide on?'

'Color?'

'For your nail polish.' She picks up a mug of tea and hands it to me. I take a sip and realize she's put in milk but no sugar, just the way I took it last night at the café. There's something about that – her *remembering* – that makes me feel like I've taken flight.

'I was going to go with cherry red, but that's so FBI,' I reply. 'A little too flashy for us DOJ folks.'

'Wise decision.'

'And you?' I ask. 'Did you glean any wisdom from *People* magazine?'

'I did what you told me to do,' she answers, and suddenly the mood has dropped like a stone in a pond. 'I saw Josef.'

'And?'

'I can't do it. I can't talk to him and pretend I don't know what I know now.' Sage shakes her head. 'I think he might be upset with me.'

Just then my cell phone rings, and I see my boss's number flashing. 'I have to take this,' I apologize, and I drift into the living room to answer the call.

He has a logistical question about a prosecution memo that I edited on a different case. I walk him through some of the changes I made, and why, and by the time I hang up and walk back into the kitchen, I see Sage drinking her coffee, perusing the front page of Reiner Hartmann's SS file.

'What are you doing?' I ask. 'That's classified.'

She looks up, a deer in headlights. 'I wanted to see if I could identify him, too.'

I grab the folder. I can't show her Reiner's file; she is a civilian. But I hold up that front page, the one from his SS file that gives his name, address, birth date, blood type, and photo. 'Here,' I say, offering a quick peek of the image – the parted hair, the pale eyes you can't quite see.

'He looks nothing like Josef now,' Sage murmurs. 'I don't know if I could pick him up out of a lineup.'

'Well,' I reply, 'let's hope your grandmother doesn't agree.'

Once, a historian in my office named Simran brought me a picture of Angelina Jolie. It was on his iPhone, and it was a party scene. There were balloons all over the place and a birthday cake on the table, and in the foreground pouting was Angelina. 'Wow,' I said. 'Where'd you take that?'

'She's my cousin.'

'Your cousin is Angelina Jolie?' I asked.

'Nope,' Simran said. 'But she looks just like her, don't you think?'

As it turns out, witness identification is frequently total crap. It's often the weakest part of the proof phase of criminal law enforcement. It's why DNA testing is continually overturning the convictions of rapists who were identified positively by their victims. There really are a very limited number of facial variations, and we tend to make errors of judgment. Which is great for Simran's cousin, but less great if you work for the Department of Justice and you're trying to get an eyewitness ID.

Minka's cane hangs over the edge of the kitchen table, upon which is a glass mug of tea and an empty plate. I'm sitting beside her; Daisy, her caretaker, stands with her arms crossed in the doorway of the kitchen.

'Voilà,' Sage announces, and she sets down one perfectly baked roll on the china.

The roll is knotted on the top. Crystals of sugar dot the surface. I don't have to wait for Minka to break it open to know that inside is cinnamon and chocolate, that this is the roll her father once baked for her.

'I thought maybe you'd missed these,' Sage says.

Minka gasps. She turns the small roll over in her hands. 'You made this? But how . . .?'

'I guessed,' Sage admits.

When did she have time to bake this? During the morning, maybe, after she met with Josef? I stare at Sage, watching her face as her grandmother breaks open the pastry and takes the first bite. 'It's just like my father used to make,' Minka sighs. 'Just like I remember . . .'

'Your memory is what I'm counting on,' I say, sensing a perfect segue. 'I know this isn't easy, so I really appreciate you making the sacrifice. Are you ready?'

I wait for Minka to meet my gaze. She nods.

In front of her, I place a photo spread of eight Nazi war criminals. Genevra has outdone herself, in both speed and precision. The picture of Reiner Hartmann – the same one Sage had been looking at earlier in his SS file – is on the bottom left. There are four photos in the row above it and three more beside it, which depict other men of generally similar appearance, wearing identical Nazi uniforms. This way, I am asking Minka to compare apples to apples. If Reiner's photo was the only picture of a man in uniform, it could be seen as prejudicial.

Sage, sitting beside her grandmother, looks down at the spread, too. The eight individuals all have the same parted, slick blond hair as Reiner Hartmann, they are all facing the same direction. They look like young movie stars from the 1940s – smooth-shaven and strong-jawed, matinee idols for a macabre documentary. 'It's not necessarily the case that anyone in this photo array was at the camp, Minka, but I'd like you to look at the faces and see if anything jumps out at you . . .'

Minka picks up the paper with unsteady hands. 'We did not know them by name.'

'That doesn't matter.'

She passes a finger over each of the eight faces, as if it is a pistol held to the forehead of each man. Is it my imagination, or does it hover over Reiner Hartmann's portrait?

'It's too hard,' Minka says, shaking her head. She pushes away the photo spread. 'I do not want to remember anymore.'

'I understand, but—'

'You do *not* understand,' she interrupts. 'You are not just asking me to point to a photograph. You are asking me to poke a hole in a dam, because you are thirsty, even though I will end up drowning in the process.'

'Please,' I beg, but Minka buries her face in her hands.

The anguish on Sage's face is even more profound than it is on Minka's. But that's what love is, isn't it? When it hurts you more to see someone else suffer than it does to take the pain yourself? 'We're done,' Sage announces. 'I'm sorry, Leo, but I can't put her through this.'

'Give her a chance to make up her own mind,' I suggest.

Minka has turned away, lost in a memory. Daisy swoops in like an avenging angel and wraps an arm around her fragile charge. 'You want to rest, Ms. Minka? Because it sure looks to me like you need to lie down a bit.'

She glares daggers at me as she helps Sage's grandmother to her feet, hands her the cane, and leads her down the hall.

Sage seems as if she is breaking in half, watching her grandmother go. 'I should never have brought you here,' she whispers.

'I've seen this before, Sage. It's a shock to the system, seeing the face of someone who hurt you. Other survivors have had the same reaction, but have managed to pull themselves together and make a valid ID. I know she spent over half a century keeping these feelings buried. I get that. And

I understand that it's painful to rip the Band-Aid off the wound—'

'This isn't a Band-Aid,' Sage argues. 'This is surgery without anesthesia. And I don't really give a damn about the other survivors you've seen going through this. I just care about my grandmother.' Standing abruptly, she heads down the hallway, leaving me with the photo array.

I look down at the spread, at Reiner Hartmann's face. There is nothing in it that suggests the evil beneath the surface. Instead, we are forced to approximate what toxic cocktail of cells and schooling might allow a boy raised with scruples to be led to an act of genocide.

The uneaten roll that Sage baked lies on the plate in two halves, like a broken heart. I sigh, and reach for my briefcase, ready to slip the photos inside. But at the last minute, I stop. I pick up the plate with the roll on it and walk to Minka's bedroom. Behind the door are soft voices. Taking a deep breath, I knock.

Minka sits in an overstuffed chair, her feet raised on an ottoman. 'Stop fussing, Sage,' she says, exasperated, as Daisy opens the bedroom door for me. 'I'm all right!'

I love that she's full of piss and vinegar. I love that she's tough as nails one moment and soft as suede the next. It is what got her through the worst era of history, I'm sure; and what has kept her going since.

And it's what she's passed down to her granddaughter, even if Sage doesn't know it.

They both look up as I enter, holding the roll and the photos. 'You have *got* to be kidding me,' Sage mutters.

'Minka,' I say, handing her the plate, 'I thought you might want this. Sage went to the trouble of baking it because she thought it would give you a bit of peace. That's what I wanted to do today, too. What you lived through? It wasn't fair. But it's also not fair for you to live in a country where you have to share your homeland with your former tormentors. Help me, Minka. Please.'

Sage gets to her feet. 'Leo,' she says tightly. 'Get out of here *now.*'

'Wait, wait.' Minka waves me closer and holds out her hand for the photo spread.

The plate with the roll lies balanced on her lap. In her hands is the photo array. She traces the faces, as if the names of the men could be read in Braille. Slowly, Minka brings her finger down on the photograph of Reiner Hartmann. She taps his face twice. 'This is him.'

'Who?'

She glances up at me. 'I told you. We did not know the SS officers by name.'

'But you recognize the face?'

'Anywhere,' Minka says. 'I would never forget the man who killed my best friend.'

We have tuna sandwiches with Minka for lunch. I talk about how my grandfather taught me to play bridge, and how bad I was at it. 'To say we lost catastrophically would be an under-statement,' I tell her. 'So when we left, I asked my grandpa how I *should* have played the hand. He said, "Under an assumed name."'

Minka laughs. 'One day you will come back here, Leo, and you will be my partner. I'll teach you everything you need to know.'

'It's a date,' I promise. I wipe my mouth with my napkin. 'And thank you for . . . well, for everything. But Sage and I probably should be going.'

She hugs her grandmother good-bye. Minka holds Sage a little tighter than normal, which is something I've seen other survivors do. It's as if, now that they have something good in their lives, they cannot bear to see it go.

I hold her hands, cool and brittle as fallen leaves. 'What you have done today . . . I can't even begin to thank you for. But—'

'But I am not finished,' Minka says. 'You want me to go to court to do it all over again.'

'If you're up to it, yes,' I admit. 'In the past, the testimonies of the survivors have been hugely important. And yours isn't just an identification. You have direct experience watching him commit a murder.'

'Will I have to see him?'

I hesitate. 'If you don't want to, we can arrange to videotape your testimony.'

Minka looks at me. 'Who would be there?'

'Me. A historian from my office. A cameraman. Defense counsel. And Sage, if you'd like.'

She nods. 'This I can do. But if I had to see him . . . I don't think . . .' Her voice trails off.

I nod, respecting her decision. On impulse, I kiss her good-bye on the cheek. 'You're a class act, Minka.'

In the car, Sage pounces. 'So? What happens next? You got what you needed, right?'

'We got *more* than we needed. Your grandmother was a gold mine. It's one thing to give eyewitness identification and to have her point out the *Schutzhaftlagerführer*. But she did something even better. She told us about something in his SS file that no one – except my office – would have known.'

Sage shakes her head. 'I don't understand.'

'It seems almost ludicrous, but there was a right way and

wrong way to kill the prisoners at the concentration camps. Officers who did not follow the rules would find themselves written up with disciplinary infractions. It was one thing to shoot a prisoner who didn't have the strength to stand up anymore, but to kill a prisoner for no reason was to kill a worker, and the Nazis needed those workers. Granted, no one in charge cared enough about the prisoners to do much more than give the offending officer a slap on the hand, but every now and then in an SS man's file, there's a mention of the disciplinary proceeding.' I look up at Sage. 'In Reiner Hartmann's file, there's a paragraph about him going in front of a review committee for an unauthorized shooting of a female prisoner.'

'Darija?' Sage asks.

I nod. 'With your grandmother's testimony that's a pretty airtight lock that this particular guy she identified – and the man who told you his name used to be Reiner Hartmann – are one and the same.'

'Why didn't you tell me that was in the file?'

'Because you don't have government clearance,' I say. 'And because I couldn't risk you influencing what your grandmother had to say.'

She sinks back in the passenger seat. 'So he was telling me the truth. Josef. Reiner. Whatever his name is.'

'It looks that way.' I can see a flurry of emotions move like storms across her face, as she tries to reconcile Josef Weber with his previous persona. It's different, somehow, once that confirmation's been made. And in Sage's case, she is wrestling, too, with betraying a man she had considered a friend. 'You did the right thing,' I say. 'Coming to me. What he asked you to do for him – that isn't justice. *This* is.'

She doesn't look up. 'Do you arrest him right away?'

'No. I go home.'

At that, Sage's head snaps up. 'Now?'

I nod. 'There's a lot I have to do before we move forward.'

I don't want to go. I'd like to ask Sage out to dinner, actually. I'd like to watch her bake something from scratch. I'd just like to watch her, period.

'So you're going to go to the airport?' Sage asks.

Does it seem like she's a little disappointed, too, to hear that I'm leaving?

But that's just me, reading into the situation. She has a boyfriend. Granted, he happens to have a wife, but the bottom line is that Sage isn't looking for anyone right now.

'Yes,' I say. 'I'll call my secretary. There's probably a flight back to D.C. around dinnertime.'

Ask me to stick around, I think.

Sage meets my gaze. 'Well, if you have to go, you probably should turn on the ignition.'

My face flushes with embarrassment. This pregnant pause between us wasn't full of unspoken words, just a vehicle that hadn't been started yet.

Suddenly her phone begins to ring. Frowning, she shifts in her seat to pull it from the pocket of her shorts.

'Yes . . . this is Sage Singer.' Her eyes widen. 'Is he all right? What happened? I – yes, I understand. Thank you.' When she hangs up, she stares at the phone in her hand as if it is a grenade. 'That was the hospital,' Sage announces. 'Josef's been admitted.'

*F*rom where we were hiding, behind the woodshed on Baruch Beiler's property, we could see it all: Casimir chained on the makeshift stage; the wild rage in Damian's eyes as he screamed at the teen, his spittle flecking the boy's face. Drunk with power, Damian addressed the villagers, who huddled beneath the blazing blue sky. Their captain of the guard had found not one perpetrator, but two. Surely this meant they were safe now? That they could go back to the way they had been?

Was I the only one who knew that wasn't possible?

No. Aleks knew it, too. It was why he had tried to atone for his brother's sins.

'My friends,' Damian announced, spreading his arms wide. 'We have broken the beast!' There was a roar as the crowd swallowed his words. 'We will bury the upiór the way he should have been buried the first time: facedown at a crossroads, with an oak stake through the heart.'

Beside me, Aleks was chafing. I held him back with a gentle hand on his arm. 'Don't,' I whispered. 'Can't you see, this is all about setting a trap for you?'

'My brother can't help himself. It doesn't make what he does right, but I cannot sit here—'

Damian beckoned to a soldier behind him. 'First, we will

make sure that he remains dead. And there is only one way to do that.'

The cadet stepped forward, holding a wicked, curved scythe. The blade winked like a jewel. He raised it over his head as Casimir squinted into the fierce sunlight, trying to see what was happening above him.

'Three,' Damian counted. 'Two.' He turned, fixing his gaze directly at the brush where we were hidden, so that I realized he had known we were there all along. 'One.'

The blade sliced through the air, a scream of metal that severed Casimir's head from his body in a single blow.

Blood flooded the stage. It spilled over the edge of the wood and ran in runnels over the ground, toward the crowd.

'Nooooo!' Aleks cried. He tore away from me and rushed the stage as soldiers ran to apprehend him. But he was no longer a man. He bit and clawed, throwing off seven men with the force of an entire army as the crowd scattered to take cover. When only Damian remained, without his protective escort, Aleks stepped forward and snarled.

Damian lifted his sword. And then he dropped it, turned tail, and ran.

Aleks was on him before Damian was halfway across the village square. He tackled the captain, turning Damian so that he landed on his back; so that the clear, bright sky would be the last thing he ever saw. In one single, wrenching tear, Aleks ripped out his heart.

Sage

Hospitals smell like death. A little too clean, and a little too cold. The minute I walk inside I have dialed my life back three years, and I am here watching my mother die by degrees.

Leo and I stand in the hallway, near Josef's room. The doctors have told me that Josef was brought here to have his stomach pumped. Apparently he had an adverse medical reaction, and a Meals on Wheels volunteer found him unconscious on the floor. It makes me wonder who's got Eva now. If someone will be taking care of her tonight.

Although Leo is not allowed into the room, I am. Josef listed me as his next of kin, which is a pretty interesting relationship for someone you've asked to kill you.

'I don't like hospitals,' I say.

'No one does.'

'I don't know what to do,' I whisper.

'You have to talk to him,' Leo answers.

'You want me to convince him to get better, so that you can ship him out of the country and have him die in a jail cell somewhere?'

Leo considers this. 'Yes. After he's convicted.'

Maybe it's because he's being so blunt – it shocks me back

to the present. I nod, take a deep breath, and walk into Josef's room.

In spite of what my grandmother has said, in spite of that photo in the spread that Leo created, he is just an elderly man, a husk of the brute he used to be. With his thin limbs jutting from a pale blue hospital gown, his silver hair disheveled, it is hard to imagine that the very sight of this man once crippled others with fear.

Josef is asleep, his left arm thrown up over his head. The scar he showed me once before, on the inside of his upper arm, is clearly visible – a shiny, dark button the size of a quarter, with ragged edges. Glancing over my shoulder, I see Leo in the hallway, still watching me. He lifts his hand, letting me know he's still watching.

With my cell phone, I snap a picture of Josef's scar, so Leo can see it later.

I hurriedly stuff my phone back into my shorts as a nurse enters the room. 'You're the girl he's been talking about?' she says. 'Cinnamon, right?'

'Sage,' I say cheerfully, wondering if she's seen me taking the picture. 'Same spice rack, different jar.'

The nurse looks at me oddly. 'Well, your friend Mr. Weber is a very lucky man, to have been found when he was.'

I should have been the one to find him.

The thought slips into my mind like the blade of a knife. As his one good friend, I should have been there if he needed me. But instead, I was the one who had argued with him and stormed out of his house.

The problem is that I'm Josef Weber's friend. But Reiner Hartmann is my enemy. So what do I do, now that they are the same man?

'What happened to him?' I ask.

'Ate a salt substitute while he was taking Aldactone. It made his potassium levels skyrocket. Could have put him into cardiac arrest.'

I sit down on the edge of the bed and hold Josef's hand. A hospital band is looped around his wrist. JOSEF WEBER, DOB 4/20/18, B+

If only they knew that wasn't who he really was.

Josef's fingers twitch against mine, and I drop his hand as if he is on fire. 'You came,' he rasps.

'Of course I did.'

'Eva?'

'I'm going to take her home with me. She'll be fine.'

'Mr. Weber?' the nurse interrupts. 'How are you feeling? Do you have any pain?'

He shakes his head.

'Could we just have a minute?' I ask.

She nods. 'I'll come back to take your temperature and blood pressure in five,' the nurse says.

We both wait until she has left to speak again. 'You didn't do this by accident, did you?' I whisper.

'I am not stupid. The pharmacist told me about drug interactions. I chose to ignore him.'

'Why?'

'If you would not help me die, then I had to do it myself. But I should have known it was no use.' He waves an arm around the hospital room. 'I told you before. This is my punishment. No matter what I do, I survive.'

'I never said I wouldn't help you,' I reply.

'You were angry at me for telling you the truth.'

'Yes,' I admit. 'I was. It's really hard to hear.'

'You stormed out of my house.'

'You've had almost seventy years to live with this, Josef. You have to give me more than five minutes.' I lower my voice. 'What you did – what you said you did – makes me sick. But if I . . . you know, do what you asked me to do . . . now, I'm doing it out of anger, out of hate. And that brings me down to your level.'

'I knew you would be upset,' Josef confesses. 'But you were not my first choice.'

This surprises me. There is someone else in this town who knows what Josef did . . . and who hasn't turned him in?

'Your mother,' Josef says. 'She's the first one I asked.'

My jaw drops. 'You *knew* my mother?'

'I met her years ago, when I was working at the high school. The World Religions teacher invited her to talk about her faith. I met her in the teachers' room during lunch, very briefly. She said she was hardly a model Jew, but that she was better than none.'

That sounds like my mother. I can even vaguely remember her going to speak in front of my sister's class, and how embarrassed Pepper was to have her there. I bet my sister would give anything to have my mother in such close proximity now. The thought makes my throat close tight.

'We got to talking, and she of course noticed my accent, and said that her mother-in-law had been a survivor from Poland.'

I notice that he uses the past tense when talking about my grandmother. I do not correct him. I do not want him to know anything about her at all.

'What did you tell her?'

'That I was sent abroad to study during the war. For years I tried to cross paths with her again. I felt it was fate, that we had met. Not only was she a Jew but she was related by marriage to a survivor. She was as close as I could come to forgiveness.'

I think of what Leo's reaction to this would be: *one Jew can't substitute for another.* 'You were going to ask her to kill you?'

'Help me die,' Josef corrects. 'But then I learned she had passed. And then, I met *you.* I did not know at first you were her daughter, but when it became clear, I knew there was a reason we had connected. I knew I had to ask of you what I did not get a chance to ask of your mother.' His eyes, blue and rheumy, fill with tears. 'I won't die. I can't die. I know you must think it is ridiculous of me to believe this, but it is true.'

I find myself thinking of my grandmother's story; of the *upiór* who begged for release, instead of an eternity of misery. 'You're hardly a vampire, Josef—'

'That does not mean I haven't been cursed. Look at me. I should be dead now, several times over. I have been locked for nearly seventy years; and for nearly seventy years, I've been searching for a key. Maybe you are the one who has it.'

Leo would say Josef has stalked me, and my family.

Leo would say that even now, Josef sees Jews as only a means to an end, not as individuals, but as pawns.

But if you seek forgiveness, doesn't that automatically mean you cannot be a monster? By definition, doesn't that desperation make you human again?

I wonder what my mother had thought of Josef Weber.

I reach for Josef's hand. This hand, which held the gun that killed my grandmother's best friend, and God knows how many others.

'I'll do it,' I say, although at this point, I am not sure if I am lying for Leo's sake, or telling the truth for my own.

Leo and I drive to Josef's house, but he will not come inside with me. 'Without a search warrant? Not on your life.'

I guess it's different, since I'm just there to pick up the dog, not to hunt for incriminating material. Josef's spare key is kept in a sliding compartment in the bottom of a stone frog that sits on his porch. When I open the door, Eva comes running out to meet me and barks frantically.

'It's okay,' I tell the little dachshund. 'He's going to be all right.'

Today, anyway.

Who will take the dog if he's extradited?

Inside, the kitchen is a mess. A plate has been overturned and broken, the food is gone (a perk for Eva, I'm guessing); a chair is lying on its side. On the table is the salt substitute Josef must have eaten.

I right the chair and clean up the broken china and sweep the floor. Then I throw the salt substitute in the trash and wash the dishes in the sink and wipe down the counters. I rummage through Josef's pantry to find Eva's dog food. There are boxes of Quaker instant oatmeal and Rice-A-Roni, mustard, rotini pasta. There are at least three bags of Doritos. It looks incredibly . . . ordinary, although I don't know what I was expecting a former Nazi to subsist on.

When I go looking for a crate or a doggie bed, I find myself standing at the threshold of Josef's bedroom. The bed is neatly made with a white blanket; the sheets are flowered with tiny violets. There are still two dressers in the room, one with a jewelry box on top and a woman's hairbrush. On one nightstand sit an alarm clock, a telephone, and a dog's chew toy.

On the other nightstand is an Alice Hoffman novel, with a bookmark still in place; and a jar of rose-scented hand cream.

There is something so heartbreaking about this – about Josef's inability to put away the trappings of his wife's life. But this man, who loved his wife and loves his dog and who eats junk food, also killed other human beings without blinking.

I take the chew toy and, with Eva still dancing at my heels, head back to the car where Leo is waiting. With the dog on my lap, gnawing at the ragged cuffs of my shorts, we drive to my house.

'He said he knew my mother,' I tell Leo.

Leo glances at me. 'What?'

I explain to him what Josef told me. 'What would he have done if he knew my grandmother was alive?'

For a moment, Leo is quiet. 'How do you know he doesn't?'

'What are you saying?'

'He could be playing you. He's lied to you before. Hell, he lied to the whole world for well over half a century. Maybe he figured out who Minka was, and is feeling you out to see if she remembers what he did.'

'Do you really think after all these years he'd be trying to clear his name against a theft charge?'

'No,' Leo says, 'but after all these years, he might still want to silence anyone who could identify him as a Nazi.'

'That's a little unrealistic, don't you think?'

'So was the Final Solution, but it got pretty far,' Leo points out.

'Maybe I would believe you if Josef hadn't asked me to kill him.'

'Because he knows you're not capable of it. So instead, he strings you along. He can snow you, the way he can't snow your grandmother,' Leo says. 'She was there. She's never met the new and improved Josef Weber. She knows an animal, a beast. Eventually, if he can get to her through you, he can kill her, or he can get you to convince her he's a changed man who deserves forgiveness. Either way, he wins.'

I stare at him, a little hurt that he would think this of me. 'You really believe I would do that?'

He pulls into my driveway, but there is already a car waiting there. Adam gets out of the driver's seat, holding a bouquet of lilies. 'People need forgiveness for all sorts of reasons,' Leo says flatly. 'I think you, of all people, understand that. And I think Josef Weber's got your number.'

He puts both hands on the steering wheel, staring straight ahead. In my lap, Eva starts to bark at the stranger outside who holds up a hand in an awkward wave. 'I'll be in touch,' Leo says.

For the first time in two days, he doesn't look me in the eye.

'Be careful,' Leo adds, a good-bye that I know has nothing to do with Josef.

The lilies would be nice, if not for the fact that I know Adam gets a deep discount with a local florist – something he told us while we were making my mother's funeral arrangements. In fact for all I know, this bouquet was just a leftover from the morning service.

'I don't really feel like talking,' I say, pushing past him, but he catches my arm and pulls me close and kisses me. I wonder if Leo is far enough down the street yet, or if he sees us.

I wonder why I care.

'There she is,' Adam murmurs against my lips. 'I knew the girl I'm crazy about was in there somewhere.'

'Actually, she's across town, roasting a chicken for your dinner tonight. I can understand that it's hard to keep track.'

'I deserve that,' Adam says, following me into my house. 'But that's why I'm here, Sage. You've gotta hear me out.'

He leads me into the living room. I realize that we do not spend a lot of time in there. When he comes over, we mostly go right to the bedroom.

He sits me down on the couch and holds my hand. 'I love you, Sage Singer. I love the way you have to sleep with one foot uncovered and the fact that you hog the popcorn when we watch a movie. I love your smile, and your widow's peak. It's a cliché, I know, but seeing you with that guy yesterday made me realize how much I have to lose. I don't want someone else to snatch you away while I'm dragging my feet over a decision. Pure and simple, I love you, and I want to be with you forever.'

Adam drops to one knee, still holding my hand. 'Sage . . . marry me?'

I stare at him, stunned. And then I burst out laughing, which I'm pretty sure is not the reaction he was hoping for. 'Aren't you forgetting something?'

'The ring – I know, but—'

'Not the ring. The fact that *you have a wife.*'

'Well, of course not,' Adam says, sitting down on the couch again. 'That's why I came here. I'm filing for divorce.'

I sink back against the cushions, shell-shocked.

There are so many ways a family can unravel. All it takes is a tiny slash of selfishness, a rip of greed, a puncture of bad luck. And yet, woven tightly, family can be the strongest bond imaginable.

I lost my mother and father, I pushed my sisters away. My grandmother had her parents torn from her. We have spent decades patching up the holes. And yet here is Adam, cavalierly throwing away his loved ones so that he can start over. I am ashamed at myself, for the role I had in bringing him to this point. I only hope it's not too late for him to realize what I'm just beginning to see myself: having a family means you're never alone.

'Adam,' I say softly. 'Go home.'

This time, it's for real.

I've told Adam that it's over, but now I mean it. And I know it's different because I cannot breathe, I cannot stop sobbing. It's as if I am grieving over someone I loved, which I guess is entirely true.

Adam had not wanted to leave. 'You don't mean it,' he told me. 'You're not thinking clearly.' But I was, possibly for the first time in three years. I was seeing myself the way Mary had seen me, and Leo, and I was embarrassed. 'I love you enough to marry you,' he said. 'What more could you possibly want?'

There were so many ways to answer that question.

I wanted to walk down the street on the arm of a handsome guy and not have other women wonder why he was with someone who looked like me.

I wanted to be happy, but not if it meant someone else would be devastated.

I wanted to feel beautiful, instead of just lucky.

The only reason Adam left was because I convinced him, through my tears, that he was only making this even harder for me. That if he really cared about me, he'd go. 'You do not want to do this,' he insisted.

The same words Josef had said to me during our chess game. But sometimes, in order to win, you have to make sacrifices.

When my eyes are so red I cannot see clearly and my nose is stuffed from crying, I curl up on the sofa and hug Eva to my chest. My cell phone starts buzzing in my pocket, and Adam's number flashes on the screen; I shut it off. My home phone starts ringing, too, and before I hear Adam's voice on the message machine, I unplug it and disconnect the phone. Right now, what I need is to be by myself.

I swallow half a sleeping pill left over from after my mom's funeral, and fall asleep fitfully on the couch. I dream that I am in a concentration camp, wearing my grandmother's striped prisoner's dress, when Josef comes for me in his officer's uniform. Although he is an old man, his grip is a vise. He doesn't smile, and he speaks only in German, and I cannot understand what he's asking of me. He drags me outside to a courtyard as I stumble, my knees bruising on rocks. There, Adam stands beside a coffin. He lifts me into it. *It's about time,* he says. When he reaches to shut the lid I realize his intentions, and I start to fight him. But even when I am able to scratch and draw blood, he is stronger than I am. He closes the lid, although I am gasping for air.

Please, I yell out, pounding my fists against the satin lining. *Can you hear me?*

But no one comes. I keep beating, hammering.

Are you there? I hear, and I think maybe it's Leo, but I am afraid to shout because it will use up too much oxygen. I struggle to breathe in, and my lungs fill with the scent of my grandmother's talcum powder.

I wake up to find Adam shaking me, and daylight streaming through the windows. I've been asleep for hours. 'Sage. Are you all right?'

I am still groggy, sleepy, dry-mouthed. 'Adam,' I slur. 'I told you to go away.'

'I was worried about you, since you weren't picking up your phone.'

Reaching down into the folds of the couch, I find my iPhone and turn it on. There are dozens of messages. One from Leo, three from my grandmother. A handful from Adam. And, oddly, a half dozen from each of my sisters.

'Pepper called me about the arrangements,' he says. 'God, Sage, I know how close you were to her. And I want you to know: I'm here for you.'

I start to shake my head, because even as fuzzy as it feels, everything is starting to fall into place. I take a deep breath, and all I can smell is talcum.

What Daisy tells me and my sisters is that Nana was feeling tired and lay down for a nap at about two o'clock that afternoon. When she didn't wake up in time for dinner, Daisy was afraid she'd have trouble sleeping through the night, so she went into the bedroom and turned on the lights. She tried to wake my grandmother, but couldn't. 'It happened in her sleep,' Daisy tells us, tearful. 'I know she wasn't in any pain.'

Me, I can't be certain.

What if the stress Leo and I subjected her to was what had finally taken its toll on her? What if the memories we brought flooding back had swept her away?

What if she was thinking of *him* in the moments before she died?

I can't help but believe this is my fault; and because of that, I am a mess.

But I can't confide in Pepper and Saffron, because I already feel like they blame me for my mother's death, even though they said it was not my fault. I cannot let them blame me for my grandmother's death, too. So mostly, I stay out of their way, grieving in private, and they leave me alone. I think they are a little afraid at how much of a zombie I have become in the wake of Nana's death. I don't mind when they invade my home and rearrange the furniture so that we can sit *shivah;* I don't complain when they go through my refrigerator throwing out yogurt that is out of date or griping because I don't have any decaf. I stop eating, even when Mary comes by with a basket full of fresh-baked pastries and condolences; when she tells me she has lit a candle for my grandmother before every Mass since hearing of her passing. I don't tell my sisters about Leo, or Reiner Hartmann. I don't try to call Josef, in the hospital. I just say that I've been spending a lot of time with Nana lately, and that's why I'd like a private moment with her at the funeral home, before the ceremony.

My grandmother lived a remarkable life. She watched her nation fall to pieces; and even when she became collateral damage, she believed in the power of the human spirit. She gave when she had nothing; she fought when she could barely stand; she clung to tomorrow when she couldn't find footing on the rock ledge of yesterday. She was a chameleon, slipping into the personae of a privileged young girl, a frightened teen, a dreamy novelist, a proud prisoner, an army wife, a mother hen. She became whomever she needed to be to survive, but she never let anyone else define her.

By anyone's account, her existence had been full, rich, important – even if she chose not to shout about her past, but rather to keep it hidden. It had been nobody's business but her own; it was still nobody's business.

I would make sure of that. After everything I'd done, by involving Leo and having him interview her, it was the least I could do.

Light-headed with hunger and heat and grief, I move

woodenly from Pepper's rental car to the lobby of the funeral home, where Adam is waiting in his dark suit. He greets Pepper first. 'I'm so sorry for your loss,' he says smoothly.

Does it even mean anything to him anymore? If you say the same words over and over, do they become so bleached that there's no color left in them?

'Thank you,' Pepper says, taking the hand he offers.

Then he turns to me. 'I understand you'd like a moment alone with your loved one?'

Adam, it's me, I think, and then I remember that I am the one who pushed him away.

He steers me through a doorway into the back of the funeral home, while Pepper takes a seat and starts texting – maybe the florist, the caterer, or her husband and kids, who will be landing at the airport any minute now. It isn't until the door to the room is closed behind us that Adam folds me into an embrace. I stiffen at first, and then just give in. It's easier than putting up a fight.

'You look like hell,' he sighs into my hair. 'Have you slept at *all* in the past two days?'

'I can't believe she's gone,' I say, tearing up. 'I'm all alone, now.'

'You could have me . . .'

Really? *Now?* I bite my lip, and take a step away from him.

'Are you sure you want to do this?'

I nod.

Adam takes me to the anteroom where my grandmother's casket is waiting, ready to be transferred to the sanctuary in time for the service. The small space smells like the inside of a refrigerator, cold and faintly antiseptic. My head spins, and I have to hold on to the wall for support. 'Could I have a minute alone with her?'

Adam nods and gently opens the upper half of the casket so that I am looking down at my grandmother. The door closes behind him as he steps outside.

She is wearing a red wool skirt with black piping. The blouse that is tied at her neck blooms like a flower against her throat. Her eyelashes cast shadows on her cheeks, which look lightly flushed. Her silver hair is swept and styled, the way she has had it done twice a week at the salon for as long as I can remember. Adam and his staff have outdone themselves. Looking at her, I find myself thinking of Sleeping Beauty, of Snow White, of women who woke from their nightmares and began to live again.

If that happened to my grandmother, it would not be the first time.

When my mother died, I did not want to touch her. I knew my sisters would lean down and kiss her cheek, embrace her one last time. But for me, the moment of physical contact with a dead body was terrifying. It would feel different from all the other times I'd turned to her for comfort, because she couldn't hug me back. And if she couldn't hug me back, I had to stop pretending it was possible.

Now, though, I don't have a choice.

I reach into the casket and lift my grandmother's left hand. It is cold and oddly firm, like the dolls I had when I was a little girl that were advertised for their lifelike feel, which was never really lifelike at all. I unbutton her cuff so that the sleeve slides backward, exposing the flesh of her forearm.

The casket will be closed at the funeral. No one will see the tattoo she was given at Auschwitz. And even if someone were to look inside, like I did, her silk blouse would cover the evidence. But my grandmother went to such great pains to keep from being defined by her experience as a survivor that I feel like it's my duty to make sure this continues, whatever comes next.

From my purse I pull a small tube of concealer, and carefully blot it onto my grandmother's skin. I wait for it to dry, making sure the numbers have been obliterated. Then I button her cuff again, and folding my hands around hers, press a kiss into her palm like a marble to carry with her. 'Nana,' I say, 'when I grow up, I'm going to be as brave as you.'

I close the casket and wipe beneath my eyes with my fingers, trying not to mess up my mascara. Then I take a few deep breaths and walk unsteadily into the hallway that leads to the lobby of the funeral home.

Adam is not waiting for me outside the anteroom. It doesn't matter, though, because I know my way around here. I walk down the hallway, my ankles wobbling in the black pumps I am not accustomed to wearing.

In the foyer, I see Adam and Pepper bent in quiet conversation with a third party, whose body is blocked by their own. I assume it's Saffron, arriving before the rest of the guests. When they hear my footsteps, Adam turns, and suddenly I can see that the person they're talking to is not Saffron at all.

The room spins like a carousel. 'Leo?' I whisper, certain I have imagined him, until he catches me the moment before I hit the floor.

*F*or a long time, I simply cried.

Every day, at noon, Aleks was brought to the village square and punished for what his brother had done. It would have killed an ordinary man. Instead, for Aleks, it was just a new circle of hell.

I stopped baking. The village, without bread, grew bitter. There was nothing to break at the table with family, to digest over conversation. There were no pastries to pass to a lover. People felt empty inside, no matter how much other food they ate.

One day I left the cottage and traveled by foot to the nearest city. It was the one Aleks and his brother had last come from, where the buildings were so tall it hurt to try to see the tops of them. There was a special building there full of books, as many books as there were grains in a flour sack. I told the woman at the desk in the front what I needed, and she led me down a curved set of iron stairs to a place where leather tomes were nestled into the walls.

I learned that there is more than one way to kill an upiór.

You could bury a body deep in the ground, weighted down in the belly with rich soil.

You could drive a nail into his brain.

Jodi Picoult

You could grind up a caul, like the one Casimir had been born with, and feed it to him.

Or you could find the original corpse and slice open its heart. The blood of its victims would pour out.

Some of these may have been old wives' tales, but this last one, I knew, was true: because if Aleks cut open his heart, I was certain that I would be the one to bleed to death.

Leo

S he looks like a raccoon.

An exhausted, dazed, beautiful raccoon.

There are black circles under her eyes – from her makeup, and a lack of sleep, I'm guessing – and two high spots of color on her cheeks. The funeral director (who also happens to be the same married boyfriend I met a few nights ago, as if this town weren't small enough already) gave me a compress to put on her forehead, which has matted her bangs and dripped a damp ring around the collar of her black dress. 'Hey,' I say, as Sage opens her eyes. 'I hear you have a habit of doing this.'

Let me just say that I'm doing everything I can not to get sick, right here in the office of the funeral director. The whole place creeps me out, which is pretty astounding for someone who scours photographs of concentration camp victims all day long.

'Are you okay?' Sage asks.

'I'm the one who's supposed to be asking you that.'

She sits up. 'Where's Adam?'

Wow. Just like that, an invisible wall cleaves the space between us. I rock back on my heels, putting distance between the couch where she's lying and myself. 'Of course,' I say formally. 'I'll get him for you.'

'I didn't say I wanted you to get him.' Sage's voice is as thin as a twig. 'How did you know . . .'

She doesn't finish her sentence; she doesn't have to. 'I called you when I got back to D.C. But you didn't pick up the phone. I started to get worried – I know you think a ninety-five-year-old isn't a threat, but I've seen guys that age pull a gun on a federal agent. Anyway, someone finally answered. Your sister Saffron. She told me about Minka.' I look at her. 'I'm so sorry, Sage. Your grandmother was a very special woman.'

'What are you doing here, Leo?'

'I think that should be pretty obvious—'

'I know you're here for the funeral,' she interrupts. 'But why?'

Various reasons run through my head: because being here is the right thing to do; because there is a precedent in the office for coming to the funerals of survivors who've been witnesses; because Minka was part of my investigation. But really, the reason I am here is that I wanted to be, for Sage. 'I didn't know your grandmother, of course, the way you did. But I could tell just by the way she looked at you when you didn't know she was looking that family came first, for her. It's like that for a lot of Jews. Almost as if it's in the collective unconscious, because once, it got taken away.' I glance at Sage. 'Today, I thought maybe I could be your family.'

At first Sage doesn't move. Then I realize that tears are streaming down her cheeks. I reach for her, right through that invisible wall, until I am holding her hand. 'So, no biggie, but is this good crying, like you're happy to set another place at Thanksgiving, or bad crying, like you just found out your long-lost relative is a creeper?'

A laugh bubbles out of her. 'I don't know how you do that.'

'Do what?'

'Make it so I can breathe again,' Sage says. 'But thank you.'

Whatever barrier I thought was between us is completely gone now. I sit next to her on the couch, and Sage rests her head on my shoulder, simply, as if she has been doing it her whole life. 'What if we did this to her?'

'You mean by getting her to talk about what happened?'

She nods. 'I can't shake the feeling that if I hadn't ever brought it up – if you hadn't shown her the pictures . . .'

'You don't know that. Stop beating yourself up.'

'It just feels so anticlimactic, you know?' she says, her voice small. 'To survive the Holocaust, and then die in her sleep. What's the point?'

I think for a moment. 'The point is that she got to die in her sleep. After having lunch with her granddaughter, and a very dapper, charming attorney.' I am still holding Sage Singer's hand. Her fingers fit seamlessly between mine. 'Maybe she didn't die upset. Maybe she let go, Sage, because she finally felt like everything was going to be okay.'

It is by all accounts a lovely service, but I don't pay attention. I'm too busy looking around the room to see if Reiner Hartmann shows up, because there's still a part of me that believes it's possible. When I realize that he's probably not going to come, I focus my attention on Adam, who is standing unobtrusively near the back of the sanctuary the way a funeral director should, trying hard not to stare at me every time Sage grabs on to my arm or buries her face in the sleeve of my suit jacket.

I'm not gonna lie; it feels pretty damn good.

When I got dumped in high school by a girl who wanted a more popular, studlier date on a Friday night, my mother used to say, *Leo, don't you worry. The geeks shall inherit the earth.* I am starting to believe this might actually be true.

My mother would also tell me that hitting on a woman who's grieving at her grandmother's funeral is a one-way ticket to Hell.

I don't recognize any of the mourners, except for Daisy, who is sobbing softly into a linen handkerchief. At the end of the service, Adam announces when and where *shivah* calls can be made. He also lists two charities, suggested by Pepper, where donations can be sent in Minka's memory.

At the graveside, I stand behind Sage, who sits between her two older sisters. They look like her, but overblown; birds-of-paradise flanking a primrose. When it is time for Sage to throw dirt into the grave, her hands are shaking. She tosses three handfuls. The rest of the mourners – a collection of both elderly people and friends of Sage's parents, from what I can gather – throw handfuls of dirt as well. After it is my turn, I catch up to Sage, and without saying a word, she slips her hand into mine again.

Sage's house, which has been commandeered by her sisters to host a post-funeral gathering for friends and family, looks nothing like the home I was in just a few days ago. Furniture has been rearranged to accommodate the crowd. The mirrors have already been covered for mourning. Food is spread on every horizontal surface. Sage looks at the throngs of people streaming in the front door and takes a shuddering breath. 'Everyone's going to try to talk to me. I can't do this.'

'Yes, you can. I'm not going anywhere,' I promise.

As soon as we walk inside, people swarm around Sage to offer their condolences. 'Your grandma was my bridge partner,' one nervous, birdlike woman says. A meatball of a man with a gold pocket watch and a handlebar mustache who reminds me of the guy on the Monopoly Chance cards hugs Sage tightly, rocking her small frame back and forth. 'You poor thing,' he says.

A balding man holding a sleeping toddler in his arms catches my eye. 'I didn't know Sage was dating someone.' He awkwardly sticks out his hand, which is caught under the chubby knee of his son. 'Welcome to the circus. I'm Andy. Pepper's other half.'

'Leo,' I say, shaking his hand. 'But Sage and I . . .'

I realize I have no idea what she's told her family. It is certainly at her discretion to explain what's going on with Josef Weber, if she sees fit. But I'm not going to be the one to break the news to them if Sage hasn't.

'We're just working together,' I finish.

He looks at my suit dubiously. 'You don't look like a baker.'

'I'm not. We met through . . . well, Minka.'

'She was something else,' Andy says. 'Last year for Chanukah, Pepper and I got her a trip to a fancy salon for a manicure. She liked it so much she asked if, for her birthday, we could get her a *pedophile*.' He laughs.

But Sage has overheard. 'You think it's funny that English wasn't her first language, Andy? How much Polish and German and Yiddish do you speak?'

He looks horrified. 'I don't think it's funny. I thought it was sweet.'

I put my arm around Sage's shoulders and steer her in the opposite direction. 'Why don't we see if your sisters need a hand in the kitchen?'

As I lead her away from Pepper's husband, Sage frowns. 'He's such a dick.'

'Maybe,' I say, 'but if he wants to remember your grandmother with a smile, that's not such a bad thing.'

In the kitchen, Pepper is putting sugar cubes into a glass bowl. 'I understand not buying creamer because of the fat content, but do you really not have milk, Sage?' she asks. 'Everyone has milk, for God's sake.'

'I'm lactose intolerant,' Sage mutters. I notice that when she talks to her sisters, her shoulders hunch and she seems like a smaller, paler version of herself. Like she's trying to be even more invisible than usual.

'Just bring it out there,' Saffron says. 'The coffee's cold already.'

'Hi,' I announce. 'My name's Leo. Is there anything I can do to help?'

Saffron looks up at me, then at Sage. 'Who's this?'

'Leo,' I repeat. 'A colleague.'

'*You* bake?' she says doubtfully.

I turn to Sage. 'Okay, so which is it – do bakers wear clown suits or something, or do I dress like an accountant?'

'You dress like an attorney,' she replies. 'Go figure.'

'Well, good,' Saffron says, sailing past us with her platter, 'because it's completely criminal that there's not a single decent deli in this entire state. How am I supposed to feed sixty people with pastrami from Price Chopper?'

'You *used* to live here, you know,' Sage calls out after her.

When her sisters bustle out of the kitchen and we are alone, I hear crying. But it's not Sage; and she hears it, too. She traces the sound to the pantry, and opens the doors to find Eva the dachshund trapped inside. 'I bet this is a nightmare for you,' she murmurs, picking the dog up in her arms, but she is looking at all the people gathered to celebrate her grandmother's life. People who want to make her the center of their attention, as they share memories.

While she is still holding the dachshund in one arm, I pull

her through the back door of the kitchen, down a set of stairs, and across her rear lawn to the spot where I've parked my rental car.

'Leo!' she cries. 'What are you *doing*?'

'So,' I ask, as if she has not spoken. 'When was the last time you ate?'

It's only a Courtyard by Marriott, but I order a bottle of crappy red wine and a bottle of even worse white; a French onion soup and chicken Caesar salad; buffalo wings and mozzarella sticks and a cheese pizza; fettuccine Alfredo, three scoops of chocolate ice cream, and a colossal slice of lemon meringue pie. There is enough food for me, Sage, Eva, and the rest of the fourth floor, were I inclined to invite them.

Any reservations I have about kidnapping a grieving girl from her own house, where she is supposed to be sitting *shivah* for her grandmother, and smuggling a dog into a pet-free hotel, are allayed by the fact that the color has started to come back to Sage's face as she works her way through the bounty in front of her.

The room, made for business travelers, has a small sitting area with a couch and a television. We have it tuned to Turner Classic Movies, with the volume low. Jimmy Stewart and Katharine Hepburn are on the screen, arguing with each other. 'Why do people in old movies always sound like their jaws are wired together?' Sage asks.

I laugh. 'It's a little known fact that Cary Grant suffered from TMJ.'

'No one from the 1940s ever sounds like trailer trash,' Sage muses. As Jimmy Stewart leans close to Katharine Hepburn, she dubs a line for him. 'Say you'll go out with me, Mabel.

I know you're out of my league ... but I can always start bowling on Tuesday nights instead.'

I grin, speaking over Katharine Hepburn's scripted response. 'I'm sorry, Ralph. I could never love a man who thinks loading the dishwasher means getting your wife drunk.'

'But, sugar,' Sage continues, 'what am I gonna do with these NASCAR tickets?'

Katharine Hepburn tosses her hair. 'Hell if I care,' I say.

Sage smiles. 'This is a missed opportunity for Hollywood.'

She's turned off her phone, because her sisters will be calling her nonstop, once they discover her departure. At one end of the couch, the dog is snoring. The screen abruptly fills with the carnival colors of a commercial. After watching something that's so black and white, it's overwhelming. 'I suppose it's done now,' Sage says.

I check my watch. 'The movie's got another half hour.'

'I was talking about Reiner Hartmann.'

I reach for the remote and mute the television. 'We don't have the possibility of a deposition from your grandmother anymore, much less a video testimony.'

'I could tell a court what she said—'

'That's hearsay,' I explain.

'It doesn't seem fair.' Sage tucks her leg beneath her on the couch. She is still wearing her black dress from the funeral, but she's barefoot. 'That she would die, and he would still be alive. It feels like such a waste. Like she should have lived to tell her story, you know?'

'She did,' I point out. 'She told it to you, for safekeeping. And now that she's gone, maybe it's yours to tell.'

I can tell Sage hasn't thought about her grandmother's death that way. She frowns, and then gets up from the couch. Her purse is an oversize black hole, from what I can see; I can't imagine what's inside it. But she rummages around inside and pulls out a leather notebook. It looks like something Keats might have carried around in *his* purse, if that was in style back then.

'The story, the one she talked about that saved her life? She rewrote it, after the war. Last week, for the first time, she showed it to me.' Sage sits back down. 'I think she'd like you to hear it,' she says. '*I'd* like you to hear it.'

When was the last time someone read aloud to you? Probably when you were a child, and if you think back, you'll remember how safe you felt, tucked under the covers, or curled in someone's arms, as a story was spun around you like a web. Sage begins to tell me about a baker and his daughter; a soldier drunk with power who loves her; a string of murders linked like pearls throughout the village.

I watch her as she reads. Her voice begins to take on the roles of the characters whose dialogue she's speaking. Minka's tale reminds me of Grimm, of Isak Dinesen, of Hans Christian Andersen; of the time when fairy tales were not diluted with Disney princesses and dancing animals, but were dark and bloody and dangerous. In those old tomes, love took a toll, and happy endings came at a cost. There's a lesson in that, and it's tugging at me; but I am distracted, held spellbound by the pulse in Sage's throat that beats a little faster the first time Ania and Aleks – the most unlikely of couples – meet.

'Nobody,' Sage reads, '*who looks at a shard of flint lying beneath a rock ledge, or who finds a splintered log by the side of the road would ever find magic in their solitude. But in the right circumstances, if you bring them together, you can start a fire that consumes the world.*'

We become the *upiory* in the story, awake all night. The sun is already crawling over the horizon when Sage reaches the part where Aleks falls into the trap the soldiers have set. He's jailed, and scheduled to be tortured to death. Unless he can convince Ania to kill him first, out of mercy.

Suddenly Sage closes the book. 'You can't just stop there!' I protest.

'I have to. It's all she wrote.'

Her hair is a mess; the circles under her eyes are so dark it looks like she's fielded a punch. 'Minka knew what happened,' I say decisively. 'Even if she chose not to tell the rest of us.'

'I was going to ask her why she never finished it . . . but then I didn't. And now I can't.' Sage looks at me, her heart in her eyes. 'How do *you* think it ends?'

I tuck Sage's hair behind her ear. 'Like this,' I say, and I kiss the ridged trail of her scar.

She sucks in her breath, but she doesn't pull away. I kiss the corner of her eye, where the skin pulls down because of a graft. I kiss the smooth silver flecks on her cheek that remind me of falling stars.

And then, I kiss her mouth.

At first, I hold her in my arms like something fragile. I have to exercise every fiber of my body not to crush her tighter against me. I've never felt like this about a woman: like I need to consume her. *Think of baseball,* I tell myself, but I know nothing of value about baseball. So I start silently listing the justices of the Supreme Court, just so that I don't scare her off by moving too fast.

But Sage, thank God, winds her arms around my neck and presses herself flush against me. Her fingers comb through my hair; her breath fills me. She tastes of lemon and cinnamon, she smells of coconut lotion and lazy sunsets. She is a live wire, and everywhere she touches me, I burn.

When she grinds her hips against mine, I surrender. With her legs wrapped around me and her dress tangled around her waist, I carry her into the bedroom and lay her down on the crisp sheets. She pulls me over her body like an eclipse of the sun, and my last conscious thought is that there could not possibly be a better finale to this story.

In the cocoon of the room, created by blackout shades, we are caught in a bubble of time. Sometimes I wake up holding Sage; sometimes she wakes up holding me. Sometimes all I can hear is her heartbeat; sometimes her voice wraps me as tightly as the tangled sheets.

It was my fault, she says, at one point.

It was after graduation, and my mother and I, we'd packed up the car to go home. It was so full she couldn't see out the back window, so I told her I'd drive.

It was a beautiful day. That made it even worse. There was no rain, no snow, nothing else to blame it on. We were on the highway. I was trying to pass a truck, but I didn't see the car in the other lane, so I swerved. And then.

A shudder runs down her spine.

She didn't die, not right away. She had surgery, and then she got an infection, and her body started to shut down. Pepper and Saffron, they said it was an accident. But I know deep down they still blame me. And my mother did, too.

I hold her tightly. *I'm sure that's not true.*

When she was in the hospital, Sage says, *when she was dying, she told me,* I forgive you. *There's no reason to forgive someone, unless you know they've done something wrong.*

Sometimes bad things just happen, I say. I brush my thumb over her cheek, tracing the topographical rise and valley of her scars.

She catches my hand, brings it to her mouth, kisses it. *And sometimes, good things do.*

I have a thousand excuses.

It was the red wine.

The white.

The stress of the day.

The stress of the job.

The way her black dress hugged her curves.

The fact that we were lonely/horny/sublimating grief.

Freud would have plenty to say about my indiscretion. So would my boss. What I've done – taking advantage of a woman who was instrumental in an open HRSP case, one who had attended a *funeral* hours before – is unconscionable.

Worse, I'd do it all over again.

Eva the dog is giving me the evil eye. And why shouldn't she? She witnessed the whole sordid, intense, amazing affair.

Sage is still asleep in the bedroom. Because I do not trust myself to be near her, I'm out here on the couch in my boxers and T-shirt, poring over Reiner Hartmann's file with every ounce of Jewish guilt I can muster. I can't undo what I did last night to take advantage of Sage, but I can damn well figure out a way to make sure this case doesn't get ruined in the process.

'Hi.'

When I turn around, there she is wearing my white button-down shirt. It almost covers her. Almost.

I stand up, torn between grabbing her and dragging her back to bed, and doing the right thing. 'I'm sorry,' I blurt out. 'That was a mistake.'

Her eyes widen. 'It didn't feel like a mistake.'

'You're hardly in any condition to be thinking clearly right now. I knew better, even if you didn't.'

'Marge says that it's normal to crave life when you're in the throes of death. And that was pretty lively.'

'Marge?'

'She runs the grief group.'

'Oh,' I sigh. 'Fabulous.'

'Look. I want you to know that in spite of what you've seen in the few days you've known me, I'm not usually . . . like this. I don't . . . you know.'

'Right. Because you're in love with the married funeral director,' I say, rubbing my hand through my hair and making it stand on end. I'd forgotten about him last night, too.

'That's over,' she says. 'Completely.'

My head snaps up. 'You're sure?'

'Dead certain. So to speak.' She takes a step toward me. 'Does that make this less of a mistake?'

'No,' I say, starting to pace. 'Because you're still involved in one of my cases.'

'I thought that was over, too, since there's no way to identify Josef anymore as Reiner Hartmann.'

That's not true.

The caveat flies like a red standard in the battlefield of my mind.

Without Minka's testimony, the murder of Darija cannot be linked to Reiner Hartmann. But the prisoner wasn't the only one to witness that infraction.

Reiner was there, too.

If someone were to get him to confess to the incident that was written up in his SS file, it would be a slam dunk.

'There might be another way,' I say. 'But it would mean involving you, Sage.'

She sits down on the couch, absently stroking the dog's ears. 'What do you mean?'

'We could wire you up, and tape the conversation. Get him to admit that he was reprimanded for killing a Jewish prisoner in a way that wasn't sanctioned.'

She looks into her lap. 'I wish you'd asked me first, so that my grandmother never got involved.'

I am not going to explain to her that this is a default attempt; it would never have been my first choice. Not just because of the power of a survivor's testimony but because there is a good reason we don't put civilians into the field as makeshift agents.

Particularly ones we might be falling for.

'I'll do whatever you need me to do, Leo,' Sage says. She gets up and starts unbuttoning her shirt. *My* shirt.

'What are you doing?'

'Honestly. A Harvard degree and you can't figure that out?'

'No.' I take a step backward. 'Absolutely not. Now you're a material witness.'

She vines her arms around my neck. 'I'll show you my firsthand sources if you show me yours.'

This girl is going to be the death of me. With superhuman effort, I push her away. 'Sage. I can't.'

She takes a step back, defeated. 'Last night, for just a little while, I was happy. Really happy. I can't remember the last time I felt like that.'

'I'm sorry. I love you, but it's an enormous conflict of interest.'

Her head snaps up. 'You love me?'

'What?' My face is suddenly on fire. 'I never said that.'

'You did. I heard it.'

'I said *I'd love to.*'

'No,' Sage says, a grin splitting her face. 'You didn't.'

Did I? I'm so tired I don't know what the hell is coming out of my mouth. Which probably means that I don't have the faculties to cover up what I really feel for Sage Singer, with an intensity that terrifies me.

She places her hands flat on my chest. 'What if I tell you that I won't wear the wire unless you come back to bed?'

'That's blackmail.'

Sage is beaming. She shrugs.

It's easy to say you will do what's right and shun what's wrong, but when you get close enough to any given situation, you realize that there *is* no black or white. There are gradations of gray.

I hesitate. But only for a second. Then I grab Sage around the waist and lift her off her feet. 'The things I do for my country,' I say.

*I*t was not easy to break into a prison.

First, I had baked the croissants, their bitter almond filling masking the taste of the rat poison I'd mixed in. I left them outside the door where the guard stood, keeping watch over Aleks until tomorrow morning.

Then, the new captain of the guard, Damian's second in command, would torture him to death.

Whistling like a trapped animal, I got the guard to open the door to see about the racket. Finding nothing, he had shrugged and taken in the basket of pastries. A half hour later, he was lying on his side, his mouth foaming, in the throes of death.

Nobody who looks at a shard of flint lying beneath a rock ledge, or who finds a splintered log by the side of the road would ever find magic in their solitude. But in the right circumstances, if you bring them together, you can start a fire that consumes the world.

Yes, now, I had killed a man. Surely that meant we belonged together. I would have eagerly rotted in this cell beside Aleks, if it was all the time I had left with him.

Through the cell window, I watched Aleks as he sat with his back against the dank wall, eyes closed. He was a skeleton, emaciated after a month of daily torture. It seemed his captors *had tired of the game before Aleks's body gave out; now he was not just to be toyed with, he was to be murdered.*

When he heard me approach, he stood. I could see the effort it cost him. 'You came,' he said, twining his fingers with mine through the bars.

'I got your note.'

'I sent it two weeks ago,' he said. 'And it took two weeks before that to coax the bird onto the window ledge.'

'I'm so sorry,' I said.

Aleks's hands were scarred and broken from the beatings, yet still he held me tight. 'Please,' he whispered. 'Do one thing for me tonight.'

'Anything,' I promised.

'Kill me.'

I drew a deep breath. 'Aleks,' I said. '—

Sage

I f you had told me a month ago that I would be undertaking a covert mission as an FBI field agent, I would have laughed in your face.

Then again, if you'd told me that I would be falling in love with a man other than Adam, I would have told you you were crazy. Leo, without a reminder, asks for soy milk every time we order coffee. He turns the shower on before he leaves the bathroom so that the water is warm before I get in. He holds the door open for me and won't drive anywhere until my seat belt is fastened. Sometimes, there's this expression on his face, as if he cannot quite believe he got so lucky. I'm not sure what he's seeing when he looks at me, but I want to be that girl.

And my scars? I still see them, when I look in a mirror. But the first thing I notice is my smile.

I'm nervous about taping my conversation with Josef. It is going to happen, finally, after three days of waiting. First, my sisters had to end their *shivah* calls. Second, Leo needed to secure permission to use electronic surveillance through the DOJ Criminal Division's Office of Enforcement Operations. And third, Josef had to be discharged from the hospital.

I am going to be the one to bring him home, and then, I hope, I can get him to confess to Darija's murder.

Leo has been arranging all the details from my house, where

we moved back in as a team after that first night in the hotel. It was by unspoken agreement that we decided he would check out of the Marriott and come stay with me, instead. Although I was ready to fight off my sisters' comments and questions, I didn't even have to do any damage control. Leo had had Pepper and Saffron charmed after ten minutes of conversation about how a famous thriller writer had shadowed him, taken pages of notes, and then completely ignored reality to create a bestseller that, while wildly inaccurate, had shot to the top of the *New York Times* list. 'I knew it!' Saffron had told him. 'My book club read it. We all felt there was no way a Russian spy would ever make it into the DOJ with false credentials.'

'Actually, that's not the biggest stretch. But the main character, the one who has a full closet of Armani suits? No way, not on a government salary,' Leo had said.

Of course, I couldn't really explain Leo's presence – or Eva's for that matter – without telling my sisters about Josef. And to my surprise, that made me an instant celebrity.

'I can't believe you're hunting Nazis,' Saffron said last night, the last meal we would share before she and Pepper left for the airport in the morning to return to their respective homes. 'My little sister.'

'I'm not really hunting them,' I corrected. 'One sort of fell into my lap.'

I had called Josef, twice, at Leo's suggestion, and explained my absence with the truth. A close relative had died unexpectedly. I had family business to take care of. I told him Eva missed him; I asked him what the doctors said about his condition; and I arranged the details of his hospital discharge.

'Still,' Pepper agreed. 'Mom and Dad would be delighted. Considering all the fuss you made about not going to Hebrew school.'

'This isn't about religion,' I tried to explain. 'It's about justice.'

'They don't have to be mutually exclusive,' Leo said amiably. And just like that, he steered the conversation away from a critique of me and to an analysis of the last election.

It's an odd luxury, knowing someone's got my back. Unlike Adam, whom I was always defending to others, Leo effortlessly defends *me*. He knows what will upset me before it even happens and like a superhero, bends the track of the runaway train before it strikes.

This morning, when Pepper and Saffron leave, I have a box of freshly baked chocolate croissants for them as a care package. My sisters hug Leo good-bye; then I walk them out to the driveway, to the rental car. Pepper embraces me tightly. 'Don't let this one get away, Sage. I want to hear how everything turns out. You'll call me?'

It is the first time I can remember my sister soliciting contact, instead of just criticizing me. 'Absolutely,' I promise.

In the kitchen, Leo is just hanging up the phone when I return. 'We can pick up the van on the way to the hospital. Then while you're getting Josef – Sage, what's wrong?'

'For starters,' I say, 'I'm not used to getting along with my sisters.'

'You made them out to be Scylla and Charybdis,' Leo says, laughing. 'They're just ordinary moms.'

'That's easy for you to say. They're mesmerized by you.'

'I hear I have that effect on Singer women.'

'Good,' I reply. 'Then maybe you can use that magic to hypnotize me, so that I don't screw this up today.'

He comes around the counter and rubs my shoulders. 'You're not going to screw this up. You want to go over it again?'

I nod.

We have done dry runs of this interview a half dozen times, some with the recording equipment to make sure it works properly. Leo has played the role of Josef. Sometimes he's forthcoming, sometimes he is belligerent. Sometimes he just shuts down and refuses to talk. I say that I'm losing courage; that if I'm going to bite the bullet and actually kill him, I need to be able to think about what he did as a concrete example, not a global genocide; that I need to see a face or hear a name of one of his victims. In every scenario so far, I've gotten him to confess.

Then again, Leo is not Josef.

I take a deep breath. 'I ask him how he feels . . .'

'Right, or anything else that seems natural. What you *don't* want is for him to think you're nervous.'

'Great.'

Leo sits down on the stool beside mine. 'You want him to open up without leading him on.'

'What do I say about my grandmother?'

He hesitates. 'Normally I'd tell you not to bring Minka up at all. But you did mention a death in the family. So play it by ear. If you do mention her, though, don't let on that she's the grandmother who was the survivor. I just can't be certain how he'll read that.'

I bury my face in my hands. 'Can't you just interrogate him?'

'Sure,' Leo says. 'But I'm pretty sure he'll know something's up when I show up at the hospital instead of you.'

The plan is for Leo to be parked in a van across the street from Josef's house. That way the receiver – a box the size of a small briefcase – will be in range for the transmitter of the body wire. While Leo is hidden in the van, doing surveillance, I will be in Josef's house.

We have a safe word, too. 'And if I say *I'm supposed to meet Mary today . . .*'

'Then I run in and draw my gun, but I can't get a clear shot without hitting you. So instead I break out the jujitsu moves that got me a blue ribbon in seventh grade. I toss Josef off you like a cheap coat and pin him against the wall by the neck. I say, *Don't make me do something we'll both regret*, which sounds like a movie line, and is, but I've used those before in tense law enforcement situations and they actually work. I release Josef, who collapses to my feet, and confesses not just to all war crimes at Auschwitz but also for being responsible for the colossal mistakes New Coke and *Sex and the City 2*. He signs on the dotted line, we call in local law enforcement for an arrest, and you and I ride off into the sunset.'

I shake my head, smiling. Leo actually does carry a gun, but he has assured me that ever since Camp Wakatani in fifth grade any weapon is really for show; that he could not hit a target the size of Australia. It's hard to tell with him, but I imagine he's lying. I cannot imagine that the DOJ lets him carry a weapon without having learned how to use it efficiently.

Leo looks at his watch. 'We should get going. You ready to get suited up?'

It's hard to wear a wire when it's summertime. My usual outfit, a tank top and jean shorts, is too tight to hide the microphone that will be taped underneath my shirt. Instead, I have opted for a loose sundress.

Leo hands me the transmitter – it's the size of an iPod mini, with a small hook that can be affixed to a waistband or belt, neither of which I have. 'Where am I supposed to put it?'

He pulls aside the neck of the dress and tucks the transmitter into the side of my bra. 'How's that?'

'*So* comfortable,' I say. '*Not.*'

'You sound like you're thirteen.' He threads the wire with the tiny microphone under my arm and around my waist.

I pull down the top of the sundress so that he has better access. 'What are you doing?' Leo says, backing away.

'Making it easier for you.'

He swallows. 'Maybe *you* should do it.'

'Why are you so shy all of a sudden? Isn't that like locking the barn door after the horses are gone?'

'I'm not shy,' Leo grits out. 'I'm trying very hard to get us to the hospital on time, and *this* doesn't help. Can you just, you know, tape it down? And pull up your damn dress?'

When the microphone and transmitter are in place, we make sure the channels are synced to the receiver that Leo will have in the van. I am driving the rental car; Leo sits in the passenger seat with the receiver on his lap. We go first to Josef's house, where we drop off Eva and test the transmitter for distance. 'It works,' Leo says when I get back in the car, having filled Eva's water bowl and spread her toys around the living room, promising her that Josef is on his way.

I follow the GPS directions to the parking lot where Leo is meeting someone from the DOJ. He is quiet, running through checklists in his mind. The only other car there is a van, making me wonder how the other officer will get back home. It's blue, and says DON'S CARPETS on the side. A man gets out of the driver's side and flashes his badge. 'Leo Stein?'

'Yup,' Leo says, through the open window. 'Just a sec.'

He hits the power button so that the window rolls up again, so that our conversation is private. 'Don't forget to make sure that there's no background interference,' Leo says.

'I know.'

'So if he likes to listen to CNN or NPR make sure you turn it off. Power down your cell. Don't grind coffee beans. Don't use anything that could affect the transmission.'

I nod.

'Remember that *why* isn't a leading question.'

'Leo,' I say, 'I can't remember all this stuff. I'm not a professional . . .'

He mulls for a moment. 'You just need a little inspiration. You know what J. Edgar Hoover would do, if he were alive today?'

I shake my head.

'Scream and claw at the top of his coffin.'

The response is so unexpected, so irreverent, that a bark of laughter escapes before I can cover my mouth. 'I can't believe you're making jokes while I'm freaking out.'

'Isn't that exactly when you need them?' Leo asks. He leans forward, and stamps me with a kiss. 'Your gut instinct was to laugh. Go with your gut, Sage.'

As the doctor relays the post-discharge instructions to us, I wonder if Josef is thinking the same thing I am: that a dead man, which he hopes to be, does not have to worry about salt intake or rest or anything else on the printout we are given. The candy striper who wheels Josef down to the lobby so I can bring my car around recognizes him. 'Herr Weber, right?' she asks. 'My older brother had you for German.'

'*Wie heißt er?*'

She smiles shyly. 'I took French.'

'I asked for his name.'

'Jackson,' the girl says. 'Jackson O'Rourke?'

'Oh yes,' Josef says. 'He was an excellent student.'

When we reach the lobby, I take over and wheel Josef to a spot in the shade outside. 'Did you really remember her brother?'

'Not one bit,' he admits. 'But *she* didn't need to know that.'

I am still thinking about this exchange when I reach Leo's

car in the parking lot and drive it under the portico so that Josef doesn't have to walk as far. What made Josef such a memorable teacher, and such a devoted citizen, was his ability to make these connections with individuals. To hide in plain sight.

In retrospect, it's been a brilliant plan.

When you look someone in the eye and shake his hand and tell him your name, he has no reason to think you are lying.

'This is a new car,' Josef says, as I help him into the passenger seat.

'It's a rental. Mine's in the shop. I totaled it.'

'An accident? You are all right?' he asks.

'I'm fine. I hit a deer.'

'Your car, and your relative passing . . . so much has happened in the past week that I do not know about.' He folds his hands in his lap. 'I am sorry to hear of your loss.'

'Thank you,' I say stiffly.

What I want to say is:

The woman who died was my grandmother.

You knew her.

You don't even remember, probably.

You son of a bitch.

Instead, I keep my eyes on the road as my hands flex on the steering wheel.

'I think we need to talk,' Josef says.

I slide a glance toward him. 'All right.'

'About how, and when, you are going to do it.'

Sweat begins to run down my back, even though the air conditioner is on full blast. I can't talk about this, now. Leo isn't close enough, with the receiver, to record the conversation.

So instead I do exactly what he told me not to do.

I turn to Josef. 'You said you knew my mother.'

'Yes. I should not have kept this a secret.'

'I'd say *that* little white lie is the least of your problems, Josef.' I slow at a yellow light. 'You knew my grandmother was a survivor.'

'Yes,' he says.

'Were you looking for her?'

He looks out the window. 'I did not know any of them by name.'

I sit at the red light long after it turns green, until a car behind me honks, thinking that he has not really answered my question.

When we pull up to Josef's house, the carpet van is exactly where it's supposed to be, across the street. I cannot see Leo; he's somewhere in the cavernous back with his receiver ready and waiting.

I help Josef up the porch stairs, giving him an arm to lean on when he cannot bear his own weight. Leo, I'm sure, is watching. In spite of his earlier superhero story, I know he's ready to rescue me if necessary, and he doesn't find it unreasonable to think an elderly man who can barely walk is capable of doing harm. An eighty-five-year-old subject once came out of his house and started shooting, he told me, but luckily he had cataracts and lousy aim. *We have a saying in our office,* Leo had said. *Once you've killed six million, what's six million and one?*

As soon as the key turns in the lock, Eva comes running to greet her master. I lift her squirrelly little body and place her in Josef's arms so that she can lick his face. His smile is as wide as the sea. 'Oh, *mein Schatz,* I missed you,' Josef says. I realize, watching the reunion, that this is the perfect relationship for him. Someone who loves him unconditionally, who has no conception of the monster he used to be, and who can listen to any tearful confessions without ever betraying his confidence.

'Come,' Josef announces. 'I will make us tea.'

I follow him into the kitchen, where he sees the fresh fruit on the counter and then opens the refrigerator to find milk, juice, eggs, and bread. 'You did not have to do this,' Josef says.

'I know. But I wanted to.'

'No,' he corrects. 'I mean, you did not *have* to.'

If, that is, I was willing to kill him anytime soon.

Here goes nothing, I think.

'Josef.' I pull out a chair and gesture for him to sit down. 'We have to talk.'

'You are not having second thoughts, I hope?'

I sink down across from him. 'How could I not?'

I hear the drone of a lawn mower outside. The kitchen windows are open.

Shit.

I fake an enormous sneeze. Standing up, I walk around and start ratcheting the windows shut. 'I hope you don't mind. The pollen's killing me.'

Josef frowns, but he is too polite to complain. 'I'm afraid of what will happen after,' I admit.

'No one suspects foul play when a ninety-five-year-old man dies.' Josef chuckles. 'And there is no one left behind in my family to ask questions.'

'I'm not talking about the legal aspect. Just the moral one.' I find myself fidgeting and force myself to stop, thinking of the rustling of fabric that Leo must be hearing. 'I feel a little silly having to ask you this, but you're the only person I would know who might even understand, because you've been there.' I look up at him. 'When you kill someone . . . how do you ever get over it?'

'I asked you to help me die,' Josef clarifies. 'There's a difference.'

'Is there?'

He exhales heavily. 'Maybe not,' he admits. 'You will think of it, every day. But I would hope you could see it as mercy.'

'Is that how you thought of it?' I ask, the most natural flow, and then I hold my breath for his answer.

'Sometimes,' Josef says. 'They were so weak, some of them. They wanted to be released, like I do now.'

'Maybe that's just what you told yourself so you could sleep at night.' I lean forward, my elbows on the kitchen table. 'If you really want me to forgive you for what you've done, you have to tell me all of it.'

He shakes his head, his eyes growing damp. 'I have already. You know what I was. What I am.'

'What was the worst thing you did, Josef?'

It strikes me, as I ask the question, that we are gambling. Just because Darija's murder was the one written up does not mean it was the most heinous crime Reiner Hartmann committed against a prisoner. It only means that it was the one where he got caught.

'There were two girls,' he says. 'One of them worked for . . . for my brother, in his office, where he kept a safe with the currency that was taken from the prisoners' belongings.'

He rubs his temples. 'We all did it, you know. Took things. Jewelry or money, even loose diamonds. Some officers, they got rich working in the camps for this reason. I listened to the news; I knew that the Reich was not going to last much longer now that the Americans had gotten involved. So I planned ahead. I would take what money I could, and I would convert it to gold, before it was worthless.'

Shrugging, Josef looks at me. 'It was not hard to get the

combination to the safe. I was the SS-*Schutzhaftlagerführer*, after all. There was only the *Kommandant* above me, and when I asked for something, the question was not whether I would get it but how quickly. So one day, when I knew my brother was not at his desk, I went to the safe to take what I could.

'The girl – the secretary – saw me. She had fetched her friend from her job outside, and brought her to the office while my brother was gone, to warm up, I suppose,' he says. 'I could not let the girl tell my brother what she had seen. So I shot her.'

I realize I am holding my breath. 'You shot the girl who was the secretary?'

'I meant to. But I had been injured, yes, on the front line – my right arm. I was not as steady with the pistol as I should have been. The girls were moving, frantic, they were clutching at each other. So the bullet went into the other girl, instead.'

'You killed her.'

'Yes.' He nods. 'And I would have killed the other one, too, but my brother arrived first. When he saw me there, with the gun in one hand and the money in the other, what choice did I have? I told him that I had caught the girls stealing from him, from the Reich.'

Josef covers his eyes with one hand. His throat works, the words jamming. 'My own brother did not believe me. My own brother turned me in.'

'Turned you in?'

'To the disciplinary committee at the camp. Not for stealing, but for shooting a prisoner against protocol,' he says. 'It was nothing, a simple meeting where I was reminded of my orders. But you see, don't you? Because of what I did, my own brother betrayed me.'

I am not sure what element of this story makes it, in Josef's warped mind, the worst thing he ever did – that he murdered Darija, or that he destroyed the relationship he had with his brother. I am afraid to ask. I'm more afraid to hear the answer.

'What happened to your brother?'

'I never talked to him again, after that. I heard he died a long time ago.' Josef is crying silently, his hands trembling where they rest on the table. 'Please,' he begs. 'Will you forgive me?'

'What will that change? It won't bring back the girl you killed. It won't fix what happened with your brother.'

'No. But it means that at least one person will know I wish it had never happened.'

'I'll think about it,' I reply.

I get into the rental car and blast the air-conditioning. At the end of Josef's block I turn right, into a cul-de-sac, and pull over at the curb. Leo is driving toward me in the van. He swerves so fast that the van goes over the curb, then hops out and pulls me out of the car and twirls me in a circle. 'You did it,' he crows, punctuating each word with a kiss. 'Goddamn, Sage. I couldn't have done a smoother job.'

'Are you hiring?' I ask, relaxing for the first time in two hours.

'Depends on what position you're looking for.' Leo frowns. 'Wow. That came out wrong . . . C'mere.' He opens the back of the van and rewinds the digital recorder so that I can hear my own voice, and Josef's.

You killed her.

Yes, and I would have killed the other one, too.

'So it's done,' I say. My voice sounds hollow, with none of the bright ring to it that Leo's has. 'He'll be deported?'

'There's just one more step. I already called Genevra, my historian, and she's headed here tonight. Now that we've got Josef on tape confessing, we'll see if he's willing to cooperate and talk to us voluntarily. We drop in unannounced – usually to see if the subject has an alibi, but clearly that's not the case here. It's just a way for us to get even more information, if that's possible, to secure the case. Then Genevra and I head back to D.C. . . .'

'Back?' I echo.

'I need to write a pros memo, so that the deputy assistant attorney general can approve it, start legal proceedings, and issue a press release. And then, I promise you, Josef Weber *will* die,' he says. 'Miserably, in prison.'

Genevra the historian is arriving in Boston rather than Manchester, because that was the quickest flight she could book. That means a five-hour round-trip drive for Leo, but he says he doesn't mind. He will use the time to fill her in on the aspects of the case that she's missed.

I stand behind him, watching him knot his tie in the bath-room mirror. 'Then,' Leo says, 'I will drop her off at the Courtyard. From what I understand the beds are pretty comfortable.'

'Are you going to stay there, too?'

He pauses. 'Did you want me to?'

In the mirror, we look like a modern *American Gothic*. 'I thought you might not want your historian to know about me.'

He folds me into his arms. 'I want her to know everything about you. From the way you are the consummate double agent to the way you rock out to John Mellencamp in the shower, and sing all the wrong words.'

'They're not the wrong—'

'It's not "you pull off those Barbie books." Trust me on this. Besides, Genevra's going to get to know you when we go out after work in the District . . .'

It takes me a moment before the words sink in. 'I don't live in the District.'

'Technicality,' Leo says, shyly. 'We have bakeries in D.C.'

'It just . . . doesn't feel right, Leo.'

'You're having second thoughts?' He freezes. 'I come on strong. A hundred and forty percent. I know that. But I just found you, Sage. I don't want to let you go. It can't be a bad thing to know what you want, and run with it. One day, years from now, we can read the press release about Reiner Hartmann aloud to our babies and tell them that Mommy and Daddy fell in love because of a war criminal.' He looks at my face and winces. 'Still too over the top?'

'I wasn't talking about moving. Although that's still up for discussion . . .'

'Tell you what. If you can find a Department of Justice job up here, *I'll* move—'

'It's Josef,' I interrupt. 'It just doesn't feel . . . right.'

Leo takes my hand and leads me out of the bathroom, sits me on the edge of the bed. 'This is harder for you than it is for me, because you knew him as someone else before you knew him as Reiner Hartmann. But this *is* what you wanted, isn't it?'

I close my eyes. 'I can't remember anymore.'

'Then let me help you out. If Reiner Hartmann is deported or even extradited, it's going to be news. Big news. Everyone will hear it – not just in our country, but all over the world. I'd like to think that maybe, the next person who is about to do something horrific – the soldier who is given an order to commit a crime against humanity – will remember that press release about the Nazi who was caught, even at age ninety-five. Maybe in that moment, he'll realize that if he carries out his order, the United States government or some other one is going to hunt him down for the rest of his life, too, no matter how far he runs. And maybe he'll think, *I'm going to have to be looking over my shoulder forever, like Reiner Hartmann.* So instead of doing what he has been told to do, he'll say no.'

'Doesn't it count for anything if Josef wishes he hadn't done it?'

Leo looks at me. 'What counts,' he says, 'is that he *did.*'

Mary is in the shrine grotto when I arrive. I'm a sticky mess; the air is so humid that it seems to be condensing through my skin. I feel like I've replaced all my hemoglobin with caffeine, I'm that jittery.

I have a lot to do before Leo gets back tonight.

'Thank God you're here,' I say, as soon as I reach the top of the Holy Stairs.

'That means a lot, coming from an atheist,' Mary says. She is silhouetted against the dusk, in the kind of light that would make a painter swoon: fingers of purple and pink and electric blue, like the salvia she is weeding. 'I tried to call you, to see how you were doing, with your grandmother and all, but you don't answer messages anymore.'

'I know; I got it. I've just been really busy . . .'

'With that guy.'

'How did you know that?' I ask.

'Honey, anyone with two functional brain cells who was at the funeral or the gathering afterward could have figured that out. I have only one question for you about him.' She looks up. 'Is he married?'

'No.'

'Then I already like him.' She strips off her gardening gloves and sets them on the edge of the bucket she's using to collect the weeds for composting. 'So where's the fire?'

'I have a question for a priest,' I explain, 'and you're the closest thing around.'

'I'm not sure if I should be flattered by that or if I should find a new hairstylist.'

'It's about Confession . . .'

'That's a sacrament,' Mary replies. 'Even if I could grant penitence to you, you're not Catholic. It's not like you can sashay into a confessional and wipe your slate clean.'

'It's not me. I was asked to do the forgiving. But the sin, it's truly, truly awful.'

'A mortal sin.'

I nod. 'I'm not asking about how Confession works, for the person who's confessing. I want to know how the priest does it: hears something he can barely stomach, and then lets it go.'

Mary sits beside me on the teak bench. By now, the sun has sunk so low that everything on the shrine's hill is glowing and golden. Just looking at it, at so much beauty in one place, makes the tightness in my chest loosen a little. Surely if there's evil in the world, it's counterbalanced by moments like these. 'You know, Sage, Jesus didn't tell us to forgive everyone. He said turn the other cheek, but only if you were the one who was hit. Even the Lord's Prayer says it loud and clear: Forgive us our trespasses, as we forgive those who trespass against *us*. Not others. What Jesus challenges us to do is to let go of the wrong done to you personally, not the wrong done to someone else. But most Christians incorrectly assume this means that being a good Christian means forgiving all sins, and all sinners.'

'What if, even tangentially, the wrong that was done *does* have something to do with you? Or with someone close to you, anyway?'

Mary folds her arms. 'I know I've told you how I left the convent, but did I ever tell you why I entered it?' she says. 'My mother was raising three kids on her own, because my father walked out on us. I was the oldest, at thirteen. I was full of so much anger that sometimes I woke up in the middle of the night with the taste of it in my mouth, like tin. We couldn't afford groceries. We had no television and the lights had been turned off. Our furniture had been reclaimed by the credit card company, and my brothers were wearing pants that hit above the ankle because we couldn't afford to buy new school clothes. My father, though, he was on vacation with his girlfriend in France. So one day I went to see our priest and I asked what I could do to feel less angry. I was expecting him to say something like, *Get a job,* or *Write your feelings down on paper.* Instead, he told me to forgive my dad. I stared at the priest, convinced he was nuts. "I can't do that," I told him. "It would make what he did seem less awful."'

I study Mary's profile as she speaks. 'The priest said, "What he did was wrong. He doesn't deserve your love. But he does deserve your forgiveness, because otherwise he will grow like a weed in your heart until it's choked and overrun. The only person who suffers, when you squirrel away all that hate, is you." I was thirteen, and I didn't know very much about the world, but I knew that if there was that much wisdom in religion, I wanted to be part of it.'

She faces me. 'I don't know what this person did to you, and I am not sure I want to. But forgiving isn't something you do for someone else. It's something you do for yourself. It's saying, *You're not important enough to have a stranglehold on me.* It's saying, *You don't get to trap me in the past. I am worthy of a future.'*

I think of my grandmother, whose silence all these years had accomplished the same goal.

For better or for worse, Josef Weber is part of my life. Of my family's story. Is the only way to edit him out of it to do what he's asked; to excuse him for his actions?

'Does any of that help?' Mary asks.

'Yeah. Surprisingly.'

She pats my shoulder. 'Come on down with me. I know a place you can get a good cup of coffee.'

'I think I'm going to stay here for a little bit. Watch the sun set.'

She looks at the sky. 'Can't blame you.'

I watch her move down the Holy Stairs until I cannot see her anymore. It is dusk now, and the edges of my hands look fuzzy; the whole world seems like it's unraveling.

I pick up Mary's gardening gloves, which are draped over the edge of the bucket like wilted lilies. I lean over the railing of the Monet garden and cut a few stalks of monkshood. In the pale palm of Mary's glove, the blue-black petals look like stigmata – another sorrow that can't be explained away, no matter how hard you try.

There are so many ways to betray someone.

You can whisper behind his back.

You can deceive him on purpose.

You can deliver him into the hands of his enemy, when he trusts you.

You can break a promise.

The question is, if you do any of these things, are you also betraying yourself?

I can tell, when Josef opens the door, that he knows why I've come. 'Now?' he asks, and I nod. He stands for a moment, his hands at his sides, unsure of what he is supposed to do.

'The living room,' I suggest.

We sit opposite each other, the chessboard between us, set neatly for a new game. Eva lies down, a donut at his feet.

'Will you take her?' he asks.

'Yes.'

He nods, his hands folded on his lap. 'Do you know . . . how?'

I nod, and reach for the backpack I've worn while biking here in the dark.

'I have to say something first,' Josef confesses. 'I lied to you.'

My hands still on the zipper.

'What I told you earlier today . . . that was not the worst thing I ever did,' Josef says.

I wait for him to continue.

'I did speak to my brother again, after. We had not been in contact after the investigation, but one morning, he came to me, and said we had to run. I assumed he had information that I didn't, so I went with him. It was the Allies. They were liberating the camps, and any officers who were lucky managed to escape instead of being shot by them, or killed by the remaining prisoners.'

Josef looks down. 'We walked, for days, crossing the German border. When we reached a city, we hid in the sewers. When we were in the country, we hid in barns with cattle. We ate garbage, just to stay alive. There were those who sympathized with us, still, and somehow, we managed to get false papers. I said we needed to leave this country as soon as possible; but he wanted to go back home, to see what was left.'

His lower lip begins to quiver. 'We had picked sour cherries, stealing from a farmer who would never notice the handful missing from his crops. That was our dinner. We were arguing as we ate, about which route we would take. And my brother . . . he started to choke. He fell to the ground, grabbing at his throat, going blue,' Josef says. 'I stared at him. But I did nothing.'

I watch him pass a hand over his eyes, wiping them dry. 'I knew it would be easier traveling without him. I knew that he would be more of a burden to me than a blessing. Maybe I had known that my whole life,' Josef says. 'I have done many things of which I am not proud, but they were during a time of war. The rules don't apply, then. I could excuse them, or at least rationalize, so that I stayed sane. But this, this was different. The worst thing I ever did, Sage, was kill my own brother.'

'You didn't kill him,' I say. 'You chose not to save him.'

'Is it not the same?'

How can I tell him it isn't, when that's not what I believe?

'I told you some time ago that I deserve to die. You under-stand that, now. I am a brute, a beast. I killed my own flesh and blood. And that is not even the worst of it.' He waits until I meet his gaze. 'The worst of it,' he says coldly, 'is that I wish I had done it sooner.'

Listening to him, I realize that no matter what Mary says, what Leo claims, or what Josef wants, in the end absolution is not mine to give away. I think about my mother in her hospital bed, pardoning me. Of the moment the car spun out of control, when I knew it was going to crash, and I was powerless to stop it.

It does not matter who forgives you, if *you're* the one who can't forget.

In the anecdote Leo told me before he left, I realize that *I* will be the one looking over my shoulder forever. But then again, this man – who helped murder millions, who killed my grandmother's best friend, and who reigned in terror; this man – who watched his brother choke to death before his eyes – has no remorse.

There is an irony to the fact that a girl like me, who's actively struggled against religion her whole life, has turned to biblical justice: an eye for an eye, a death for a death. I unzip the backpack and remove one perfect roll. It has the same intricate crown at the top, the same dusting of sugar as the one I baked for my grandmother. But this one, it's not filled with cinnamon and chocolate.

Josef takes it from my hand. 'Thank you,' he says, his eyes filling with tears. He waits, hopeful.

'Eat it,' I tell him.

When he breaks it open, I can see the flecks of monkshood, which has been chopped finely and mixed into the batter.

Josef tears off a quarter of the roll and places it onto his tongue. He chews and swallows, chews and swallows. He does this until the bread is gone.

It's his breathing that I notice first, labored and heavy. He starts fighting for air. He slumps forward, knocking several pieces from the chessboard, and I take him in my arms and settle him on the floor. Eva begins to bark, to pull at his pants leg with her teeth. I shoo her away as his arms stiffen, as he writhes before me.

To show compassion would elevate me from the monster he was. To show revenge would prove I'm no better. In the end, by using both, I can only hope they will cancel each other out.

'Josef,' I say, leaning over him and speaking loudly, so that I know he hears me. 'I will never, ever forgive you.'

In one last desperate effort, Josef manages to grab my shirt. He bunches the fabric in his fist, pulling me down so that I can smell death on his breath. 'How . . . does . . . it end?' he gasps.

Moments later, he stops moving. His eyes roll back. I step over him and retrieve my backpack. 'Like this,' I answer.

I take a sleeping pill when I get home, and by the time Leo slips into bed beside me, I am long gone. I'm still groggy, in fact, the next morning when I wake up, which is probably better.

Genevra, the historian, is not at all what I was expecting. She's young, just out of college, and she has a tattoo up one arm that is the entire preamble to the Constitution. 'It's about time,' she says, when she is formally introduced to me. 'I suck at playing Cupid.'

We drive to Josef's in the rental car, with Genevra sitting in the backseat. I must look like a zombie, because Leo reaches for my hand and squeezes it. 'You don't have to go in.'

I had told him yesterday that I wanted to. That I thought Josef might be more likely to cooperate if he saw me. 'I may not have to, but I need to.'

If I was at all worried about Leo thinking I am acting strange, I shouldn't have been. He is riding on such a high I'm not sure he even hears me respond. We pull into Josef's driveway, and he turns to Genevra. 'Game on,' he says.

The point of having her here, he has explained, is so that if Josef panics and starts fudging details to make himself less culpable, the historian can point out the inaccuracies to the investigator. Who can, in turn, call Josef on his lies.

We get out of the car and walk to the front door. Leo knocks.

When he opens the door, I'm going to ask him if he's Mr. Weber, Leo told me this morning as we were getting dressed.

And when he nods yes, I'll say, But that's not your *real* name, is it?

However, no one answers the door.

Genevra and Leo look at each other. Then he turns to me. 'Does he still drive?'

'No,' I say. 'Not anymore.'

'Anywhere you think he might be?'

'He didn't say anything to me,' I reply, and this is true.

'You think he flew the coop?' Genevra asks. 'Wouldn't be the first time . . .'

Leo shakes his head. 'I don't think he had any idea she was wearing a wire—'

'There's a key,' I interrupt. 'In the frog, over there.'

I walk numbly to the corner of the porch, where the frog sits in a potted plant. It makes me think of the monkshood. The key is cold in the palm of my hand. I open the door, and let Leo enter first. 'Mr. Weber?' he calls, walking through the foyer toward the living room.

I close my eyes.

'Mr—Oh, shit. Genevra, call 911.' He drops his briefcase.

Josef is lying exactly the way I left him, in front of the coffee table, chess pieces scattered around him. His skin has a tinge of blue to it; his eyes are still open. I kneel down and grab his hand. 'Josef,' I yell, as if he can hear me. 'Josef, wake up!'

Leo holds his fingers to Josef's neck, feeling for a pulse. He looks at me across Josef's body. 'I'm sorry, Sage.'

'Another one bites the dust, boss?' Genevra asks, peering over his shoulder.

'It happens. It's a race against the clock, at this point.'

I realize I am still holding Josef's hand. Around his wrist is the hospital bracelet that he never removed.

JOSEF WEBER, DOB 4/20/18, B+

Suddenly, I can't breathe. I drop Josef's hand and back into the foyer, where Leo threw down his briefcase when he saw the body lying on the living room floor. Grabbing it, I slip away from the front door, just as the local police and EMTs arrive. They start speaking to Genevra and Leo as I walk down the hall to Josef's bedroom.

I sit on the bed and open the clasp on Leo's briefcase, take out the SS file that he had not let me read just days before.

On the first page is the photo of Reiner Hartmann.

An address in Wewelsburg.

The birthday, which was the same as Hitler's, Josef had once said.

And a different blood type.

Reiner Hartmann had been AB. This was something that the SS would have known, and reflected not only in his file but also in the *Blutgruppe* tattoo, the one Josef said he had carved out with a Swiss Army knife after the war. However last week, when Josef had been admitted to the hospital unconscious, phlebotomists had drawn his blood and typed it, B+.

Which meant Josef Weber was not Reiner Hartmann after all.

I think of my grandmother, telling me about the *Schutzhaftlagerführer* and the pistol that shook in his right hand. Then I visualize Josef sitting across from me at Our Daily Bread, holding his fork in his left hand. Had I been too stupid to notice the discrepancies? Or had I not wanted to see them?

I can still hear voices down the hall. Gingerly, I pull open the nightstand on Josef's side of the bed. Inside there is a packet of tissues, a bottle of aspirin, a pencil, and the journal that he always carried with him to Our Daily Bread, the one he had left behind that very first night.

I know what I am going to find before I open it.

The small cards, with their scalloped edges, have been carefully taped at the corners to affix them to the page, picture side down. The tiniest, most careful handwriting – handwriting I recognize, with its precipitous spikes and valleys – fills each square. I cannot read the German, but I don't have to in order to know what I have found.

I carefully peel the card away from the yellowed paper, and turn it over. There is a baby in the photograph. Written in ballpoint pen along the bottom is a name: Ania.

Each of the cards is a picture, labeled. Gerda, Herschel, Haim.

The story stops before the version that my grandmother gave me. The version she re-created when she was living here, and thought she was safe.

Josef was never Reiner Hartmann, he was Franz. This is why he could not tell me what he did all day long as an SS-*Schutzhaftlagerführer*: he never *was* one. Every story he had relayed to me was his brother's life. Except for the one he had told yesterday, about watching Reiner die before his eyes.

The worst of it is that I wish I had done it sooner.

The room spins around me, and I lean forward, resting my forehead against my knees. I had killed an innocent man.

Not innocent. Franz Hartmann had been an SS officer, too. He might have killed prisoners at Auschwitz, and even if he didn't, he was a cog in a killing machine, and any international war tribunal would hold him accountable. I knew he had beaten my grandmother, as well as others, badly. By his own admission he had intentionally let his brother die. But did any of this excuse what I had done? Or – like him – was I trying to justify the unjust?

Why would Franz have gone to so much trouble to paint himself as the more brutal brother? Was it because he blamed himself as much as his brother for what had happened in Germany? Because he felt responsible for his brother's death?

Did he think I wouldn't help him die if I knew who he really was?

Would I have?

I'm sorry, I whisper now. Maybe it is the forgiveness Franz had been seeking. And maybe it's just the forgiveness *I* need, for killing the wrong man.

The book falls off my lap, landing splayed on the floor. As I pick it up I realize that although the section written by my grandmother ends abruptly, there is more toward the back of the journal. After three blank pages, the writing picks up in English, in more uniform, precise penmanship.

In the first ending Franz has created, Ania helps Aleks to die.

In the second, Aleks lives, and suffers torture for the rest of eternity.

There is one vignette where Aleks, nearly drained of his own blood, is resurrected with Ania's and becomes good again. In another, even though she transfuses him back to health, he cannot shake the evil that runs through his veins and he kills her. There are a dozen of these scenarios, each different, as if Franz could not decide on the outcome that fit the best.

How does it end? Josef had asked. Now I realize he lied twice to me yesterday: he knew who my grandmother was. Maybe he had hoped I'd lead him to her. Not to kill her, as Leo has suspected, but for closure. The monster and the girl who could rescue him: obviously, he was reading his life story into her fiction. It was why he had saved her years ago; it was why, now, he needed to know if he would be redeemed or condemned.

And yet the joke was on him, because my grandmother never finished her story. Not because she didn't know the ending; and not because she *did,* as Leo had said, and couldn't bear to write it. She had left it blank on purpose, like a post-modern canvas. If you end your story, it's a static work of art, a finite circle. But if you don't, it belongs to anyone's imagination. It stays alive forever.

I take the journal and slip it into my bag beside the re-created version.

There are footsteps in the hall, and suddenly Leo is standing in the doorway. 'There you are,' he says. 'You okay?'

I try to nod, but don't quite succeed.

'The police want to talk to you.'

My mouth goes dry as bone.

'I told them you're basically his next of kin,' Leo continues, glancing around. 'What are you doing in here, anyway?'

What am I supposed to say to him? To this man who might be the best thing that has ever happened to me, who lives within the narrow boundaries of right and wrong, of justice and deceit?

'I-I was checking his nightstand,' I stammer. 'I thought he might have an address book. People we could contact.'

'Did you find anything?' Leo asks.

Fiction comes in all shapes and sizes. Secrets, lies, stories. We all tell them. Sometimes, because we hope to entertain. Sometimes, because we need to distract.

And sometimes, because we have to.

I look Leo in the eye, and shake my head.

Author's Note

Readers who want to learn more might be interested in the following resources, all of which were instrumental to me while writing *The Storyteller*:

The Chronicle of the Łódź Ghetto, 1941-1944. Edited by Lucjan Dobroszycki. New Haven: Yale University Press, 1984.

Gilbert, Martin. *The Holocaust: A History of the Jews of Europe During the Second World War.* New York: Holt, Rinehart & Winston, 1986.

Graebe, Hermann. 'Evidence Testimony at Nuremberg War Crimes Trial.' November 10 and 13, 1945. Nuremberg Document PS-2992. www.holocaustresearchproject.org/einsatz/graebetest.html.

Klein, Gerda Weissmann. *All but My Life,* expanded ed. 1957. New York: Hill & Wang, 1995.

Michel, Ernest W. *Promises Kept.* Fort Lee, NJ: Barricade Books, 2008.

———. *Promises to Keep.* New York: Barricade Books, 1993.

Salinger, Mania. *Looking Back.* Northville, MI: Nelson Pub. and Marketing, 2006.

Trunk, Isaiah. *Łódź Ghetto: A History.* Bloomington: Indiana University Press, 2006.

Wiesenthal, Simon. *The Sunflower: On the Possibilities and Limits of Forgiveness,* rev. and expanded ed. 1976. New York: Schocken Books, 1998.

About the author

Jodi Picoult is the bestselling author of twenty-one novels including *My Sister's Keeper*, *House Rules*, *Sing You Home* and *Lone Wolf*.

Since studying creative writing at Princeton, Picoult has worked as a technical writer for a Wall Street broker, a copywriter at an ad agency, an editor at a textbook publisher, an English teacher and as the author of five issues of the *Wonder Woman* comic book series. She is an international Number One bestseller with her novels translated into forty languages in forty countries. Three have been made into television movies and *My Sister's Keeper* was released as a major motion picture starring Cameron Diaz, Alec Baldwin and Abigail Breslin in summer 2009.

Most recently Jodi's first co-authored novel came out – she wrote *Between the Lines* with her teenage daughter Samantha van Leer.

Jodi Picoult and her husband Tim van Leer live in New Hampshire with three children, three springer spaniels, two donkeys, two geese, three ducks, six chickens, and the occasional cow.

Jodi Picoult on Researching The Storyteller

A transcript of Jodi's talk at
Kings Place, London, 27 March 2013.

My mother lives part-time in Arizona and she has been to a bunch of Anti-Defamation League talks. I knew she had heard some survivors speak, so I wrote her an email and said, 'Do you think you can maybe arrange to talk to some of those people and ask them if they'd be willing to talk to me?' And I swear to you, in half an hour I had a list of nine names, contact addresses and phone numbers – she had phoned them all and told them that I would be calling. My mother should work for the government: she's amazing.

I wound up speaking to six people. Of those six, four told me stories which I used and braided together to create the character of Minka. Even though they were willing – or thought they were willing – to talk to me, it was too hard for some of them, and I wouldn't push them to experience something again that they weren't willing to experience. One of the things you see in *The Storyteller* is that Minka has never before spoken about what happened, and I found that to be very true. The survivors I spoke to have either dedicated their lives to going to museums or to schools to talk about what happened over and over, or they've never said anything. It's one or the other: there's no in-between. Minka falls into the latter camp.

So I started with my mum, and what I'll do is tell you about a few of the survivors that I did wind up speaking to. The first one is a man called Bernie. Bernie grew up in a small town in Poland which contained 5,000 Jews. By the end of the war there were 36. He told me that when the Germans began to occupy his village, residents would go underneath their homes into the basement and hear German soldiers walking around upstairs looking for people to take off to the camps.

One night, they were there with a friend of the family who had a newborn who was crying. They started to feed the baby bread, but the baby was still crying, so the mother juggled it up against her shoulder. She accidently smothered her own child, and ended up walking upstairs, sitting on a kerb and waiting for three days until the soldiers came back because she didn't want to be there anymore. When they finally came to take Bernie away, he was grabbing onto the doorframe of his house so tightly that he managed to pry – from its nails – the mezuzah that was nailed into it. If you don't know what a mezuzah is, it's a strip of metal with a scroll inside that's been blessed and is meant to bless a Jewish home. He pulled this thing off and held it in his hand with his three fingers curled under it for the entire war, so that when it was over he had to have his hand surgically opened because his fingers had fused shut. When I met him, he showed me the mezuzah he had carried all that time. He was finally taken off to Tarnopol in 10 wagons full of Jews from his village. He was with his mother and father. The German soldiers stopped to have a drink in a pub and told the Jews not to move. After several hours, his father – who had a bad back – stood up to stretch. A villager saw him and went to the pub to tell the soldiers. One came out and shot him in the head.

This would have been devastating for any son to see, but Bernie was particularly freaked out because you can see brain tissue when someone is shot in the head. His mother then made Bernie promise that when he died, it would be with a bullet to the heart, not to the head. Just imagine being a mum and making your child that kind of promise.

The next survivor I spoke to was a woman named Gerda Weissmann Klein. Very famous as survivors go, she was awarded the Presidential Medal of Freedom by President Obama a few years ago. Gerda also grew up in Poland in a very integrated neighbourhood. In June 1942, the Nazis came and separated her from her parents. They were taken off and killed in Auschwitz, while she was sent to a variety of work camps. In January 1945, after several years at these camps, she and 4,000 other women were put on an enforced 350-mile march because the Allies were advancing. They marched through the snow; less than 150 of them survived. Gerda told me that the reason she held onto her life was because she was wearing ski boots that her father had told her to wear when she was taken. Her best friend Ilsa died in her arms during that trip. When she was liberated by the American Allies, she weighed 60 pounds, her hair was white and she had not showered or bathed in three years. An American soldier held the door open for her to walk through first. This surprised her and she said, 'I am a Jew, you know,' and he said, 'Yes, I am too.' They wound up getting married. Everybody likes that one.

The last woman I'm going to talk to you about is a woman named Mania. Mania is the survivor I grew the closest to. When I was doing my interviews, I actually stayed in her house with her. After I had left to go back home to write, she kept sending me emails saying, 'Are you done yet? I'm a very old woman and could die soon!' She's still alive and kicking, and she's great. Mania also grew up in a hugely integrated Polish community.

She was very bright and wanted to go to the state high school because it would've given her the best education. But there were only two Jews allowed entry each year and they were already enrolled. So instead, her father's accountant – who was a Christian – managed to get her into Catholic high school. She studied everything that Catholic kids studied, but during catechism she would sit outside and do her homework. In a Catholic high school, you had to take a language and you had a choice of French – taught by a very large, unattractive nun – or German, which was taught by a young, hot teacher. Mania took a lot of German. She became the star German pupil and in fact this saved her life multiple times during the war because she was routinely put into secretarial positions instead of working hard labour. When she was rounded up and sent to a ghetto, one of the first jobs she had was at a 'German factory' (which meant 'workshop') working for a man called Herr Beiker. She was his personal secretary, and a bunch of other young girls worked in the workshop underneath them. Herr Beiker was a really nice man. He cared about the girls and called them 'meine Kinder' ('my children'), which is why one day, when he suddenly became very angry and very mean, it scared her. Herr said, 'Nobody leaves this factory. You will stay here working through the night. I don't want to hear anything; I don't want to talk to any of you.' He was very, very angry and Mania became scared and ran home. She was talking to her parents when a soldier showed up and said, 'You must come back now. Mania must come back to the factory.' She found out later that one of her best friends had pawned her watch to get that soldier to bring her back. When she got to the factory, she saw Herr Beiker standing outside holding a rifle to keep the girls inside, but, more importantly, to keep the Nazis from coming in, because that was the night of the first round-up in their village.

It was also the last time Mania saw her mother and her baby brother who were taken off to a place called Treblinka.

After that, Herr Beiker arranged for his girls – his children – to be sent to a farm where he thought they would be safer. While Mania was working on this farm, a boy showed up and said, 'I know what happened to your mother and baby brother.' He told them about Treblinka, where there were these showers that a hundred people went into at a time. But they weren't really showers: they were gas chambers. Mania and her friend listened to this description and said it sounded insane: Why would anyone do that? That's ridiculous! They completely dismissed him. After the farm closed, Mania was sent to another work camp called Pianki. There, she was reunited with her father. Her father was sentenced to hard labour and she was once again a secretary. She saw how the efforts of hard labour were killing her father so one day, she took an empty folder, closed it, and using her fluent German, marched herself to the commandant's office saying, 'I cannot speak to anyone about the contents of this file. Only the commandant's eyes can see it.' They finally let her into the commandant's office; he opened the folder up, looked at it and then looked at her because it was empty. He was not a nice man and had recently hanged someone who tried to escape. Mania said, 'I don't know if you have a daughter, but if you do I hope she would do for you what I have to do for my father.' She told the commandant that her father was dying. The commandant listened to her and a moment later wrote something down. He then changed her father's job so that he lived to survive that camp.

When the camp closed, they were sent to Auschwitz. The loading ramp at Auschwitz was the last place Mania saw her father. He was killed there. Mania was not killed: she was sent to the showers, where she suddenly remembered everything that boy had said about Treblinka. She expected to die but she did not. She was deloused, she was given a uniform, she was given a tattoo, her hair was shaved and six days later she was shipped out to yet another work camp. This one was in Hindenburg, where she was assigned to carry out night welding. She was speaking German when one of the guards heard her and said, 'Have you ever done inventory?' 'Yes,' she replied, 'I've done plenty of inventories.' She had never done inventory in her life. They moved her into an office where she was working with Germans and she was routinely locked in a closet during observations because, had she been found working with Germans in her striped uniform, she would have been shot on the spot. Finally, after four years of working in the camp, she was sent to Bergen-Belsen. Nobody worked at Bergen-Belsen; you went there to starve and to die. She was living in a barracks with 900 other people when she cut her arm and it became infected. She contracted typhoid. One morning, feverish and near death, she climbed over a mound of bodies to get some fresh air, rolled out onto her back and looked up to see that there was no one in the guard tower – there was only a white flag. The Allies had come to liberate them. The British came and set up medical tents and when Mania got there they said, 'You need to have your arm amputated.' She begged them not to take her arm and they wound up giving her the last shot of penicillin which they'd been saving for an Allied soldier. To this day, she still has use of her arm.

Book club discussion questions *for* The Storyteller

1. Sage has been a part of the grief group for three years. Why has she stayed?

2. The paradox of loss: How can something that's gone weigh us down so much? (p. 12) Discuss.

3. How 'religious' is Sage's family? Does this matter, given what happens to her?

4. 'Sharing a memory with someone is different from reliving it when you are alone.' (p. 46) Discuss.

5. How do Mary, Sage, Rocco, and Josef react to the image of God in the loaf of bread? How do you think you would react?

6. What request does Josef make of Sage? What do you think you would do?

7. The periodic pages in italics are a continuing story – a Gothic fairy tale. In what ways does it parallel the present day story? In what way does this story-within-a-story add to the moral dilemma Sage faces?

8. Why does Sage go to the police station? Would you do the same? Why or why not?

9. When Jews were being taken by the Nazis, many Germans turned a blind eye. How easy would that be to do?

10. Grandma Minka and her father were also bakers. How important are the family recipes? The baking of special breads? Is baking a metaphor for something else in this book?

11. 'If my grandmother could reinvent herself, why not Josef Weber?' (p. 75) Have you ever had the opportunity/desire to reinvent yourself? Did it work/help?

12. Leo has a passion for his job as a Nazi hunter. Why does he think it's important?

13. Does Josef have the right to ask Sage to forgive him? Why or why not?

14. Josef explains how you can develop brutality (p. 133). Discuss his explanation in terms of bullying today.

15. Josef/Reiner's brother, Franz, says: 'Power isn't doing something terrible to someone who's weaker than you. It's having the strength to do something terrible and choosing not to.' (p. 164) In what ways does this reflect upon the actions of Reiner? Franz? Sage?

16. 'So everyone from the guards to the bean counters at Auschwitz is culpable for what happened there, simply because they were aware of what was going on inside its fences, and performed their duties.' (p. 198) Do you agree? Disagree?

17. What is the importance of having Christian papers? If you were Minka, would you have used them?

18. What does Rubin do to save his son? What does Basia do to save Rubin? How have their circumstances changed their actions?

19. While working in Kanada, going through luggage, Minka comes across her father's suitcase. What does she do with her father's sweater? Why is this a pivotal moment?

20. What purpose does the fairy tale serve for the Hauptscharführer? How has the fairy tale evolved from when Minka first wrote it until the time she is writing for the Hauptscharführer?

21. 'There was no black and white. Someone who had been good her entire life could, in fact, do something evil. Ania was just as capable of committing murder, under the right circumstances, as any monster.' Discuss.

22. When Minka and Darija see the bride, dressed in white, it gives them hope. Why?

23. How does the Hauptscharführer save Minka's life? (p. 382) Why do you think he does that?

24. 'So you see, this is why I never told my story. If you lived through it, you already know there are no words that will ever come close to describing it. And if you didn't, you will never understand.' (p.412) Discuss.

25. 'Forgiving isn't something you do for someone else. It's something you do for yourself.' (p. 518) Discuss.

26. What do you think Josef really wants to be forgiven for? Would you have forgiven Josef? Why do you think he lied?

27. As she often does, the author has a double meaning for the title. 'The Storyteller' could be several people and mean different things. Discuss.

28. There are groups that say the Holocaust never happened. As we get further and further away from World War II, fewer people are alive who would remember. Why is this story still relevant?

Here's what I know about me as a writer: I would write no matter what – even if there was no one out there to read what I'd written.

But the fact that you are there? That's amazing.

I love to hear from you. If you want to let me know what you thought about the questions I raise in this novel, or find out more about what I'm doing next, here are some easy ways to stay in touch:

- Follow me on twitter @jodipicoult
- Like my Facebook page
  www.facebook.com/JodiPicoultUK
- Visit my website www.jodipicoult.co.uk, and sign up to my newsletter.

Thank you for reading!

Your Questions

In the hardback edition of *The Storyteller*, we asked readers to send us their questions for Jodi, with the chance for them to appear in the paperback edition. Below are the lucky few which were selected.

Is Minka's character based on a real person's story? How much of her account is true and how much is fiction?

Margareth Sackett

Minka is based on several people who I interviewed as part of the research for the book. I was amazed and horrified by what I learned from them, and we cried together and also cheered survival. All of what you read in the prison camp parts of the book is extrapolated directly from my conversations with these amazing people.

Did you speak to a specific person with regards to Josef Weber, or are the happenings of the book taken from a wide range of written evidence?

Denise Dacillo

Most fictional characters are composites of what I learn through talking to people and reading. However, although I had many survivors willing to speak to me, it was much more difficult to find willing Nazis, for obvious reasons. In lieu of that, I worked very closely with the senior historian for the US Holocaust Memorial Museum, and with the head of the HRSP (Human Rights and Special Prosecutions Division) of the Dept. of Justice – which even today searches out Nazi war criminals. By reading transcripts that had been taken from those men who were interviewed and who eventually confessed to being Nazi war criminals, and by struggling through the history of the war to piece together a viable course for Josef, I created his character.

SPOILER ALERT: Why does one character spend his life pretending to be his brother? Isn't he 'less evil' than his sibling?

Barbara Freeborn

Had a different officer been the one to find Minka's fragmented story, she might have been killed immediately. Yet this man sees it as a mythological study of himself and his own brother – a truth that he could never utter aloud because it would lead to his own punishment. It is the opportunity for 'what if?' – for an ending other than the one assumed to be inevitable that keeps this particular officer reading, and that ultimately is Minka's salvation. The Nazi cannot imagine a future other than the hell he is living. And yet, there is the unspeakable horror of realising one's own brother is monstrous – and that you did not stop him from committing atrocities. Pair that with the knowledge that you yourself were not completely blameless during the war, and you wind up with a character with so much individual guilt that it is crushing; and a belief that he is just as culpable as his brother for the crimes committed.

What inspired you to write about the subject of the Holocaust?

Emma Bennett

This book actually began with another book – Simon Wiesenthal's *The Sunflower*. In it, Mr Wiesenthal recounts a moment when, as a concentration camp prisoner, he was brought to the bedside of a dying Nazi, who wanted to confess to and be forgiven by a Jew. The moral conundrum in which Wiesenthal found himself has been the starting point for many philosophical and moral analyses about the dynamics between victims of genocide and the perpetrators, and it got me thinking about what would happen if the same request was made, decades later, to a Jewish prisoner's granddaughter.

Did you find this story, more than any of your others, hard to write? Were you worried that the research that would go into it would be too much to bear?

Alison Killoran

This research was amongst some of the most emotionally gruelling I've ever done. Some of those details went into the fictional history of my character, Minka. It was humbling and horrifying to realise that the stories they recounted were non-fiction. Some of the moments these brave men and women told me about will stay with me forever. I am agnostic but I was raised by Jewish parents and so, like Sage, I find myself in the odd situation of being a spokesperson for a religious group I do not personally affiliate with anymore. And yet, I firmly believe that the Holocaust was not a Jewish problem. It is a human rights issue.

6 million Jews were killed during the war, but 11 million people overall were murdered by Nazis. For this reason, we all need to keep telling these stories.

Most writers say that they come up with different endings: did you write a different conclusion before the one you finally selected?

Charlotte Hall

I always know the ending before I write a book. I knew the big twist right off the bat. There was, however, a smaller psychological twist that I can't give away that revealed itself to me near the end as I was typing and it was so PERFECT I could not believe I hadn't known it was coming! And so no – I didn't change the ending!

How long does it take you to research the theme of your book before you begin to write it?

Portia Mthethwa

My books are like pregnancies! Each one takes nine months. Sometimes the research takes longer than the writing – and sometimes the reverse – but every book seems to pop out after those nine months!

If you enjoyed *The Storyteller*, why not share Jodi's writing with the teen in your life? Read the new novel from

JODI PICOULT
written with her daughter
SAMANTHA VAN LEER

Between the Lines

Delilah knows it's weird, but she can't stop reading her favourite fairy tale. Other girls her age are dating and cheerleading. But then, other girls are popular.

She loves the comfort of the happy ending, and knowing there will be no surprises.

Until she gets the biggest surprise of all, when Prince Oliver looks out from the page and speaks to her.

Now Delilah must decide: will she do as Oliver asks, and help him to break out of the book? Or is this her chance to escape into happily ever after?

Whether you keep it all for yourself (we won't tell!) or share this treat of a book with a younger reader you know and love, *Between the Lines* is sheer enchantment.

Out now in paperback and ebook

Luke Warren would sleep in the dirt if it meant he could be under the stars.

He lives by the laws of nature, and would surely want to die that way.

But Luke is in a coma, and his family must make an unbearable decision.

As tensions and secrets rise to the surface, the tragic accident which brought them back together against the odds could well tear Luke's family apart forever.

They know Luke would not want to live like this.

But how can they choose to let him die?

Out now in paperback and ebook

JODI PICOULT
Sing You Home

Zoe Baxter has lost everything.

Struggling to rebuild her life, the last thing she expects is to fall in love.

It changes her world.

Until she discovers there are those who will do anything to stop her from living her life the way that she believes.

Sing You Home is accompanied by a soundtrack of original songs created for the novel by Jodi Picoult and Ellen Wilber, available to download or listen to online.

www.hodder.co.uk/singyouhomemusic

Out now in paperback and ebook

HODDER

The best books live on in your head long after they are finished. As you read, you are turning the pages faster and faster to find out what happens next, only to feel bereft when you reach the end.

If that is how you feel now, you might like to join us at www.hodder.co.uk, or follow us on Twitter @hodderbooks, and be part of our community of people who love the very best of books and reading.

Whether you want to find out more about this book, or a particular author, watch trailers and interviews, have the chance to win early limited editions, or simply browse our expert readers' selection of the very best books, we think you'll find what you're looking for.

And if you don't, that's the place to tell us what's missing.

We love what we do, and we'd love you to be part of it.

www.hodder.co.uk

 @hodderbooks

HodderBooks

HodderBooks